CHEST OF STONE

BOOK 2, THE AFTERWORLD CHRONICLES

VICKI STIEFEL

COPYRIGHT

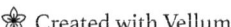 Created with Vellum

PRAISE FOR VICKI STIEFEL

THE AFTERWORLD CHRONICLES

"The writing style is innovative, the world is very interesting and provocative. It's a great story! I's a bunch of crazy, but it's GOOD crazy, with some super vivid scenes and fascinating characters."

—Nocturnal Book Reviews

"The story is fast-paced, with non-stop action. The plot is complex and intriguing with unpredictable twists."

—Sujitha Alexander

"*Chest of Bone* was full of action, magic, suspense and deception. The magic was mysterious and intriguing, and the way it was described was beautiful. I highly recommend this book if you're a lover of the fantastical with loads of mystery and lots of explosive kisses!"

—Tiffany Roberts, author of *Dustwalker* and Isle of the Forgotten series

To Rosemary Hill
For your warm heart, fiery spirit, and beautiful friendship
And
To the Illuterati Group
Your support, knowledge, and generosity has seen me through

It takes courage to grow up and become who you really are.
—e.e. cummings

1

WHERE'S THE MAGIC?

The glowing Celtic spiral tattooed on my wrist hurt like a bitch. It pulsed, too. Maybe this time. Maybe...

Plop. Plop. Plop. Dammit to hell. Blood dripped from my nose to plop into the brownie mix. That sucked. My magic sucked. Everything sucked.

All I'd wanted to do was light the burner with my fireflies. Easy peasy, right?

I'd moved a bus with my magic. Beheaded a rapist with my magic. Defeated a mage with my magic.

But for six frigging months, I couldn't do shit with my magic.

That final battle with Tommy... I'd tapped out my magic!

I tossed the brownie pan into the sink where it spidered into a million threads. Damn.

Without my magic, how was I supposed to find the frigging Chest of Stone?

My fingers curled against the counter. Breathe. Think.

I slumped at the kitchen table. My headache spiked. I pulled off the band wrapping my dreads, curled a finger around one and twirled. Nothing was normal anymore, not even my dreadlocks, which were a shiny blonde that glistened so brightly, strangers commented. So not helpful to my staying under The Union's radar.

Dammitall, I wasn't giving up on my magic. I would not give up.

I entered my bedroom, pulled by the forbidden. My bare feet padded across the cool wood, the lush area rug, until I stood beside my bed before a painting. Danger and desire threaded through me, caresses of smoky tendrils.

The Chest of Bone.

A scent tickled me, rosemary and sage.

I lifted the painting that covered the hidden safe and pressed my palm to the safe's door keyed only to my print. The small door whooshed open. There it was, the velvet-smooth ebony box. Deep in my bones, I grasped what lay inside the box. When I drew the box from the safe, it warmed to my touch.

On the edge of the bed, I set the plain rectangular box on my lap. So smooth, so lush, glazed by the moonlight streaming in from the window.

The box had no lid, no opening. But that was a lie. I was The Key. No other could open the box. None. Not even a Guardian. I touched the top, and the lid yawned, an awakening lotus flower.

There, inside the box—the Chest of Bone. Its curved lid beckoned me. Did I dare?

I'd first glimpsed it as a teen's plastic jewel box, complete with twirling ballerina, not the oval bone coffer sitting before me. I bit my lip. Odd, semi-sentient thing. The five chests changed to suit their environment. So much pain and death could have been avoided if I'd only first touched the jewelry box with my flesh. Instead, I'd been wearing gloves, and the chest hadn't responded. Seven months ago? More like centuries.

Each of the five chests contained universes, as well as slivers of souls. Each ordered the magic of a particular species, the one before me belonging to the mages, like me. Each only responded to The Key. How ironic, how amusing, how absurd.

My dark mood deepened.

When I reunited the five chests with their accompanying

guardians, the magic retwining with the mundane world would synchronize, harmonize, become one, as it once was millennia ago.

Now? The replaiting was chaos—destroyed Sedona and St. Petersburg, created the flower fields in Australia, vanished the Golden Eagles. How many other events hadn't reached my ears?

As The Key, I mattered, a fact I found ridiculous. Because of that, The Union, my brother, others sought to possess me, control me.

But if I opened the Chest of Bone, I'd be in control.

I'd wield its power and... unearth the Chest of Sone, solve Lulu's and Ronan's problems, find James, my lost love. Then we'd be a family, a happy one.

Except the chest wasn't mine. I wasn't to touch it, just keep it safe. It was a terrible and dangerous thing. Anouk said it could destroy me, but...

I set the box on the bed, brushed my fingers across the rich velvet lining. The chest's lid glowed warm and welcoming. It knew me. Although I hadn't touched it, pins and needles feathered up my fingers.

Outside its protective container, it would assume a new form. Camouflage. I could hide it on my dresser or in a drawer. Use it at will.

Its ancient patina glowed. It throbbed like a human heart.

My index finger atremble, I touched the chest's lid. A thrill rolled through me. Golden runes slid across its lid and down its sides, their swooping letters, Tolkienesque, interspersed with The Ouroboros, The Dragon, The Eye. When the symbols covered the entire box, they stilled.

The chest hummed, the sound oscillating inside me, a half-remembered melody, alluring and inscrutable.

If I lifted the lid, the cosmos would be mine.

Calm caressed my shoulders, my back, my mind. Delicious melodies wove inside me and coiled toward my pool of magic.

Now. Do it now!

I slid my fingers inside the ebony box to free the Chest of Bone.

"Fuck you, asswipe!" screamed my ward, Lulu. "Kids call me Bloodsuckerhead."

"That's a cool vamp!" Ronan shouted back.

No. Stop fighting. My fingers crept further inside the box.

"You're not my boyfriend anymore!" she hollered back.

"News to me!" he said.

No. I savored the brush of cool velvet, the warmth of the chest.

"They call me Agent Orange, too." A shriek.

"Your hair's copper, a gorgeous shade."

Tingles skating up my hands. Remembered power.

"And Burning Bush!"

"Don't, Lulu!" Ronan hollered.

"Bite me!" Another scream. "Help!"

I snapped back to the now, stared at my hands cupped around the chest.

Shit. Was I crazy? What had I been thinking?

I shoved the box back into the safe, slammed shut the door, and raced from the room. "Lulu! Ronan!"

The bathroom door was open, cold light splashing into the hall. I stepped inside. Half of Lulu's luxuriant hair pooled on the floor like a bloody stain as she struggled with Ronan, the scissors way too close to his chest.

"Stop!" I said at her bathroom entrance. "Stop it now!"

They froze, grappling statues.

Lulu, the high school girl, my mentor's daughter—a girl I loved with my whole heart. Ronan, the huge orphaned boy we "adopted" back in New Hampshire, now a college student. Both oozed pain and sorrow, both of their lives as off-kilter as mine.

"Oh, Lulu," I said.

Her freckled face whitened with anger. "I cut it, all right. I cut it, and I'm gonna finish cutting it until it's gone, gone, gone."

I lay in bed, darkness cradling me, so hot I sipped my bourbon on the rocks, rather than neat.

The bourbon was a palliative. Certainly not a cure for the emotions pinballing around inside me. Dave... Lulu's dad, my beloved mentor, homicide victim, and former Guardian of the Chest of Bone. He'd tell me I'd experienced emotional overload, in that kind-firm way he'd possessed.

Lulu and Roman, acting out, behaving as only teens could. Gods, how could Dave think I'd be a good guardian for his daughter?

I was so screwed up. I'd almost fallen into the chest's cosmos, imagined its magical infinity, aching to feed on the power of those souls who'd given themselves to strengthen it.

It would fix all our ills. Right. Of course it wouldn't.

Only I could do that.

Time to cancel the pity party and get my act in gear.

Thoughts awhirl, not sleepy in the least, I picked up my iPad and read.

I press my face to the glass. On the other side, it rains, pouring down in liquid sheets. Darkness cloaks the space beyond. A man steps into the picture. James. His eyes widen. He lays his hands on the glass, biceps bulging, and pushes. The glass spiderwebs, but doesn't break. He pushes again and again, his face rigid with effort. The glass remains whole. His big hands form a fist. He pulls his arm back and pistons into barrier. Blood dots his knuckles. He does it again and again until his fists are bloody.

My hands rise and I lay them on the fractured surface that refuses to yield. "Stop."

He doesn't. He can't hear me.

I'd swear I catch the crunch of bones as he smashes his fists over and over into the glass.

"Stop, James!" I place my lips on the glass.

He halts, his eyes widening. Then he places his shattered palms on the glass, matching his huge hands to mine. His eyes close and he bows his head.

WHAT HAD AWAKENED ME? That dream? Gods, it was awful. My

bourbon tumbler sat empty on the bedside table. The lights were out, and who knew when I'd fallen asleep.

I listened, eyes scratchy with exhaustion, and reached out with my empath senses.

Someone. Something was in the living room. I tuned my emotional senses, tried to understand. Hunger. Animus.

Grace slept at the end of the bed, her usual snores wuffling her cheeks. The thing hadn't awakened her. Odd. My movement did just that, but I hushed her with a gesture, whispered her to stay.

My hand found the throwing knife I kept between the mattresses, then I padded to the closet, eased it open. With habitual movements, I geared up with my gun, several throwing knives, and my small Bowie. I brushed the katana James had gifted me. Not to self: learn to use katana.

James. Where are you?

Knife in my left hand, Glock in my right, I eased into the hall and again unfurled my empath senses.

Shit. Whatever was downstairs wasn't human, its emotional signature off-the-charts strange. The thing was in our living room, still as a rock.

Was it listening for me? Had it heard me? Damn.

I stood still as ice, doffing my emo baggage, while donning that familiar, pre-battle calm.

My bare feet schussed across the wood floor, down the hall toward the three steps that led to the living room. Faint moonlight from the picture window filtered through the Stygian dark. I peered around the hall corner. A bead of sweat traced its way down my temple.

I took a cleansing breath, then slid around the corner, back pressed to the wall. Clear. I had a straight line to the living room's three steps and moved forward.

The closer I got, the more that "otherness" clung to my skin like mucous. What the hell?

Ten steps, eight, three.

The living room's darkness yawned. A shape, cloaked in the room's inky black, little more than a shadow, its overriding emotions ones of hunger, desire, death. Tall, about seven feet. Shit. Arms, yes, long ones, outstretched, ovoid head, strangely elongated legs, but skinny.

From a crack in the curtains, a moonlit beam brushed the creature's head.

My brain scrambled to process. Splotchy pinkish-red shiny skin, hairless, long canid jaws—a Daliesque version—teeth overlapping, small deep-set eyes, and strings of drool stretching downward. Gross. And scary as shit.

What was it doing? Smelling. Its amplified snuffles sounded like dogs scenting prey.

What would James do?

That pierced my brain just as the thing's head swiveled slowly in my direction, eyes now a putrid glowy lime green, staring right into mine.

It made a chittery sound, like a thousand bug legs scraping together. I hated chittery.

Goosebumps erupted across my flesh. A few fireflies swirled my hands, the first in months. Yeah, but I doubted they'd come through in a pinch.

Its lips peeled back, exposing dozens of teeth, the canines unnaturally long.

My fireflies sure caught its interest. "Yeah? You want a piece of me?"

Its jaws opened, a growl. It leapt.

I did the same, shooting as I did, hit its shoulder, knife slicing upward as it plowed into me.

Shit, it weighed a ton.

My gun flew from my hand as the thing plastered me to the ground. I kicked out, twisted my legs around its torso, tried to flip it. Not happening.

My arms, trapped beneath its chest. I pried my hands open just as that canid head, jaws wide, ran up my neck, slow, sniffing, coating me with drool, licking me. Gods. Why didn't it bite me? Rip out my throat? Tear my face off?

Screw this.

I head butted it, got my hands open and clawed whatever fricken' flesh I came into contact with.

The creature howled, jumped back, but I hung on with my right hand, tore a knife from its sheath with my left, leapt high pushing off the creature and slammed the knife down on its neck. Rolled away and into a crouch.

A bony hand pressed to its throat, it swayed as it watched me. Assessing its next best move? I didn't wait, but forward rolled, came underneath it and sliced at its femoral artery.

The thing moved, fast, too fast, missed the artery, but caught its thigh. I jonesed on the grate of bone against steel.

"What's going... Eeekkk!" Lulu's scream slammed into me, a deadly distraction. Any second Ronan would join her, and I didn't want the creature anywhere near those kids.

The creature's attention snapped to her, hunger in its lime-green eyes, and I threw a knife straight to its...

Damn! Not its heart, but its back, as it turned, snarled, and smashed through the picture window, a trail of drool and blood in its wake.

Lulu stood there hyperventilating. I sat on the floor, bleeding. Ronan stared at the two of us, hands on hips, eyes ablaze, vanished, returned with bandages. That kid sure had his act together.

"What the hell was that, Clea?" he said, scooching down in front of me.

"Ohhhhh..." My voice trailed off. "Some weird creature I've never seen before."

It had shredded my arm, my hip—and it hurt, dammit.

He plucked away fabric, then doused my cuts with hydrogen peroxide.

"Shit!" The peroxide killed.

While he wrapped my bloody arm and plastered a bandage to my hip, I focused on how gross I felt. The thing had drooled all over me.

I'd been slimed, like in Ghostbusters. Would I suffer the effects of poison in its saliva or in its claws or...?

Gods, what time was it? I pushed myself up and, given the twisted ankle I hadn't noticed, limped over to Lulu, whose wide eyes, pale face, and rapid breaths said she wasn't over Mr. Pinky's attack.

I wrapped my good arm around her and hugged tight. "It's cool. It's all cool, Lu. Whatever it was, it's gone. I don't think it's coming back, either. At least not tonight."

"What makes you so sure?" Ronan said from the kitchen where he was washing up.

"Well, I'm not sure-sure, but we were no easy take down."

He tromped back into the living room, finger pointed at me. "You, you mean."

"You would have joined in if you hadn't been so shocked."

He plucked at his soul patch. "True."

I laughed, and it felt good and clean. "True."

Lulu pressed her forehead to mine, and I was pleased to see her breathing had evened out and her eyes no longer had that deer-in-the-headlights stare.

"That thing was disgusting," I said. "It slung its drool all over the carpet and table and me. Yuck."

She plucked at her nightshirt. "Eww. It's on me, too."

"Hey, yo, Instagrammers," I said. "Anyone happen to get a photo?"

"Dammit, no!" Ronan spat out.

"You guys always have your phones!"

Ronan shrugged. "It would've been so cool to post, man."

"No, Ronan," I said. "It would not have been cool. But I do wish we had a photo."

Given Mr. Pinky's magical bent, once again I was at a loss as to what IT was. Grimm had that book with all those creature pictures. I wanted a book, too. How about a Magical Creatures and Their Origins or a Guide to the Magical Realm? So where was it when I needed it?

I sighed. Back to the mundane, and our giant broken living-room window.

Ronan drove to the Pico Rivera Walmart for sheets of plywood, which he now nailed across the destroyed window. I'd call window repair the following day. Or maybe I shouldn't, given that Pinky thing might plan a return visit. Time to move from our Beachwood rental? Sure looked like it.

The following day, on the way to a possible new rental, I passed L.A.'s FBI office. Boy, how easy to slip on my interrogator persona. I'd walk through the Bureau's portals and return to a job I did very well.

Yeah, right. More likely, I'd be arrested or kidnapped.

What would the FBI make of that Pinky thing? A hysterical laugh burst from my lips.

The rental was a bust, so when I returned home, I slipped on my neglected ballet slippers and did my pliés, stretches, splits, and a bunch of other forms that killed, then went for a run in the wilderness of Griffith Park bordering our rental. I remained jagged of mind, not to mention of body. Why had that thing attacked us? Why hadn't it killed me when it had the opportunity? Next to the Cardillo, it was the creepiest thing I'd ever seen. I needed to get in touch with Anouk bad. She hadn't appeared since we'd left New Hampshire, scarcer than Odin's ravens. Note to self: find Anouk.

Only the Grace Draven novel pouring from my earbuds gave me any surcease. I swiped an arm across my dripping forehead, paused the book, and swayed. I'd busted ass today, and that was good. I glugged some water to hydrate.

Early September's high temps had scared off most hikers. I looked around. No cars dotted the access road, where dried grasses spiked in the breezeless day, the hill at my back craggy and wild and beautiful.

My Spidey sense—my dead mentor's term for my heightened empathetic senses—raised the hairs on my forearms. I stilled, even as I expanded my mind outward. Someone was watching me.

I tilted my head back and took another drink, closing my eyes to slits, and without moving my head looked to my left, then to my right.

Up ahead, a man stood with his back to me beside a large tree.

Tall and broad shouldered, with raven black hair that brushed his shoulders. A thrill frissoned through me.

James. The man I adored. The man who'd promised to return. The man who'd vanished for six interminable months.

The guy turned and gave me the once over as he zipped up his fly. He winked. My heart deflated. I almost gave him the finger, but instead walked away. The hand I swiped across my face shook.

I had faith in James, was sure he'd return. But he sure wasn't that bozo with the handlebar mustache.

Alone, I bucked it up. Time to call my magic, yet again. I stretched out my right arm, palm facing ahead. I focused, calling my magic.

Three children's bodies miraged before me. Dead children. Awash with blood. Naked. Broken. Devastating.

I froze, unwilling to lose sight of the children.

The vision winked out, and I staggered.

What the hell? Shaken, I bent and rested my hands on my knees, took some calming breaths. Where had that come from? Why had I just seen that?

I shook myself to clear my head. Erased the mirage from my empathetic senses. Found my calm. I closed my eyes and delved deep to where my magic pooled.

Yes, there it was. Finally. I pushed the energy from my mind, my soul, down my neck, over my shoulder and across my right arm, picturing a cascade of power streaming to my raised hand and out my palm, to firefly. My mind's eye saw a shattering burst of fireflied light that poured from my hand, a massive release of energy. My spirit lifted, the wildness calling to me, singing its immense song, blazing. The power, so much power. I was the locus, I was the magic, I was doing this.

This would crush the Pinky, easy-peasy.

Except where was the commingled pain and pleasure from my magic expenditure?

I peeked through narrowed lids.

The space in front of my hand was empty of fireflies. Except a yellow-helmeted woman on a bike stared wide-eyed at me. *Damn.*

"You're bleeding," she said. "You okay, lady?"

"Uh, yeah." I swiped my nose with one of James' old polka-dotted handkerchiefs, fisted it. "I'm fine. Thanks for asking. Just doing some exercises. For acting class."

"You looked…" She shook her head. "Okay. Bye."

She pedaled off, pumping muscular legs hard, as if chased by a horde of zombies.

2

TOLLING BELLS

J ust as I stepped inside the front door expecting to find Lulu, my phone chimed. Lulu had varsity volleyball practice. My ward had texted me to remind me she'd be home late, said she was sure I'd forgotten the time. Of course I had.

After I let the dogs out back, I trolled the rental ads, noted a few that might suit, and called a window-repair place. They'd come in a week. Swells.

After many "come get us" barks, the dogs thundered back into the house. Lemonade and knitting in hand, I sat on the sofa and clicked on the TV. The scarf I'd begun a few days ago for James was one of the many I'd been obsessively knitting since we'd landed in L.A. six months ago. I'd crafted quite a pile of wooly goods, to say the least. Right. L.A. Made no sense.

The TV reporter jumping up and down. *What?* I stabbed the button to unmute the sound. My hands flew as I knit, the soothing cashmere threaded between my fingers while...

I dropped a stitch. *Holy shit!* A giant squid had eradicated the Palm Islands in Dubai. The pictures, shot by observers' phones, showed gargantuan tentacles wrapped around stories-tall buildings as if they were Lego toys. People flailed. Cars exploded. Fires erupted.

The videos were worse than the photos, complete with screams, weeping, and, yes, shots of the giant squid.

Palm Jumeirah and Palm Jebel Ali had vanished, consumed by a fifty-tentacled, thirty-foot-high squid. The newscaster said its tentacles first scraped the islands raw of buildings, people, monorail, cars, and any other human detritus, then scraped again, destroying what remained of the islands.

"This event is unprecedented!" the reporter said, struggling to keep his composure.

Horrible, but not unprecedented. The squid disaster wasn't the first, nor would it be the last Ripley's Believe It or Not. Cataclysmic events would only increase in severity and frequency until I returned all *five* Chests of Unity to their Guardians.

More disasters would occur, more people would die, and I felt hopeless and helpless to stop it.

After I fixed the dropped stitch, knit a couple more rows, I put my knitting away. I leaned forward and pet Gracie. "So where are the damned chests, Grace?" Why wasn't there a help line for clueless mages like me?

AN HOUR LATER, deep into torturous research on my laptop, my fingers froze on the keyboard. The back of my hand, my neck, prickled. My Spidey sense. At least *that* worked.

Lulu wouldn't set it off. Nor would Ronan.

My heart sped up. Maybe James had returned.

Except he wouldn't set it off, either. Not like this, with that whole danger vibe thing happening.

I flew to the closet, strapped on my waist belt, and slid my Glock into its holster. The linen shirt I donned fell low enough to hide it, but I'd still have easy access.

I padded to the front door and pressed my right eye to the peephole.

A man, no a guy, a surfer-guy. Early thirties, tanned, about six two, broad shoulders, but leaner than James, in low-riding faded jeans and one of those crazy Hawaiian shirts. Unbuttoned, the shirt blew in the breeze above a white tee. He paused where the drive met the walk and surveyed our home with sun-glassed eyes the same way I imagined he'd check out a curling wave.

Straight hair, pale gold, pooled on his shoulders.

He raised his head and looked right at me, well, at our door, then moved forward. His walk was silky, powerful thighs flexing beneath his jeans.

Gorgeous, and quite possibly lethal.

The closer he came, the more my hand itched for the Glock. I slid it from its sheath and held it at my side, parallel to my thigh.

When he neared the stoop's overhang, his face tightened into a lopsided grin I'd call self-deprecating. Strong bones, straight nose, assertive jaw. Those shielded eyes. I wanted to see them. Here I was in LaLa Land, with an extra from... *Game of Thrones?*

Why had I thought that? But, yeah, this guy was strange. My honed empath senses reached out to read his emotions. He blocked me, and he did it with finesse. When he pressed the buzzer, I opened the door, moving my arm behind my thigh to hide the gun.

"Hey," I said, looking up, way up. "Can I help you?"

There went that grin again, and I inhaled his salt water and sunlight scent.

"Can you?" he said, in a voice that echoed the warmth of his scent, but held a slap of power. Lots of it.

I gasped, caught a low note of pain. From him. Whoa. He'd *let* me sense those, *knew* I could, then slammed that brief window closed. A slither of fear tickled my spine.

"We've met before," he said, voice bright light, with notes of humor, even irony.

No, we hadn't. "I'm afraid I don't recall."

He reached up, and I tensed, but all he did was draw his Ray Bans off his face. Eyes like ancient gold coins. Mesmerizing. Beautiful.

"And, now?" His grin was open, friendly.

I rocked back on my heels. I'd seen that eye color only once before, many months ago in a beautiful cemetery where I'd been attacked by the monstrous Cardillo. The creature from the magic world would have killed me had a group of shapeshifters in the form of immense white wolves not battled beside me.

Their leader's eyes matched those of the man standing on my door stoop.

He nodded. "You can put the gun away."

Not yet.

"You're..."

"Yeah." His grin widened, and it was beautiful. "I'm Alex. Alex Arctos. Welcome to the world of the weird. Welcome to L.A."

THOUGHTS of our battle at Mt. Auburn cemetery and the wolves' aid bombarded me as I sat Alex on the sofa and got us drinks. Okay, so I was a little stunned, but, hey, I was still functional.

He had to be the wolf alpha. I'd seen only one shapeshifter change from human to animal—Anouk. But one shapeshifter does not make a person comfortable with the idea of people transforming into magical animals. No, siree, it does *not*.

I holstered my gun, but I wasn't ready to release my fear, a useful tool when danger comes calling.

I seated him and offered drinks. In the kitchen, I retrieved a tray. *Why was he here? How had he found me? What did a shapeshifter wolf drink?* Clueless, I filled the tray with two glasses, OJ, ice water, and two Sam Adams.

I scrubbed my face to clear my head and returned to the living room. And my guest. He could be here to guide me, teach me the ways of magic. Yeah, that could be it.

Anouk had abandoned me, but perhaps she'd handed me off to him and he would help me find the Chest of Stone.

With my crappy luck, he was with those Union freaks who wanted me as their lab rat. Or maybe my evil brother Tommy, who wanted me and my power, not to mention the chests.

Golly, so many exciting options.

I plastered on a non-committal smile as I set the tray on the coffee table. "Which drink...?"

He snagged the beer, and I sat in the club chair across from him, gun by my side, and poured myself a glass of water.

His swig of Sam Adams was long and deep, those arresting eyes never leaving mine. Scoping me out. Searching for weakness?

Lucky was unaware of my fireflies. Or lack thereof.

Should I mention the Pinky thing? Maybe later, depending on how our convo went.

Alex nodded as he thumped the bottle back on the table. "Thanks, I needed that."

Gods, his eyes sparked with hunger, like he wanted to eat me, and not in a good way, but with a side of AI.

Okay. I slid into defense mode, morphed into my interrogator persona. Confidence seeped through me. I let it fill me as the silence grew, waiting for the bloom of his words.

Could I help? He'd said. Perhaps a trade. A wolfie thing, maybe. Anouk, my alleged and quite-missing guide, was a shapeshifter, too, but a humongous bird, and a panther on occasion. Wolves were different, right?

I hated, *hated*, understanding so little about this world I now inhabited.

He stretched one long arm across the back of the couch. "You really have to chill. Tone it down, Clea. Settle. This is L.A., after all."

What the *hell*? "Tone it *down*?"

He waved his hands. "The vibe."

"Are you kidding me?"

He shook his head, that mane of liquid gold shifting as he moved. Distracting.

"Nope," he said. At a loss for words, I changed course. "Um, I have to thank you. Thank you for saving my butt that day in the cemetery."

Head tilted to the side, he nodded. "The pleasure was ours."

The wolves *had* seemed to enjoy themselves ripping those deadly Cardillo tendrils to shreds. Senses expanding, I tried to read him again. Nothing. "If you're not here to do me in, why are you shielding yourself from me?"

"To protect you." He shrugged. "Sure you want to have a go?"

"Of course." My senses reached for him, delved into this shapeshifter, this man who...

Gods. Pain, so much pain. Agony. Loss. Tears and howls and shards of grief ripping flesh. I closed my eyes, and image scraps... A weeping brunette, hugging a floppy rag doll. A man's face, back bowed in pain, hands fisted as he howled into the morning sun. A white wolf, licking a woman, her face scored and bloody, cleaning, nuzzling, loving.

I withdrew. Hand trembling, I took another drink of water. Vivid. Too vivid. For the first time I'd seen, *experienced*, in movie-like clips, not just emotions.

Raw with it, I said, "What happened?" His pain had roughened my voice. "Tell me, please."

He leaned forearms on thighs, all sunshine dowsed, and threaded his hands together. "You've grown, sweetheart."

I frowned. "I'd prefer you not call me that."

He held up his palms up. "Sorry. Just a term of affection. Nothing more. But you *have* grown."

"Not enough."

He frowned. "No."

Still shaken from the bath of pain and loss, I ran the cool glass across my forehead, trying to buy time, desperate to understand. "You're not here to kill me, are you."

"No."

Truth.

He shrugged, strands of that honey hair brushing his face. "I'm here to use you."

Boy, that sounded oh-so-familiar. "I might owe you, but what makes you think I'd allow that?"

He blinked, a sardonic smile curling his lips. "Word has it, you always pay your debts."

"Not with my life," I said. "Or my soul."

His eyes tethered me. "Yeah, sometimes that happens. But I'm not looking for your life or even your soul. Just your skills."

I shook my head. "I hate to disappoint, but whatever 'skills' I possess, they're pretty useless at the moment."

His sunshine fled beneath a smoky cloud of anger. "I suspect your magically enhanced empath skills work just fine." Claws distended, breaking the skin of his clasped hands, white-knuckled with contained anguish. "Three children are missing."

That rocked me. I didn't intend to mention that afternoon's vision. "I... I know."

He growled. "How?"

"I saw them. Today. Like a vision." I shrugged. "Or how I imagine a vision would look. Then you allowed me inside."

He pulled a handkerchief from his jeans pocket and wiped the blood from the backs of his hands where his claws had pierced them. The cuts had already begun to heal. "Sorry. I'm usually more... in control."

"It's understandable," I said. "The children?"

A rabid animal's eyes shined back at me. "They're ours."

"*Shapeshifter* children?"

"And why should that make a difference?" he said, words like crushed rocks.

"Hey." I spread my hands. "Well, of course it does. Another layer to their kidnapping, a more complex one."

He swiped at his face. "These kids... My control is shredded."

Forcing myself not to sit beside him, to draw his pain to me, I fisted my hands.

"You're a softie, Clea."

"A part of me, yeah. I don't plan to change that."

He grinned, all wolf. "Nor should you. I saw you fight, remember. I'd bet your granite core is in good working order."

"The children...?"

With a deliberate calm, he raised the second beer to his lips and drank. "The police, the FBI are looking for kidnapped children."

"I haven't heard anything on the news about them."

"They're keeping it on the down-low."

"What do you want from me?"

"You are to find their kidnappers, Clea."

My eyes widened. "I can't." My mission—recover the chest.

"Oh, you can." His grin never reached his eyes. "And you will."

You are the only one. Anouk's words. *The Key. Life or death. Immense power. The world.* Grandiose expressions of a mission that seemed both profound and miles beyond my reach "Let me explain—"

"About the fucking chest?" he said. "I know that's your task. End of days. You're The Key. All sorts of crap the magic realm loves to dish out. And, truthfully, I don't give a rat's ass."

Damned if he hadn't echoed my thoughts. But I still needed a guidebook on how to deal with creatures of magic. I'd bet a billion bucks woo-woo figured into these kidnappings, and that the hunt would be ten-times harder than any mundane search. I was tempted, almost blurted out *Yes!*

I needed to think. "Want something to eat?" I dashed to the kitchen. Except he got there before me, was leaning against the counter, a leg crossed over the other, waiting.

Fear slammed back into me.

"I don't know how you did that," I said. "Why should I trust you?"

His hands banded my upper arms. Damn, I'd left my gun in the living room.

"You should trust me because you once did so, with your life."

"I had no choice."

"We all have a choice."

"My ass." He lifted me so I dangled a foot above the floor.

I blinked. Terrified? I'd faced worse. Godsdammit, I would not be intimidated. "Stop it."

His canines lengthened. He snarled.

I fought those implacable eyes, calmed my breathing, my fear, all the while hating that not one firefly swirled in my palms.

"To trust is hard. I know." He lowered me to the floor. "I also have a trade for you, one I think you'll like."

"I don't do trades."

The slam of a door. "Hey, Clea. Volleyball practice got called early. Where are you..." Lulu barreled into the room. "Whoops!"

Alex stepped back, Lulu's eyes saucered, and I could almost taste her teen hormones going into overdrive.

"Alex," I said, "This is Lulu, my ward. Lulu, Alex. He lives..."

Wolfie waved and Lulu stared.

"In Los Feliz," he said. "Just a ways over."

And Lulu stared harder, her eyes saucer wide.

"Lulu!" I said.

She bobbed her head, as if awakening from a trance. "Oh, yeah, sorry. Hi, Alex, nice to meet you. How come you're here? Selling insurance?"

He cut me a glance that said trouble was coming for me in the guise of a red-headed teen.

And didn't I know it. "No, he's here on business. Not insurance business either."

"Yeah, yeah," Lulu said as she bounced her way to the cookie jar, scooped out a handful.

"Dinner!" I said.

Large violet eyes begged.

"Two. That's it. And no soda. Water, mademoiselle."

She pursed her lips. "You're no fun."

And didn't I know that, too.

She poured some water from the Brita. "Do you surf, Alex?"

A lazy nod. "A little."

Lulu's body vibrated with excitement.

Uh, oh. She was going to ask this male a completely inappropriate question. "Lulu, I—"

"Will you teach me, Alex?" she said.

Gods, just what I didn't...

"How serious are you?" Alex's tone was dark, a glimpse of the Alpha peeking through. "Or is this some teen fantasy? You know, surfers, fun, all crazy."

Her head bobbed. "No, no, I mean it. Really. I love to swim, and I thought boarding would be cool and fun."

About to speak, to tell her no, I paused. Lulu needed this, needed joy in her life. Since her father's murder, she'd had so little. "She'd be good at it. She's got great balance."

"Well, then," he said. "You're on."

"We'll *consider* it," I said, adding a note of caution. I'd find out more about Alex, but gods, Lulu would have a blast.

She turned to me, stuck out her tongue so Alex couldn't see, then pirouetted back to him. "Thanks! I mean, really thanks!" She varoomed from the room, trailing the words, "Gotta do homework. Math, yuck, test tomorrowwww!!"

Alex chuckled. "Don't *you* have your hands full."

"Yeah. And I love it." Most of the time. But, damn, I was lucky to have her. Kids. I sighed.

"Forgive me, little mage. I've acted poorly. Our pack needs your skills. We'll talk. I'll explain... more."

I bowed my head. Again, I saw three children. Three bloodied children. Nor could I forget that this man, this wolf, and his pack *had* saved my life. He was right about one thing. I always paid my debts. "Your kids... All right. I'm willing to listen."

He notched his head. "Better yet, I'll show you."

"Our compound," he began as he drove through roads that snaked over and around the Hollywood Hills, "is in Los Feliz. Protected by walls and gates and magic. Zach, Cami, and Paul used to sneak out to adventure in the park."

"Griffith?"

"Yeah. All the pack kids do it. That's where we run as wolves. More than four thousand acres, most untamed, rugged, perfect. It's shrunk since our pack settled here, centuries ago, but still viable." He chuckled. "For us city types."

Outside the car window, a small lake shimmered, ringed by a path, with walkers and runners and people pushing strollers. "Silver Lake?"

"I want you to see where we found them."

"But they're—"

"No," he said. "They're not missing, although the authorities believe that. We have them safe now."

Safe. But not alive.

I turned away. Outside, the world blurred.

He snagged a space across from a small, fenced area where dogs of all sizes romped. Face tight, shades in place, he crossed to the park and opened the gate, held it for me. He nodded, and I walked forward while he stayed by the gate.

Here was where they'd found the children's bodies. Dogs bounded over, owners calling "no!" and I petted several, before they all streamed by me to lay quietly at Alex's feet. Several gave him their bellies.

He sat on his haunches and stroked many of them, then at whatever signal he conveyed, most bounded off to resume play. A few, however, remained, and he continued to stroke their fur while watching me.

The dogs. A distraction. I didn't want to do this, feel this. But I would. I began my empathetic scan. I was rusty, so it took little time for me to arrive beneath the spreading boughs of an oak, my feet stapled to the ground.

Pins-and-needles rose from my feet to my legs. Faint, almost whispers. I'd felt similar magic in the presence of Anouk, the shapeshifter Guardian and golden eagle. Yet the notes differed, and as I quieted my mind, I tasted three separate magics, all similar, but... The children. Yes. Their residual magic.

My mind brushed aside those magics, and I probed deeper for the knowledge of who or what had been there, and of the events that led to their deaths.

I flinched. A low hum, jagged, sharp. A cauldron of emotion—no magic—yet as I pulled it to me... Another power roiled into me, strong, staggering. I stumbled back and bumped... Alex, who must've moved behind me at some point.

"Please get back," I said. "Your emotions. Too much."

His presence evaporated, and again I reached for those harsh, sharp notes, trying to understand, to define them.

Exhilaration. Triumph. Yes, I caught it now. The thrill of victory. But... I pulled on a thread, fainter and strange.

It was an odd emotion. Elusive. One I couldn't quite grasp.

WE WERE HEADED toward Alex's Los Feliz compound, where I'd meet with the families. Once I saw them, I'd feel their all-encompassing grief, taste their anger and their agony. My empathic senses were my gift and my curse from my mage ancestors, my shielding subpar. But this was what I did, whether as an FBI interrogator or as an individual committed to alleviate suffering. No matter how much it hurt, it was who I was.

The images I'd seen through Alex's pain, ones of weeping and screams and blood, made sense now.

I kept trying to grasp that puzzling emotion, the low note I sensed. The harder I tried, the more fleeting it became.

The kids had disappeared two weeks earlier, which was when Alex's pack had reported them missing to the LAPD. Three days later, the pack sensed they were dead, their remains nearby. They immediately recovered their bodies, which the killer had deposited at the dog park. They'd tracked them through their blood signatures, and Alex's interwoven connections to all his pack.

"You didn't tell the authorities you'd recovered the bodies."

"No. Nor will we. We might be the Arctos pack, but we have first and last names, just as humans do. We have jobs, families, traceable histories in the mundane world. The pack has been part of this world for centuries, far longer than most magical creatures."

"I see." Of course, I didn't. Not really. But now wasn't the time for a history lesson. I wished I'd brought my knitting. It soothed me like nothing else, especially when I was about to walk into an emotional tsunami of grieving parents, confused kids, and wrathful shapeshifters.

Alex's grip turned white knuckled. "Why would he leave them at a dog park? Why not leave them in Griffith as carrion? Bury them? Throw them into the sea?"

"Perhaps because the killer equates the dog park with shapeshifter wolves? But there's more," I said, pausing, waiting. And there it was, dandelion-fuzz-light as it drifted down into my conscious mind. "Gratitude. He felt gratitude. He or she was *grateful* to the children. And, no, I can't read thoughts, only sense feelings."

"What the fuck?" he said, grinding the words.

I sensed joy and triumph, but underneath it all... "He was thanking them."

3

DREAMS AND SCHEMES

Fury, grief, and confusion showered me as I walked beside Alex through the gates of the Arctos pack's perimeter wall.

I was prepared. These past hours with Alex enabled me to see, to *know* much of the true man, the true shifter. He was dominant and demanding, yet honorable and fair. He'd spoken truths and showed his pain. I'd tried to do the same—well, at least the truth part. Thus I had enough trust to walk into a den of shapeshifter wolves and not fear being eaten alive.

The crowd was subdued, angry, grieving. Three men and two women who stepped from the waiting crowd projected excitement. They howled a greeting. I almost did the same, but smiled mine instead. They must be the five other wolves who, along with Alex, fought the Cardillo that grim day. Without them, my death would have been inevitable. I owed them my life.

"Thank you," I said, holding each one's gaze. "Thank you so much."

In a flash they surrounded me, hugging, slapping my back, and talking at once. "That was a badass day," someone said. "Shit, yeah," said another. One woman chuckled. "You were on fire!"

A cleared throat. Alex reigning in our happy-reunion party. Yeah, not the time.

"Later?" I said.

"Sure as shit, yeah."

"That day," Alex said. "It was a good one."

And today was not.

Four of them slid back into the crowd, while one man remained, shorter than Alex, brawny, with defined muscles beneath his grey t-shirt and keen emerald eyes flecked with gold.

"My First," Alex said, nodding at the beefy man. "Erick."

"Clea." Erick nodded, all business now, and stepped beside Alex.

The huge courtyard and surrounding two-storied buildings recalled an old Spanish hacienda, with mellow stucco walls and curved red-tiled roofs. Cholla, yucca, and other succulents greened up the area before the massive entrance doors of the central building.

No one spoke as we entered and much of the crowd trailed behind us. Alex turned to them, face grim. "Now is for the families."

The crowd melted away except for six people—two couples, one with a child who looked about eight, a lone man, and Erick.

"Can I come?" the child said.

The bronze-skinned woman who held his hand shook her head. She leaned down and whispered in his ear.

He stamped his foot, shook his head, straight black hair flying in every direction.

"*Non*, Bron," she said with a French accent, exasperation oozing from her pores. She pointed to the dissipating crowd. "Go with Heather."

Arms crossed, anger fizzing around him, he stomped off. But I caught the sheen of tears in his eyes. Not of anger, but sorrow, and guessed one of the murdered children was his sibling. My heart stuttered.

With faces hard as the stone floor, we walked through the large salon filled with sofas and club chairs, where a wall of two-storied windows faced the expanse of Griffith Park. Breathtaking. No wonder the kids snuck out to play. As wolves, they could run across acres of wilderness.

Alex led us through the salon, through winding corridors, and down a narrow staircase that twisted. No one spoke, the families' emotions oppressive in the silence.

We spilled out into a cave-like hall, encompassed by rock, odd for this SoCal location. Walls broken up by doors and, again, we wound through corridors and deeper into the earth's belly until we came to an immense windowless room crouched at the corridor's end.

I took a breath, inhaling the grief and anger now amplified by stone. I felt buried alive and would have run topside if I'd had my druthers.

When Alex waved us in, Erick nodded for me to go ahead, where we took seats at a large live-edged redwood conference table, scarred and scratched by what must be wolf claws.

Mutterings by the parents, and that sense of anger... directed at me.

The emotional pitch rose, and I grew dizzy.

A hand pressed the small of my back, the brush of blond hair across my cheek. "You okay?" Alex said.

A faux chuckle. "Yeah, yeah."

"This should help."

He stood beside me, close, a large presence dampening the cascade of emotion, then tapped something under the table. A creak, then a smooth, whooshing noise as ten feet of wall slid away like a barn door, revealing...

Griffith Park undulated before me, a hot breeze sweeping away the claustrophobic sensation. "Holy shit."

He grinned. "Every den needs an escape hatch."

I suspected there were more. "The kids got out here?"

He shook his head. "One of the smaller doors leading to the park."

"But down in these caves."

"Yes."

"She doesn't belong here," mumbled the lone father with the braid.

Erick grunted. "Shut it, Reidar. She's proven herself to me, to four of our brothers and sisters, and to our alpha." He sat beside me, reclining as if the chair couldn't quite contain him, eyes a cool emerald, dark chocolate hair brushing his nape. "We tracked the children."

"Your noses," I said. "Super sensitive like—"

"Dogs?" He winked. "But better."

Alex finally sat, directly across from me. The room quieted, the emotions tamped down to a hum of confidence in this man, their leader. He gave an affectionate nod to the couple on his right—a black-haired mother and her mate, whose narrowed blue eyes bored into mine. "This is Mira and her mate, Justus. Parents of Camilla." His eyes slid left, to the man with the braid. "Reidar, father of Zach."

The woman across from him, bronze skinned, her hair a tempest of curls, mother of the little boy, Bron, held the hand of the blond man beside her. "I am Melike," she said, her French accent strong. "And Carlos is my mate. Paul was our son."

Alex leaned forward. "We traced the children to the peak of Mt. Chapel."

"A favorite of theirs," Mira said, face dreamy with memory.

"*Tais tois!*" said Melike. Claws extended from her paw and a bristle of white fur undulated up her forearm to her human elbow. Five gouges appeared in the table.

Alex shot Melike a dark look until her forearm and hand morphed back to human. "Yes," Alex said, shifting his eyes to mine. "A favorite. That's where the assassins captured them. They sprayed the children, as well as themselves, with perfume, and they all took off."

"You said 'they'."

Erick snorted. "Yes, four. We followed the scents. Man, did we ever. But however they carted the kids, we lost 'em. Fucking bastards."

Alex turned to me. "They knew," he said, his voice a dark growl. "They knew we were shapeshifters."

"How could they possibly... Damn." I understood why they hadn't shown the FBI or LAPD the bodies and their retrieval site. "The kidnappers had to be knowledgeable mundanes or magical."

Reidar lasered his eyes at Alex, then glanced away, unable to hold his alpha's gaze. "What the fuck use is she? I objected to her presence before, and I object now. She's an outsider and human."

"No, Reidar," Alex said. "She isn't human, but even if she were, *I* brought her in. So shut up. Point of fact, she's mage, and you were told of this. You—"

"What good is a mage?" Reidar said.

"*Oui!*" Melike's voice a near screech. "What can she do that we can't?"

"I agree!" Justus said, as his fist slammed the table.

Alex reclined, eyes hooded. Erick wasn't so patient. His growl grew until it drowned out the protesters.

Silence.

Alex pinned each parent with a gaze that oozed power. In turn, each person lowered his or her eyes. "Not one of you is an investigator. Not one of you is an empath. Not one of you comes with the skill set of this mage and her history with mundane law enforcement. She has graciously, *graciously,* offered us aid. And you will treat her with the respect her gifts, her skills, her humanity, yes, humanity, deserve."

Hell, he wasn't describing me, but Wonder Woman. I almost snorted.

Alex slid a folder across the table to me. I tilted my head, a question.

"Crime scene photos. We used shifter techs, the bobcat pack's. They're damned fine."

Bobcat pack? I flipped open the cover, reviewed the photos, and much like hundreds of others I'd scanned, I wished I'd never seen them.

I turned inward and processed.

Broken children, but staged like the spokes of the wheel, feet outward, their heads pointing inward and touching, supine, hands facing upward. They'd dressed the children in white, the girl in a dress—obviously not their original clothes—and little blood spattered the clothes or scene. No visible injuries, but each child was unnaturally pale.

I shuffled through the pictures again, and a certainty coalesced inside me. The killer or killers had drained the children of their blood.

The images pointed to a weird, ritualistic killing.

Why? Why the blood? What would he or they *do* with the blood?

More photos, and I paused, drew one closer. Scribed into the dirt at the dog park, what looked like droplets of blood in five curling configurations. Four appeared to be runes while the fifth resembled the Celtic spirals on my wrist tattoo. Again, that sense of ritual.

Otherworldly magic? I hadn't sensed any at the dump site.

I raised my eyes to Alex. "Have you been able to decipher the runes?"

He scraped a hand across his chin. "Our historians looked into it. She's knowledgeable. She believes they're nonsense, mumbo jumbo."

Then what did the ritual *mean*?

ALEX, Erick and I stood on the peak of Griffith Park's Mt. Chapel, buffeted by warm winds. Constellations blanketed the night-dark expanse. A quilt of lights, of Hollywood, downtown Los Angeles, and much of the Southland covered the earth far below us.

I'd insisted we follow the path the children had taken. Much of the dirt trail had been smooth and wide, with a steady incline until the path turned steep and rocky to reach the peak. A tough climb.

During our trek, the only resonant emotions I'd picked up had been ones of laughter and glee and excitement.

Having understood the kids' joy, my eyes burned. I let the tears fall and turned to Alex. "In wolf form, they were racing each other, yeah?"

Golden eyes filled with poignance, but his lips twitched to an almost-smile. "Yeah. Best friends. They competed in *everything*."

Here at the peak, the emotions evoked a tangled skein of yarn. I shooed the two men away, far enough so their anger and pain wouldn't bleed into the already complicated emotional mess.

Eyes closed, senses open, I drew in the lingering feelings of the children and their captors to sort the sensory snarl. I thumped down hard on my butt, rested my forehead on my knees, overwhelmed by the children's fear. I sifted out anger. The kids were angry, pissed off at their captors. Good for them. I brushed those emotions aside and allowed the perpetrators' hunger and triumph to rise. Cold. Their feelings chilled. And then... a hint of... metallic, yet not metal, but a taste half-familiar, and... No, that couldn't be right. I sifted again, muffled the unwanted emotional notes and...

That hint, that taste... it reminded me of James Larrimer.

I peered up at the two men. "I'm worried."

Alex frowned. "About..."

"The killer or killers taking more children."

Erick snorted. "Crime of opportunity."

"No." I shook my head, voice a croak. Alex and Erick crouched before me. "This wasn't a crime of passion. Not of lust, nor sexual depravity. Opportunity? Possible, but I doubt it. I didn't sense any greed. Not an accidental killing, say a kidnapping gone wrong. But ritual? Yeah, it feels like that." I looked at the two men, both shaking their heads.

"We've got nothing that even comes close," Alex said. "Shifters aren't a ritualistic people."

"We don't do the woo-woo thing." Erick's laugh was bitter. "We leave that to you mages."

Except for Anouk, the shapeshifter Guardian. But even she was mostly pragmatic.

The wind stole Alex's hair as he tilted his head. "So maybe this is a mage thing."

"I admit I'm new at this mage gig, but I didn't sense any magic or..." I smiled at Erick. "Woo woo."

And I kept that half-familiar taste to myself. James. My absent lover, crafted of nanotech and magic, would never take and kill children.

But that taste... So similar.

He'd mentioned others who were nanoteched beings, all created by DarkPool, all property of The Union.

But that made no sense, either.

I stood, as did the two men, their eyes glowing silver in the moonlight. "The children were alive on this mountain, taken to another location, drained and killed, then placed at the dog park. Whatever took the children," I said, "must have been watching the compound."

Alex fisted his hand, moved to Erick, and the men talked quietly between themselves.

"How will you protect the children?" I said.

Alex tilted his head. "Do you doubt us?"

"Of course not. But how will you keep them safe to and from school? After-school activities? Daily life?"

"We will." He scoffed. "You can't know it's only shapeshifter children they're after."

I filtered again all that I'd sensed and shrugged. "I just... do."

ALEX WAS DRIVING me back to Beachwood through Griffith Park. Since the emotional overload had died down, my injuries reasserted themselves. With precision, I detailed the Pinky attack.

"I'll check with our historian," he said. "But I've never heard of anything like you're describing." He morphed into protective Alpha mode.

"I'm fine," I said.

Those golden eyes bored into mine. "Dammit, woman, you're not. I can tell you're in pain."

His anger and protectiveness and... desire overwhelmed me. Shit. I leaned back against the seat cushion, too beat up to deal with any of it.

Except I couldn't leave it alone. Part of me felt I was betraying James and part of me responded. From his luscious mouth to his carved jaw to his Alpha stare, Alex was a fine, fine male. I inhaled his sunshine scent. It soothed me.

"Clea." He shot me a cocky grin.

"Yeah. Sorry. Woolgathering."

"Was that what you were doing?" His smile widened.

Mr. Alpha knew just what I'd been thinking, and he liked it. Double shit. "So number one question: why did the Pinky attack us?"

"That's easy. You're a powerful mage."

I snorted. Useless, more like it.

"And The Key."

I waved a hand. "Question number two: why didn't he kill me when he had the chance?"

"Easy. He was on some scouting mission."

For whom or for what? No point in reviewing the legion of people and organizations hunting me. I wasn't even sure the "who" mattered anymore.

"You're quiet." He turned down Deronda Drive, his lips bowing to a slow smile. "You haven't even asked about our trade."

That strong profile, the smile lines carved beside those lush lips —Alex was a man who preferred to smile. To find joy. Who hid a vein of devilish humor. A good man.

I laughed. "Do I dare ask about that trade?"

"You're getting a twofer." A wolfie grin.

"Smartass." I raised a fist. "Shall I beat it out of you?"

He barked a laugh. "No, just the opposite. I plan to beat it out of *you*. You're in pathetic shape."

"Am not."

"Look what happened when that thing attacked you. There's no getting around it. You're a physical wreck."

"My ass!"

He chuckled, low and sexy, and I got the point.

"Later," he said. "My first trade is that Melike will train you, physically and with weapons. Erick, too, when he has time."

"Melike. She can't stand me."

He nodded. "Exactly."

"This is going to hurt, isn't it?"

"Exceedingly."

But the idea of being trained by the wolves? Oh, yeah. "Bring it on. That twofer?"

He threaded the car around three hikers hogging the road and hooked a left into my dooryard, a term Californians didn't get.

The car purred, Alex unhooked his seatbelt, and moved to face me.

"Let's talk inside," I said.

He shook his head. "I've got to get back. I've arranged—"

"This is gonna be bad, isn't it?"

"Clea-us interruptus. I hear it can be fatal."

My amusement bubbled, but I kept my trap closed.

"As I was about to say, I've arranged for you to meet a mage of considerable power."

I opened my mouth to speak.

A growl.

I closed it.

"He will work with you on your mage skills."

"Really? Really?" I clapped, kissed his cheek. Strong arms banded my back, pulling me close, then his head turned and his tongue traced the seam of my lips.

His warmth, affection, and hunger engulfed me. So good to be held after months of holding others, being the go-to gal, hoisting a weight that increased by the second.

I sighed, slipped out of his embrace. He wasn't James.

"I... I..." Stuttering. I was so uncool.

His smile was gentle. "You're a beautiful woman. Can't blame a wolf, right?"

I hid my smile with the shake of my head. "I'll take it as a compliment."

"I'll be in touch."

"Me, too." I lifted the folder from the dashboard.

The pack's children needed me. My adopted children might be older, but they needed me, too.

EACH NIGHT since that first surreal dream of James and the glass, I'd dreamt of him, vivid dreams so real I sometimes felt his smooth skin beneath my fingertips and his soft lips on mine. I pulled back the bedcovers. I could hear Ronan playing a video game in the living room. The clock read one a.m., but he was a college student now, and it wasn't my place to tell him when to go to bed.

I slipped between the soft sheets with trepidation. I was afraid. I *wanted* to dream of James, but... Over the past six months, I'd dreamt plenty of James, sure, and a few of those dreams had been pleasant, even sexual. But these recent ones felt too real, too visceral. They scared me.

Perhaps my nightcap of bourbon was the culprit, so I abstained. After an hour of reading, I put aside the book, turned over, and snapped off the light. I shivered.

THEY'RE BEATING HIM! *Half-a-dozen huge men and women with knives and claws and whips. Blood smears James' body, drips across his face. He strikes out. His fists and teeth rend his attackers. Three lab-coated men look on, bored. I go to cover my eyes, but I have no eyes, no body, no presence. I am merely an observer.*

A knife to the gut doubles him in half. I scream, and it might've only been in my mind, but in a massive burst he throws off his attackers, pivots, and stares straight at me, Pacific-blue eyes blazing.

4

LET'S GO FOR A WALK

The following morning Alex reappeared at our home. When I opened the door, he held out a hand. "C'mon. Let's go for a walk."

Taking his hand would have meaning. I hesitated. No, it didn't have to mean anything, just a gesture between two friends. I wrapped my paler fingers around his larger tanned ones and we walked out the door.

We climbed the dirt road toward the Hollywood sign. "The blood analysis will take a week or two at the least," I said.

"Mari's fast," Alex said.

I sighed. "Blood isn't. But at least we have something. Blood tells many tales. I can only imagine how the FBI techs would freak."

He wiggled his brows. "That could be fun."

"Yeah, right." I kicked at the road, sending a puff of dust into the air.

We walked in silence for another fifteen minutes. Damn, but I still hurt. I raised a hand to my neck, tried to work out the kinks.

"Here, let me." He massaged my shoulders, long fingers digging into muscles tight with strain.

Boy, did that feel heavenly. "Thanks," I said when he released me.

He lifted my hand to his lips and kissed the back. "My pleasure."

Ouch. Definitely more than a friendly shoulder rub.

His eyes narrowed. "I want you, lady."

An electric shiver zapped me. "And I'm not ready for that."

"Soon."

"Alex. I..." I drew my hand from his and we walked on.

"Soon." He grinned.

His smile was deadly and told me way too much info.

The image of a large raven-haired man, stoic faced, blue Pacific eyes that stole my soul. *I was so* not ready to give up on James. "I wish I understood my instincts better," I said. "The fact that the killer is targeting shapeshifter kids. Why them?"

He narrowed his eyes, face serious, and his profile echoed one I'd seen on an Icelandic sculpture of Thor, the chin arrogant and fierce. "A mystery," he said. "For now, at least. The attacker doesn't know we've involved you."

I could think of only one reason shapeshifter children would be targeted. Just one. "I can't stop thinking about—" "The Chest of Stone." A whisper. "The air has ears."

"Knowledge is power. And again I feel powerless." Just like with the Chest of Bone and Dave's death. I'd sworn never to feel that way again. Talk about a fail.

Well, *hell*. Not this time, dammit.

"Come." He tugged my hand to a side trail that led downward, where we spilled onto a paved road. "Your chariot awaits."

Said "chariot" was a beast of a motorcycle, a vintage Harley or an Indian, a little dusty and bruised, which only added to its hotness.

When he oozed that Alpha charm, it was obvious stuff came easy to him. Well, I wasn't easy. So when he handed me a leather jacket and a ginormous helmet for his bike, I gave him a dirty look. "It's nine million degrees out. Cars have A/C and comfort."

He shrugged, in full surfer-guy mode.

Deeply curious, I had to ask. "Where are we going?"

"You'll see. Trust me."

That usually never ended well. I slipped on the jacket, zipped up, then slid the helmet over my head. "This is ridiculous," I mumbled to myself.

His voice boomed in my ear. "Better ridiculous than—"

"What the hell!"

"Microphone. Speakers. They have those back in New Hampshire, right?"

"Oh, shut up." I lifted my leg over the bike and fastened my hands on his waist. "Like I said, where—"

"Sshh. I'm taking you to see Rae, the mage I told you about."

Yes!

"He's not what you'll be expecting."

I chuckled. "No one ever is."

The machine blazed down a side road, and the only thing between me and the pavement were my two hands going numb from my death grip on Alex.

"Chill, sweetheart. You can ease up on your claws."

"I don't *have* claws," I sniped.

"You wish."

"No. I don't."

A snort.

But I loosened my hands enough to resume circulation. Yes, I was a little excited to meet Rae. Okay, really excited, even if the timing sucked.

We threaded in and out of traffic, zoomed up ramps and down them. Understanding L.A. was still beyond me, but I recognized Melrose, and... We were in Hollywood. Soon, on Fairfax, maybe.

I was finally enjoying myself, the ride, the excitement. Hell, yeah.

A beat began to thump in my head. Rap, hip-hop, the words muffled by my helmet. The traffic slowed, and couples and trios strolled the sidewalks—black, white, Asian, and everything in between. L.A.'s tapestry of cultures and ethnicities and blends excited me.

We slipped into a tiny parking space in front of a black-fronted store with a starburst carved over the door. Alex removed his helmet and shook out his hair, then took my helmet and locked both onto the bike.

He grinned, ruffled a hand through my dreads. "Hat head."

I laughed. "Riding was fun."

"Told you."

"Smartass."

Men in gold chains, ball caps reversed, pants sagging walked the sidewalk, as did girls in spiked heels, tight dresses or low-slung jeans that hugged their asses. "What is this place?"

"The urban streetwear clothing capital of L.A. Maybe the world."

Streetwear, urban hip-hop, skateboarders. "Rae is *here*?"

Another grin. Alex was having way too much fun with this.

Inside the store fittingly called Starburst, the walls were black, the ceiling lit with blue tube lights, and the music pounded, customers tried on hats, shirts, and sweats.

A tall ebony-skinned young man trotted over in low-slung black jeans, work boots, and a shirt stamped with a woman's lips, lush and red.

"Hey, man," the kid said to Alex.

They slapped palms, gave quick man-hugs. Then the kid turned to me, giving me the stink eye. I returned the favor.

"Rae," Alex said. "Meet Clea. Clea, Rae." This was the powerful mage who would teach me? *Really?*

His sleepy smoke eyes stared in a way I didn't much like. The body might look like a twenty-two-year-old's, but the eyes... Beneath those heavy lids, eyes old and sharp as shards looked at me with disdain.

"Hey, hon, y'all done lookin' yet?" he said, his accent Georgia-peach thick.

"No. I'm not." Damn me for being snippy, but he felt like nails on a blackboard.

He tittered a laugh. "Well, y'all got somethin' anyways."

"Fuck you." Had I really just said...?

Kissing sounds. "Now *that* ah might like, sugah." He looked me up and down and smirked, then lifted one of my dreadlocks and sniffed.

"Cut that out!" I tugged it away.

He picked it up again. "Oooh, shiny!"

I pulled my dreadlock out of his hand. Steaming, I turned to Alex... *who wasn't there!*

The music thumped. Someone had turned up the volume. Customers, salespeople swirled around me as a small wave of power surged. I tried to push it back, but it crested over me, sending nasty prickles across my skin accompanied by Rae's grin.

"Stop it," I said.

"Y'all gonna hav'ta *make* me stop." With a two-fingered salute, he walked off to help a customer.

As I turned, a cute gal pierced to the gills handed me a Starburst bag. "From Rae."

"Thanks." I took the bag and stormed out of the store, making a beeline for the wolf alpha.

Alex leaned against his bike, texting on his phone.

I beaned him on the arm with the bag. "There's *got* to be another teacher."

He winced, laughed. "He's the best."

I swung my leg over the bike, slipped on the helmet, and slammed down the visor. The quiet, the blackness enveloped me as we peeled out of the parking spot.

I hadn't even used my empath abilities, just reacted to Rae's button pushing. He'd gotten to me good. Alex was right. Rae was nothing like I'd expected.

CONTEMPLATION STOLE my focus as we wound through L.A.'s busy streets. I had no idea where we were. L.A. was crazyland, after all. Alex varoomed by one too-slow car, then zoomed down the pavement between lanes, and...

"We could've crashed!" I said, sounding funny inside the helmet.

"Could've, sweetheart. That's the operative word."

We stopped for a huge lunch at a taco truck, and once back on the bike, I got the sleepies as we wove through L.A.'s streets. The bike swerved to the left, barely missing a car that should've turned right, but hadn't. *Shit.* Pay attention. My grip on Alex tightened. He was warm and hard, his jacket butter-soft beneath my fingers. And I shouldn't be thinking those things.

I'd been alone too long.

We peeled onto another side street. When he hooked a right, and varoomed up the hill, a sense of the familiar hit me. "This isn't Beachwood."

"Nope."

"Well, where are we going?"

"The compound."

"I've got to go home. Meet Lulu and—"

"Lulu's at the den already. So's Ronan. And the dogs. And even the cat, though I was tempted to leave it behind. I don't like cats."

I sputtered. "You moved my family!"

"My team assessed your house." Another turn, and we climbed a hill. "Beachwood is too dangerous, too exposed to the park for you to stay there."

"I like it *because* it's by the park."

"Too much glass. Too many exits and entrances. Easy to break in. Easy to attack."

Another turn, and directly in front of us a car backing out of its driveway. Alex slowed the bike.

I took a quick look around, swung my leg over the seat, and leapt. *Ouch, dammit this might be stupid, but...* I thudded hard onto a grassy lawn, and rolled to a stand.

Within seconds, Alex stood in front of me, his bike sprawled on the lawn. "What the fuck?"

"Yeah, what the fuck. You had no right to take my family, my critters, and my stuff and hold them all hostage at your compound. No right."

A growl rumbled from his chest, his face tightened, shifted. Fur sprouted beneath golden eyes and teeth lengthened. He sliced the air with a clawed hand. "You weren't safe!"

The fury, the feral anger told my hindbrain to run. Instead, I stepped forward, nose to nose with Mr. Alpha. I'd been herded, directed, pressed into service by other forces. Not given a choice. Never given a choice. I was done with that shit. No one would rule me. Arms stiff, hands fisted, I said, "I don't give a flying fagarwe! You will not control me."

His face eased into its human form, and his eyes morphed to a soft silver-gray. "Forgive me. I didn't understand. Please, accept this change for yourself, for your charges, and for your quest."

I shook my head. "No. I can handle it. I can take care of them."

He snorted. "You so can't."

"Swear to gods, Alex, I feel like punching you."

His open smile was disarming. "Many in the den feel the same. Please. Think." His face tightened but remained human. "If you say no, I will return you and yours to Beachwood."

"You should have asked."

"I should have."

"I'll handle living at Beachwood." He had offered to take us home. The way out was open.

But I heard the lie. And I saw Lulu coming home from school. And what if I wasn't there? Gracie running around in the backyard. Ronan leaping into a fray that could kill him.

Life was never what we expected. "I need my privacy, my own space."

"That's manageable. Plus, you'll adapt."

My MO for the last eight months. I nodded. "Let's go, get this over with."

HE PULLED up in front of the Arctos compound, entered a code, and when the gates swung open, drove inside.

"What about my knitting? If you manhandled it and some of the stitches fell off the needle on one of my projects, I'll kill you. It's a complicated pattern. A scarf designed by Romi. And it could..."

He chuffed a breath.

Yeah, I was rattling on, and I knew it. I didn't want my little family living at the Arctos den. But it was the smart thing to do. For now.

Packed everything, had he? I bet he hadn't found the wall safe. The Chest. Yeah. Not everything.

For now, the Chest was safe, shielded from magical hunters, and no one mundane or magical could code it but me. Given my injuries and exhaustion, I'd do a Scarlett O'Hara and think about it tomorrow.

DINNER WAS AT SIX. I'd explored our family suite, with sprawling windows and a view onto the wildness of the park. I'd unpacked, checked out Lulu's and Ronan's bedrooms, as well as my own. In each, I found a small carved wolf placed on a redwood shelf that gleamed in the afternoon light. A welcome I'd tucked in my jeans pocket, the smooth wood soothing where little else in my life was.

As I explored the den, I found the river-stone floors and adobe walls beautiful. Soon, the fifteen-foot ceilings of the communal rooms gave way to the cozier arched pathways where I presumed families and singles lived. No skylights—Alex had said for security reasons—but plenty of diffuse light from wall sconces and streams of LED tubes overhead that he said dimmed at night.

Philodendron and ferns covered the walls, and down one corridor savory cooking scents made my stomach rumble.

I was hunting for the control room where computers and high-def screens and audio feeds measured the den's pulse and the pack's safety. The feeds covered the compound, down into the park and out onto the street.

Given the attack, the windows in our rooms and the communal spaces unnerved me until Alex assured me automated steel shutters would cover them at the first whisper of danger.

Down an arched corridor, alive with blossoming red geraniums, where tapestries hung depicting wolves at play, a tendril of grief and fear scraped my senses. Concern crawled through me, and I paused.

I drew closer to one door, carved in a black wood with a bas relief of a family—two adult wolves, two pups.

The grief was stronger here, the sorrow, the fear, along with a low note of anger that threaded beneath the other emotions.

I raised my hand to knock, stopped. It wasn't my business.

Yeah, well, I rapped my knuckles on the door anyway, too foolish to heed my wiser rational mind.

"Go away," came the small voice on the other side of the door.

Well, that wasn't happening. Never with a child in pain.

"I'd like to come in," I said, projecting vibes of comfort and caring. "I'm new here."

Shuffling feet. The door flew open so hard it banged the wall.

"Fine!" said a red-faced boy who looked up at me with defiance, blackberry eyes shiny with tears. "Who are *you*?"

He must be *Bron*. Melike's and Carlos' son. Brother of Paul, who'd been drained of life and of blood. I dropped to my haunches, eyes now even with the eight-year-old's. "I'm Clea. We met earlier. Remember?"

He stomped to the sliders that overlooked the park, his back to me, arms tight at his sides, hands fisted. "Yeah. I remember."

I stepped into the apartment, cozy and woodsy and inviting. Carvings and weapons adorned its walls, and a huge leather sofa and coffee table sat atop a Turkish rug in golds, greens, and blues. Beneath the glass-topped table, carved trout swam in a stunning 3-D rendition of a stream.

Afternoon light poured in from the glass sliders, silhouetting the boy whose body vibrated with anger.

He jammed his hands into his pockets.

"Shall I stay or leave?" I said.

The boy didn't turn. "Why should I care?"

I moved forward, but not too close. "I don't know. I thought you might like some company."

He flipped around to face me, lower lip quivering until he got it under control. "Yeah, I would. My brother, Paul."

I sat cross-legged on the floor, projected warmth and concern toward the boy. "You know that's not possible."

He moved forward with that wolfie grace I'd seen in all the shifters, then stopped about a foot away. His hand thrust to his hips and his eyes bored into mine. They were filled with a child's fury and bottomless sorrow. It hurt, my head throbbing with pain.

"This is a nice apartment," I said. "Your dad's a woodcarver."

Eyes narrowed. "Yeah, so?"

He seeped with grief. "Your mom, she's a warrior."

Chin notched. "One of the *best*."

"But she couldn't save Paul."

The faintest tremble of that notched chin. "She didn't!"

"He went off on his own, Bron. You know that."

He loomed over me, vibrating with pain and fury. "She *should've*."

"I'd like to hear about Paul. You have some good stories, I bet."

In one fluid motion, his bum was on the floor, legs crossed to mimic mine, still furious, still hurting. "Maybe."

I smiled. "Only maybe?"

"Yeah, okay. I've got some good ones."

Bron talked, and I listened to tales of the boy Paul, who played and fought with his beloved younger brother, who idolized him in return. Paul had been a carver, too, and Bron pointed to a less refined carving of a deer Paul had completed only last week.

"Your brother sounds amazing."

"Yeah, well, he thought he was all grown up. And he *wasn't*."

"You're right," I said softly. "He wasn't."

He stomped from the room. I almost followed, but forced myself to wait. Minutes later, he returned with a Wolverine bobblehead, old and scarred, clutched in his hand. He resumed his seat, eyes on me, hands absently bobbing the figure's head.

"He's cool," I said. "Always one of my favorites."

"You, and everybody else."

I chuckled. "True."

"Neddy gave him to me."

"A buddy?"

"Sorta. He's so neat. He was Paul's pal. He's older, like fifteen, maybe. He gives me his old action figures and stuff. He liked Cami a lot. Y'know, not *like* liked. But like a big brother. He's really sad, too."

"Because his friends died."

"Yeah, but..." He spread his arms wide. "He was supposed to go. He would've protected them. He's really big."

I suspected Neddy would have ended up dead, too. I opened my mouth, but Bron spoke first.

"*They* won't let me talk about him. Paul." A sniffle. He swiped the back of his hand across his nose.

"That's because your mom and dad hurt," I said.

"I don't care. I want to talk about him."

He let me take his hands in mine. "You care about your mom and dad, Bron. I can feel it."

"Whatddya mean you can feel it?" Eyes wide, curious.

"Your mom's a warrior. Your dad's a carver. I'm an empath. I feel things others do."

He looked at me, and I could tell he didn't understand. "You know how you taste ice cream and chocolate and—"

"Cherries! I love cherries, especially the hard one. The soft ones are gross."

I laughed. "Yeah. You know how you taste those things, well, I taste other people's feelings the same way."

"Oh, that's weird."

My forehead crinkled. "And turning into a wolf isn't?"

"No."

"Of course it's not," I deadpanned. "Everybody turns into wolves, right?"

His face scrunched up. "Maybe not. But we do."

"And I taste feelings. See? And I help heal feelings, too. I'd like to help you."

Lower lip thrust. "Whaddya mean? How?"

"It's something I've been practicing."

He nodded, all sage.

"I go inside a person, and I try to smooth things out. Like your dad does with sandpaper and wood."

"Inside where?"

"You."

More scrunching. "How? I don't know anybody who can do that. Like, inside me?"

"Yeah. Just like that."

"How?"

I took a moment. "I'm not really sure. It's sort of new. At least, my awareness of it is."

He leaned on his fisted hands, forehead scrunched. "Um, er, will it hurt? Not that I can't take it. I'm a warrior, too."

I bit back a laugh. "I know you are. And, no, it won't hurt. May I try?"

He snorted. "I'm not afraid. I'm tough."

So very tough. "How about it?"

I glimpsed the hesitation in those deep black eyes. "Yeah, sure. I'm not scared."

"I didn't think you were."

His hands were warm, a little calloused, and though my nerves prickled, I was determined to give it a shot. He closed his eyes when I told him to, and I closed mine. I regulated my breathing, and soon our breaths mingled, in sync.

I'd been practicing, sure, on Lulu and Roman, with this new ability that fit like a second skin. But I knew them well. Bron? He was different, a broken child whose cover of bravado hid a well of pain and incomprehension.

I sent tendrils of love and care through my hands to his, up his arms, his shoulders, into his chest and lower body, then to his face. Still, I went deeper to enfold his spark of life, the elusive part of all creatures that I sensed with my inner talent. And that was where it got hard, where I "saw" cracks and fissures that I smoothed. I couldn't erase them, but I could soften the edges, narrow the fissures, dampen the pain. At the same time, I poured warmth and healing into that same heart, scraped away much of that anger and replaced it with images of his mother and father and ones of a healthy, happy Paul I'd seen online.

Exhaustion turned my efforts static-y. I began to withdraw, as if I were surfacing from deep in the blackest of oceans, the solid world pricking my senses, telling me I had little more to give before I passed out. Tears dampened my face, but I didn't open my eyes, not yet, needing to make our transition back to the tactile world a smooth one.

"What the *fuck*!"

The fury of the voice jerked open my eyes, senses screaming with the shock of departure. The whites of Bron's eyes gleamed back at me and as his hands slipped from mine, he fell sideways to the floor.

Someone wrenched my shoulder and hauled me to my feet, the blade of a knife pressed to my throat.

As if I'd leapt off a tilt-a-whirl, I swayed, felt the blade bite skin. Warmth trickled down my throat.

"Stop it, Melike!" Male, a thread of command.

"Why should I?" Words ground out like broken glass.

"She's under our protection."

"Fuck that," she said, her French accent thick with hatred.

I wanted to shake my head loose of the dizzy. Bad idea with that knife pressed to my throat.

"She wasn't hurting Bron," the male said.

What was his name? Ah, Carlos. Yes. I blew out a breath. "Carlos is right. I wouldn't hurt Bron."

"So you say." A growl low in Melike's throat.

I kicked back, my foot connecting with Melike's knee, rotated as I jumped away. Swayed a little, but found my footing. "I was not hurting Bronson. If you hadn't jerked me out of there, he'd be fine."

She spit at me. "Bah! Think you know, *putain*."

Did she mean "damn," or was she calling me a prostitute? Whatever she meant, it definitely wasn't nice. Then her boulder of pain smashed into me. "I do know."

"Stay away from our boy." Her knife pointed at my gut.

"Mom?" Bron said, all hazy and distant.

She dropped to the floor and scooped up her son, hugging him tight, so tight.

Carlos' eyes met mine. They told me he was sorry, told me to be wary, told me to leave.

"He'll be better," I said to Carlos, then stole a glance at Bron. "Talk to him about Paul. He needs that."

Carlos shook his head as if clearing cobwebs.

Only after I'd left, walking back to our suite, did I touch my fingers to my throat. They came away smeared with blood, and though that achy pain that comes with a cut was minor, my fingers shook.

Melike. This was the woman who'd train me to fight?

Wasn't that shit-tastic.

5

A WHITE STRIPE

That night, dinner was an unpleasant affair with Lulu having added a white stripe to her newly short, newly *black-dyed* hair. It was okay if you liked that sort of thing. Ronan didn't. He made it apparent in the way his stiff-backed frame retreated to a table of older teens and twenty-somethings in a dark corner of the dining hall.

Given the knife cut I sported on my throat, I'd considered wearing a turtleneck, but with the high temps, I'd opted for a snap shirt done up to my throat. All I needed was a pocket protector. I ignored Alex's strange looks as we ate, surrounded by shapeshifters he'd introduced at the onset of the meal.

The only positive note to the evening was the friendly overture by Mira, Camilla's mother.

Now I sank into my bed, more tired than I'd been in months. The bed was big, plenty big for two, and I ran my hand over the covers, thinking how sweet it had been those few days I'd slept beside James. For the first time in months, I allowed myself to remember how his body had curled around mine, his warmth enveloping me in a kind of comfort alien to me.

That was just stupid, remembering that. Just stupid.

I smashed a fist into my pillow and allowed my eyes to close.

I DIVE into warm Caribbean waters and swim. Over and over, turquoise blue parts before my hands. Smooth, as if limitless freedom accompanies each stroke. I turn my head for a breath, the sun warms my cheek. Divine bliss.

Except...

The waters chill, darken. No, not the translucent Caribbean, but the Pacific, where waves crest over me with increasing force. I bob, try to ride them, but...

Something tugs at my legs, binds them together. A rope! And me, gasping a breath, then another, mouth choking on salt water. Shaking my head, no, no...

I'm pulled deeper and deeper into Stygian dark. Plunging, twirling, inexorable.

I must reach down, untie the rope, free my legs, but my speed's increasing, heavy, weighted with stones, a bag of stones.

Yes, stones pulling me down, boulders so heavy I can barely reach my ankles. Pulling, scraping at my legs, fighting so hard to reach them skin peels beneath my nails.

Down and down and....

James' face emerges from the murk. And in a swift movement, he slices the rope in two. His arm clamps my waist, and he propels us, soaring upward through the deep.

We break the surface, and I suck in a massive breath, then begin to cough.

"You okay?" he says.

"Now I am. I wish you were real."

He smiles, that dragon grin a mixture of arrogance and love. "I'm real."

I rest my head on his chest, and then we paddle to shore.

THE FOLLOWING MORNING, the shit hit the fan, a gross image, but all too accurate. Melike bitched to Alex about my convo with Bron, then she beat me bloody in our first training session. My honed blade of a body turned out to be more gummie bear-ish, only my ballet and runs saving me from complete annihilation. And that fricking dream. It amped up my compulsion to find the Chest of Stone, already sandpaper on flesh. It was important, sure. But murdered kids trumped a mythical chest, at least to me. Not to mention finding the source of my assault by what I now called the drooly Pinky thing.

I grabbed a bite in the dining hall, where I spotted Ronan with one group of kids and Lulu with another, which hurt my heart. They were drifting away from each other.

When I spotted Bron in a group of boys and waved, he turned away.

Like I said, shitty.

As I shoved another bite of tempeh-and-veggie salad into my mouth, Alex appeared in the doorway and did the c'mere thing with his head. I frowned, scarfed the rest of the salad, snagged my water bottle, and walked down the stone-paved aisle knowing, yeah, *knowing* that more crap was about to land on my head.

"Ready?" he said.

"Damned if I know."

Hands on hips, he threw back his head and laughed. "You are one funny woman."

That infectious laugh brightened my mood. "I aim to please."

His lip curled. "Yeah?"

Oh, gods. "Not that way. What's up *now*?"

His eyes narrowed at a particularly nasty bruise on my arm. "I'll talk to Melike."

"Don't. At least she has someone to work out her pain on."

"She's amply aware humans and mages don't have our shapeshifter strength or resilience. She crossed the line."

Given shapeshifter ears, I tugged him into a darkened corner well away from the dining hall. "I don't want to be here, you know that. But because it makes sense, I am. So I have to make my own way. I'll work it out with her."

His pause said volumes, with a few chapters that spoke of Alex's alphaness, the others of sex. Rusty pheromones sparked, and I tamped them down. I might find Alex drool-worthy, but I'd be damned if I'd do anything about it before I resolved my relationship with my MIA lover.

"So what am I to be ready for *this* time?" I said.

"Rae."

Swellsies.

I WANTED TO BE PSYCHED, all tingly and stuff, as we drove toward the 101 on Alex's bike. I was going be taught how to access my mage powers, call my fireflies whenever and wherever I needed them. Yippee! Not so much. Rae had played me yesterday, and I didn't like it one bit.

We ended up on the 101 in traffic. Just another typical, clichéd day in L.A. Except Alex started threading the bike like a banshee between the lines of cars inching along the highway. And I got it. I laughed. "Whooee. This is cool!"

He chuckled. "Yeah."

We zigged and zagged down the road, heart in my throat, but only a little, flew down the ramp for Topanga Canyon, then past shops and suburban streets lined with trecs, until we started to climb. The world transformed.

We varoomed into the canyon. Trippy and deeply strange. Gnarled trees, million-dollar houses and shacks crouched on hills of ochre and green. Funky signs and women in hippie dresses and men with long locks swinging across their backs. Dogs trotting on hidden streets that wound narrow and tight up hills and down into valleys where streams burbled and sang.

Joni Mitchell and Neil Young and Will Geer. Trailers and yurts and expansive estates. Love beads and Mercedes and ganja.

I'd seen no other place like it in L.A., and it sang to my heart. Home. It said "home."

Deep, old magic was here, pulsing the earth and brushing the blue, blue sky.

We wound a circuitous road higher and higher until Alex slowed the bike. I raised my visor, smelled the Pacific, saw gulls circling above.

"Almost there," Alex said.

"Gods, it's beautiful."

"True. We almost relocated the pack here, but the commute down the 101 is a beast."

"Worth it."

"Some of our members didn't think so. Maybe someday. You feel it?"

"The magic, close? Yeah."

"Topanga's a thin spot where the two worlds, magic and mundane, mingle. One of the first places where the magic started replaiting half a century ago. Scared the shit out of some pack members."

"Really? It didn't you, though, did it?"

"Naw. I loved it. Loved the fuckin' feel of it."

"Me, too. Home."

"Home." He squeezed my hand that rested on his waist. "You're nervous."

"You *have* met Rae, right?"

"He's not so bad."

"Neither is a plague if you're already dead."

His snort reverberated through my microphoned helmet. "Your nerves are like pins and needles on my skin. They hurt!"

I snickered. "Poor baby." But he was right. My stomach cramped. Working with Rae's snarky attitude was only part of it. What if I failed?

Down a long dirt road near the top of a mountain, around a bend, and a leafy canopy hid... a treehouse! Clapboard redwood siding and a three-sided porch. Its three stories rambled across the branches like a living thing while a winding staircase led to a carved door. What a gorgeous construct, one that seemed so at odds with the man I'd met.

Alex's bike ground to a halt, all noise and dust. I removed my helmet and corralled my long Medusa dreads with a scrunchie. I puffed out a breath, then lifted my leg over the bike. I wobbled. The forty-minute trip, not to mention Melike's pounding, had exacerbated my injuries. My legs were jelly.

"Alex, I..."

Visor up, face ablaze with a grin, he shouted, "Back in four hours!" and drove off.

What the... "Alex!"

He held up four fingers, then disappeared around the treed bend, the bike curved so low, I was amazed he didn't spill. Show off.

He'd left me, damn him. Oh, hell.

I shook out my legs, brought them back to life, which was when power oozed across me. I flipped around, my body set in a relaxed, battle-ready stance. That power crested like a wave, too reminiscent of my dream for my liking. It peaked and curled around me. I staggered, determined to hold my ground, expecting to see Rae slinking toward me.

Instead a young woman sashayed in my direction, all hips and long legs and wavy auburn curls. She wore skinny jeans, a red silk shirt unbuttoned enough so a lacy black bra peeked out. Long chandelier earrings bobbed as she strolled closer. She wore Rae's face.

"Hey, girlfriend," she said, waving long fingers polished with red. Another power wave hit me.

Who the hell? My fury ignited. Some *prank*. Some clever...

Whoa. Was this a trap?

I released my anger, cloaked myself in calm, just as Dave had taught me.

Now my empath senses could read the woman, girl, really, sauntering toward me as she jived to some music humming from her black earbuds.

"That's better without all that nasty anger, sugah," she said, with Rae's accent, but a woman's voice.

"I am not your sugar." I sucked in a breath, focused, and tasted her humor and calm. She/He was silently laughing at me. Whatever Rae was playing at, I didn't like it.

Prickles covered my body, like fuzzy caterpillars crawling across flesh.

"Cut it out," I said. "I've had a shit day already."

She plucked out the earbuds and chuckled. "It's only gonna get worse, hon."

The buds kept thumping music. Hip-Hop. Dre. Yup, Dre. *Gods.*

Breathe, calm.

"That's a start, girlfriend."

Prickles again, poking and prodding. "Stop it."

Rae's face transformed to a feral sneer. "Make me."

I was so screwed.

"I can't." My body vibrated with anger and aggression. "And you know it."

"Sure you can, punkin'."

I dug deeper, raised my right palm, demanded my tattoo ignite, insisted my fireflies spark and stream and shut this girl up.

Nothing. "Dammit. That's why I'm fucking here."

"No need to swear, punkin'. I sure can't see y'all accessing any power. Y'all a minor leaguer. Alex is full a rubbish."

I walked close, nose to nose and toes to toes. "No, he's not." I bunched my fists, blinded by the asshole's button pushing.

A viscous slime crept over my hands, then up my arms, much like my twisted brother Tommy's ooze had done, except this burned.

The invisible goo crawled up my arm, searing, scorching, the pain intense.

"All right, dumplin', listen up. Y'all hear?" She sucked on a long, red nail, shook her head, curls bouncing. "You don't have It. Too bad, sugah'." Her hand made a shooing wave.

"Oh, I have It, all right." I was so damned mad. Maybe this was a test. Maybe I was to be humbled. Maybe she just liked playing with people. The goo hit my breasts, and the pain increased. "It's asleep, and I'm not going anywhere until you teach me how to wake it up. Got it?"

"Why should I? My time is val-u-able."

"*I'm* valuable."

The goo vanished, nerves achy with released pain.

"*That's* a start," she said. "Good thing you stopped pitchin' that hissy fit."

She would drive me batso. But I needed Rae. So I'd lose my anger and play this smart. I bent at the waist, pressed my palms together. "I am yours to command, sensei."

"I ain't no sensei, but at least you got your 'tude in check, sugah."

I approached Rae with wariness. "Alex said you're the best mage teacher around."

She notched a hip, big grin, grey eyes turned silver. I read pleasure. No, satisfaction.

"Now that's more like it, dumplin'."

If Rae's training didn't kill me, her Southernisms would.

AT EXACTLY FIVE O'CLOCK, Alex varoomed up the driveway on his bike. I was in no shape to ride. But I'd take a go-cart to escape from Sadist Rae. I'd thought Bernadette, my deceased grandmother, defined hardass. Rae made her look like a pansy. But at the end of our torturous session, I'd felt something deep inside me crack. A small thing. I didn't know what it was, couldn't access it voluntarily, *yet,* but I'd felt it, and knew it was the key.

"How pissed are you?" Alex said, removing his helmet.

I shook my head as I donned my passenger's helmet.

"Rae?" he said.

"He... she... didn't deign to walk me outside. Said you were on your way and I should wait in the driveway. What a prick."

He placed a finger beneath my chin. "He's all that, sweetheart. But Rae's the best."

WE SPED up the 101 on his bike, while people in cars pretty much sat there, although one woman thrust a middle-fingered salute our way.

I was antsy to retrieve the Chest of Bone. But until it was locked away at the den, I'd keep mum about it.

"I have an idea," I said via the helmet's mic.

"Stoked."

"You know, sometimes you sound just like a surfer guy."

"Aren't you noodled?"

"What the heck does that mean?"

"Beat. Exhausted. I'll teach you if you want."

"To surf?"

"Best high in this mundane world."

Tempting. Just like Alex. "Someday. Now about my idea. Yeah, I'm... noodled, but not totally. Let's stop at the Beachwood house. I need to check you got everything."

"We did."

"Maybe we could trap that thing that attacked me."

He chuckled softly. "Stones, lady. You got stones. What makes you think it'll come back?"

"Because it was scenting for something. And once I appeared... Yeah, it was scenting for *me*."

Ten minutes later, Alex stopped the bike a ways down Beachwood, removed his helmet, and tucked it under his arm. He flipped around on the bike, his sweat-soaked hair stuck to his head, but his eyes—ancient coins stared into mine, serious and deadly.

"Why was it scenting you and why this crackbrained idea?" he said.

"Crackbrained? You're really going there? Look, we agreed it didn't try to kill me. It smelled me, tasted me. I want to know what it is and why it's after me."

"Okay, I listened. Too dangerous. Not worth it." He pulled the helmet back on his head.

So I slid mine on to talk to him. "You're not shutting me down that easily."

"I just did."

Screw it. I wasn't a prisoner. I'd do it on my own, armed to the teeth, of course.

He inhaled, deep and long. "No," he said. "You won't."

"What, you joined the California Psychics Association?"

His lips twitched, fighting a grin. He failed, and his warm laughter filled the air. "No. I'm coming to learn the way your twisted mind works."

"I see. So you're now the shapeshifter police?"

"You bet I am."

"What am I doing that's so interesting to the otherworldly Mr. Pinky? Item One: searching for the Chest of Stone. Item Two: searching for the killer of three shapeshifter children, who were taken, I might add, for reasons we don't understand. Makes sense, right? Either way—"

"Item Three: the most interesting thing you're doing, sweet Clea, is being *you*. They want to end you, a powerful mage."

"*They*? Pinky could have killed me. He didn't. Didn't even try. Rather creepy, in fact."

"He hurt you bad enough."

"Because I fought him. So let's say I agree with Item Three. Great. Yet another reason to capture the beast. Proactivity are us."

"Father Fenrir, save me."

"Praying to your wolf god? He won't help."

"Nor am I stupid enough to think he will. Terms: I'll go tonight. With Erick. You will stay at the den. We'll take some clothes of yours and make sure your scent's concentrated in one spot."

Thoughts careened around my head. I had to make it sound real, sincere. "I still think I should go, but I bow to your wisdom, and all that crap."

Yeah, that *so* wasn't happening.

6

THE BRAIDING OF TWINS

I stood in the compound's tower room and watched the sun dip deeper into the Pacific, the moon a small crescent dangling just above the horizon.

I loved the moon. Magic retwining, magical creatures, beings who could fly and dissolve, two worlds—Magic and Mundane, twins, braiding together again after a millennium apart. I rested my hands on the open window frame, the stone warm beneath my fingers. Impossible to get my head around it, the concepts too big, too vast, unknowable. But the moon. That I could love.

The sea had swallowed the sun, with only its last rays now parting the dark. A noise behind me. I whirled.

A muscled boy, teenaged, stood in an aggressive stance, weight on the balls of his feet, only his tousled brown curls to soften the leaf-green eyes narrowed with hate. The knife in his hand glistened in the light of the wall sconces. I stilled, found the threads of his emotion, like worn stones on a path well-trod.

"Hello. I'm Clea."

He thrust the knife out further, not touching me, but close. "You stay away from my friend."

He went for the dominance thing, holding my eyes, his Alpha-eyes bright, expecting me to cave.

Yeah, perhaps he'd be alpha someday, and though his 5'10" or so didn't match Alex's height, I suspected he hadn't finished growing yet. I held my gaze to his, our near-matching eyes ablaze. "Why should I stay away from Bron? I like him."

"Because he's not yours, he's mine."

His wave of guilt staggered me, and I blinked, which he took as winning the Alpha stare out. I didn't mind letting him think that. "I can see you believe that he's yours. I bet you're Neddy. You're devastated by Paul, Cami, and Zach's deaths, aren't you?"

The bold boy didn't drop his stare, yet his free hand fisted around the claw and tooth that hung on a leather cord from his neck. An ooze of horror, but this boy had guts. He'd be a fine alpha someday. If he made it that far.

"I didn't do anything," he said.

Now, guess time. "Perhaps you made a bet with them?"

"No."

A truth. *His* truth? "Dared them?"

He snickered. "Yeah, right."

If not those, then...

"You teased Cami. You scared her."

His hand tightened on the knife just before his muzzle and canines elongated and he came at me.

My right hand flew upward, palm out, and for the first time in months, my fireflies swirled. They streamed from my palm, magic lights—a knitted web of feather-and-fan, searing pleasure and pain —and stopped the jaws snapping closed an inch from my throat.

Okay, then. I held him there, frozen. Muzzle drawn back from sharp teeth, snarls ripped from his throat.

"Neddy," I said, breathless in my struggle to hold the boy inside my fireflies.

That alpha stare again, fury at being trapped, fear roiling off him.

"Listen to me," I said. "It wasn't your fault. Evil took your friends. They went up that mountain on their own."

That stare dropped. Had he chased them?

I released him from my fireflies and rested my hands at my sides. His muzzle receded, canines shrinking, and his face reshaped into Neddy's belligerent one.

"Whatever happened, you didn't take them or kill them. You're not to blame."

A boil of horror, and he wrenched his eyes from my grasp and ran down the stairs. "You're as creepy as they said!" he shouted back at me. "I'm gonna tell everyone!"

That was me, creepy ol' Clea.

Breathing hard, I checked my phone. I was late. Shit. Erick and Alex had left for Beachwood forty-five minutes earlier. Hyper aware of whom I might meet on those ambush-ready stairs, I trotted down them to check on Lulu and Ronan before I left.

When I entered our suite, Ronan was nuking something in the microwave. "Have you seen Lulu?"

He notched his head toward her bedroom, snatched the mug from the microwave, and stomped out the door.

Lulu was in her room, all right. She lounged at the small table surrounded by three shapeshifters, two boys and a girl, who couldn't keep their eyes off her while she focused on the tarot cards laid in front of her. Gods, she'd gone Goth. The air smelled of incense, heavy and dark, and a small smile played over her black-slicked lips.

I stepped inside and sneezed. "Where's Ronan off to?"

She shrugged, eyes glued to the cards.

"The dogs?"

"Out with some pack guy. He said he was gonna take them for a romp."

"I'll be out for a little while." I did a one-eighty and left, averting a blowup when I asked her why the hell she looked like an extra from the *Rocky Horror Picture Show*. I tried to tamp down my niggle of worry that I was screwing up with Lulu, breaking Dave's trust that I'd do well by her. She was a teen, my mantra of late. It didn't help.

I peeked into the den's basketball court, where a shirtless Ronan guarded a shirted boy half his size as a bare-chested shapeshifter dribbled the ball up the court.

Okay, onward.

Back in my bedroom, Calico Kitty sprawled at the foot of my bed. I geared up, knives, guns... and again looked longingly at James' katana. Note again to self—get Melike to teach me to use it. I thrummed with anxiety as I grabbed my black ankle-length raincoat. I should have told Alex about the Chest of Bone, and I would once I had it safe in the compound.

I strode out of the bedroom to face a five-foot-eight bundle of hatred lounging in the doorway to the corridor.

"Melike," I said. "What's up?"

"I'm your guard," she said, eyes glittering with fury. "You want to leave, *cheri*? *Bien*! Nothing better than beating you shitless."

I pulled my Bowie. "Not with this in my hand, you won't."

She laughed. "You won't cut me." She stepped forward.

So did I and beaned her in the temple with the butt of my knife.

She crumpled, still conscious, but barely. I ran.

I BURNED rubber on the way to Beachwood. Melike wouldn't hurt Lulu or Ronan. Me? I would pay for tonight's work in painful ways.

On our street, I slowed, passed our house, and parked up the dirt road to Hollyridge Trail. On "soft feet," as Dave once called them, I padded back toward the house while berating myself for beaning Melike. "*Snap out of it!*" shouted the memory of Bernadette. Yeah, she'd been a *Moonstruck* fan, too.

Crap. Focus.

I neared the edge of our Beachwood rental, where tall trees and a fence screened the front of the house. I left the road, clambered over rocks, and headed to the back of the property. The house was silent, but a soft thread of shapeshifter vibe came from inside. If I could sense it, could the Pinky, too?

And if I could sense the wolves... *Damn!* I'd bet they could smell me.

So I dumped my stealth mode, walked up the path to the front door, and twisted the knob.

Inside the darkened living room, all I could see were the outlines of shapes, sucky night vision and all. But, boy, did I ever *feel* the wolves. Three of them. Alex seethed, apparently so furious he couldn't utter a word. Erick? Annoyance, yes, but his silent laughter bounced around the room pinball-like. The third's wary indifference came from a shifter I hadn't met.

"Hey, boys, how's it hangin'?"

A choking sound. Not sure if that was from Alex's apoplexy or Erick stifling a laugh. Ah, definitely Alex.

"Do wolves get high blood pressure?" I said. "Unhealthy."

More choking, then a pulse of red-hot. "Erick," Alex ground out. "Take her back."

The third shifter, who was leaning against the wall, growled.

"That's gonna be tough, boss," Erick said. "She's armed to the teeth."

I really hoped I was wrong about the high blood pressure thing because Alex was streaking toward supernova.

"Take. Her. Back."

Erick stepped forward, in front of the picture window. I side-stepped into the umbrella stand which was there for no good reason, since it rarely rained in L.A.

"I'll wait in the bedroom," I said. "How's that, Alex?"

All went to hell when a trio of pink creatures crashed through the plywood window, knocking Erick to the floor beneath them.

Alex leapt atop me, but a creature plucked him away like so much tissue paper. Chittering. There was that damned chittering. I drew my knife just as a glob of drool splashed my face. "Shit!"

The creature pulled me close, sniffing, its huge nostrils distending. It whined something, and the other two flanked it. The third shifter leapt onto a Pinky's back, wolf jaws wide to bite its neck. Another Pinky ripped him off and threw him across the room where he thudded to the floor.

I was bizarrely calm, unafraid for my life, grossed out by the creatures but trying to sense them, too. The Pinky holding me snaked out its purple tongue and dragged it from my chin to my forehead. *Gross!*

I registered a ping, so fleeting, so shocking, I couldn't process it.

Released, free, and I caught my balance just as two Pinkys disappeared in a tumble of arms and legs as they grappled with two immense white wolves. The Pinky holding me hadn't let go, and even though we stood by the door, it dragged me to the now-gaping picture window.

Snarls and growls came from the wolves trying to rend the two Pinkys apart.

The Pinky tugged on me, and I dug my fingernails into the hand holding my throat. It dragged me ever closer to the empty night, and I drew my knife, hacked at the wrist, the Pinky screeching, its grip tightening to where I could barely breathe.

Tighter and tighter, and through the haze of my dimming consciousness, I kept hacking and sawing.

The hand fell away, still attached to me, the Pinky howling, and I pushed the creature from me, and ripped the severed hand from my throat, preparing to leap back into the fray.

Alex sprang in front of me, half wolf, half human. "Go to the bedroom, godsdammit. You're distracting us!"

I nodded and ran, leapt up the three stairs, stumbled into a wall, and aimed for my bedroom.

More screaming and growling and a high-pitched keening.

I slammed the bedroom door, locked it, and shoved the disgusting hand into my coat pocket. I pulled out my gun and stood in my darkened bedroom, knife and gun at the ready, eyes never leaving the door.

Should I not have listened? Should I go back downstairs and fight? I shook as I waited, panting, assessing, unnerved by the growls and shrieks and... silence.

The perfect time to get the Chest of Bone, but, no, not with Pinkys around.

I *stepped* toward the door, planning to help the guys. Except... Was

Alex right? *Was* I a distraction? Would they fight harder and better without me? Be more lethal?

I *really* wanted back in the fray.

I reached to unfasten the door lock.

Think, my brain insisted. *Be wise.*

So I waited.

I hated waiting.

James would have had a good laugh over this one.

A THOUSAND HOURS LATER, the knob turned and met the lock's resistance.

"Clea," came the hoarse, exhausted voice.

I scrambled to unlock the door, and it blew open. I still couldn't see, but it was Alex. I'd know that vibe anywhere.

I pressed my hands to where I imagined his shoulders would be. "Alex?"

"They're gone."

"The Pinkys?"

"The *what*? Yeah, they're gone."

I helped him to the bed, where he sat, hard.

My groping fingers found the wall switch, the light blazed, and I got a look. "Oh, gods."

Slime and blood covered Alex from head to boot. A deep cut lacerated his cheek, another his chest. And bite marks... everywhere.

"Oh, Alex."

He waved a hand. "We heal fast. I'll be fine. Nice necklace of bruises you got there."

"Choke hold. Almost got me."

He rubbed his thumb gently across my throat.

"Erick?" I said.

"He'll be okay."

"Your other packmate?"

His jaw tightened. "Eido. He's hurt bad."

"Oh, Alex. I'm so sorry."

"He'll recover, too. Slow. But he'll get there."

I slumped beside him, tucked my arm into his. "So much for my plan to trap Mr. Pinky, huh?"

A bloody-toothed smile. "Not bad, sweetheart. Not bad."

Which was when I reached into my pocket for the hand, except my fingers recoiled. Gross. In the heat of battle was one thing, the aftermath quite another.

"I, um, I've got something."

"Huh?"

"A hand. I cut off one of the Pinkys' hands."

He chuffed, harder and harder until he sounded like a maddened wolf, moon-mad and feral.

A SHIFTER ZOOMED Eido to the pack's healer, while the rest of the crew patched Alex and Erick up. Both still looked like crap. A woman I didn't recognize put a cold pack on my throat. Heavenly. With reluctance, I dropped the bomb about the wall safe and insisted they take the whole safe to the compound without me telling them what was in it. Hey, I'd paid a huge security deposit.

After Alex examined the hand—patches of pink flesh, tufts of wiry brown hair, claw-like black nails, the stump with coagulating purple blood—disgusting. He passed it over to a tech, who took photos and collected blood from the scene. Efficient, just like mundane techs. "Mundane," not "human." I was starting to think in otherworldly terms even if I hadn't yet met a vampyre. I shivered. I wasn't ready for that little joy.

Once they'd nailed the plywood back in place, we locked up and left for the den, the safe in my possession. I'd bet Melike was waiting for me. Yippee.

Alex rode in the car with me, the silence deafening. He wore clean clothes, but the dried blood and other fluids remained. Here it comes. I was so not eager for him to ask me about the safe. Thunderclouds built. Distraction time. "Bet you can't wait for a shower."

"True."

"The Pinkys could follow us," I said.

"They know where you're at, sweetheart."

"What makes you—"

"Noses. They've got noses good as ours. But we whipped their asses. Right now, they're probably licking their wounds."

Literally. Yuck.

"Don't worry. They won't get inside the compound. Ever."

"Your tech... What makes you think DNA analysis will work?"

"Oh, ye of little faith," Alex said. "You think they'll only use mundane tests?"

"I guess I hadn't thought about it."

He swiveled toward me. Uh, oh. "So what's in the safe?"

"The Crown jewels. I stole 'em."

He growled. He actually *growled* at me.

"We're almost home," I said.

"I wish you trusted me."

"I do."

"Not enough." He straightened and donned his mantle of alphaness. "Just like you, Lulu, and Ronan, we'll keep the Chest of Bone safe."

He'd guessed. Understandable, I supposed. And now he thought I didn't trust him. His ripples of anger, disappointment, and a note of longing soaked my senses to the bone.

He touches the woman's breast, and she moans. His hand, bronzed skin on the woman's white belly, meanders downward to her thatch of black curls. His fingers dip into her cleft, and the camera pulls away. Her delicate face is a portrait in bliss, head thrown back, neck taut, her long fall of dark hair spilling across her pillow.

James, no, please!

The kiss he gives her sears my soul.

His fingers massage her cleft, and she writhes in his arms. He moves to his side, and I see his erection, huge and pulsing. He dips his head low, laves her breast. Her fingers dig into his shoulders.

James rips himself away from her and sits on the edge of the bed, his fingers scraping through his long hair. Then he shakes his head, a dog shucking water. "No. I will not do this."

A male voice slithers from the woman's mouth. "Yes, you will."

7

BODY ART

Drunk from the previous night's dream, I stepped into the shower the following morning too aware that my body resembled a black and blue splatter painting. My eyes watered. *Why? Why was I having these dreams?*

I dried off, hung up the towel, and walked into my bedroom to find Melike on her haunches before the safe, now tucked in a corner.

"Melike." I had no intention of mentioning last night's conking her on the head.

Her body swiveled like a snake's, disgust pouring out of her.

Forcing myself to ignore my nudity, I strolled over to the dresser, donned underwear—gods, everything hurt—and slipped on a pair of jeans and a white button down.

She spat. "*Bah! Vous êtes un diable.* We have training. Or did you forget?"

Damn. "First, I need to check on Lulu and Ronan, and I—"

"Excuses." Her lips curled.

"No, my kids. As soon as I touch base with them, I'll come to work out, yeah?"

She shrugged, as if my plans were inconsequential, and turned to go.

"Wait a sec." I retrieved James' Katana. "I'd like to learn to use this."

"*Bien sûr.*" She twirled and left.

Yup, soon I'd be in a world of hurt.

WHEN I TEXTED THE KIDS, Ronan said he was in class. Only silence from Lulu. Assuming she would text me from school on her break, I changed into my workout clothes.

I waited, but thirty minutes later, my worry rose to the orange zone. By now, Lu should have texted me back. I went in search of Pris, a twenty-something shapeshifter and Lulu's friend.

I halted when I passed a suite, door open, TV on, newscaster shrieking. Smoke billowed behind him, and sirens wailed, people shouted and horns bleated.

The male reporter, rumpled suit, tie askew, waved his arms. "Gone! The top fifty-four stories of our beloved 108-storied Sears Tower is gone." He looked off camera, spat. "No, I will not call it the fucking Willis Tower."

I stepped closer. Tears coursed down the reporter's cheeks, dirtied with soot, and what might be blood. "At nine this morning, something sheared off the top of the tower. It *vanished*, along with all the desks, phones, elevators, and, tragically, all the people in those top 54 floors. Is this yet another, new kind of terrorist attack?"

The man's hand shook as he tried to right his tie.

An off-camera female hand wrenched the mic away, and...

From down the hall, laughter, giggles. I backed out of the doorway and followed the sound.

No, the Sears Tower disaster was no terrorist attack, but yet another magical eruption caused by the arrhythmic retwining of worlds.

What if smaller, less noticeable eruptions hadn't reached the news from far-flung sites around the world? How often were they coming? How severe were they? Like that squid in Dubai? The flower fields? Sedona?

What precipitated the individual eruptions? Where had the Sears-tower people gone? Were they alive... somewhere?

Until I gathered all the chests and handed them to their guardians, the events would only get worse.

More giggles, and moans, as I neared Pris's door.

Later. I'd think about magical eruptions later and deal with what I could fix now.

I knocked, and after a few heartbeats, a pretty blond cracked the door.

"Hey, Pris. Do you know if Lulu got off to school okay?"

Her toffee-brown eyes stared into mine. "Yup. Fine."

A lie, one so blatant I almost choked.

"Really," I said, deadpanned. Tried not to panic that Lu might be off having "an adventure," as she liked to call them.

"Can I come in for sec?" I said.

A slow dip in eyes now filled with calculation. "It's a bad time, Clea."

Bad time, my ass. I was tired, hurt, and cranky as all get out. And Melike was waiting for me. I might not be shifter strong, but surprise does wonders. I shoved hard on the door.

There sat Lulu and another girl I didn't know, both *a la* Goth, fingers pressed to a Ouija board planchette.

I tamped down my fury. I would not blow this. I would *not*. "Not feeling well?" I said in my most conversational tone.

Her one-sided shrug spoke both of indifference and guilt.

"I'll drive you. That way, you can make some classes."

Her lips bowed downward. "Not in the mood."

I would not blow this.

The other girl popped her gum. "She doesn't need school."

She looked about twenty-one, the same age as Pris. I walked further into the room. "No? Is that your point of view? Or, perhaps, it's that of your alpha's?"

The girl blanched.

"Don't talk to Zoe like that," Lulu said.

I rounded on Lulu. "In what way am speaking inappropriately?

I'm curious if the unimportance of school is the pack's point of view or Zoe's and Pris's."

Pris shot me a grin. "Don't include me in that! I graduated from UCLA at 20."

I nodded. "Impressive. Then why is it okay for Lulu to miss school to do the Ouija board?"

"We were doing more stuff than that," Lulu said.

"You're not even a shifter." Zoe notched her chin. "What do you know?"

I chuckled. "You're trying so hard to be a smartass." I gave her a smile with teeth. "Careful, little girl. I might not be a wolf, but I bite."

She snapped her head around. Her earrings swished to and fro. Mesmerizing.

I blinked. Something. Yes... *something.*

Those earrings. They weren't huge, maybe an inch-and-a-half long, and so at odds with her Goth persona. Golden, burnished s-shaped dolphins, held to her ears by a pearl stud or wire, with another smaller pearl adorning the dolphin's lower "s" shape.

"Clea?" Lulu said.

I shook myself. "Lulu, go change for school."

"I don't need to change, and I'm not going. You can't make me."

I rested my hands lightly on Lulu's shoulders and leaned forward to whisper in her ear. "You're right, I can't. But what I can do is change our Wi-Fi password, as well as take away that iPhone I bought you. *That* I can do."

Her eyes widened. "You wouldn't."

"Wanna put it to the test, kiddo?"

"*Fine.* But you're acting strange."

I walked closer to Zoe.

"You going to hit me or something?" Zoe said.

"No," I said in a husky voice. Hard to focus on anything but her earrings.

I closed my eyes and allowed Zoe's essence to seep inside me. No bad vibes. Just a kid looking to get by, which felt like enough for her.

"Can I see one of those?" I touched my finger to an earring's pearl.

She jerked back. "They're just fakes. I didn't steal them."

I pushed calming waves through the room. "I didn't think you did." My softest, most convincing voice. "I used to have a similar pair. I just want to see how alike they are."

"This isn't some trick, is it? I heard you're weird."

"She is not!" Lulu said.

"It's okay, Lu. No, Zoe, it's not a trick." I offered her a smile filled with trust.

"You want to hold my earring, eh?" she said. "Sure. For a twenty."

Gods save me. "Be right back."

I ran to my room, drew out twenty bucks, and stuffed it into the pocket of my workout pants.

Back at Pris's room, Zoe held out her palm, fingers waggling. "And...?"

"That's awful," Lulu said.

I chuckled. "Life is full of surprises, Lu." I slipped Zoe the money. "How about that earring?"

Eyes sly with calculation, she slid it out of her ear and handed it to me. "See? I can play good girl."

I held the earring in my palm, wrapping my fingers around it, closed my eyes, shut out the "real" world in favor of the sensory one.

Threads of promise, a thing that hinted at a need so strong my gut churned. But I kept my focus tight, refusing the distraction. Not blood. No, but a lure, skating across shimmering waters, the knowledge coming from deep within.

Different, but the same. I shook my head. Not exactly these, but *like* these. Made no sense.

I held up the earring. "Where did you buy them?"

"You want to know? That'll cost you."

Lulu stood. "No, it won't. She got them at the Eagle Rock Goodwill. I was there, and I got a sweater."

I nodded, and while my conscious mind felt the oddness of our conversation, my subconscious obsessed on the earring.

"How about you loan them to me?" I asked Zoe.

Zoe snorted. "For forty more bucks." Again, she held out her hand.

"Dream on, little girl." I whipped out my phone and took some snaps of the earrings, then shot Zoe a pointed look. "Enjoy your Ouija game."

"Wait," Lulu said, standing. "Can I walk with you?"

"Sure."

Pris chimed in. "But Lulu, we—"

"I'll see you later. *After* school."

I'D BLOWN off my practice time with Melike, had lunch with Lulu, and we'd talked and laughed and painted our nails, hers white, mine turquoise blue. I wanted to drive to the Eagle Rock Goodwill, but if I did that, I'd be late for Rae in Topanga. Since I didn't need more grief from her... him?, I headed up the 101.

Today Rae's costume flapped around him like the Harbinger of Death, reminding me of the Saint-Gaudens statue I'd seen in Washington. It was titled "Grief," which fit, given the grief he laid on me again and again. His face was Asian featured and pale, at least it was before he disappeared. Poof. So annoying when he did that. I'd given up being stunned by his transformations and poofing.

I stood in a circle of dirt surrounded by white stones, bent over, hands on knees, gasping as sweat soaked my tank top and trickled beneath my loose workout pants.

"You're a damned beast," I said to empty air. He'd attack me again, I just didn't know from where.

Invisible Rae slammed my shoulders, and my ass slammed the dirt hard. *Damn him.* I sat there, ignoring the sparks of pain Rae could turn deadly with ease.

"What's up with me, Rae?"

He poofed in beside me and sat, his robes floating to pool around him.

"Somethin'," he said. "That's for sure."

"Wow. Wisdom for the ages."

He chuckled. "You could piss off the pope, white girl."

"For all I know, you're not even black or Asian or African American. A man or a woman? Who knows? Or *Southern*."

He examined his hands. "Yeah. I'm all a those. Sometimes."

"You can be anything. That's pretty magical."

His lips tugged into a frown when he sat beside me. "It's my gift. It's my curse. It's all clothing I wear. Doesn't change who I am. Most people, they're caught up in the clothes. They don't see *me*."

Yet when I unfurled my empath senses, he was always the same. Always Rae. "I do. I will."

Which is when I sensed it. A tendril of familiarity wound around me like a song. I pushed to my feet, did a 360. There, across the stream and just up the hill. It tickled my senses, compelled me. Similar to an essence I'd touched at Mount Chapel, from one of the killers who'd taken the children. Were they after me? Had they tracked me?

The shiver down my spine transformed to anger. We'd see about that. I was no child.

I sprang to my feet, took a step, halted.

The taste, that low note. Different. Off. Unrecognized, yet... *Fuck*. I was having trouble reading the signature.

I closed my eyes and delved deep into the source of my magic, a swirling place of quiet and certainty.

"Back to work, sugah."

"Hush."

I used caution, padded on silent feet, and followed the thread. The chilly stream I crossed soaked my bare feet, and mud squished between my toes as I ascended the slope. I stopped. An unnatural quiet cloaked the wood. I dropped to a crouch, mouth dry, sure any second something vicious would slice me to ribbons. I scanned the surrounding trees and vegetation.

Gods, I'd love to get one of those killers. Rae would back me up. Maybe.

The guy was near, maybe ten yards away. I could feel him, his fragmented essence streaming across my exposed flesh.

I moved to all fours, using vines as ropes, and crept up the increasingly steep hill. A vine I clung to gave way, but I dug my fingers into the soft earth, panted. He was close. So close.

Vegetation hid me as I inched forward. There, projecting from the lip of a small precipice right above me. A pair of booted feet, jeans bottoms.

If I sprang, I'd grab an ankle, maybe bring him down, slow him down.

I slunk forward another foot and leapt.

My hand closed around...

What are you playin' at? Rae said *in my head.*

My hand fisted on air.

Damn. I hoisted myself up onto the rock. I didn't need eyes to see the watcher had fled. I walked around the small clearing, found a clump of sage scrub crushed by a large booted foot.

"What are y'all *doin'*?"

I shrieked—Rae had proofed right in front of me—reeled and almost tumbled off the precipice.

"I'm investigating!"

He tugged his lower lip. "And...?"

"He got away. Someone's been watching us."

"I know."

"You know! And you didn't check it out because...?"

"Bidin' mah time."

Grrr. I did one more circuit. Something black balled beneath a sage bush caught my eye. Something that didn't belong. "I'll be down in a sec."

He snorted. "Y'all best be. We got work to do."

After he poofed away, I dropped to my haunches by the sage and reached out a finger. The black thing was springy. I burrowed my hand into the bush and drew it out. Weird. Worrisome. I knew what it was and how it was made. I smoothed out the glove on my thigh.

Wool. Hand knit. A half-fingered mitt, one of a pair. I sniffed, but only the sage scent remained.

My fingers curled around the glove.

Many months ago, I'd knitted an identical mitt for James.

Since Goodwill was closed by the time I made it back to L.A. proper, I spent my evening researching ritualistic killings and Zoe's dolphin earrings, while I knit on James' scarf.

I admit I hunted for James, too.

When I'd told Rae my suspicions, his eyes had narrowed. He called him a freak. "Fuck you," I'd said.

Once human, James had been recreated by DarkPool from nanotech, a wyvern's blood, and a spark of fae. Only his brain remained fully human.

But he wasn't a monster, as he often referred to himself. He was *mine*.

I knit a final stitch on a row and began another.

The last time I'd seen him...

He stands by my open car window. The moon shines. His eyes glitter. But he is serious. So serious.

"Please come with us, James." I cup his cheek.

A slow grin, all white teeth and warmth. Then he dips his head and kisses me. Our song grows and twines between us, electric and haunting.

When he releases me, he says, "I've got things to clean up. I'll find you, Clea. I'll always find you. Promise."

He'd promised.

My knitting slowed, the butter-soft yarn settling beneath my fingers.

He told me once I made his life bearable. He mine the same. No, more than that. *So much* more than that.

The night I'd almost been raped, almost died, he'd held me, bent his head and nuzzled my neck, said gentle things to comfort me in that husky voice of his.

That was the first night we'd slept together. We hadn't made love, but just slept. He'd curled around me, enveloped me in his warmth, his strength, his calm. We lay together until our breathing slowed. I turned, nestled in the crook of his shoulder, my hand mapping his face, his brushing my body. He'd drawn the covers over us, stroked my wild hair. "You're a warrior," he'd said. "Remember that."

I wasn't a warrior, just a woman who'd overreached and luckily hadn't died. Yet. I set my knitting aside.

He wore his stoic mask like armor, but for me his Pacific blue eyes held laughter and love. I replayed his many acts of kindness. And how such a small thing like my knitting him a pair of mitts had touched him deeply. How his katanas blurred when he fought beside me. How his eyes burned the first time we made love.

He'd pulled me to him and kissed me just the way I liked. His lips teased, and he deepened the kiss, his tongue sliding inside my mouth. I grew dizzy as we kissed and caressed, felt his hardness straining against his jeans. I wanted to touch his flesh, needed him stroking mine.

When we were naked, I explored all of him—his face, his muscled chest, his cock. He blazed with warmth and with hunger, and gods he felt so good when he buried himself inside me. He licked me, pounded hard into me, over and over, and his hands touched my breasts and his tongue....

My nipples ached and my cleft throbbed. My hand slid down my body, across breasts painful with need, beneath my jeans' waist and over my belly to find that aching sweet spot.

I touched myself there, sparked with remembered desire for James.

"You're at it again."

Holy shit. My hand jerked, eyes flashing open, and I turned my head to meet her eyes. Thank the gods my back was to her. Miss Goth. Except her concerned expression was pure Lulu. I swiveled my chair around. "What do you mean, Lu?"

She thrust a hand on her hip. "Oh, c'mon, Clea. I'm not *that* dumb. You've been looking for James."

I massaged my forehead. "Yeah, well, okay. Maybe."

She smiled, sad. "He'll be back."

"Thanks, sweetie. He will."

"I stopped to tell you I'm going out."

"Did you finish your homework?"

She rolled her eyes. "That's so, like, knee jerk."

Truth. I puffed out a breath. "Not out-out, right?"

"I can do stuff, and I'm gonna. Later."

"Wait." I tried to stay casual. "Who are you meeting up with?"

She shrugged. "A friend."

Gods save me. "Okay. Who?"

"He's a shifter." She tossed her head. "He's pretty cool. He's got some ideas about who took the kids. You know, detective ideas."

The urge to ask about Ronan made me bite my tongue. "What's his name?"

"Neddy." Her violet eyes sparked, almost a tease.

Two Neddies in the den? Unlikely. Ohboy. Had he told her about our confrontation? Was he using her in some twisted way to get at me? Or did he just like her? "I met him."

Her face blanched, and she fisted a hand. "Look, his mom and dad grounded him that night, *the* night... Don't you dare tell me not to see him."

That was my right, *dammit*. "I wasn't going to say that. Detective ideas, huh? As long as you're not going out-out. I mean it, Lu. You don't leave the compound or I'll fry your ass."

More eye rolling. "Whatever." She vanished around the corner.

Calico Kitty jumped onto my lap, and I absently stroked her fur. What brain cells had died to make Dave *ever* think I could be guardian to a teenaged girl?

The following morning, Melike growled and hissed and tore into me big time, payback for that missed class. I got in a few licks, too, before she kicked my butt to the curb. After my shower and a few stretches, I checked my phone. Whoa. Rae had texted me. *Y'all up for adventure?*

Was this some scheme to ferret out my secrets? My trust factor was hitting negative numbers. Alex never said Rae was a standup guy, just that he was the best at what he did.

The mage knew his request was irresistible. I texted him back, and we agreed to meet at Starburst. All that hip-hop. So much hip-hop.

A quick shower and change of clothes, and I beelined it to Alex's office. I needed his take on the mage. If I hurried, I'd have enough time to make the Eagle Rock Goodwill before I met Rae.

In the office off his bedroom, Alex sat with his back to me, tapping away at his computer. He waved me to a seat without a pause. Busy, busy man. I sat in a chair near his desk and smacked into the cloud of anger surrounding him.

"What's wrong?"

He swiveled his chair, forearms on thighs, hands clenched. "Neddy's missing, he's—"

Oh, gods. "I know who he is. I met him." And Lulu went out with him last night. I pulled out my phone and texted her. "When, Alex? How?"

"His mother thought he was out with a friend."

I looked at my phone. No answering text. I'd been asleep when she'd come in. "He went out with Lulu last night. At least that's what she told me before she left to meet him. I was asleep when she came in."

"Did she say anything this morning?"

I tugged on one of my dreads. "No. I was out when she left for school. *Oh!* What if she's gone, too?"

Face taught, cheekbones like blades, he inhaled deep and long. "Don't you know kids need watching?"

"Yes. *Yes!* But she said she wouldn't leave the den. It was an innocent date. I…"

He covered my hand with his. "Sshh. Clea. I know you're new to this parenting gig."

"I've had six months. You'd think I'd have gotten it right by now." My gut roiled, my head about to explode.

Ping.

I clutched my phone hard enough to shatter it.

Math class sucks, Lulu texted.

My eyes burned with happy-sad tears. I looked up Alex. "She's okay. She's fine."

He squeezed my shoulder as my pressure valve gradually released. Lulu might be safe, but... "Neddy?"

"We tracked him to Griffith Observatory."

I leaned forward. "And...?"

"Once again, a pristine site except for the sprayed perfume."

"I'd like to see it, get a sense of it, like I did the earlier one."

He nodded. "We may have one thing." He leaned back in his chair and handed me an eight-by-ten photo that lay on his desk. "This."

Scratchings in the dirt—a lightning bolt with a star fastened at the bottom.

I forced my hands not to tremble as I handed him back the photo.

"We think Neddy drew this before he was taken. We have no idea what it means."

But I did. A lightning bolt attached to a star was tattooed on the back of James' neck. My throat dried. I had to say something. Tell him. But I couldn't. I trusted James. He wasn't a kidnapper of children.

I groped. "I've been doing a lot of research. It's a symbol of some kind, but seemingly nothing from the mundane realm. I was think-ing... it might have meaning in the *magic* realm. Do you have a book of magical symbols or maybe a database of them?"

He shook his head. "Our books on that world are sadly out of date. Hundreds of years out of date. And to my knowledge there is no database, at least on the mundane plane. Our pack has existed for so long in the mundane world, we can no longer safely travel to the magical one. We've been told by reputable sources that it will kill us."

"Could they be wrong?"

He scraped a hand across his face. "Any pack member who's ever tried has never returned."

"And the realms' retwining? How will that affect you?"

He jammed his hands into his jeans. "We'll find out, won't we?"

I slung my backpack onto my shoulder as I stood, eager to leave.

He nodded, kissed my cheek. "We'll get there. We'll find Neddy."

"I knew a man once." I licked my lips. "He had a tattoo. Similar to the drawing in the dirt."

Molten eyes nearly fried me to a cinder. "*Where* is this man?"

"I don't know. I've tried to find him, but... I have no idea."

8

ANTS IN THE PANTS

On my way to Eagle Rock, I wondered if I'd done the right thing. I hadn't given him James' name, even when he pressed me. But I reassured him that "my friend" had disappeared without a trace. He knew I was hiding things. But for the moment he'd accepted that I wouldn't say more. He trusted me as I did him.

I believed in James. Understood him well enough to know he'd never kill or kidnap a child.

But sooner or later, I'd have to tell Alex everything.

And I'd completely forgotten to ask him about Rae. As opposed to what I'd just learned about Neddy, the tattoo, and the magic realm's deadly effect the pack, the question felt microscopic.

I parked on Colorado Street, just down from Eagle Rock's Goodwill, a far more chichi building than I'd expected. The large shop was filled with a myriad of stuff, but I focused on the wiry man behind the U-shaped counter talking to an older woman.

With ants in my pants, I waited for him to finish, hoping, praying I'd learn a crucial detail about Zoe's earrings. I'd examined the photos closely. I'd bet big-time they weren't fakes, but pure gold, or at least vermeil. The clerk finally finished and looked at me, no smile, but he raised his bushy eyebrows.

I walked over and held up my phone. "Is there any chance you remember these?"

He leaned closer, his eyes glued to the image. "Yes," he said, in a faintly Latino accent. "I do."

I brokered a smile. "And...?"

Teeth. He gave me lots of teeth. "The unusual thing was that nobody bought them for many months, which is why, my dear, I recall this pair. Not until a Goth-looking girl saw them and, to quote her shrill reaction, 'couldn't live without them.'"

Interesting. "Any idea where they're from or—"

"The Getty. More specifically, the Getty Villa's gift shop."

"The Getty Villa. You mean the museum that parallels the 405?"

"Oh, no, my dear. That's the larger main museum. The Villa is on the Pacific Coast Highway and quite spectacular."

"I've never heard of it."

He raised a shoulder. "Your loss."

The expansive store contained hundreds and hundreds of items, yet... "I'm pretty amazed you remember them."

"I've visited the Villa many times. I saw these in the gift shop." He brushed a thumb across the picture on my phone. "I found them... entrancing."

Interesting. "Do you recall who brought them in to sell?"

He pulled his reading glasses further down his nose and peered at me. "No. The paperwork's long gone. As I mentioned, they stayed in our case for a very long time. Do you know the girl who bought them?"

"Yes, not well, but—"

"Perhaps she would consider selling them to me?"

How odd. "I don't know."

"They would look pretty on my wife. I should have bought them..."

"Thank you so much for your help." His acquisitive gleam struck me as deeply strange. I punched the "home" button and slid my phone into my pocket. "Zoe loves them. I doubt she'd sell."

He folded his hands in front of him and beetled his bushy brows. "She didn't seem the type."

"They appealed to her inner classicist."

WHEN I FINALLY MADE IT to Starburst, the joint was rocking. Or I should say hip-hopping. Thank the gods for the A/C, since the September day was another L.A. broiler. A dozen people milled around the store, including one ginormous athlete who I was certain played for the Bruins. Low-slung jeans on the guys, tight tees on the gals were the order of the day.

In my salmon-colored tank and black cargoes, I almost blended. Well, okay, not so much, but I didn't care.

When Rae appeared, he wore his urban-streetwear uni of ass-riding jeans and flag t-shirt paired with purple high-top Cons. The smile he offered gave me goosebumps, but when he crooked a finger, I strode forward.

We passed the dressing area, a bathroom, and walked through a door into the stockroom, where a dim narrow hall ended in a door to what I assumed was the outside. So far, no adventure that I could see. I followed Rae down the hall, and he reached for the outer door.

"Are y'all ready, sugah?"

"For what?" I'd circled the block earlier, and all that was out back was an alley street and employee parking.

He swung the door open and blazing light blinded me. He took my hand. Mist and smoke and spectrum colors rippled before my eyes.

"This," was all he said, and dragged me outside.

He released my hand, and I reached for my backpack to don my sunglasses. Except my eyes adjusted and... The pack fell from my limp hands.

Twilight. A grassy verge painted in muted colors of red and gold and purple lined a hill greener than any I'd seen on this earth. I inhaled air that smelled of roses and lilacs and a strange, delicious indefinable scent. Buzzed by the heady brew, I was about to turn to

Rae when a jackalope hopped across the verge, paused, stared at us, then hopped away.

Yeah, right—jackalopes don't exist. Not in the real... "Where? Who? Huh?"

"Darlin', sounds like you don't know whether to check your ass or scratch your watch."

Except... that might be *what* he said, but not *how* he said it. His words... musical notes? Ones I understood as language.

Holy shit.

I focused before a frigging unicorn trotted out from the trees. "We're in the magic world."

"*Our* world. And it's only magic if you don't understand it."

"Your voice is music. But not. You're saying words, but—"

"That's because this is your first time." He flapped a hand. "Next time, you won't notice. If there *is* a next time, sugah."

A gold, mouse-sized scarab beetle flew by my nose. It landed on my upper arm. "Eepp!"

Rae brushed it off, and it darted away. *The damned mage was laughing again!* I gave him the side-eye. "Why did you bring me here?"

"To Flow."

"What the hell is... oh, my fireflies."

"Some mages can. Others, not so much." He clicked his tongue. "Which one are you, dumplin'?"

Was I ready for this? I did a 360. Nope, no door back into Starburst`s rear entrance, but rather a valley of that neon-green grass dotted with Aspen-like trees, but with round blue, fluttery leaves. *Wow.*

I was stuck with Rae, of all people, but the magic realm was definitely cool. Now if I could only firefly... Flow.

I nodded, walked in a circle. "Yeah, yeah I get it. You figure if I can firefly—Flow—here, I'll be able to do it back home."

"You're not in Kansas anymore, sweet pea."

"Did we have to go there?"

He did that '*he, he, he*' laugh of his. Grrr.

And his words, all music. Were mine that way, too? Oh, who cared? I took a step forward.

He vised a hand around my upper arm. "No."

"I want to explore."

"Nonononono."

"Why?"

"Here be dragons."

I brightened. "Really? I've always—"

"I was speaking metaphorically."

"You mean they're not real?"

"Of course they're real, sugah. Yes they are."

Woohoo! Dragons. Like the wyvern, maybe. No, the wyvern had two legs, and dragons had four. Didn't they? Ohhhh. I wanted to see. Were they the eating-human kind or the sexy kind?

I was in the magic realm. *Wheee.*

"You be bouncin'. Cut it out."

Okay, okay... calm. "Why can't I explore?"

He grinned, all toothy, eyes sparking, and held up his hand, extending two fingers like the peace sign. He tapped one. "First, because we've got different time streams in our world. Like ocean currents. You dig? Sometimes time flows here same as in the mundane one. But streams can be fast, fast, fast. You could age a year in a month."

"You mean I could enter at 29, be here for a month, and when I returned to the mundane world, I might be 30?"

He nodded. "Or older. That's bad shit. Or a time stream can be slow as a tortle."

"A tortle?"

He shook his head. "Listen up. In a year here, you could age only a month. Sometimes slower. It's bad when you return to the mundane world. Everybody's older but you. Remember the reverse can happen, too. Either way you're screwed."

I opened my mouth to speak, but he tapped the second finger.

"Two. I was referring to *metaphorical* dragons, and they will eat you. Can't have that. You're The Key. And my boss'd fry me if somethin' ate you, sugah."

"You're confusing me. Metaphorical dragons as opposed to real ones, ones who'll kill me, and who's your boss?"

"Immaterial! Now *Flow*."

Temporarily putting aside my curiosity, I breathed deep, gathered, and turned back the clock to when I was three. Da was right beside me, alive and whole. Oh, how I wished. Da's words rang in my head. *Remember the Magics. The Magics. Trust your feelings. Bold, like a Jedi.*

And I laughed, because, yeah, that's what Da always said when he was teaching me. And I heard his voice, and it was beautiful.

Right hand, thumb out, palm open, open to the magics. Gather, gather. I hold out my hand and push.

My fireflies shot from my palm. *Gods!* The pain near brought me to my knees, but, oh, the pleasure radiated through my flesh, too. *Delicious.*

My fireflies, my Flow knit itself into the waterlily motif. Elegant. My wrist tattoo's fiery Celtic spirals glowed. Familiar, natural.... normal.

And I threw back my head and laughed and laughed, shaking with joy. As my white-gold fireflies swirled from my palm, scents of citrus and cedar exploded around us. I inhaled, relishing the aroma as thousands of fireflies surrounded me, and I pulled with my mind, shaped the knit motif, so they coated me and Rae and spread...

A far-away screech.

Rae snagged my shirt.

"Not yet!" Rapture. *Ohmygods.*

"Cut them! Cut the Flow! Now!"

I gasped. "No!"

"Yes! Now! Or she will fry us like marshmallows."

A swift breeze, and a taste so alien and enticing my mouth watered. A cloud in the distance, moving closer, purple-green, like a bruise. I turned away.

"Now!" Rae barked.

Dammit. A breath, and I clenched my hand, cut off my fireflies. But here in the magic realm they hovered for a moment in stasis—suspended, glittering motes—until they dissipated.

Dizzy, unfocused. That was some magic mushroom trip. I stepped forward, and a cold hand enclosed mine. Rae's. A tug. Blurry eyed, I slipped. A gluey thing beneath my feet. Another furious screech—hunger thwarted. Another tug. *Shit!* What was happening?

Burning embers coated my back. Nailed by pain, I tripped, and Rae righted me. A stab in my head. Focus splintered.

More splinters, barbed wires, and I stumbled, thrust out my hand, smashed into hardness.

I staggered into a wall, bounced. Deafening hip-hop music—the store?—and I clutched the knob to the bathroom we'd passed earlier. I made it to the toilet before my breakfast erupted from my mouth. Oh, gross. Gross, gross, gross. I hated puking.

"That was close," Rae said. "Holy shit, darlin', too badass close."

Rae, the full Southern, hip-hop reality of him, was back.

A few heaves later, I pushed my face away from the porcelain throne and rose.

"Sugah, you look like you been chewed up and spit out." He dabbed at my ears, and it sucked seeing shiny red on the paper towel.

"Let me." I washed off my ears and beneath my nose, then rinsed out my mouth.

Rae flushed the toilet, and as he blasted the Febreze, most of the stink abated. He flopped down the toilet seat.

The boom made me cringe. "Could you do that much louder?"

"Sure could."

"Don't you dare." I slid to the floor, hygiene be damned, and leaned against the wall. "Better. The time slippage thing. Are we the same age?"

He stared at his hand, turning it over and over again. "Seems so."

"You're a wiseass."

Rae kicked the door shut.

"Will you stop that!"

"Sorry about the pain. Too fast a reentry." Elbows on knees, he plopped his head into his hands, covering his face.

"What?" I said, in a thready voice.

"She knows."

"Who knows?"

"*She*. Knows."

"Is this *really* the time for cryptic?"

"You're screwed, sugah."

"Tell me something I don't know."

"That bitch Tatianne wants to suck yo' essence right out a you."

"Huh?" I closed my eyes.

A warm finger tucked beneath my chin. "Open your eyes and look here."

When I complied, he did that two-fingered eye thing from *Meet the Parents*.

"Tatianne?" I blurted out.

Rae raised his brows, but only said, "She's got many names, Tatianne, Soul Eater, Dom, Tanya."

My mouth dropped open. My brother Tommy's girlfriend was named Tanya. I'd never met her, but... *Couldn't be.* Except... His intense powers. His whacked moral compass. His delusions. She'd leeched away his love for me, I suspected. I sighed. If it looked like a duck and quacked like one, too. "Is she mage? Fae?"

"Once she was fae. Now she's a hybrid, part fae, part vampyre." He tapped his hand to his lips. "Some say shapeshifter and mage, too. She's got this talent. Once she sucks the life out of her victims, she acquires their attributes. She's an eater of souls."

"In other words, a real treasure."

"Y'all not as stupid as you look."

"Just 'cause I'm blonde doesn't—"

He chortled. "You're one funny woman."

"I live to make you laugh. Tell me more about Tatianne."

His face grew serious in a way I hadn't seen before, and his eyes... they were old and tired.

"Rae what *are* you?"

"I'm me, that's all." "You're more." He shrugged. "Most folks from the world you call magic, they welcome the retwining of the worlds. That's how it once was long ago. The worlds commingled. That's how it *should* be. But other folks?" He shook his head. "They refuse to accept Mama Nature's laws. Stupid fucks. Tatianne is one a those. To stop this replaiting, she'll make mincemeat of you, not to mention the whole absorption thing."

No, my brain definitely wasn't in gear. "Absorption?"

"You're a powerful mage."

I snorted. "So they say."

"Wake up, girl! If she gets ahold of you, she'll suck up your powers like chocolate milk."

"There must be other mages as—"

"Yeah, but they know what they're doing. They protect themselves but good."

And I didn't know how. I was open season. Nice. It sounded way too *Lord of the Rings*, not to mention woo woo. "I'm just—"

"See, you're a bonus. You're The Key, darlin'. By collecting the chests for the guardians, you're uniting the species, givin' them back power they once held. Tatienne purely hates losing power. Absorbing you... she could retrieve the chests. So stay alive, save the world."

"I'm a slogan from that old show, *Heroes*. Or maybe I'm Buffy." Yeah, Buffy was cool.

He laughed again, shook his head. But his eyes were so very sad. "Like I said, y'all are one funny woman. Don't get too big on yourself. The Guardians will find another Key. Trouble is, that takes time *we don't have. You* don't have, little Miss Clea Reese."

"Oh, shut up. Except, don't. If Tatianne's so uber-powerful, why doesn't she just come get me?"

"Now, you're bein' smart, sugah. Figure it out."

My brain was a sludge puddle, but rattling around in there somewhere... The answer poked me in the ass. "She can't cross to the mundane world."

He did the slow-clap thing. "Give little Miss Clea a candy apple."

"She'll come after me if I go back to the magic world, won't she?"

He grinned, all wiseass. "Faster than green grass through a goose. So if you plan to keep breathin', leave it be."

I pushed off the wall and stood. Dizzy, I slapped out my palm to steady myself, then held out my right hand to firefly. A wave of nausea bent me in half.

"Too fast, girl. You need to power up again. Takes time."

"How much?"

"Enough."

I shoved Rae off the throne, lifted the lid, and barfed.

A knock at the door.

"Give us a minute here!" Rae shouted.

I repeated the cleanup, Rae dittoed the Febreze, and we passed a petite girl as we exited.

"Sorry, Chelsea," he said.

"What were you two doing in there?" she said, wrinkling her nose.

If she only knew.

It dawned on me that I couldn't do research within the magic realm. The thought of being sucked dry by Tatianne, my soul devoured, made me queasy. *Damn.* As I drove back to the compound, I realized I'd forgotten to ask Rae about the Pinkys. The minute I arrived, I texted him.

You nuts? I never heard a those Pinky things. Scary shit.

Yeah, right. And today wasn't?

Back at our suite, I found the kiddos and our critters safe, Gracie and Miss Kitty curled up together on my bed. Irresistible. I pulled out my phone and snapped a pic. After I brushed my teeth and showered, I crawled into bed, eking out a minuscule space beside them.

Tomorrow. The Getty Villa. Absolutely.

I crashed.

9

WOLF ALPHAS

Pounding. I checked the time, then staggered to the door. My two-hour nap hadn't been bad. I hadn't dreamt, but I still felt out of it. I opened the door to the wolf alpha, one jeaned leg crossed, arms crossed, too, as he leaned against the doorframe. His eyes laughed and his smile that said he was trouble.

"Alex!" I said. "You found Neddy?"

He breezed by me. "No."

"Lulu? Ronan?" I rubbed my eyes. "What?"

He moved closer, tucked a finger beneath my chin. "You smell... odd."

"Gee, thanks."

"You look off, too."

"Wow, the compliments just keep coming. What's up?"

He winked, held up his other hand, which clutched a bottle of bourbon.

"How did you know that—"

"It's your favorite? We packed up your stuff, remember?"

In the kitchenette, he trolled the cabinets and produced two glasses. "You good?"

"Swell." I slumped at one end of the couch. Hostess are us. Not.

He set the glasses on the table and poured us each two fingers. "You want to share?"

I took the glass and sipped. Heaven. "Yeah."

Alex took the other end of the sofa, well, more like about half of it, since he was a sprawler. He was also one of those rare people who had the ability to listen with deep intent. He appeared relaxed, one arm across the sofa back, one leg bent on the sofa, the other on the floor. Yeah, relaxed, but alert, too. His eyes never left mine.

It had been a long time since anyone watched me and waited for my words with such keen anticipation. No, not just my words, me. All of this wolf alpha was focused on me. Everything, including that one warm tendril of desire.

I told him about my journey to the other world. He never interrupted, not once. When I finished, and polished off my bourbon, he poured me another, as if he had all the time in the world and wasn't in charge of a den of hundreds.

"What was it like?" he asked.

"Strange. The air was light, but moist. More like New England than here. A green band ran in an arc across the sky. Like the piece of rainbow. That jackalope. It made me wonder. Things like..." I bit my lip. "The yeti. Mothman. Nessie. Are they all real in the magic world?"

He shrugged, muscles tightening beneath his gray t-shirt, a sense of sadness he tried to conceal, but couldn't, not from me. "Never been."

"I understand. But Anouk says magic has always been here, in this world. It's bled over. Just not much of it."

"Alien abductions?" He smiled, waggling his brows.

"Yeah, not so much."

"That Tatianne. I've read about soul eaters. Man, they're rare, but big-bad news. Be wary. Be *careful*."

"I don't even know how. How are you careful of a creature with that much power? Could Tommy..." And there it was, that niggle. Except now I *knew*.

Alex leaned forward. "Your brother. Didn't you end him?"

I shook my head. "I don't think I did. I damaged him, really badly. But dead? No, I suspect my brother isn't dead."

"Your twin."

"My nemesis," I ground out. "The Master. Long ago, before all... this, before he tried to kill me, steal the Chest of Bone, before I even *knew* he was my brother, he was my best friend." I laughed, and it hurt. It still hurt, dammit. "After he left the Army, and came home for a visit, he told me about his new girlfriend. Tanya. Ty, he called her. My bets are on her being Tatianne." Oh, the damnable irony.

"This *abomination* wants to absorb you."

"Apparently. She can bite my ass."

"But she doesn't want to absorb him?"

Gods, I wished I smoked. "Guess not. Maybe he's not as tasty."

He laughed. "I'm sure he's not."

And... we were talking about two different things entirely. "He's not The Key, which I guess makes me the olive in the martini."

"Clea." He set down his glass and moved closer. "Clea."

Now we were most definitely talking about one thing. He was a beautiful man in many ways.

He leaned forward, his hair brushing his shoulders, his lips, soft, wanting, and those eyes, they boiled with hunger. For me.

It felt good to be wanted.

I lay my palms on his chest, hard, firm. Solid, like the man. I'd intended to stop him, but I didn't even try, as he eased closer still, to where our faces were inches apart. His lips brushed mine, soft, a whisper. Then the tip of his tongue licked, quick, across my lips. He deepened the kiss, cupped the back of my head with his large hand, his other sliding around my waist to press us tight together. My breasts burned. He explored my mouth as a man skilled in the arts of love, of sex. Easy, slow, thorough.

Heat, the kind I'd forgotten for months on end, pooled in my cleft. I ached.

My arms found their way around his back, and I held him, felt the muscles move and shift beneath his shirt as he left my lips, his tongue taking a final lick and nip, before nuzzling my cheek, my jaw, my neck.

He shifted me, so that my legs straddled his lap, my heated center pressed to the hot erection that bulged beneath his jeans. I moved, trying to assuage that familiar ache, *wanting*, desperate, for it to be soothed by a man, this man. Yes, this man.

Except I was imagining him as James, and that was plain *wrong*.

"What do we have here?"

How? What?

Alex and I leapt into matching crouches, knives in hand, facing the threat. Except it wasn't a threat. At least, I didn't think so.

"Refreshing to know you two are prepared." Anouk stood before us in all her human-form glory, her languid body a chocolate-skinned tall drink of water as she leaned against the far wall, one hand holding a lit cigarette that swirled smoke. Once again, she'd poofed in, something I hated.

"What the hell?" I said. "Ever heard of knocking?"

Alex growled as he sheathed his knife.

"Caught you at a bad time, have I?" she said in that precise and faintly foreign accent of hers.

Alex dipped his head. "Guardian."

"Oh, do not be so formal, Alexandros Arctos. Sit, sit. Do not let me interrupt you. I have always enjoyed watching."

"Really." I plopped my ass back on the couch.

He slid me a glance, one of annoyance. Hard to miss his anger at her and his hunger for me. "You break protocol, Anouk."

"So formal. I *am* a guardian after all."

He snorted and sat, crossed an ankle over a knee, his posture relaxed, his emotional signature, anything but.

"Put that thing out." I waved a hand at her cigarette.

A spark of amber in those sloe eyes, before they morphed back to blue-black. I'd pissed her off. Good. She pissed *me* off, too.

She stabbed her cigarette out in the sink, which left a noxious smell. Her head swiveled toward me as only a bird's could. "Do you have it?"

"Six months, and that's all you can say?" I shook my head. "Not very friendly, Anouk."

She hissed. "I am not feeling very, as you so graciously put it, friendly."

With no idea whether she'd take a seat or not, I waved her to the club chair.

Rather than comply, she turned toward Alex. Her eyes glowed.

He laughed. "You really think you can glare me into leaving? It's my den, my territory."

A slow smile across her lips exposed gleaming teeth. "So, Alex Arctos, you protect the mage."

"Like I just said, my den, my territory, *my people*."

She gave a dismissive shrug as she glided to the club chair and sat, crossing her slim legs. "Yes, well I expected nothing less."

"Where is that creature?" she asked me.

Who...? Then I got it. James. Which sizzled me big time. "He's a man."

"A thing. No soul."

I notched my chin. "Oh, he's got plenty of soul. Why are you really here?"

She tapped one finger to her lips. "You have grown. Yet you cannot Flow. You are having trouble of late?"

Alex threw me a silent question.

"Flow," I said to him. "My mage fireflies. Which worked perfectly fine in the otherworld." And I finally caught what I'd been sensing from Anouk. I turned back to her. "*That's* why you're here."

"Yes, foolish Clea. Rae should never have taken you there."

"Water under the bridge," I said.

She leaned forward in the chair, petting the black beads that hung from her neck. "You have little time left to find the Chest of Stone."

"So what else is new?" I said.

"New?" She drew the word out like a lover. "Word is, Tatianne has sent the Cardillo."

My throat dried. The snaky-headed creepy thing that attacked me in the cemetery where I'd met the wolves, and again at the bridge, where James and I fought my once-beloved brother, Tommy. And Bernadette had died. "Tommy?" I choked out.

She shook her head. "While I do not feel your brother, my bet would be yes." A half-lidded pause. "And my bets are seldom wrong. Helps when I visit the track. Find the chest, save—"

"Yes, yes. Save the world." Gods, did any of these woo-woo people *not* speak in clichés?

She thrust out her hand, which held what looked like a black oval block of wood. Similar to the one that contained the Chest of Bone, the boxes were added protection from both magic and mundane hunters for the five chests. "Is it warded and keyed only to me?"

She smiled. "Of course. I intended to give you this earlier."

When I took the box, feathery tingles skated up my arm. "And you didn't because…?"

She shrugged. "I seem to have forgotten. I have been busy, you know, while you have been diddling around."

"Diddling?" Why that pain-in-the-ass shifter.

Her eyes slid to Alex. She plucked the box from my hands, handed it to him, and nodded.

"Why did you do that?" I said.

That Cheshire grin of hers appeared. "A surprise. Now get to work!" Smoke swirled about her, a murky multicolored cloak, and dissipated. The great golden eagle sat beside the chair, looked at me, then Alex, and blinked those gorgeous eagle eyes… and vanished. Poof.

The woman *loved* to poof.

"Can you poof?" I said to Alex.

He chuckled, shook his head. "Her Highness is the one who transported us to that cemetery. Handy trick."

"Her Highness, huh."

Laughter in his eyes. "I call her that to piss her off."

"You going to tell me about the surprise and why you're in charge of the box?"

"Can't."

"The box is for the chest, thus for me. Tell me."

"If I do, she'll rip off my head. I like my head."

I did, too. Frustrating. I'd find out... somehow.

He waggled his eyebrows.

"You did that to make me laugh, Alex."

He ran a finger down my cheek. "I'd like to make you do other things."

A flush heated my cheek. "Yeah, well..." I shook my head. "I'm sorry. For before. I don't know what got into me."

He smirked.

"Okay, poor choice of words."

"Not in my book." His gold eyes sizzled, and he stepped closer.

I tilted my head back. Nope, no answers on the ceiling on dealing with this situation. "I can't. I *can't.*" I hadn't told him about James. Made sure the kids didn't breathe a word about him, either. It was too private, too personal, too dangerous.

He took my hand, kissed each fingertip, one by one. "One day, I'll take you to Yosemite.

"I hear it's beautiful."

"Perhaps the most beautiful place in the mundane world. For wolves, at least."

He didn't smile, but his eyes did. For all his deadliness, his Alphaness, Alex was sunshine and light. He drew me to him, the proverbial moth to flame.

"Can I see your wolf?" I said. "Oh, shit. That's probably impolite."

A growl, deep in his throat, nothing human, all animal. Smoke rose, pulsing with a deep gold light, the color of Alex's eyes, cyclonic, flickering bright, glorious, accompanied by the scents of sunshine and the sea. Incredible.

The smoke and scent retreated, and nothing had changed except an immense, pony-sized white wolf stood in front of me. But the eyes, they remained Alex, and they held me tight.

I reached out a hand. Maybe he'd mind. I fisted it. He tilted his wolfie head as if wondering why I'd stopped.

He padded slightly forward, nudged my thigh with his massive head. I kneeled in front of him, so we were eye to eye, ran my hands down his sides. Silky, soft, but not too soft, like the coat of a recently groomed German shepherd. I laughed aloud. "You are gorgeous!"

He yipped.

I Eskimo-kissed his nose. Cold. Laughing again when he licked my throat. I tugged those ancient coin eyes to mine, hoping he could feel my joy, sense the beauty I saw in his wolf form. I rested my cheek against his neck, inhaled. Yes, Alex, but different.

Another golden burst of sparks, warm, almost hot against my cheek, and I was nuzzling him, the man, the brush of his long blond hair tickling my nose. I pushed back and stood, eyes squeezed tight, realizing he might be naked. So not ready for a nude Alex.

"Hey," he said.

I slitted my eyes so I could sort of see. He wore the same jeans and t-shirt as before, thank the gods. A small burst of disappointment. Hell, I didn't know myself anymore. "Oh, that was amazing, Alex. Amazing! I mean I've seen Anouk and all, but you, oh…"

He stoppered my words with a kiss that delved and probed, his tongue hot on mine, lips soft and intense and needing. I was needing, too. Except…

I pulled away. The kiss was good. Very good. But it didn't affect me the way my Dragon Dude's kisses did. Should I expect it to? Was I genuinely interested in Alex? Or was I simply desperate to fill that black hole left by James? I didn't know.

"Gotta go, sweetheart," he said, oozing pride and maleness. Devastating.

"Um, clothes!"

"Huh?"

"You're wearing clothes. How come?"

Soft laughter. "Disappointed?"

"Oh, hell, Alex. Tamp down the sexual innuendo, or I'll turn you into a toad."

Jaw clenched, he narrowed his eyes.

I laughed. "Of course I can't do that. It's all that came to mind."

He tilted his head in that wolfie way. "You *sure*?"

I wasn't positive, but I wouldn't tell him that, either. I smiled. "It got you to lower the sexual temperature, didn't it?"

He grunted, shoved his hands in his pockets. "Clothes. What you see is of the mundane realm. My wolf is of the magical. They don't interact, not that way." A slow smile meandered across those gorgeous lips. "So like I said, you disappointed?"

"Out." I handed him the box, which he'd place in the warded room to await the chest, and pulled open the door. "Out!"

Deep masculine laughter followed him down the hall.

THE GETTY VILLA didn't happen the following day, or the next, or the next. Life—damn its interference.

Days later, over dinner with Ronan and Lulu—her hair was pink! When had that happened?—steak for them, eggs and salad for me, I told them I'd gotten tickets for the show they'd been begging to see.

"Yes!" Lulu said, all Goth darkness banished by *The Book of Mormon*.

"It'll be fun," I said, grinning. "Normal. Family time, right?" And maybe, just maybe, Ronan and Lulu would be in harmony again. They were good kids. Once they'd been wonderful together. Now? Republicans and Democrats harmonized better.

Ronan nodded, and his pleasure cascaded over me, dissolving his almost-constant aura of confusion and anger that scraped my senses. All because of Lulu. Made me sad. But evolution was inevitable. Change, the only constant.

"Saturday night, the Pantages Theatre."

Lulu frowned. "But I was going to—"

"What?" Ronan said. "Meet up with your new friends? Blow me off? What?"

"Guys," I said.

"Screw you, Ronan!" Lulu said. "I can do whatever I want. I've got friends now. Just because you don't like—"

"No, I don't." He threw down his napkin and stood, a tall boy-man wearing a thunderous expression. "They're idiots. And you frigging don't see that."

"Oh." She wiggled her shoulders. "And your new friends are all cool and neat. Not! They're boring. Traditional. So uncreative!" She pursed her lips, crossed her arms, and glared.

"Cut. It. Out!" I captured both their eyes, which wasn't easy given Ronan's height. "Sit down, Ronan."

"I'm sorry, no," he said in a quiet, firm tone. He took my hand, pointedly ignoring Lulu. "I want a new place, a new room. I don't mean to leave the den. I get the security situation. But I can't live here, with *her,* anymore."

I started to protest, except I realized the sense of his request. I sighed. "I understand. I'll talk to Erick."

"I'd like to be bunked with the soldiers. As a trainee."

Almost nineteen. How could I refuse? He'd seen a lot in his young life. Too much. But the hint of sorrow in those gentle eyes pained me. "All right. Erick will know about that, too."

He disappeared into his room.

When I turned to Lulu, her lower lip was quivering.

"I don't know what happened," she said. "How things changed so much. Ronan and I... I love, loved, him."

"Sometimes it's hard to know what we feel. Feelings can be confusing, Lu. And conflicted."

"I don't know. I don't know!" Hand covering her mouth, she shook her head, pink locks wild, and ran from the room.

Her sobs were loud enough to wake zombies.

10

RAE = FRUSTRATION

Training with Rae was an exercise in frustration. His taking me into the magic world helped with my fireflies. The magic inside me had cracked open, widened day by day, but in an annoyingly random fashion. Some days it felt like I was riding a rodeo bull, others, lolling in a tepid pool. On command, I could swirl my fireflies in my palms. They looked like tiny cosmoses. Magic. But streaming them outward? Not so much. One out of five times meant a good day. My other magical senses were heightening, too, but in a more controlled, incremental way. We worked on my shields, so I could block others' emotions, a task that was starting to feel natural again.

"How will I recognize the chest, Rae?" I said the day he was lobbing black motes of energy at me like the Enterprise shot photon torpedoes. Though I was battered and bloody and wobbling, I managed to deflect three out of seven. A win in my book. "Anouk says they take different forms."

"Their disguise," he said. "I reckon you'll get hints."

"I didn't feel anything with the Chest of Bone. Not until I touched it."

"The same with the Chest of Stone and the others, but you're stronger, more sensitive." Another torpedo.

I dodged. "But I'll still have to touch it?"

"Sure will, sugah." Bottles of water and Mountain Dew poofed into his hands. He handed me the water, and I glugged. "What if I can't get to the chest? What if I can sense it, but I can't touch it?"

"Y'all gotta." He tugged his lower lip, eyelids drooping, scrutinizing me. "Y'all still blockin' your powers. Holdin' back, sugah. Think about all you've done. Hell, y'all ended two vampyres."

I narrowed my eyes. "What?"

"Ivor and Ivan." He took a swig of Dew. "Pretty famous ones."

"*Vampyres?* But neither tried to bite me. I saw them in the daylight." I'd killed Ivan, Blondie2, but James had ended Ivor, Blondie1. Not that Rae needed to know the particulars.

He waggled a finger back and forth. "Today's not the day for learnin' about vampyres."

The Blondies were creeps, not because they were vampyre, but because they were bad.

"Y'all lucky y'all ain't dead."

I grinned. "Maybe I'll make that my mantra. Or add a tattoo?"

"That battle against The Master. Your gramma. She died."

"Her grandson killed her." I stared at the small Zen garden beside the house. If I met his eyes, he'd see my tears.

"You know how I said you're holding back? In your head, you still *believe* you're mundane," Rae said, his Southern accent disappearing as he got serious. "See, magic—*mage* magic—it's like a battery. You used it, lots, but you had no control. Without control, your power, it burns out. To find the chest, you need to control your power. The chest's not gonna plop in your lap like the Chest of Bone. Right now, y'all's battery's depleted. Couple that with your mundane POV, and you're one big-assed mess."

"My ass isn't big. And, dammit, I want my magic back."

He chuckled that annoying malevolent laugh. "It'll come back, natural like."

He waved hands too large for his thin frame. "Think of a spring, one deep in Mama Earth. You drain the thing, it takes time to rise again. But with control, it builds. With control, if you deplete it, it comes back fast. With control, y'all got power enough to spare."

I was getting stiff. I bowed my back, stretched, straightened. "So it's gradually coming back on its own. Too gradually."

"Your problem. You did it."

Not intentionally. "I came to L.A. because I sensed the chest was here."

He laughed. "Oh, it's here all right, punkin'."

"Where? Where do you think it is, Rae?"

"No idea."

How very *helpful*.

With a flick of those clever hands, he flung me across our training ground. I pushed to my hands and knees, every muscle and bone aching, put one foot under me, then the other, and pushed to my feet. My face burned, scraped raw, but screw that. Hands on hips, I stalked him. "You're pissing me off."

His eyes blazed, and his hands shot sparks. "You wanna give me some respect, sugah."

Nose to nose, I shoved him. "No, I don't."

Iridescent black motes attacked my body, surrounding me, enveloping me, pinching me with a million bee stings. Tears, or maybe blood, wept from my eyes and nose, my mouth a silent howl. I curled my fingers into fists. "Damn you!"

I slammed my hands forward, palms out, and called my fireflies. I screamed. "Fuck you!" Pleasure-pain arced through my body. My fireflies erupted to form knitted Gothic Arches, and I traveled beyond myself, my hands and arms swooping in an intricate, symphonic pattern. I pushed my fireflies to encircle the black motes. My Flow contained them, bound them, and in a furious motion I flung the writhing sack away.

Clap. Clap. Clap. Rae eyes danced with laughter, face wreathed in a huge grin.

I grinned back, one hand pressed to a tree trunk. Collapsing was not an option.

"About time, sugah. Now let's do it again."

MY EYES ARE CLOSED. Hands on me, naked as I am. No. My lids fly up. James hovers above me, face tight with longing. He lies beside me and touches me with a reverence I don't deserve. I reach for him, but my arms are leaden. I want to brush my fingers across the smooth skin of his neck, trace his pectorals, follow the arrow of black hair to his cock that juts proudly across my belly.

He slips his arms around my back and crushes me to him. "This isn't real, but fuck, Clea, I wish it were."

I try to answer him, but my mouth is glued tight.

He buries his face in crook of my neck. "I want to smell you, feel you, hear your smoky voice. Clea, I ache. When we're together, my world is right."

His words are a prayer and a promise, but I lie limp in his arms, a useless rag doll.

I fight and fight and manage one word. "James."

EXHAUSTED as I was from my torturous dreams, day after day, I practiced growing my power with Rae, who continued to mantra patience. Yeah, well mine was rice-paper thin. I needed control. I needed to understand. I needed mastery of things nonsensical to me. Rae said I must think like a mage, not a human. I needed to become the magic. Without that belief, I would fail.

I pictured Neddy, a boy with eyes the color of mine and a fierce attitude. How long before the killers destroyed him?

"I need my senses honed to find Neddy, to uncover who killed those children." Neither I nor the pack had made progress in our hunt. The shifters were going crazy about it, and so was I. The key was me accessing my powers. I was sure of it. "When we find him, I'll need my fireflies to fight those Pinky things."

"Well, y'all's fightin' yourself as much as them. You sound like dead meat to this black boy."

NEDDY. I couldn't stop thinking about him as I walked down the hall from our suite, having showered the day's sweat away. Friday afternoon had thankfully come, and I might be a hot mess of bruises, sharp pain, and bone-deep aches from Rae's and Melike's workouts, but I had plans.

My legs flew out from under me. Fuck! Airborne, I twisted in time to land in a crouch, knife out, ready for my attacker. Melike. She was grinning that evil smile of hers.

"In the hall?" I said. "What the hell was that?"

"You need to learn surprise and how to react to it," she said. "Again!"

That final word, and I flashed on Bernadette, my beloved nag, my grandmother, whose ashes lay beneath a cairn in the cold New Hampshire earth. "Not now. I have an appointment." The Getty Villa. Finally.

"Cancel it." Her beautiful face tightened with command.

"I can't. I *won't*."

"Again!"

I gave her the finger, sheathed my knife, and headed for den's underground parking garage. A hand grabbed my dreads and hauled me close.

"You," she said, breath hot on my neck, hands banding my forearms. "Are a poser. You say you want to learn. Bah. All I see is a weak woman who relies on men to do her dirty work. Don't think I haven't missed how Alex hungers after you. Well, I'm not Alex."

I'd had it. I clamped my hands around the one that clenched my dreads and pushed downwards. I held on, dipped, turned, and stepped partially behind her, bending her arm inwards. I added pressure to the back of her hand, which hyper extended her wrist joint.

Melike released my hair. But I held on to that hand and continued my motion until I was completely behind her. Her other arm flailed, but she couldn't reach me, and I tamped my empath senses down hard to ignore her inner howl of pain. Right hand on her bent wrist, I yanked her backward, my left hand locking around her jaw, which I turned violently to the side opposite her bent wrist. I tugged her downward, and she fell to the floor onto her side. I pinned her.

"I'm so tired of your shit. I appreciate you training me. Dammit, I do. But I'm not the reason you lost Paul. So quit taking it out on me. I'm only trying to help."

I released her and bounced up, knowing she might attack, knowing she could rip me to shreds in an instant.

She didn't. And my little spurt of pleasure at her defeat morphed into an awareness that the next time we met, she'd slide out the claws.

I pounded out the door and down the steps. The Getty Villa closed in two hours. Some thirty to forty-five of those would be spent traversing L.A.'s traffic-riddled highways. I arrived in the compound's lower parking garage, and came to screeching halt. Melike leaned against my mini-van, wearing a shit-eating grin. She was flipping a knife over and over.

Screw this. I walked toward her. "We are not doing this here. Not now."

"I'm your bodyguard."

I laughed. "Yeah, right."

She waltzed to the passenger side and flung open the door.

"No way," I said.

"*Oui.*" From inside, she pushed open the driver's door. "Way."

If I didn't know she was a wolf, I'd swear I saw cat in her eyes.

I was tempted to argue. Instead, I slid behind the wheel and shut the door. Not hard, not gonna give her that satisfaction. "Okay," I said, keeping my tone light. "Here's the deal. I'm doing some investigating. Can you hang back? Not look like a frigging predator about to eat one of the humans?"

She shrugged. "Of course."

"If you screw this up..."

She hissed. There was that cat again. "I know my job."

And off we went.

WE ENTERED the Getty Villa's Romanesque grounds less than forty-five-minutes later. Not bad, except when I'd tried to make conversation on the way over, the cloud of silence had thickened with each mile, each stoplight, each traffic snarl. Rather than kill her, I beelined past the amphitheater that sat across from the Villa's colonnade courtyard, entered the gift shop, and meandered around until I made it to the jewelry case. But I failed to spot the dolphin earrings. At least Melike hung back.

A shopkeeper walked over, a smile on her elderly face. "Can I help you?"

I showed her my photo of the earrings. "I'd like to look at a pair like these."

She frowned. "I'm afraid we no longer sell them."

"I'd appreciate anything you can tell me about them?"

Her lips pursed. "Dolphins were sacred to Aphrodite, since she was born of the sea, but they were beloved by many of the Greek pantheon. In Egypt, too, because of Aphrodite's cult there, but mostly during the Ptolemaic Egypt or Cyprus eras. They're replicas from our collection here at the Villa. Greek. Oh, dear—or perhaps Egyptian. Or Roman. My memory's not what it used to be, and it's been a long time since they were in stock."

I smiled. "Thank you. How old do you think the originals are?"

"I'm afraid I don't know." She sucked on a tooth. "I'm forgetting something. Well, doesn't matter. But these earrings are quite beautiful."

"They are," I said. "Not gold."

"No," she said with a smile. "Oh, no. Although the originals would have been. These are vermeil—gold over sterling—with cultured pearls. If they were authentic, they be of 24 karat gold and natural pearls."

"Thank you so much." Maybe I'd buy them from Zoe. Gods, I could only imagine how much the avaricious girl would charge.

The earrings had drawn me to the Villa with delicate tendrils of power, power which could easily be an elaborate trap. I fisted my hand. Trap or truth, it was all I had.

When I entered the museum proper, Melike would follow, whether I wanted it or not. Her vibe, angry storm clouds, prickled my skin. After I checked the map, I climbed the stairs to the second floor, aimed for the Coins, Gems, and Jewelry room. As I walked down the hall—hard not be distracted by the gorgeous art and artifacts—my shoulders began to tingle.

Not because of Melike, either. While she remained a good distance behind me, I could still read her emotional signature as *her*. No, this was someone different. A tingling, but no anger, no desire, no... anything. Yet it shivered across my shoulders and chilled the back of my neck.

I stopped, examined a painting, then gripped my cell and pressed the mirror app. No one to my left or my right. I tucked my phone away, rotated my shoulders and walked on.

When I entered the Men of Antiquity room, the hinky feeling dissipated. I walked around, then through to the Victorious Youth room, another walkabout, until I finally entered the jewelry room, my target.

The room was relatively small, and I was alone, but I had to clamp down my shields as I was near drowning in the room's vibe. Most of the artifacts were worn close to those ancients' skin, the essence of the long-dead a faint shimmering. Cumulatively it was like a thousand pricks to my senses.

The displays of crafts and jewels from thousands of years earlier mesmerized me. Glass, gems, gold. So much gold. Not the cool modern version, but mellow and deep, with the richness of warm amber. I went from case to case, amazed that so many ancient artifacts remained in our world. They trapped me in time, and I marveled at the fantastical creatures depicted on the necklaces and bracelets, earrings and rings. Were those strange creatures imaginary or from the magicworld?

What better place for the Chest of Stone to rest, hiding in plain sight?

Furry caterpillars crawled up my spine. I whirled. A shadow, like smoke, in the corner by a statue. I didn't move, unafraid, yet curious. I took a step toward it. Emptiness. No shadow. Just a marble male torso.

I peeked into the far room, titled Athletes and Competition. Statues, plenty of them, and people, four or five. But no shadows there, either.

Keeping my focus was a bitch. The Getty's vibe reminded me of champagne bubbles. I could get giddy from it.

A deep breath later, I resumed my hunt. In every case, gorgeous earrings. But none like Zoe's replicas.

Frustrated, I turned to hunt down a docent.

A muscled arm snaked around my waist, another on my upper arm, lifting me. "Want."

I jammed an elbow into his solar plexus, kicked out with my heel and caught his balls. A grunt, and he hurled me across the room. I flew, a rag doll, so fast I smashed into a case, shattering glass. Alarms screamed. I bounced off the case, my knee hitting hard, and landed on my belly. Dazed, pain shooting up my leg, I stumbled into a fighter's stance expecting to see my attacker.

What I saw was a blur, dead ahead, as if a chunk of the world were smeared, out of focus. Heard grunts, barks of anger, and the smudge of two shadow figures twisted and turned through the archway into another gallery. I raced after whatever "they" were, except my knee crumpled. I landed hard, head thudding on the marble floor. Silver stars on black until Melike came into focus, as did the horde clustered around me—guards, and men and women in suits.

Oh, this would be fun. Not.

THE GRILLING WASN'T as bad as I expected, mostly because of my cuts, bruises, and the immense black-and-blue handprint curled around my upper left arm. An attack at the Getty Villa wasn't normal. So after I was patched up and did the police report thing, they offered me a bunch of freebies, I guessed out of fear I'd sue.

I could have asked them for anything, like about the earrings, but I wanted to keep my search on the down-low. The good news was my injuries were superficial, although I sported fresh bandages on my knees, thighs, arms and cheek.

I'd never been more ready to scram.

Except after the herd dispersed, one woman lingered, maybe thirty-five, draped in a gorgeous black dress with a deconstructed hemline and an artisanal scarf. She pulled up a chair across from mine, slid one long slim leg over the other, and smiled.

Ouch, fake smile and shielded vibe.

"Would you mind telling me your story," and she paused at that word, "once again?"

"Yes, I would mind."

Another fake smile, her eyes a raptor's. "Oh, please. Just once more." Her voice had a long-time smoker's raspy quality.

"Who are you?" I said.

"Sandra Yevtukh. Chief of Security at the Villa."

All righty, then. "Swell. You've been here the whole time, heard what I have to say."

She smoothed her hand over her blond chignon, not moving a hair. "And I'd like to hear it again."

I was pooped, hurt, and in a pissy mood. But the smart road was not making an enemy of this woman. I complied.

"Thank you," she said when I'd finished. She offered me a glass of ice water.

I accepted and took a long pull. "Done, then?"

"Not quite. I'd like to hear what your shadow has to say."

I started at the word 'shadow' before I realized she meant Melike. None of those who'd questioned me had sniffed out the shapeshifter.

"Melike?" I said.

She moved forward, all shapeshifter glide and precision.

"And who might you be?" Yevtukh said.

Melike grinned. "Clea's buddy." Her broad Jersey accent was perfect. I almost snorted into the water glass.

"Her... buddy." Yevtukh narrowed her eyes.

"Yeah," Melike said. "She wanted to come here. Since she's my pal, I came. When it happened, I was looking at some weird statue in one of the other rooms."

"You mean galleries," Yevtukh said.

"Yeah. I heard the ruckus, and hot footed ovah heah. And all you people were around her. So I hung back."

Not even a twitch gave Melike away.

"Why don't you tell me what *you* saw?"

Boy, the woman loved dramatic pauses. But shielded or not, she was more than her California-sophisticate appearance.

"Not a thing," Melike said, her accent hurting my ears. "I feel bad about that."

"All right." Yevtukh stood. "Thank you for your time. Again, so sorry about what happened. Do check in with me next time you visit the Getty. I want to make sure your next visit is smooth as silk."

I bet she did.

"LET'S GO." Melike banded her hand around my uninjured arm, her natural French accent firmly back in place. Ditto for the attitude, too.

"Wait a sec."

"*Dieux!*" she said.

"I doubt the gods can help me. C'mon." I went docent hunting.

The middle-aged man in the blue shirt stared at my bandages, then asked if he could help me, like I might bite or something. His docent's tag read Mr. Harper. I showed him the earring photo, repeated what the shopkeeper had said.

His eyes widened. "You must realize this is only part of the vast collection. While I don't doubt the earrings exist in our collection, they very well may be stored."

I didn't need stored, dammit. "Any way I could find out? See them, Mr. Harper?"

His brown eyes twinkled. "Write a note. I'll see what I can do."

"Thank you!" I hastily wrote down my request, along with my name and number, and handed him the note with another thank you.

I exited through the Athletes room, ventured into the Wine in Antiquity room, and reached the main hall just as the loudspeakers boomed that the museum would close in fifteen minutes.

As I turned toward the staircase leading to the first floor, I again felt that tingle across my shoulders. Someone, *not* Melike, was following me. I whipped around. Nothing, although I caught Melike's smirk that said I'd lost it. I gave her a one-fingered salute and left.

Other than being attacked and trailed by an entity I now dubbed "The Tingler," I hadn't found squat at the museum. But I would. I was on the right track.

If and when the docent found the original earrings, perhaps I'd understand better.

WE GOT JAMMED up in traffic on our way back to Los Feliz. I expected Melike to scream at me, saying I'd put myself in danger, I was an idiot, blah, blah, blah. Instead, she sat and fumed.

I peeled away the layers of her vibe and thought. Figured it out. "You're upset."

She slid me a venomous glance.

"Because you didn't protect me. It wasn't your fault."

A wolfie growl, low in her throat.

"Here's why." I explained about the attack from behind, then watching a blur twirl and hearing grunts.

She slammed her foot onto the dash. "*Merde.* What do you mean, a blur?"

"Well, it was strange. Like someone smeared Vaseline across part of the room. All out of focus and...blurry. I've never seen anything like it before."

"*Dieux.* That petite love hug you've got on your arm. That's real enough."

"Did *you* see anyone following me?"

"*Non,*" she snapped, looking straight ahead. "*Pas un seul.* No one."

Sometimes I was so guarded. It wouldn't kill me to open up to Melike, let her see me as vulnerable. Sure, it would give her ammo, but so what? "I felt a 'something', Melike. A presence. Not the guy who attacked me. Something else. Some*one* else."

"Are you saying I don't know my job?" She snapped her teeth at me like a wolf.

"Not at all." And we inched forward, almost to the light. "Like I said, I felt a 'something' several times. Each time I tingled, like the aftermath of a small shock. My Spidey sense."

She snorted a laugh. "You didn't just say that."

My arms went rigid on the steering wheel. I forced them to relax. "My *mentor*, a man who taught me, who skilled me, who was murdered seven months ago, used to call it that."

She tilted her head in a very wolfie way. "*Je suis désolé*. I'm sorry you lost your friend. And for snapping at you."

"That was sorta cool."

She growled, very wolfie, and I grinned.

"So...," she said, pursing her lips. "Tell me more about what you felt in the museum."

I did. "And that shadow. Sometimes, I'd turn, glimpse something." I shook my head. "But all I *saw* was that shadow out of the corner of my eye. Then someone grabbed me, and the two of them, the 'shadow' and the guy who attacked me, they fought. At least I think they did from the sounds they made." She'd get a good laugh if I told her my attacker said *Want*. As if I were a prize.

"No one was following you," Melike said. "No one corporeal, at least."

"Ghosts don't exist."

"*You*, so certain. Always. Some of my packmates think they do."

Oh, why the hell not ghosts? I could just add them to my catalog of the weird, along with fae and vampyres and jackalopes. "Valid point. The shadow didn't do anything. Just watched. At least until that guy went after me. I've got too much real to worry about, so let's bag the ghosts."

She laughed, a bawdy sound. The first genuine one I'd heard from her. "That's an understatement. I'd love to take on those pink things Alex told us about."

"No, you wouldn't. They're disgusting. They drool."

She laughed again, harder. And for the first time, she allowed me to see the woman beneath the shell of pain and anger and violence.

That other Melike was gone. My aching muscles knew she'd be back. But *this* woman was complex, composed of nooks and crannies of kindness and humor, along with the jagged edges of fierceness and fury.

Her low inhuman growl startled me.

"They still have Neddy," she said.

"They do. I try not to think too hard about what he's experiencing. It makes me nuts."

"Cuts deep."

"Yes."

"Will they take more of our pups?" Her voice, controlled, contained, but the low notes of desperation told the story.

"I wish I knew. But until I understand the 'why' of it..."

She pointed to a street on the right. "There. Take that. Longer, but less traffic. *Sacre bleu*, turn!"

I did, uncaring of the driver's honks or the squealing tires. We rode the rest of the way home in silence.

FRANKENSTEIN'S SHADOW

What a day. My evening was worse. I talked to Erick, and Ronan would move out of our suite tomorrow and in with the warrior trainees. He was thrilled. Lulu pretended she was, too, as they spat at each other over dinner. Later, Lulu's unappealing sulk left me feeling helpless, and her shouted, "I wish my dad was here and not you!" clenched my heart. Her words, her mood stemmed from confusion and hurt. All I could do was kiss her cheek goodnight and give her an unwanted hug. As much as I wished to help, to comfort, she'd have to find her own way.

After I punched my pillow for the eightieth time, I rose and turned up the blower that circulated air up from the cool cellars, then lay down again. I said my nighttime prayer, one I'd learned as a child from Da. That always helped. But as I closed my eyes, they snagged on the small wolf carved as a welcoming gift when we moved into the den.

And arrowed my thoughts straight to Alex.

His touch, the softness of his lips, the strength of his arms, the beauty of his sunshine-and-sea aura. I was drawn to it. To him. He was a light in the void, his desire for me, a living, breathing thing.

Except...

I pictured a dark, brooding man. Closed. Distant. Troubled. He'd say not even a man, but a Frankenstein lab creature. A construct. A thing.

And I ached for him.

That presence watching me at the Villa. That shadow. It had moved in perfect synchronicity with me. Like a dance partner who anticipated my moves. I'd only ever had one shadow in my life, one who danced perfectly to my rhythm, and mine to his. James.

I snagged the knit glove that I'd found at Rae's off the shelf. It was comforting beneath my fingers. I padded over to the bedroom window, secured by filigreed iron and peered through the darkness. Maybe I'd see a shooting star. But even at three a.m., the lights of L.A. blazed too bright. So I imagined the star and wished upon it.

For James.

I STAND, not knowing where I'm headed. My bed is rumpled. I'm asleep, but I toss and turn. I shrug. It makes no sense. Wait. The faintest of notes, of music. Our fae song, calling to me, distant, but...

I race, feet slapping on the corridor's stone, out the front door, across the courtyard. I stumble, scrape my knees, but launch again into a run. I stop, breathless, at the top of the hill. Down below, a few lights dot the compound. A soft rain mists my face and body.

The call has stopped. I pause.

A large man steps from the shadows. My breath catches. I walk toward him, as he does toward me, then I run and jump. He catches me. James always catches me.

I hitch my arms around his shoulders, my legs around his hips. I laugh.

He grins, crinkling lines that fan from his eyes.

"I'm going to kiss you now," he says.

"You are, huh?" I ache for him, long for his lips. Our song rises.

He bows his head, his mouth closer to mine, his breath warm, his honey-pine scent tantalizing. He licks my top lip, nips the bottom one. "Want me to?"

"You're a tease," I say.

His eyes blaze. "Pot, kettle, m'dear. I look at you and..." He fastens his mouth on mine. I open, then our lips are smooshing and our tongues are dueling and I'm eating James up, my James. His one arm presses me firm against him while his other hand sneaks beneath my PJ bottom and inches lower and lower. The spot between my legs is wet and hot and achy. So achy. I moan into his mouth, our kiss frantic, me clawing his shoulders. My hips jerk. If he doesn't hurry, I may kill him.

His hand reaches my cleft, and one finger finds my clit. It moves, back and forth, faster and faster, and those other fingers are caressing my slit, and I'm building, building, wanting—gods, it feels so good. I need more, more, more...

He rips his mouth from mine. "Love you always."

I explode, our song crescendoing, arching backward as wave after wave of pleasure undulates through me. He clenches me to him, nuzzles my neck, my hair.

I slump against him, boneless, and he raises his hand, licking those fingers with a slow precision that gets me hot all over again.

"You are a devil," I say.

"I am that."

"I love you, too. Always."

He inhales deeply. "Your smell of cedar and lemongrass drives me mad."

"I'd rather smell of you."

"Soon."

THREE DAYS LATER, Ronan was all moved, Lulu was all attitude, and I was all aches, not to mention the colorful black and blues and scabs blotching my bod. The delightful handprint? The thing was huge.

Alone, getting dressed for our dinner and the theater, I paused, troubled. For three nights, I hadn't dreamed of James. I'd slept soundly, undisturbed by dreams or nightmares.

That troubled me more than I wanted to admit.

Instead, I concentrated on the positive and called my fireflies.

I cupped my hands. Palms up in supplication as Rae had taught me, I called to them. They coalesced within me, and I watched with awe as they swirled in my palms, each a mini-cosmos of magic and light.

When I stopped, when they dissolved, my heart squeed in triumph. My bod, not so much. I'd felt almost no pain and little plea-sure, only the wave of exhaustion Rae assured me would pass as I strengthened my psychic muscles. I sat my ass down on the edge of the bed.

Damn, but I didn't care if it tired me out. I would get better, stronger, badder.

Rae said that when I could call them at will to my palms *every time*, we'd start with streaming. Well, there you go, Mr. Smartass Rae. Tomorrow, I'd start learning to stream my Flow at will. *Hell, yeah.* Tomorrow.

MY GOAL for my night out with the kids was peace. No sniping from the kids. No snark. No bitching.

For the first time since we moved to the compound, we were out on the town—our first stop, a shopping mall, which the kids loved. I hated shopping and figured sainthood was just around the corner.

California's malls were different from those on the East Coast. Oh, not the stores. But the ambiance, since back home in the chilly Northeast, they're all enclosed. In L.A., many were open to the sky, with fountains and trees and here at the Grove, a trolley car, which had once almost run me over. The trolley stops for no one.

So far so good, as we ate alfresco at Marmalade, a favorite of Ronan's and Lulu's. Conversation flowed like it once had, with little conflict and much laughter. We people watched, and a delicate truce held through the meal of artichoke soup, artisanal burgers for the kids and grilled portobello, asparagus, and tempeh for me. Our guards—yes, Alex had talked me into bodyguards. Beth, a raw-boned woman with an easy smile, and Reidar, a murdered child's dad who dripped sorrow, gave us space by eating a few tables over.

I wanted tonight to be special, a family outing.

As I scooped another bite of portobello and asparagus, a guy in a kilt, bagpipes and a mohawk passed by with a snap to his step. Hard not to smile. Glam and funky, plain and gorgeous, quirky and preppie. All normal for L.A. But I couldn't help but wonder—were any of them mages, like me? Or fae or vamps, or other creatures I'd never knowingly met? I wouldn't even recognize a shifter in the stream of people. Otherworlders hiding in plain sight. Had been for centuries upon centuries. Fearing mundanes, who so outnumbered them. Did all fae have pointy ears? Were all vamps pale? What magic could they do? Shifters looked like mundanes, though many were built sturdier. There, a pretty girl with a perfect face and a fall of golden hair that shimmered in the fading light. She could be fae. Or could she?

No matter what I was, no matter my knowledge of the magical, I still felt mundane.

But the Union wanted me, allegedly for study... Yeah, right. Scientists of the government/DarkPool coalition, the Union, were studying the magical, the Union desperate to acquire it, harness it, wield it.

I looked around, suddenly paranoid. They'd carve me up, dissect me, like the lab rats and monkeys they used and discarded.

No wonder otherworlders cloaked themselves.

Could the Union be causing the disastrous anomalies?

No. Anouk said it was the chaotic retwining of the two worlds.

"C'mon," I said to the kids. "Let's walk around the Grove, do some shopping. We have a little time."

When I walked between Ronan and Lulu, I felt pigmy-sized. I wrapped my hands around each of their forearms, which they tolerated, and smiled up at them.

"Fun?" I said.

Ronan nodded, his grin wide.

"Yeah," Lulu said. "It's so neat here." She squealed. "There's Zac Efron!" Her head swiveled, following his path.

Ronan shrugged. "He's okay."

"Okay!" Lulu said, whipping around to face him. "He's hot. That's how much you know."

She stormed off, I followed, and Ronan trailed behind me like the tail of a comet. I found her in an antique shop.

She prowled around, enraptured, while the besuited shopkeeper wearing several strings of love beads hovered, showing her this and that artifact.

Few males could resist the lure of a passionate Lulu on a hunt.

Seeing that she was safe and her good humor had returned, I scanned the shop. My eyes caught on an unsheathed blade, a katana, hanging on the wall. I walked over and reached for it.

"Careful!" said the shopkeeper. "It's sharp."

I nodded. "Thanks."

After Ronan's long reach assisted me in bringing the weapon down, I gripped the hilt, a near match to the one James' had given me. I turned it over and almost dropped the damned thing.

The price—five thousand dollars. The tag noted it was the standard two shaku, 3 sun or 27+ inches in length, from the sixteen hundreds, the early Edo period, and attributed to the Echizen Seki School. The blade came with a silk brocade carry bag, sword maintenance kit, sword stand, plus a copy of the book *Bushido: The Soul of Japan*.

The mountings, the hilt, the blade, even the weight—I'd swear they were identical to the one James had given me.

"Put it back for me?" I asked Ronan, and I turned to the shopkeeper. "Um, sir? I have a katana that matches this sword. Can you—"

"I very much doubt that." He hastened over. "This is a rare blade, particularly for the U.S."

I wasn't going to argue. "How about I bring mine in for you to examine?"

His eyes gleamed. "Of course."

"I can come back in two days. Will you be here?"

His smile widened. "I'll make a point of it."

I noted the appointment on my phone's calendar and saw the time. "We're going to be late. C'mon, kids."

"I want to come back with you," Lulu said.

"In two days, you'll be—"

"Please!"

"Sure," I said.

Ronan placed a hand on the small of Lulu's back and she smiled up at him.

Their truce held all the way to the theater.

THE GLAMOROUS PANTAGES theater sat smack on Hollywood Boulevard, a street that defined "crazy." A person could buy anything, see anything, do anything at this epicenter of LaLa Land. In the right mood, I loved it, this town of consumerism and history and aching dreams. It was often noisy and sometimes silly and always jumped with so many disparate vibes I'd get dizzy. Literally.

Lucky for us, around theater time, the vibe ratcheted down.

We queued up to the ticket taker. Just behind us, a handsome blond guy wearing braids and a gray suit eyed Lulu, in all her Goth glory. No matter how Lulu dressed, her aura attracted men like virtual reality attracted geeks.

I ignored the blond, knowing Beth and Reidar were nearby, steered us inside the gold and bejeweled Art Deco lobby, and then toward the left.

In the auditorium, an usher led us to our prime orchestra seats.

"You dropped this," came the sensual voice behind me.

I flipped around. Lulu was looking with hunger at the braid-wearing blond, who held up a theater program.

Just what we needed.

"Thanks," she said, her voice Monroe breathy.

"Hey," Ronan said. "Fuck off."

Ronan's reaction—the cherry atop the sundae.

I braced an arm on Ronan. "Hey, Ro. Cool it."

Lulu jerked her chin up. "You're not my boyfriend anymore, so shut up."

Braid-boy turned to Ronan and offered a snarky grin. "Why don't *you* fuck off."

We'd stalled the line, the usher bristled, and testosterone billowed between the two men. Beth and Reidar shoved bodies aside to get to us.

Oh, goody.

I lay one hand on braid-boy, the other on Ronan's shoulder, and poured calm into both. Not having a third hand, I couldn't do anything about Lulu. The men calmed, Beth and Reidar slowed, but Lulu snapped at Ronan.

"You just stop!" she said.

"We need to get to our seats," I said in a soothing voice. "We're holding things up."

She stormed in the opposite direction, back up the jammed aisle. I handed Ronan his ticket. "Get seated." Turned to braid-boy. "Get lost." I pushed my way up the aisle.

When I passed Reidar, I told him to stay with Ronan and make sure the two didn't escalate.

Beth moved to follow Lulu, but shouts behind us halted her progress. All three men, including Reidar, were engaged in a pissing contest. "Dammit. Switch with Reidar and send him after me. Just in case." She snapped me a nod and shoved through the aisle crowd.

Whatever. Ours was supposed to be a fun, family evening, not another three-ringed circus. Didn't matter. I was the one Lulu needed.

When my foot hit the lobby carpet, the lights flickered. Five minutes to curtain.

I scanned the large space, now thinned of people, but failed to spot Lulu. She wouldn't have left. She was dying to see the show. I trotted toward the sign pointing to the ladies' room around the corner. When in crisis, hit the can. I'd be she was there.

As I neared the entrance, women queued up inside the alcove that led to the bathroom. I unfurled my senses. Lulu. Inside the lav. My muscles relaxed a fraction. She was safe. But I still had to calm her down. At sixteen, hormones were a bitch.

I took a step. From an arched alcove to the lavatory's left, wrongness tickled the hairs on my arms. I whirled. Something sharp grazed my shoulder. My hands whipped up to grip the beefy wrist digging into my shoulder. I pulled on the wrist, shot my foot back to a vulnerable knee—a satisfying crunch—dropped my shoulder. I tugged my opponent forward as I spun back toward the bathroom with its many women.

"*Clea!*"

My stride hitched.

Reidar raced toward me across the lobby.

A sting on my neck.

Lights out.

12

DARKNESS, ACID, AND STEEL

I awakened to darkness, the scents of acid and steel, and the sounds of liquid dripping. No rainbows or unicorns here. I was woozy, must've been drugged. Naked, too. I shivered from the chill and...

Yeah, okay, so I was scared.

I lay on my back, a burning sting in my shoulder, and my head pounded to the rhythm of the drips.

Someone had stretched and bound my arms above me, palms flat together, in a bizarre prayer pose, with something tight wrapped around them. Duct tape. Cold hard things manacled my wrists. Forehead taped, attaching me to a bed, not too hard, not too soft. Christ, I was thinking in fairytale metaphors. Lips dry as the Mojave. I tried to wiggle, but my waist was bound, too, as were my legs, cuffed tight together. My mind scrambled.

Gods, who... what... had taken me? Why? What would they do to me?

Pinkys! I pictured Pinkys pawing at me, drooling on me, licking me with their purple tongues.

A wave of nausea.

Woozy.

Out.

TIME. Mutable. Fluid and endless. Drugs and dreams. Pain and machine sounds. Whoosh, click. Whoosh click. Slaps and pinches... and a scent. *Whose scent, but he...* Probes and pricks. Over and over and over. Tired. Weak. A broken doll. The warmth, my blood. My face, my heart, my mind. My mind!

Fading.

I couldn't do this.

Oh, that was just stupid. Of course I could.

I CAME BACK to myself slowly.

Wheeze, thump. Wheeze, thump.

Everything hurt. Toes, shins, knees, chest, arms—bees stinging again and again. My face. Slaps, pinches, punches. My brain... *Fuck this!*

Deep, deep inside, I groped for my magic. For its warmth. Comfort. It felt small, shrunken. Had they taken that? They couldn't. *No, they could not.*

So who was I convincing?

Wait. *They.*

Two. There had been two of them. Men.

That scent.

And voices. One, *his.* No. Impossible. Mouth dusty, my reflexive swallow brought up a cough. We'd battled. I'd maimed him. My twin, *Tommy.*

Except laughter had followed each pinch and slap and punch to my face. *His* laughter.

Or was this some drug-induced hallucination of my addled brain?

Didn't matter. None of that mattered. Had to get free.

Wheeze, thump. Wheeze, thump.

That damned sound. I remembered that damned sound. Pervasive. Constant. Abhorrent.

Focus.

Fingers. The tape was gone, and I wiggled them. Ouch. One appeared broken. Left hand. Dominant hand. Lousy. At least it was only one.

But manacles still bound my wrists. *Damn.*

A crust of tears stuck my eyes closed. I couldn't reach them, of course. Without hands, no one realizes how hard it is to open eyes glued closed.

My stomach heaved. Smells of puke and poop and urine. And blood. Something about the blood. No, no, no.

I worked the eyeballs, squeezed, tried to open them. A glimmer, then, bam—got it!

The room. Where I was bound. Cement walls, ceiling, huge creepy refrigeration unit—I hated those, given the sucko memories they resurrected—damp chill, like I was buried beneath the earth, another non-fave of mine.

Wheeze, thump.

My head swiveled toward the sound. Whoa, my forehead wasn't taped anymore. Cuddled up to my bed stood a pole with two bags of blood hanging from steel arms. Half full. A slow drip of blood plopped into each bag. Plop, plop, plop.

Gods, I was still half stoned.

A sound by the door!

I stilled. Listened. Nothing.

Paranoia are us.

Beside the pole crouched a machine. The wheezing thing. Twin tubes snaked from the machine's belly to each of my purpled thighs, connected to needles that pierced my skin.

Holy shit, they were draining my blood!

Whoa. My thighs were mottled purple. Had they beaten me that badly?

I blinked. No, my legs weren't purple. Glops of purple and black covered them. My boobs, too. My belly.

My breath hitched. A glutinous eyeball rested in the hollow of my bellybutton, like some grotesque navel ornament. On the wall, a chiaroscuro of light cement and long trails of dark blood. And guts. Strings of purple guts splattered the surface, mingled with gobs of pink flesh and hair and...

I squeezed my eyes tight, stomach cramping, controlling the puke. Not gonna do it.

What had happened?

Was it day? Night? Twilight? No clue.

Someone was watching me. Who? He'd leap out of the shadows if I moved.

Stop. I unfurled my mind, cast outward, though an icepick jabbed my brain. I was alone. Took a deep breath, and I sucked it up. I peered to my right. Fog dissipated to memory—two men. One standing beside me, dark, shadowy, the other dead center at the foot of the bed. I could almost make out his features.

He was big. Huge. Most definitely not my brother. Like a fuzzy black-and-white image. I blinked fast, tried to clear my head. Bigger than Alex. Taller than James. And more massive. If James was a mountain, this guy was Everest.

Light had reflected off his bald head.

His vibes. Yeah, he had strange, erratic vibes that bounced from one emotion to the next. At some point, I'd tasted his emotions. His essence... chaotic. Hungry. Obsessed. Determined. Fearful. Worshipful.

And mad as a hatter.

He'd left the lights on when he'd left. No, *a* light, sticking out from the wall and caged in metal.

I'd held off, but finally cut my eyes to the floor. My head thundered. *Oh, shit.* More blood and mucus and splotches of pink flesh. And legs. Six of them, some with feet, others... Bones poked through flesh, more like ground meat than anything anthropoid. They were ... the Pinkys. No more chittering for you guys, huh.

I'd done that?! Ended three beings. They might have been monsters, but they'd had some sort of lives.

Did I give a shit?

I did.

A glance at the gray door. Push-down handle. Locked, chained. Not that locks or chains would make a difference to *Him*.

A shiver took me. Where had they gone? When would they be back? Why were they taking my blood? My fuzzy mind failed to provide answers.

But I'd killed the Pinkys, saw it like a movie, someone else playing the part of me. But it wasn't someone else.

I'd been in the moment when I'd fireflied them, hadn't thought ahead to what killing my jailers would mean.

Foolish Pinkys. When they'd untaped my palms—fuckers wanted me to pet them, stroke them—they'd prompted my fireflies with a wham, bam, thank you, ma'am. Rae would love it.

Gods, I felt drunk, stoned, whatever. Guess my magical motes had worked on overdrive.

Even with no tape around my forehead and hand, my wrists and ankles remained manacled to the bed. I tried to firefly. *Naturellement*, as Melike would say, nothing happened. Must have spent all my moola on the Pinkys. Rae'd be ticked.

Slaps, punches, pricks... *Don't go there.*

Mouth parched, I ran my tongue across my split lips, tasting my own blood and his. Whose? Foul. The Pinkys? Him? Tommy? I'd bitten someone, hoped it was Tommy.

No way would I wait until they returned, went at me again. *Shit. Shit. Shit.*

And damn that tear sliding from my left eye, salt stinging my cut cheek as it meandered down the swollen hills and valleys of my face.

I'd try once more—just for the fun of it—captured my energy, focused it, jerked on my ankles, my wrists hard, harder.

No fireflies, just pain. *Screw it.* I did it over and over. "Fuck!"

Muscles collapsing into the softness of the mattress.

They'd be coming. Soon? No idea the time. No idea the day. Tick tock. Big bucks on this pair having stolen the children's lives. I'd pray for madness, except then I'd never catch the bastards.

If I rocked hard, side to side, could I tip the bed over, land on my belly, and crawl with the thing turtling me to the door. Absurd idea. Sure, why the hell not? Better than sitting still.

Side to side, back and forth. Again. Again. Again. The bed didn't budge. Not. One. Inch.

Bastard had it bolted to the floor.

I laughed, which hurt like hell. It was a lame plan, anyway.

Cold blasted through me. I shook, couldn't stop. Coated with a black roiling oil of panic. Can't breathe, panting, freezing.

Need to breathe!

What was that?

I eyeballed the door, stilled, breath vanishing in the perfection of fear.

A scrape of footsteps?

I took shallow quiet breaths through my mouth.

No. Nothing. Not a sound.

My captor, the big one—Him—walked heavy. Thud. Thud. Thud.

My face stung as I dripped wetness onto the mattress. I was a frickin' leaky faucet. Talk about a waste of good hydration.

Had to get out of there. Had to.

No more blood for you, buster.

Gather, gather. Bold, like a Jedi. Find the magic. Feel the magic, little one.

Da. So long gone. A sob stuttered from my lips.

Was I going to lay there like some beached fish? Or was I gonna get my ass in gear?

My long, deep inhale relaxed me. Another. And another. I dived deep to that place where my magic lay, like a gold pool, opaque and mysterious. Dormant, yet slow, sinuous curves moved on the pool's surface. I coaxed it, soothed it, nurtured it.

Control. Rae said it was all about control. Positive manipulation and discipline.

I focused on that warm, safe place in my mind, just as Dave had taught me. Bathed in it. Washed in sweet memories of Dave, Lulu, and James.

The pool brightened, widened, grew to a luminous spinning ball of gold laced with blue fire. I pulled it up from my belly, to my legs, my arms, my fingers and toes.

Fists clenched, I relaxed them, unrolled them, bent my right wrist so my hand tipped toward my ankles.

I unleashed my Flow.

Streams of light danced from my palms, and my fireflies speared toward the manacles. It tickled the tops of my bare feet to my ankles. My shackles fell to the floor with a clank.

Yes! My grin had widened the crack in my lip, and coppery blood dribbled into my mouth.

I twisted my hands, so my palms faced each opposing wrist. Again I gathered, found that bright pool inside me, nurtured it, grew it, encouraged it again. Then I freed the Flow to do its work.

The release of the cuffs felt divine.

Free.

A moment to pause, and some stupid song about freedom earworming my head. Really? Now? I pushed to a sitting position. The room spun carousel fast, and I clutched the gurney's side, breathed through my nose.

The door to my cell smashed open, framing a man, backlit, impossibly large, guns in hand.

I leapt off the bed into a crouch… except I flopped on the floor in a heap of pudding muscles and pain amidst Pinky guts. *Gross.*

I crawled beneath the gurney, raised my palms to firefly.

The man was tall, but not as tall as Him. Raven haired, not bald. And eyes… a storm darkened those Pacific blues, scanned me now, saw me, yet not a flicker of…

"James?"

Hoarse, just a whisper. Throat scoured raw.

His eyes swept the room, the flesh-strewn floor, me.

"James!"

But he turned away, left my field of vision, ghosting deeper into the cellar. I couldn't hear him, couldn't see him.

Had I passed out? Was this a fantasy of my muddled brain?

A presence coming back, almost into view. A shadow. But I still couldn't see him. I shook, chills rushing my body, teeth a-chatter.

He approached, glided closer, muscled thighs bunched beneath worn jeans, bronzed arms in a black tee. He holstered his guns, and his hands, large, scarred, reached for me. Everything ached when he gently gripped my shoulders and drew me out from beneath the gurney. I stood.

Legs jelly, I collapsed toward the Pinky puddle.

He caught me and lifted me, then seated me on the gurney so we were eye to eye. Mine burned, hot with relief and joy, and my tears spilled free. After six long months he was *here*.

Except he was silent. So silent. Why was he so silent?

He stared at me, those blazing blues, up close, too close, examining me. A specimen in a jar?

I raised my arms toward him, hands lifted to encircle his neck. Except my arms were jelly, too. They dropped, limp, dangling. It hurt, but I opened and closed my hands to bring feeling back into them.

He tugged a blanket over my nakedness. It was putrid, smelled of blood and Pinky death.

Why couldn't I sense his thoughts? He'd opened to me so often. I noted the tiny changes from the months we'd been apart. Hair worn longer than before brushed his shoulders. His beautiful chiseled face, tight and bronzed, cheekbones crosshatched with faint scars, and a long one that wound down the left side of his jaw. One new scar ran parallel to the laugh lines that fanned the corners of his eyes. I reached to touch it. But my arm failed to comply.

He wasn't looking at me, but intent on his task, wrapping the blanket tight around me, tucking in the ends.

One arm slid beneath my knees, the other around my back. He lifted me.

"I can walk."

"No, you can't."

His voice, hardened granite. He was in "mission" mode. I pressed my head to that chest I'd stroked more than once. I inhaled scents of honey and pine and... something bright and metallic. Odd. "I'm so glad you're back, James." I sniffled a little. The situation's surreality was getting to me.

He laid me over his shoulder, and I bit back my groan. Then he redrew his 9mms and slid me from his shoulder back into his arms.

Silent, so silent, he moved toward the wrecked door, stepping over bodies, avoiding smears and spatters of blood and guts and pink flesh.

Not once did he glance down at me.

Sunflowers, bourbon, sex. Nope, not the reunion I'd pictured.

Thundering footsteps.

No! Him!

James' arms stiffened, legs widened to a ready stance, shoulders tight. Tense, but a sea of calm. No time to put me back on the bed, but the 9mms, yeah, they were ready, too.

White wolves poured through the door, large and small, muzzles drawn back, teeth shining, feral growls breaking the silence.

"Don't shoot!" I screamed at James, my voice a raw thing.

A whoosh of magical smoke, and jeans and t-shirted men and women surround us. A shifter ripped me from James' arms, hugged me close, all sunshine and sea and sorrow, drowned out by the sounds of feral growls as they took James down.

"No!" I shouted.

Alex turned and ran.

He picked up speed inside the narrow cement tunnel, with caged ceiling lights strobing his face. The lights blurred, the world blurred. Then up and up and up, out into the daylight. It hurt.

I winced, drew into myself.

"Sorry, sweetheart."

"Alex, wait." Words stolen by air.

He paused, arms banding me, cradling me, tense, restless.

Hammers pounded me, spikes of glass. A hideousness crept over me like ugly goo, smothering, suffocating.

"He wasn't the one who..." I stuttered a breath. *All in my mind. Stop it.*

"Later," he said. "When we're home."

Again, he moved, all liquid precision, and we were in the folds of hills peppered with paintbrush and sedge and deer weed. The air, so sweet. Running, still running. And there, in the distance, were houses and roads, and we whooshed past middle-class homes, one-storied stuccoes, and trees, some blooming cacti, a pink-stoned front yard, whoosh, whoosh, whoosh across a street, down another, eyes so heavy.

To an SUV parked on a side street, a big, black thing shaded by a palm.

Alex slid me into the shotgun seat and began to buckle me in.

"Stop it," I said, slapping his hand. "I can do this. I'm not a doll." I snapped the buckle home.

Seconds later the driver's door clicked closed, and the car hummed to life. We eased out, slow, and the thrum of the road took over.

A water bottle in my hands, but the twist top. Couldn't get it off. Guess I'd expended all my mojo on the seatbelt. A tanned hand reached for the top, turned it, released the bottle. I greedily sucked.

Cooling water sluiced down my throat.

He took the bottle and set it in the cup holder. "Enough."

"But—"

"How about in a few minutes?"

I licked my swollen lips, tried to explain. "He wasn't the—"

"Just chill, sweetheart. You're safe. Okay. You can tell me everything once I get you home."

I wanted to protest, but my gut churned and the dizziness took me, and I was gone.

13

MEMORIES

The smooth scents of herbs teased my nose. Sage, rosemary. Citrus, too. Comforting. My other senses came online. The brush of a cooling breeze, the light cotton of a soft quilt. I waited for my brain to catch up, tried to clear the fuzzies. That was a flop. A man. No, two men, one hurt me, and then later, the other who... But everything was gray. And pain. Yeah, a memory of pain, except... All I felt now was discomfort, aches too, but no sharp stabs, no bones ground, no skin raw.

Not too bad.

But I needed to remember.

I lifted my lids. No sticky tears sealing them shut. I recalled that. I sniffed the room. No blood anywhere. There had been a lot of blood. So that was good, yeah, that was good.

"Clea!"

Ouch. My ears rang. A body flopped onto mine, and I stiffened until the smell of bubblegum and cashmere awakened memories of Lulu.

Oh, gods, the kid was sobbing. I couldn't have that.

"Lulu." Voice, a rusty utensil. "Lulu."

Eyes stared into mine, tears drowning the violet.

"Hey, kiddo," I said, ghosting a smile.

"You're better!" Her short hair, now a coppery red, tickled my cheek.

"What happened to the pink hair?"

Sniffles, twice. "I thought you'd like this better, so I changed it back."

My hand brushed her face. "I like you any way, Lu."

A soggy laugh. "Thanks."

"Guess we'll have to re-buy tickets to *The Book of Mormon*."

Another snuffly laugh. "Guess so."

The air grew thick with others' emotions, and I peered over Lulu's shoulder to see Melike and Ronan.

"Hey, guys," I said.

Ronan kissed my head, his eyes watery, too, before he stomped from the room.

"Finally." Melike snorted, but the vibe said 'joy.' Wow. Wonder of wonders.

Lulu was smothering me, and panic orgied through my body. A caterpillar of shakes.

Melike took her arm. "Lulu. Hon. Ease up."

"Oh!" She sprang back. "Sorry, Clea." She clapped her hands, big smile on her face. "Gotta go tell my pals you're okay."

So not okay, but I smiled again, and she flew, trailed by her two Brittanys. Which was when I realized she wore a diaphanous hippy chiffon dress. No more Goth, I guessed. At least not today.

More assessing. I was in my bedroom in our suite inside the compound. Cool afternoon light filtered in from the window. Gracie snored at the foot of the bed. Kitty, tail swishing, sprawled on the footstool. Normal.

Yeah, right.

Melike pulled my desk chair across the room, flipped it backward, and sat. "Took you long enough."

I scooched up to a sitting position. Given my brain fry, I had no clue what she was talking about. "What did?"

She frowned. "For you to wake up. *Mon dieux*, you slept forever. Days."

"How many?"

"Three."

No way. I snagged my phone off the bedside table. Stupid. I had no idea how long I'd been in that basement of horror.

A headline snared my attention. All the children in Nepal twelve and under had fallen unconscious simultaneously. They'd just awakened after a week asleep. Some said they'd visited Disney World, others Narnia, still others *Where the Wild Things* lived.

Another magical eruption? Had to be. Maybe I...

No, that wasn't what had happened to me.

I reached for the bedside glass of water, drank. "Have you found Neddy?"

"*Non*." Her eyes slid away from mine. "How much do you remember?"

"Right now? Not much. I think I was in a lot of pain, but... My brain hasn't come onboard completely. Do you know what happened?"

She nodded.

"And...?"

A very French shrug, except her fingers played with the knife at her waist. Okay, so it was bad. Though I seemed to be in one piece. That was good, right?

"So," I said. "Tell me what happened. It'll come back. You'll just speed up the process."

"*Non*. Forbidden."

"'Forbidden,' huh. Alex, Mr. Control Freak. Where the hell is he, then?"

"With the prisoner. *Merde!*" She bit her lip.

The prisoner... An avalanche pounded me, buried me, subsumed me. I curled into myself, clutched my head.

No. *No*. I didn't want to remember.

I AWAKENED CRADLED in a man's arms. Sunshine and sea, warmth and compassion. Worry.

Well, hell. "Alex. Alex, put me down, dammit."

He chuckled. "You're back."

"Enough, yes. Now put me down, wherever, in a chair, I don't care. Just do it."

"I don't feel like it."

"Tough."

With a dramatic sigh, he sat me in the club chair, then plopped down on the edge of my bed across from me. His eyes narrowed. "Do you remember what happened to you? Who came? What you did?"

"Remember? Not much. Its patchy. Someone was hurting me. Another someone came. Then the wolves." I shook my head. "It's all fuzzy." I examined my body, dressed in loose workout pants and a tank top. Squeezed my legs, my arms, my face. "I feel like crap, but superficial crap. My injuries... I'm sure they were worse, far worse."

His forearms rested on his thighs, hands fisted, white knuckled. "Yeah."

I waved an arm. "So? Even out of it for three days, I wouldn't have healed so much."

"Our healer and medics worked together. That helped. Rae came by, too."

Rae was a healer? I peeked under my tank top. Green and yellow bruises splatted my flesh. I looked like Camo Clea.

"Yeah," Alex said. "Rae helped us find you. He was with us. He'll come back to..."

"What?"

He crossed his arms, the movement showing dots of blood on his shirt.

"Why are you bloody?"

His was smile was nasty. "I cut myself chopping vegetables."

"Lying."

"Never mind that."

I stood fast, clutched the chair arm for balance. "Y'know, I did some badass work in that bunker. I'm sure of that, at least." Weaving now, but I wasn't going to sit down until I had my say. "I need to know everything. I have that right. I've got patches of memory and lots of holes, and I'm only going to recall it all with help. So give over." There. I said it. I flopped back down.

"You shouldn't remember."

"What are you, my father?"

"No, damn you." An enraged alpha towered over me.

"You're not scary, y'know," I said. "Not to me."

He crouched, one hand on my thigh, thumb rubbing back and forth. "You're the only one, sweetheart."

I cupped his cheek. "Alex, please help me. It's horrible, the not knowing. I need to find Neddy. To understand. To fix things."

His hand smoothed over mine. "It was bad, Clea. He beat you. Drained your blood. From what Rae could see, repeatedly."

"He didn't rape me, though."

Dark shadows danced in the gold of his eyes. "No."

I squeezed my eyes tight, flashed on BlondieII. Rape. It had almost happened once. But my mind was stronger now. At least this bastard didn't violate me that way. But why take my blood? "Any, um, permanent damage?"

"Not that we can tell."

I didn't miss the thread of fear in his voice. We'd see what came. Enough. One single step at a time. Just one. "I'll deal with it. But, there's more. What more? And go sit over there, Alex." I waved at the other chair. "You're hovering."

He stood. "I should get going. Don't you think that's enough for now? You haven't been awake long and—"

"I need it *all*." My voice, rusty still, was firm. I liked that. "I need it, Alex." He was trying to shield me, to be kind. I didn't want kind. I could drown in that kindness just as much as *He* had drowned me in cruelty.

He glanced at his hands, then back at me. "He, someone, was inside... your brain."

I grew very still. Wait for it. Wait. Nothing came. "What?"

"Rae's not sure. But someone poked around, searching. So Rae said."

Keep it together. "What *is* He? The one who took me? How could he do that?"

"We're not sure. He's different. Other. We've been interrogating him and—"

"Interrogating him?"

His lips thinned. "Nothing you need to know."

"But when did you capture him? I don't understand."

"He had you in his arms when we found you."

"No, he..." Lightning speared me. Pictures. No, a movie. The door crashing in, a man, lifting me, 9mms, cradling me in his arms.

I lurched across the room, gripped Alex's shoulders, shook him. "James. That's James Larrimer. My... He's my friend. He didn't *do* anything to me. He came to rescue me. Where is he? What have you done?"

I latched onto his shirt and pulled hard. Yeah, right, like a boulder would move. I tried harder. His shirt ripped. Shit. "Show me. *Show me!*"

He gripped my wrists. "Calm down."

"I'm not going to calm down when you've been interrogating someone who tried to rescue me from that hell hole."

He jerked to his feet.

I tugged on his hands. "Let me go!"

He freed me. "Rae said he was one of their constructs."

"What?" I scraped a hand through my hair, frantic, crazy. James, James. They... How to make Alex understand? I wobbled, and Alex caught me around the waist.

"Sit down before you wipe out."

"I won't wipe out, dammit!" I was screaming now.

Lulu and Erick barreled into the room.

"Where the fuck is he?" I said.

"What the hell?" Erick said.

"Clea!" Lulu's cry.

My resolve spiraled around me, calm and strong. "I am fine," I said to them. I glared at Alex. "You will take me to him. You will release him. He has done nothing to me except try to save me from the creep who kidnapped and tortured me. Am I clear, Alex Arctos?"

Erick and Lulu crept closer, fascinated horror on their faces.

"Clea," Alex said.

His look of hurt and betrayal cut deep. I couldn't blame him, but I didn't relent. "Now, please."

The glance he shot Lulu and Erick said 'back off.' Both looked away. I sure as hell didn't.

"Drink something," he said, and retrieved a juice bottle and sandwich from the mini fridge. He held them out. "You've been on IVs. Eat. You're weaker than a cub."

I kept my eyes clamped on Alex, took the bottle, uncapped it, and glugged it down. I slammed the empty onto the side table. "Now."

"You need to eat." He shoved the sandwich at me.

I boiled with anger. "Now, Alex, or I swear..."

He gripped my upper arm and dragged me out of the room. Even in his fury, his hold was firm, but not painful.

"I don't need help," I said as we marched down the hall.

Doors opened, packmates gawked, Alex glared, and all I could think about was how they'd hurt James.

People started to follow us, like the tail of a comet. One glance backward from Alex, and they dispersed.

"He's a thing," Alex said, his voice guttural, near inhuman.

"No," I said. "He's as human as you or I." I pushed at the hand that circled my arm. "Let go."

"I'm afraid you'll fall on your ass."

"At least it'll be my fault, right? You're manhandling me. Haven't I had enough of that?"

He released me so abruptly I bounced into a wall. I steadied myself, then shoved forward. We walked through the den's central salon, down the hall I'd traversed when I'd met with the dead children's parents, to the same staircase that led to the cellars.

Minutes later, we rounded a corner at the back of the cellars and faced a door. The guard stationed outside bore enough firepower to take down the Hulk. Alex gestured me forward, and I entered. The room was large, clean, and dry. Three barred cages sat against the back wall, each maybe eight by eight. Two were empty. The third held a man tied to a chair, head slumped on his chest, arms bound behind him. Above him hung a steel chain and hook and a single lit bulb.

I staggered. Alex reached for me.

"Don't," I said.

Alex moved away and spoke to the guard, who left the room.

The closer I came to the cage, the more I saw and smelled. The air stung of iron and copper, and blood smeared the floor beneath the prisoner. What I thought at first was a shirt and pants proved to be blood, dried blood that coated his naked body. I couldn't see his face.

I walked to the bars and wrapped my hands around them. "James?"

Nothing.

"Release him," I said.

"Not yet."

I whirled on Alex. "How could you? Alex, release him. Please. He's done nothing. Why are you doing this?"

His face hardened. "He's a thing."

"He's not!"

"A construct. A creature not of our world. He smells wrong, feels wrong. He's perversely powerful and swift. He barely breathes, heals abnormally fast."

Strange Alex didn't smell the fae in him. Or the wyvern. "Except for the breathing part, that sounds like you."

His face contorted into a snarl. "He is nothing like me."

"What were you doing to him? Why were you torturing him?"

"To discover the truth."

"And you learned...?"

"Nothing."

I looked back at James—blood, bone, hair, heart, soul. Yes, soul, dammit, even though he was reborn via nanotech, a fae spark, and a wyvern's blood. I knew this man. I loved this man, and why was that so hard to admit? I pressed my face to the bars. "James."

The bars felt cold and greasy from my sweat. I wiped them on my pants as I turned back to Alex.

"He may not be of the magic world, Alex, or even as the mundane understands human, but he is a man. A good man. And what you've done to him…"

If anything, Alex's face grew more rigid. "It's him, isn't it?"

I didn't pretend to misunderstand him. "That's between me and James Larrimer."

The guard returned with a folded stack of clothes, a basin of water, cloths and a first-aid kit. He reached for his keys.

Alex flicked a finger, and the guard froze. "We aren't releasing him from the cage, Clea. Not yet. He's unnaturally strong. Insanely powerful. Why was he in that room with you? What was he going to do with you? How sure are you that he wasn't involved in the deaths of our children? I have a pack to protect."

"And a child to find," I said. "And a killer to dispatch."

He notched his head toward James. "I'm not convinced he's not both their killer and your tormentor. What makes you so sure he wasn't your kidnapper, the one who abused you, then reappeared as your savior?"

"I know," I said quietly. "You'll have to trust in my truth."

Back straight as the steel bars, Alex said, "For now, he stays in the cage. He's the enemy, Clea. Don't forget it. He had three trackers on him. Some creative carving removed them from his flesh."

Bile surged into my mouth as I took the clothes and such from the guard. "All right. I'll go in and clean him up. Release his manacles. Give him a bed, at least."

Alex gestured to the guard to unlock the cage.

"Lock me in," I said. "I'll call when I want you to let me out."

"Too dangerous," he said. "You're not yourself."

"Yeah, I am, Alex. And you're not my keeper."

Alex leaned close and whispered in my ear. "All we've ever done is care for you, help you, rescue you."

I fought my galvanic temper. "He came for me, Alex. He rescued me, too."

"If he ends you, it's not on us."

Cold words that I carried with me into the cell.

I WAITED while the guard unlocked James' ankles and wrists. He slumped forward, arms dangling at his sides. The guard vanished, but I couldn't take my eyes off James. He might attack me when he surfaced, but he wouldn't hurt me. Well, not much.

I brushed the filthy, blood-soaked hair from his forehead. A hand clamped my wrist, and growls, not James', but Alex's and guards, filled the room.

"I'm fine," I said. "He won't hurt me."

The slam of a door, the snick of the key echoed in the cavernous room. Guilt rode me hard. To me, Alex had been nothing but kind. But what they'd done to James broke my heart.

"James, it's me, Clea. I'm here to wash you off, to help you."

He raised his head, and his eyes burned ice cold. "I'm not in need of help."

Right. "Will you let me go?" I looked at my wrist.

"Yes." He sat back in the chair, face gray and tight with what I believed was pain.

I felt his eyes on me as I dabbed the cloth in the water and washed his face, his arms, his chest, trying not to cringe at the many cuts and burns that marred his body. His legs and ankles were raw, the water now a muddied red. My hand shook. I tried to stop it, failed. I was so not nurse material. I picked up the antiseptic tube.

"Not necessary," James said.

More sounds, and when I looked over my shoulder, the guard outside the cell pointed to a mattress, a large pitcher of water, and a tray of food.

I peered up at James. "Will you stay in the chair while I get them?"

"Yes," he said, firm, but toneless.

James had the most beautiful voice, honeyed granite. Today, it rang flat in my ears.

At the cell door, three shapeshifters, all now white wolves, padded in a semicircle around James' jailer. I recognized Erick's wolf, and Melike's, but Alex's wasn't there.

In quick minutes, I carried in the food and water and set them on the floor. The jailer dragged in the mattress, and when he re-locked the cell, only he and Melike in wolf form remained in the outer room.

"If you stand," I said to James, "you can lie down on the mattress. Then I can tend to your back."

He stood, shoved the chair out of the way, lifted the pitcher and drank. The pitcher crashed to the floor when he dropped to his knees on the too-small mattress, then sprawled face down, his back a slab of bloodied meat. Whip marks scored his buttocks, the back of his legs, the soles of his feet. I almost lost it.

My grandmother's back had looked like that after Tommy. And she'd died.

I snatched up the basin and threw the bloody water at the jailer. It coated him, spattered Melike's white fur, too. "How could you? How could you do this?"

The jailer remained silent.

"Dammit, get me more fresh water."

On my knees, the pain staved off my tears. I saw another time, many months ago, when James' body had been scored with my vile twin's magic needles. Tommy had shot them into his torso where they'd embedded so deep they'd damaged organs. James had recovered. He'd healed quickly then. Like he would now. He *would*.

Except his pain, it twisted me up. I threaded my fingers together not knowing how to help him, where to put my hands that wouldn't hurt him further.

"I told you to leave it," he said.

"I... I can't."

The cell door opened and closed. A huge plastic bucket of water and another drinking jug and more clean cloths sat inside the locked door. I soaked one of the cloths, squeezed it out and laid it over James' back and shoulders.

"I'm going to do your buttocks, legs, and feet."

James remained silent, but I felt his intense expenditure of energy, and his pain.

With more soaked cloths, I wiped away the blood and grime that covered the rest of him. "When you're ready, there are clothes here for you. And some food."

He said nothing, but his eyes were open.

"James, talk to me. Please."

"The name is Larrimer."

"I know, of course I know, but—"

"I prefer it."

Alex talked about what *He'd* done to my body, my mind. But what had the pack done to James? He was strong. Stronger than any man I knew. But this wasn't him. Maybe... I scooched beside him, where I could make eye contact. "Do you remember me?" I kept my voice low and soothing, when I wanted to scream. "Do you know me?"

"I do. Clea Reese."

"No, I mean me. Me."

"I remember."

"But what's wrong?"

"Nothing. I'm healing."

As upset as I was, it took me a while to focus, to calm myself enough so I could truly sense him. I needed to feel his persona of protection and caring, heart and strength, pain and passion. Finally, I delved inside him, and lucky for me, his titanium shields were down.

I tumbled into emptiness, but, no, it was more like gliding through a sea of white noise. Did he have some new shields I couldn't penetrate, ones keeping me from his pain? That would be so James.

"Something wasn't right." His profile, strong, harsh, beautiful. But the vibe, it was all wrong. Had they tortured him so badly, he'd broken? He might be a nanoteched construct, but his brain, that was organically James. Had the pack damaged him somehow? Beaten him so badly that... Gods, I couldn't go there.

He rolled onto his side, stretched out his other arm and swiped a hunk of sausage from the tray of food. That was normal. He was one hell of a voracious eater. He chewed slowly, deliberately. He went for the steak, ripped it with his teeth until it was gone. The block of cheese vanished, too, then the apple, next the brownie. After that, he sucked down more water from the jug.

He tossed the plastic jug, and it bounced off the cell bars. "How so?"

"How so what?"

"You said something wasn't right."

I nodded, tired, shaky. "Yes. Hard to explain. You feel different. You're acting different."

"My body is healing itself. It's faster now than when we knew each other before."

"Before?"

"Before my tune up. Before they fixed my dissonance."

"They" were the scientists at DarkPool led by Taka, conjoined with the government to form The Union. The same Union that was desperate to find me. In the past, I'd foiled them. James had thwarted them, too, and protected me, although he was their "creature," as he'd called himself. "Your dissonance?"

"My emotions. They tuned up my limbic system so I would no longer feel emotion, which was interfering with my missions. They corrected it."

No. I sat back on my heels, opened my mouth to scream. I snapped it shut. No way I needed the wolves racing to my rescue.

The fucking Union had struck again. Bastards. How could they do that? Take away that essential part of him. Steal yet another thing from James Larrimer when they'd already stolen so much. They stole it from me, too.

Well, fuck that. Fuck them.

I was going to tune him right back up again.

14

BARS AND WALLS

When I awoke, I was stiff, sore, and pissed. I cranked open my eyes. I'd fallen asleep next to James. Last night, when I'd tried to wrap my hand around his, he'd pulled it away. Now, a dressed James sat against the far wall, knees up, hands resting on them, eyes open, watching me.

I turned to the guard. Reidar, who'd tried to help me at the Pantages Theatre. Zach's dad. What was Alex thinking, having him guard James? "What time is it?"

"Five a.m."

Melike's wolf sat on the floor beside Reidar, one yellow eye peering at me.

I had to pee. Bad.

"James." I pushed to my feet and padded over to him, a quick journey given the size of the cell. I hunkered down.

"Larrimer," he said.

"Fine." And, yeah, I was being all snippy. "Larrimer, how are you feeling?"

"Almost healed."

"Your back?"

"Tolerable."

He'd never been verbose, but this was ridiculous. I looked at him, really looked, raised a hand to touch that beautiful, scarred face.

He clamped my wrist. "Don't do that."

"Why not?"

"Touch is unpleasant."

I just bet it was. Feeling. Any kind. Yeah, that was my goal. I moved my free hand to caress him. He gripped my forearm.

"I'd prefer not to injure you," he said.

"Then let me go."

"Don't touch me."

"I can't promise that."

"If that's the case, I can't promise not to hurt you."

He'd once called me a warrior. Bring it on, Dragon Dude.

I stood, shaky but determined. "I'll be back in a few."

MELIKE, returned to her snarly human self, led the way to the bathroom. I took care of business and washed my hands, but when I opened the door it was to a blast of anger. Melike sneered as she stalked inside and slammed the door.

"*Him*?" she said. "*He's* the reason you reject Alex? You disgust me."

"And you can go fuck yourself." I brushed past her, and reached for the knob, but she snagged my hastily woven braid.

"Ow! What the hell, Melike?"

"*Non*. You and me, we're gonna talk."

"Not your business."

"My Alpha is my business." She gestured wildly. "*You* are my business."

I powered down to a slow simmer. "Can I have my head back, please?"

She released my braid and leaned against the wall, crossing a leg. "So talk."

"About?" I said, feigning confusion.

"*Him*."

Why the hell not, right? "I met James Larrimer eight months ago.

We worked together to find my mentor's killer. He had an agenda I was unaware of, to bring me in to the scientists doing tests on the magic reappearing in the mundane world and kidnapping magical creatures."

She snorted. "Bah. I knew it. Bastard."

I fisted her shirt. "I'm not finished." Why her understanding mattered to me, I didn't know. But it did. I released her. "He risked his life for me, helped me, comforted me, fought with me. He valued me in ways I can't explain. Ultimately, he turned against his employers, his keepers. For me."

She shrugged. "So you feel an obligation."

"No. I..." and stumbled over the "love" word, said it anyway. "I love him. Very much. He's complicated. Kind, and funny in his own odd way. Protective and gentle and fierce. A fascinating, interesting man. He doesn't say much, but when he talks, he says things that matter. He *gets* me. He has a beautiful soul." That did it. I teared up, talking about *my* James. The man who awaited me in the cell? I would get my James back.

Her dark brows beetled. "But he's not human, not shifter, not fae or even, yuck, vampyre. Not... real."

An image of our bed play and... whoa. Melike didn't need to know about *that.* "You're right. He's a construct of the lab. But that doesn't define him."

"*Je ne comprends pas.*"

"His spirit is bright, beautiful. He feels deeply."

She sliced a hand downward. "No, he does not feel. He is a *machine.*"

"He *did* feel. Before they got to him again. He was to meet me here soon after I left New Hampshire. But they caught him, did something to him, violated him. But he's not lost." I blinked rapidly, staving off the burning in my eyes. "He's not."

She snorted. "You are so emo it hurts."

Her arms came around me, and I tensed. A hug. Holy crap. Melike was giving me a hug. I hugged her back, clung to her, and the floodgates opened. What He had done to me... the stealing of my blood, trolling in my mind, the pain, it all deluged out, and I couldn't stop. Those bastards had done the same thing to James. Worse. They'd raped him. And, Melike, she'd lost her child, her *bebe*, her Paul. I cried harder.

The bathroom door flew open. "What the fuck, sugah! You two gettin' it on?"

I knew that voice. Craptastic.

Melike sprang back like I was infected. She plucked at her shirt. "You got snot all over me!"

"I'll buy you a new shirt," I said, and turned to the mage who was dressed in a long-skirted Chanel suit. "What?"

Rae patted my cheek. "Dumplin', y'all one hot mess."

I swiped some toilet paper and blew my nose. "So?"

"I'm here to help you sort out that pretty brain of yours."

Melike disappeared. Talk about abandoning ship. "Not right now, Rae. I might be a fricking disaster, but I've got stuff to do."

"Y'all listen to me." The finger she waggled at me was painted deep red.

I slapped her hand away. "Later. And stop poking at me."

Her eyes laughed. "Y'all are better. I like. You were one big train wreck."

"Thanks for the reminder." I splashed water on my face and paper toweled it off, reached for the door... and froze. "Let. Me. Go."

Rae placed her hands on my head, and glittering motes swirled around us, blurring faster.

"Release me!" I shrieked.

I AWAKENED IN MY BEDROOM. Didn't move. Peered around the room. Morning sunlight splashed in, patterning the floor from the window's iron scrollwork.

Fuzzy-brained again, I dug for memories that failed to come *again*. And... Rae massaging my head? What the hell had he done?

Whatever it was, I had the worst hangover *ever*. I rolled to my side and puked into the thoughtfully placed bucket.

Someone sure knew what was going on with me.

Unacceptable.

I reached for the glass of water. Considerate. Premeditated. Everybody knew stuff but me, dammit. I took a sip, spat. Did it again. My throat burned, and I sipped the water. Slow. Real slow.

I slumped back down on the bed. My stomach heaved, my head pounded. And I was pretty much sick of being everyone's flotsam.

James. Right. A mess. All I wanted was to get back to James.

I dug deep inside. Beneath the headache and nausea. Beneath the pain of loss and violation. Beneath the hurt of James and the cruelty of Him and the manipulation of Rae. There. To that crack inside me opened by my training with Rae. I widened it, slipped inside, through it, to the source. The pool of light inside me, always there, always fiery bright. I pressed a hand over my sternum, the other one over my breasts, and pulled.

Soft motes of light, my fireflies, surrounded me. No pain. Only a sense of joy, of rightness, and I directed them to cocoon me, circle me, heal me. The feeling, incandescent, like champagne bubbles rising to the air. Faster. I pulled them to zoom, a wellness, a—

A roar of fury burst my focus, and I flew to my feet, knife in hand. "What!"

Erick's open mouth flapped.

"What, dammit!"

"You.... You were being attacked."

Rather than plunging the knife into him, I sat my butt on the bed. "I was trying something new, and... Forget it. I'm okay. How's James? The prisoner?"

"Alive." Erick waved a hand in front of me, like one of those airport wands. "What the hell were those things?"

"Me." I slid the knife back between my mattress and box spring. "How long was I asleep?"

He shrugged. "Don't know."

Typical Rae, knocking me out for hours. Getting all weirdly paternalistic. "I'm going to shower. I have things to do."

"But—"

"No, buts."

"You are one wacko lady." He sniffed. "Your smell's changed. Better."

"Gee, thanks."

"No, no, you don't understand. Ever since you were taken, you smelled different. You smelled *bad*."

"And now?"

He stepped forward, sniffed at my neck. I batted him away. "Enough. I know you guys don't have to get so close to scent."

A devilish smile. "But you smell so good, *chica*. Like citrus and cedar." He inhaled deeply. "Mmmm. So good."

A smile burst inside me. I pushed at him. "Go away."

A one-shoulder shrug. "If you insist." The frown he so seldom wore appeared. "I came to tell you we've got a meeting in a half hour, in the cellars. It's bad."

I DASHED INTO THE SHOWER, dressed, then ran downstairs to see James. I flew through the door, and my steps slowed. It was dark, the room large enough to swallow the guard pacing in front of the cell. James stood in the center of the cell, in jeans and a t-shirt, arms at his sides, relaxed, eyes closed, head tilted as if listening to some inner dialogue. So different, yet the same as the night I met him, when he'd tossed pebbles at the bathroom window to draw my attention.

But different how? I neared the cell, and his head straightened, his body tightened. His eyes flew open. I tried to journey through his static of non-emotion, to work my way inside renewed shields adamantium strong, to reach his song, our song.

Because of our fae natures, we each had a song. Ours resonated one with the other, had bound us together, tethered us one to the other, like a DNA helix. Had they destroyed that, too?

In the past, as I probed, his lips would have tilted upward as he sensed my presence. Now, no change of expression, just watchfulness.

"Do you want in?" the guard asked.

I did, but not the way the guard meant. "No."

James took a few steps forward, so only the bars separated us. I pressed my face closer, and his warm breath tickled my cheek.

"Are you all right?" I said.

"Yes," he said.

"Good." I licked my lips, the words stuck in my throat. "I have a meeting, but I'll be back after. We have to talk."

He nodded. And more than anything I wanted to touch him, brush my fingers across his face, through his hair. He compelled me. He always had.

"Yes, we must talk," he said. "I need you."

My heart warmed, then froze, cracked and splintered all over again. I looked away, the emptiness in his eyes too much to bear. "*How* do you need me?"

"When you return."

I RUBBED my arms as I took a seat at the conference table, unable to get warm from the chill of James. Someone had put out platters of food—meats, cheese, fruit, and bread. I wasn't hungry, but I made a plate. A thing to do, a place to put my hands, a task to occupy my thoughts.

Pack members took their seats—Erick, other warriors, Justus and Mira, Camilla's parents, and Reidar, Zach's father, and Melike's husband, Carlos. A woman sat beside Carlos, a combination of Norse-Polynesian features and complexion, she was stunning, her eyes a light green like mine. Neddy's mom, perhaps? Soon, murmurs of conversation peppered the table.

A scrape beside me, and Melike swiped a hunk of cheese as she sprawled in the chair. She bit down and chewed. "I am fucking starving," she said through a mouthful.

"You ditched me in the bathroom, leaving me to Rae's not-so-tender administrations. I thought you were my bodyguard or something."

"Hey," she said. "I know when to cut and run. I made sure you were okay. You were out, like, for twenty hours."

I'd lost another frickin' day. "Yeah, well. I want to talk to your son again.

"*Non.*" Her voice, a low hiss.

Alex entered the room, his vibe dark with fury, alongside a short man in his fifties.

Melike straightened.

"We'll talk about Bron later," I said to her.

"No, we won't."

Alex took the chair across from me, and the stranger sat beside him. The alpha gave each person at the table a stare, skipping me like water over smooth stone. A click of the door, and Rae—male, dressed in black cargoes and a white button down—made his way to the table and sat on Alex's other side.

Rae winked at me. I rolled my eyes. *Now? Really?*

You got that right, girlfriend.

I jerked, glared at him. *What the hell?*

Silence, except Rae's face slid into smug self-satisfaction.

"This is Garth," Alex said, gesturing to the man beside him. "Of the bobcat pride. Some of you know him. He's the best forensic tech in the state. Garth?"

Garth straightened his already-straight stack of papers. "I'm sorry. This will be hard for you. It was for me. We tested the creature that attacked Ms. Reese at her home. The hand she, er, recovered. Blood, DNA, magic. Like nothing we'd ever seen."

Murmurs around the table. "Those things have magic?" Erick said.

Garth grimaced. "Some." He glanced at Alex, who nodded.

He continued. "Several days ago, we received more samples from the room where Ms. Reese was held captive. It proved helpful, given we had a control sample."

The remnants of the Pinkys I'd killed.

"The DNA," he said, "We continue to analyze it, but we believe we know enough to report." His chest heaved as he took a deep breath. "Parts of the DNA, of the blood, and *all* of the magic come from shifters."

The room exploded with chatter—anger, fear, horror—buffeting me. My heart pounded, and sweat beaded my forehead and upper lip. I closed my eyes. A hand, warm and calloused on mine, a soothing calm. I breathed it in. Better, yeah, much better.

I looked up to see Alex's stern face, eyes burning. Of course it was his arm that stretched across the table, his hand that held mine. I mouthed 'thank you,' and he released me.

"Silence," he said to the room.

In the deafening quiet, Garth cleared his throat. "The additional samples from the creatures enabled us to differentiate them. While we don't have all the magic results back from the lab, we do have the blood and the DNA, which enabled us to draw our conclusions. Each creature bore a different blood stamp, as well as differentiated DNA." He paled. "Each of the three creatures bore fragments of the DNA and shifter blood of one of your deceased children, Paul, Camilla, and Zach." After the horror, the weeping, the fury at Garth's revelation, Garth returned to his notes.

He believed that the blood needed to create the creatures was more than one child could provide. I'd drawn Justus' ire when I'd said it struck me that the children's deaths hadn't been intended, given the ceremonial way they'd been arranged, like the spokes of a wheel, and dressed in white. Garth noted that a constant source of blood was more efficient than killing multiple children. I agreed with him, as did Alex. By taking Neddy's blood for more Pinkys, their creator was allowing for Neddy to regenerate that blood before siphoning more. Alex now believed whoever was "making" these creatures was keeping Neddy alive.

The gorgeous woman, whose name was Svana and who was, indeed, Neddy's mother, brightened with what I suspected was hope. We'd need more than hope to find Neddy.

An hour later, still reeling from the aftermath of Garth's revelation, I slipped inside the room where they kept James. Not ready to enter his cell, I leaned against the outer wall, hands pressed to the cool stone. I thought I was prepared to talk to him. Wrong.

The stone against my palms, my back, was cool, soothing. My

breathing deepened, slowed. I had to get my shit together. The parents' agony at what their children had endured scraped my empath senses raw. I kept imagining Neddy's fear, his pain. If in truth the creator was keeping him alive, it sounded very much like what had been done to me.

The Pinkys' creator. *Him.* I believed them to be one and the same.

But why me? I was no shifter.

He was nameless, faceless. If only my mind could remember more, see his features.

I pushed off the wall and walked toward the cell. A shifter I didn't know guarded James. He raised his eyebrows. I hadn't looked at James, so overloaded with emotion that I feared I'd break down.

"In?" the guard said.

"Yes."

In seconds, I stood inside the locked cell. James position was the same as when I'd left him. No emotion, no vibe, which should have calmed me. I found it horrific.

He moved, pulled the mattress to the rear cell wall, and gestured. "Let's sit."

"All right." I sat cross legged and rested my back against the chilly stone. He crouched about a foot away, stiff backed, no support, feet planted on the floor, wrists loose on his raised knees.

"You look ill," he said.

"I'm not." Not the way he meant, at least. "Are they treating you better? Giving you food? Water?"

"Yes."

"Good."

"I need you."

This time, my heart didn't heat, didn't splinter. "So you said."

He glanced at his jailer, then back to me, eyes cold and deep as the North Sea. He leaned closer, brushed my hair, my ear with his lips.

A reflexive shiver washed through me. I relived the way he'd once touched me, held me, loved me, felt his long fingers smoothing my hair, stroking my cheek, holding me to him as if he couldn't bear to let me go. His being gone for six months had been bad. This was worse.

"The shifter can hear," he said. "That's not acceptable. My words are for you alone."

I stood and walked to the cell door. The guard was tall, like many shifter males, and when I looked up, his empathy flowed, a reaction to the faked tears now racing down my cheeks.

"Would you get me a box of tissues and more fresh water?"

"I should let you out," he said.

"No, I'll be fine." I sniffled. "Just the tissues and water, please. Thank you."

He turned on his heel and left.

I didn't bother scraping away my tears as I resumed my position against the wall. James moved to sit close beside me and bent his head. He was so muscular and massive, could snap my neck in a flash. From the first, he'd been protective of me. Now he felt like the enemy.

"I expect they're recording," he said. "So this works better."

He monotone didn't even sound like James. I steeled myself, unable to imagine what he wanted from me. "Of course."

He leaned even closer, and I fought my reaction. It would only weaken me. Later, when I was alone, I could unleash the agony that was clawing to get out.

"Five more operatives exist like myself."

I remembered. "You called them The Freak Team. Did they get tune ups, too?"

"We worked together for years."

"You led the team."

"No longer. But my current assignment is to apprehend one of them: Rolf."

I didn't like where this was going, yet I knew. I *knew*. "He's the one who took and killed the children, isn't he? Who created the Pinkys? Who took me? He has Neddy!"

"Yes. It was Rolf."

"Why? What's his endgame?"

"I need your help to apprehend him."

His utter stillness killed me. His flat tone. His emotionless stare that had once been warmer than a tropical sea. I wanted to shake him, slap him, to get some reaction, any reaction.

Dear gods, how would I fix this?

"Without a why," I said. "There's not a chance. And the shifters deserve in on this. He killed their children, James. Their precious cubs. Not to mention, the shifters are stronger, better fighters than I am."

"The wolves would kill him."

Sounded like a plan to me.

"You won't," he said. "My memory says you can kill, but you don't relish it. Your magic lights can control him."

"Fireflies. They're fireflies." Don't cry. Do. Not. Cry. "You still haven't told me why he's doing this. I need to know. To understand."

"Not now. Not here."

"Not me, then."

I expected his usual chuff of frustration. Stupid me. That was a feeling. James had none.

Silence.

Shit, what if... "Are you talking to them? Can you talk to them in your mind?"

"No. I was processing how to answer."

I swore. "It's like talking to Data."

"Data." A pause. "*Star Trek*. Perhaps it is."

"Correction. Data had more feeling. So tell me what Rolf wants?"

He nodded, as if reaching some decision. "He wants magic. The Chest of Bone. You."

Not that again. Geesh. The Chest... that was safe, at least. "Isn't that exactly what The Union wants?"

"Not precisely. Rolf wants to become magic."

Well, that was a gobsmacker. I almost said, *You're magic*, but kept silent.

"Wait a minute," I said. "The team, Rolf had a fae spark, just like you."

"No, most do, but he doesn't. Charlie the fae abandoned The Union before they completed the ritual on him. They have no other fae to reignite the spark."

"But shouldn't he have died?"

"The Union expected him to, but he didn't, and Rolf is desperate to become magic."

Could Rolf *become* magic? I had no idea how. "And that's why he took the children? To reclaim his magic?"

"Yes and no."

"Please clarify."

"No point. It's irrelevant."

Geesh. "Then why did he take me, bleed me, James?"

"He's not in good health. I suspect he believes that's an avenue to acquire your magic."

"And using my blood would accomplish that?" That wouldn't work... would it? "What or *who* gave him that insane idea?"

"I don't know."

I had a good bet, and her name started with T. The guard reappeared, carrying water and tissues. I got to my feet, took them, and thanked him.

When I turned back, James was standing. I moved close. "All right. I'll talk to Alex, get you released. We'll go—"

"No," he said, lips touching my ear. "The shifters can't know."

I didn't agree. Not at all. I simply had to convince James he needed them. "I want to think about all you've said. Process it."

"I need today to heal fully. Then I'll come for you, and we'll leave."

Thus speaketh the man in the cell. I had to go about this the right way. Placate James. Ease the wolves into this so they didn't take James' head off. "Look, I have responsibilities. Ronan and Lulu are mine, my charges." Not to mention finding a second chest.

"Lulu," he said, and grew still, as if a door in an unused room had opened. "Yes, Lulu."

"This isn't—"

"Are you afraid? I'll protect you."

Yeah, I'd heard those words before. "No, it's not fear. It's leaving people in the dark. If this is just your paranoia that's too bad."

He bent close again. "Not paranoia. Awareness. How do you think Rolf knew when and where the children would be?"

I paused. A beat, two. "A traitor? Someone inside the shifter compound? But that's absurd to —"

"Clea!" A bellow from beyond the locked cell. Alex. "Out. Now."

15

NOT YOUR MINION

As Alex and I walked up the cellar stairs, he tasted of brittle fury, and a quality more elusive, more compelling.

"I am not your minion," I said

"No, you're not. But *he* is my prisoner."

"And shouldn't be."

His hands gripped my shoulders, and he turned me to face him. "I don't know what he was when you knew him, but he's no longer that man. His wrongness screams at me to rip his fucking head off and burn it."

An ache. That elusive quality was an ache in his heart. His eyes searched mine, his hands tightening on my shoulders.

"Alex, please. I do see it. All too well."

He brushed a stray dread back from my face, gentle, caring. "Why are you doing this? My wolf is confused. I'm confused. You're a being of feeling, much feeling. He's... Fuck, where are the words when I need them?"

I wrapped my hands around his wrists and smiled. "I'm not used to your silver tongue being stilled." My affection for this wolf ran deep, and I desperately wanted to tell him what James had said about Rolf and the pack. But if I did. If the pack hid a traitor... So very hard to imagine. Yet if it were true, Alex should know, needed to know. What a mess.

James had assumed I'd stay silent. While I didn't reveal secrets lightly, I hadn't given my word. Except James Larrimer got me, got that I wouldn't, *couldn't* betray his trust.

And for some twisted reason, his *knowing* cemented my belief that I might bring him back.

THAT NIGHT, Ronan and Lulu tiptoed around me like I was breakable. As if Rolf could break me. My ass. The pack's disturbance from the news about the children, like pinpricks on my skin, only settled when sleep came to the wolves. Nocturnal they might be, but by two a.m. most everyone but the sentries slept. I pictured them curling one into the other for that beautiful tactile comfort so many shared. Carlos wrapped around Melike. Other couples and children holding each other tight. Even the warriors sometimes slept with each other, often in wolf form, to assuage pain.

Had I ever been more alone?

My thoughts galloped onward to pity-party town.

Nope. Not gonna happen. The healing scents of rosemary and sage lingered, and I dozed.

I fantasized about my long ago first meeting with James, a mountain of a man who took up way too much space in our New Hampshire home's little mudroom. Whose laconic "chill" made me bristle, so I demanded to see his official badge *again*. His dry sense of humor as we stared down the barrels of each other's gun.

I'll do mine, he'd said, *if you do yours.*

I'd sensed his laughter, and I was both pissed and wanted to laugh with him.

His raven hair cut ragged below his ears, casual clothes, lack of fuss—all of which telegraphed his quiet assurance. I loved that. He might be a big man, but he wasn't loud. He projected power, was one scary dude, but beautiful smile lines fanned from his Pacific blue eyes.

They hadn't crinkled once since his return.

And... here went the waterworks.

My pillow didn't fight back when I punched it, rearranged myself onto my belly.

I emptied my mind, seeking that familiar meditative state, worked at it, brushed away random thoughts of bronzed, scarred hands touching my body, finding secret needy places....

He was at me, mouth dripping with spittle, hands slapping my face. Taping my mouth, my words, my screams as he ripped into me. Giddy chittering from Pinkys watching as he probed deeper into my mind, scraping layers off me, memories, stealing them, my joys, fears, burrowing with jagged glass seeking that core of me, that magical essence. Shield after shield ripped, torn, cut, like fingernails peeled from skin.

Tried to move, to roll, to hide as he jabbed in those needles, sucked out my blood, my essence.

I sprang up, but *something was holding me down*!

Instantly my knife was in my hand. I flashed it bright and hard, felt skin part, easy, smooth.

"Stop," came the hissed order.

My eyes flew open.

A silhouette sat on the bed, gripping my shoulders, and I slashed again. Wrist in a vise, I screamed, but a hand, clamped hard and hot on my mouth, trapped it.

"Clea, stop. Clea."

No comfort in that voice, only command. Bright, metallic. But I caught a hint of honeyed granite, saw the bedroom, *my* bedroom in the den. Noted the shadow man holding me, huge, but not the size of Him. Not as big. Not Him. *James.*

I calmed, nodded.

His hand lifted from my mouth, but not my wrist.

"I'm all right now," I said.

"You dream unhealthy things."

He was but an outline in the dark. "Let me get the light." Needing to escape the blackness, my free hand reached for the lamp.

"Don't."

Something dripped onto my bare thigh, warm, his. "I cut you. I'm sorry."

"Not deep. It'll heal." He freed my wrist.

I transferred the knife to my other hand, flexed my fingers. "How did you get out? If you hurt anyone from the pack..."

"Just a tap. Nothing permanent."

"A tap, huh?" Where were the sentries? How had he gotten this deep into the den?

"Get dressed and arm yourself. We need to go."

I narrowed my eyes, furious. I wasn't going anywhere with him.

"Oh, but you are."

"What, you're a mind reader now?"

"You forget I see in the dark. Your expressions tell all."

I crossed my arms.

"I can force you."

The dream still rode me. I wouldn't be bound again. "Are you forgetting my fireflies?"

"You won't harm me."

Damn him. When he'd lost his emotions, too bad his confidence hadn't gone with them.

I'd yell for the shifters. James might get me out the window, but they'd catch us at the perimeter.

But I wouldn't. And he was banking on that. "You won't force me, either."

"You're wrong."

"Try it." I smiled, knowing his enhanced eyes would see it.

His body stiffened, each muscle bow-tight. But he didn't move. "I need your help. Come with me."

Of course I chose James. I couldn't *not* choose James, though I'd keep mum about that little ditty. "Here's the deal. I'll go with you. Freely. With your agreement to two things. First, you let me touch you whenever—"

"No."

"As I was saying, you let me touch you whenever I want and you don't keep me in the dark about *anything*. Those are my terms. Take 'em, or leave without me. I won't alert them to your escape."

Long moments passed while he stood statue-still. "Agreed."

I reached up and brushed my hand across his cheek. "Agreed."

I dressed fast. Jeans, a tank, socks, boots, knives on my arms, guns at my waist and ankle, zip sweatshirt, windbreaker, ballcap. I slipped my license, credit card and some cash into my back pocket, sunglasses into my jacket, and reached for my iPhone.

Which he snagged from my hand and tossed across the room. I stared at him, eyes burning, hands fisted. I might not see him so well, but he sure as hell could see me. It mattered that he knew I was pissed. Being pirated away without explanation or consideration sucked. *Fuck you,* I mouthed, but didn't yell or swear or scream. I knew truth when it stood in front of me.

"I'm leaving Lulu and Ronan a note," I said.

"No note."

"They're my responsibilities. And I love them. You remember what love is, huh?" I sighed, dialed it back a notch. "Sorry."

I picked up a pen and my bedside pad, paused. What to say?

I'm going to find Neddy. You'll be safe here with the pack. I love you very much. I'm coming back. Promise. I love you.

He reached for the note, scanned it, nodded.

I lay it on the bedside table anchored by the heart rock I'd taken from the New Hampshire earth. "So how are we supposed to get out of here without alerting the sentries?"

He walked to the window and broke the locked latch on the window grate, which he swung wide. The thing didn't even squeak. He cranked the grilled casement windows. Even he would fit with both open. How *convenient.*

We were really doing this. I snatched the katana from its leather scabbard where it hung beside my bed.

He whipped around, so fast, too fast.

But I'd slipped it under the comforter in time. "What?" I said, through gritted teeth.

"Come."

Any minute he'd say "fetch."

I hoped Lulu would understand when someone found the sword-less scabbard and katana. Alex would guess that I'd left with James. He even might scent a lack of violence or pain.

But only Lulu would understand my admittedly vague message. If all went well, I'd meet her at the antique shop in the Grove in two days.

WE RAN across the compound's side lawn, and he fireman-carried me over the eight-foot wall surrounding it. And kept carrying me. He ran so swiftly down the narrow streets, my eyes teared.

When he finally set me on my feet, I punched him in the stomach. "You don't just haul me places. You ask!"

He scanned the upscale L.A. homes, the street, the parked cars. A streetlight splashed nearby, highlighting his stern face.

"Did you hear me?" I said. "You ask next time. Or I'll shoot you."

"You could try."

"Was that a wiseass comment?"

"Simple fact."

James, robot man. How was I going to handle it? How did a man recover erased emotions? I shuddered, squeezed my eyes tight, forced back acidic tears.

I bit my cheek *hard*, and my blood's metallic taste focused me. Well, dammit, if I was ever to bring James back to himself, I had to handle *my* erratic emotions. "One thing matters to me. Only one thing. Finding Neddy. Got it?"

He ran, pushed a murderous pace. I managed to keep up for about an hour, and he finally slowed as we drew further and further away from the Arctos compound. The smells changed, the scents of flowers replaced by fuel and bodies and the grindings of an area that seldom slept.

When he stopped, so abruptly I banged into him, the tall buildings of Hollywood surrounded us. He merged back into the shadows, and I followed his lead.

"Why here?"

"Taxi."

"You don't have any money."

"You do."

The cab smelled of sex and yogurt. Gross. I didn't recognize the address James gave the cabbie, and I wished I'd learned more about Los Angeles since it'd been my home.

We didn't drive far, but I understood why he'd chosen four-wheeled transportation. Once in a car, the pack couldn't follow us by scent.

I paid, and we emerged before a two-storied building. Across the six-laned street sat a Liquor Mart, a 7-11, and a bank. In the glow of the streetlamps, a large, Spanish-style building wrapped around the corner of Sunset and Curson. It bore no signage, and the first-floor windows were blacked out. Tall palms flanked the sides of the building while in the distance mountains reached toward the night-starred sky.

My empath senses shrieked *run.*

James hooked a large hand around my upper arm and pulled me toward the twin front doors.

I dug in my heels. "Stop!"

He peered down at me. "Why?"

"You're not going to drag my ass around for this magical mystery tour. No way. You tell me where we're going and what's happening, or I'm outta here."

My James would have smirked, thinking it funny given, with his strength, he could haul me around like a rag doll. The new *improved* James just stared, gears grinding or whatever it was that tuned-up brain of his did.

"I see your point," he said. "The Union's L.A. Headquarters. Clothes, money, IDs, GPS, maps, transportation."

I hissed, low and guttural. "Do you *remember* the last time I encountered those people? They wanted to turn me into a *lab monkey.* To bore into my brain. To use me, my magic for their own ends. Do you *remember*?"

He let me shove him behind a palm. "Understand this," I said through clenched teeth. "There is no way, never a way, that I will voluntarily enter that building."

His vibe remained cool, unaffected by my fury. "Just like you weren't leaving tonight?"

"That was *different*." That he would even *think* to take me into that building. "The last time these people tried to take me, you saved me. *You*. Remember, dammit, remember. I will not go in there. Never. Nev—"

A door whooshed open, and I plastered my body to the trunk of the palm.

"Larrimer," came the faintly accented syllables. A command. A knowing.

Revulsion ripped through me. Taka. His handler. My nemesis. I peered around the tree trunk.

James strode toward the diminutive Asian woman with his usual gliding grace. "Yes."

"I saw you from the upstairs window. Who were you with? Have you found Rolf?"

"A homeless woman," he said, his voice smoother than velvet. "Begging cash. I have none. I have not found Rolf."

"Come inside."

I slid down the trunk to the dirt.

He hadn't forced me to go with him. What had decided him? Why didn't he tell Taka I was here? Why did he believe I wouldn't run?

Oh, *gods*, I wanted to run, fast and hard.

Taka was far more than James' handler. She was a lead scientist and agent for The Union and DarkPool, one who'd masqueraded as an FBI agent to ensnare me. I scrubbed my hands across my face, now greasy with sweat. Wiped away the residue of fear with my shirt.

A night breeze cooled me, soothed me. I rested my head on my knees and waited.

"Come," the voice commanded, awakening me from violent dreams of a shadowy figure pushing his fingers into my exposed brain.

I stood, and the tree's bark tingled my back, as if resenting my departure, my body reminding me of the beating it had recently taken.

Soft early morning light shone on James' back as he strode up Curson in tight jeans and a windbreaker. I donned my sunglasses, pushed my hair beneath my ballcap, and followed, keeping to the shadows thrown by the palms that edged the building.

"Stop," he said, voice low. "Wait."

He crossed to the drive at the side of the building and keyed in a code beside the gates, which swung inward. Minutes later he pulled out in an older-model SUV and drove off. The gates creaked closed, and I stood by the tree. James was either coming back to get me or the men in white lab coats would soon appear.

The pack would be up by now. Lulu. Ronan. Alex. Melike. They'd realize I wasn't in the den. Would they think I'd betrayed them for James? Had turned against them?

A car neared, and a door swung wide. I slid into the passenger seat, scrunched down until the Union's HQ was far behind us.

"Taka's suspicious," he said when I sat up and fastened my seat belt.

"She is." *The bitch.*

A droplet of blood fell to the leather seat.

I don't know what compelled me, but I scraped the drop onto my index finger and brought it to my lips. Iron and... an indescribable wildness filled me, an image of his wyvern drenching my mind. Did the wyvern still live? "You're hurt. What happened?"

"This." His fingers held a tiny bloodied computer chip. "They replaced one of the trackers the shifters removed. As soon as we're in a more populous area, I'll ditch it on a moving target. They won't waste the manpower sending a car after us for a long while."

I pushed his jacket aside and lifted his t-shirt. His jeans hung low, and I gaped at the raw and bloody gouge in his hip.

"Geesh." I looked around for tissues, found nothing, so I shucked off my slick jacket, pulled up the hem of my cotton tank to take it off.

His hand stopped me. "Not necessary. It'll clot and heal soon. You can't go around in your bra."

"I can zip up my jacket."

"Leave it."

Well, at least Mr. Stubborn still lived. "All right. Why did you remove the tracker? Where are we going? Why didn't you tell Taka about me? Where—"

"You still ask too many questions all at once."

I clamped my teeth. Yeah, okay, I'd give him that one.

"I may not feel, but I read your fear of Taka last night. I deemed it a good idea to see if it was justified. It was. She was angered that I hadn't brought you with me from the shifter compound. As you anticipated, she intended to keep you."

I thought about what he'd done, how he'd deceived Taka, listened to his boss, and come to his own conclusions. That room inside me where I bottled my fear clicked open to let in some light. He'd done what my James would do. Not the same. Not exactly. My love would never intentionally put me in danger.

But it was something, and it freshened the memory of who he'd once been. It also gave me hope, the human soul's most elusive and magical ingredient.

"If we find Rolf," I said, hating the way His name tasted on my lips. "We'll find Neddy. So tell me about your, um, coworker."

He remained stubbornly mute as he drove several blocks until we got on the 10 toward Santa Monica. Denizens of Los Angeles don't say things like Route 10 or Route 2. No, they had to be different. So Los Angelenos drove the 10 or the 101 or the 405. Someday, I'd research the why of that.

"Well, Mr. Silent?" I said after a good ten minutes. "You gonna speak, or do you plan to keep up the Marcel Marceau routine the entire drive?"

His nostrils didn't flare. Damn, I missed those little "tells," how he'd flare his nostrils when I got all snarky and he found it irritating... or funny, and he was trying not to laugh. Shit.

"Rolf wasn't just one of the six," he said. "He was what you would call a friend. What you would call a good man. I learned, after my tune up..."

"I hate that term."

"That they'd adjusted the others. Not the same as me, but... I started getting messages from the other four. Rolf wasn't right. Something was off. Once the most stable of the six, he was behaving in an erratic manner."

"How?"

His eyes narrowed. "Rolf is a man who insists upon order."

"You mean, order like his sock drawer?"

He nodded. "I might have been leader, but he acted as big brother to the other four. He would subtly show them the ropes, so they didn't misstep with The Union. Socialize with them. He acted, in a sense, as my lieutenant."

"Was he kind? Cruel? Funny? Serious?"

He grew quiet again. Processing, I guessed.

"From what I remember, he was sturdy, dependable. Loyal. He liked to read." He ran a finger down his scar. "I believe he told jokes."

His robo talk was making me batso. I started to choke, but managed, "He sounds, like you said, a pretty good guy."

He nodded. "I took it upon myself to go see him. Although I'm no longer leader of the six, I felt a responsibility toward him."

"Felt?"

"Just a word, Clea."

My throat dried when he used my name.

He guided the truck across lanes and took the exit. We landed on Lincoln Boulevard, which paralleled the Pacific, and headed south. Venice? Marina del Rey? The OC? Lots of wires and concrete and traffic, traffic, traffic.

"Please continue," I said.

"I never saw him. By the time I arrived at his apartment, he was gone. As I mentioned, Rolf was the neatest of men, precise, military corners on his bed. The place had been wrecked."

He turned off Lincoln, onto a two-laned street lush with vegetation and flowers and trees, with low slung homes, fenced yards, and cars lining the street. I cracked my window to scent the flowers blooming in gardens neat with care. And the sea. I inhaled the salt tang deep into my lungs, and with it a picture of Alex, whose scent always evoked the same. We took a few more turns, crossed Main, and drove down a small, narrow alley along the backs of buildings and homes.

He parked. I didn't bother questioning him. If we got towed... No, he knew what he was doing. He always did. He turned off the car and reached for the door.

"Wait. Maybe it wasn't Rolf who wrecked the place."

"I recognized his handwriting on the walls, scribbles that made little sense to me at the time. Found his prints on Play Doh sculptures of monsters tossed around the living room. Blood, his, on the creatures. He had dressed some of them. The pages of books littered the room, books on magic and mages and shifters, stolen from headquarters."

It sounded bad. Whatever had happened to the man, he'd gone wacko in a big way. Then again, I knew that up close and personal.

We walked to Venice Beach in minutes. Even this early, all the crazies were out, and nothing said crazy like the beach in Venice.

A perfect fit for Rolf.

"The doctor is in!" shouted a lab-coated pot-shop worker waving people into the bright orange-fronted store.

Please help! Penis reduction needed! screamed the sign waved by a panhandler who stood before a bucket of bills.

"Pretty, pretty! Cheap! Cheap!" said the bikini-clad girl, her fisted hand jangling a clutch of gold chains.

The crowds were thick, dense as a Mardi Gras parade's. Tourists and peddlers, rollerbladers and moms pushing strollered kids. The scents of meats, of Texas BBQ and Mexican and Chinese, the musk of too many humans, of patchouli and pot. My crowd claustrophobia kicked in and I stumbled.

A calloused hand on my elbow propelled me off the boardwalk onto the sand, where fewer walked. I could breathe again, and the breeze and sea scents simmered me down.

"Where are we going?" I said, as we started to walk again.

"Muscle Beach. Rolf often works out there."

"The tracker?"

"Taken care of."

Several minutes later, we stepped back onto the boardwalk, mingling with the press of the crowd. Just ahead, men of all ages worked out inside the fenced, but open-air gym where Schwarzenegger once played.

"I'm going inside." James pointed to the fenced-in arena. "Stay here. Get something to eat." He turned away.

I grabbed his sleeve. "I'll back you up. He could spot you and run."

"No need. Rolf doesn't run."

He was gone, into the building attached to the large gym. My stomach rumbled. I spotted a veggie corn dog seller, quickly paid for a dog and a drink, and took a seat on one of the park benches facing the bodybuilders. Yes, there were park benches for viewing the muscle. Crazy.

The corn dog tasted disgustingly great, as did the water. I unzipped my windbreaker, crossed one leg, both to gain easy access to my knives, since shooting in the crowd so wasn't happening. My nerves tingled like biting fire ants, the result of too many people and too much emotion. I'd taught myself to handle it, but I never liked it.

After I tossed the wrapper in the trash and bottle in the recycle bin, I resumed my pose.

Waiting. I hated waiting. I had less patience than a gnat, and while I'd worked on that, too, last week's events had destroyed any positive strides I'd made in that arena. My foot jiggled, fast. I probably looked like a junkie coming down off a high.

And then Larrimer appeared. Shirtless, still in jeans, tanned, a dusting of black hair on his chest, six-pack at the ready. Holy shit. Unlike most of the men working out, he hadn't oiled himself, nor waxed his chest hair, thank the gods. He was as beautiful on the outside as he was on the inside. A pain to my chest. I ached to have back the James I knew so well.

I bought another water to camouflage my drool. Nothing could hide my longing

He talked with this man and that as he moved from station to station, lifting weights, doing presses and curls, and I wasn't sure if my sweat was from the blazing sun or my hormones in overdrive.

Yeah, okay, it was the latter.

The former FBI part of me kept watch on the crowd, the juggler to my left, the skateboarder to my right.

Everything went to hell when a huge man, taller than James' 6'4", slapped him on the shoulder as he hefted some mega-weight above his head. I stiffened. The guy was bald and big and hairless.

Déjà vu… *I'm bound, peering up from the cold gurney at the man towering over me, his sweat-slicked, tatted chest muscles moving as he flicks his finger on the hypodermic filled with yellow fluid.*

I blinked. James nodded at the hairless hulk, whose tats of roses scattered on a field of skeletons didn't match my memory. Memory, yeah. *His* tats were a jumble. I saw them now. One, a snake, had slithered across his back, and its fanged jaws had moved with his muscles.

My relieved sigh drew James attention, his enhanced hearing acute even over the din of the crowd. I tossed him a tentative smile which he answered with a reassuring nod. He left the hairless man and moved on to the next station.

A meaty forearm snaked around my neck, hot breath at my ear. It tightened, cutting off my air and lifted me off the bench. My eyes sought James, but he was turned away from me, reaching for some weights. *His* other arm trapped mine, and I rose higher and higher, clamped against a hard chest.

I curled my legs, fingers seeking my ankle sheath. If he got me, took me again…

I rammed my Bowie knife deep into his forearm.

16

SHACKLES

He jerked, tightening the band around my throat. Black spots dappled my vision. I groped for my gun...

A roar, answered by my captor's bellowed "Fuck!" James scaling the fence, a blur.

The abrupt release landed me hard on my side, and I rolled forward, got my legs under me and stumbled after James, who was swifter than wind as he pursued my attacker. People flew aside as the two men ran, their pace electric.

Legs pumping, I pushed out a burst of speed as I threaded through the crowd. But I was no match for two nanoteched humans.

I ran and ran, stopping when I realized the idiocy of chasing men I couldn't hope to catch. They might be in Santa Monica by now, for all I knew. My sides heaved, and I pressed hands to knees as I fought to catch my breath.

Alone. In frigging Venice, how could I be alone? I wasn't that far from the boardwalk, but I was on a narrow parallel street, free from cars and the backs of lo-rise buildings to my left and bazillion-dollar houses facing the beach on my right. The shade cooled me, and I leaned against a building's pebbled wall, smoothing my breath, calming my mind.

Why the hell hadn't I fireflied the guy? All I'd thought about were my knives and guns. *Idiot.*

A movement. A shadow, but I'd caught it at the corner of the narrow alley. The shadow flowed close to the building. The ping of a door opening. The bark of a dog. I didn't turn my head, but saw a flash of pink and another movement. I gathered, gathered, hands relaxed, but open to the magic. The Pinky wouldn't see them, not until I was ready.

Warm lights swirled in my palms, and Rae's Southern tongue sounded in my head. *Y'all are in control.*

The creature slunk closer, movement a whisper. A runner thudded down the shadowed street, slap, slap, slap. I waited, needed him to pass, to be long gone.

When the runner was far distant, I whipped around.

A drooling, feral, claw-pawed Pinky stared down at me from its 7-foot height. I'd expected it, but still found it heart poundingly hideous. Patches of grey-brown fur bristled between patches of shiny pink. Bony broad shoulders. Skinny, with long lean muscles. Yet this Pinky was different—its head more lupine than the other ones, its ears bearing tufts of fur.

It towered over me, and I raised my hands, fireflies swirling, confident I could end it.

It craned its neck downward, drool escaping its semi-open maw, a tooth and claw dangling from a leather cord tied around its throat.

Oh, no. No, no, no. *Neddy.* He'd worn that same necklace.

And the eyes—an unusual light leaf-green, my eyes' twin.

This Pinky wasn't simply Neddy's blood and DNA. It somehow *was* the boy I'd met weeks ago. What had happened? What had that bastard done to the kid? I adjusted my fireflies, not to kill, but to trap.

The clawed construct reached for me

"No!" came the shout from behind me.

The Pinky snapped it jaws, turned, and ran.

I whipped around to face the man charging toward me.

"James, wait!" I held up my hands, fireflies swirled. "Wait!"

He didn't slow. Fuck.

I leapt, dousing my fireflies, hands pressed outward to stop his forward momentum.

We flew into the air. His arm banded my waist, he flipped us, and we whomped onto the pavement.

My breath whooshed out on our landing. The world shimmered, then focused.

"Not the smartest thing you've ever done," he said.

He wasn't even mussed, but I definitely liked the position. "Depends on your point of view."

"You're wearing an odd expression," he said.

"What's odd about it?"

"Are you going to get up?"

I liked where I was at just fine, cushioned by his body, his beautiful face close to mine. With reluctance, I rolled off him to sit on the ground. I massaged my bruised ribs. "You're almost as hard as the pavement."

He flowed to his feet. "But not quite."

"Thank you for taking the brunt of the landing."

He nodded and offered me a hand.

When I took it, he tugged me to my feet. His face didn't change, but his eyes bored into mine. "Why did you stop me from capturing that thing?"

"I thought you would kill it."

"I might have. Its death would give us the advantage with Rolf."

I sighed. "Yeah, well, that 'thing' is a new wrinkle. That was Neddy, a teenaged shapeshifter. Not just his blood or DNA. Him. Whatever Rolf did to the boy..." I didn't want to think about it.

Instead my stupid brain pictured Him, his arm banding my throat, squeezing tight, tighter. I shivered.

"Are you injured?"

"No." Not this time.

"You did fine with that knife. Good style."

"I wanted to kill him."

"No, you wanted to not be afraid anymore."

I gave him teeth. "Maybe. But killing would have been sweet." I'd lived so long with fear, it was a cozy old pal. "C'mon, let's go."

AT JAMES' insistence, we ate first. He downed three burgers, while I had a salad, the veggie corn dog and my stomach not entirely happy with each other. I sipped a chocolate milkshake that was so damned delicious it hurt. We sat in the car, James deeming it the safest place for me, which I thought was stupid, and we'd argued. Well, I'd argued. He'd gone into stoic mode, and I was a gnat beating against a stone wall.

"If we bring in the shapeshifters," I said, trying to convince him yet again, "they can track Neddy."

"So can I."

"Not as well."

"There, you're wrong."

Some tune-up he'd had. "Then why didn't you?"

"Because you stopped me—"

"Stop bringing that up. I know what you would've done."

"Speculation."

"No, judgement. I couldn't let you kill the boy."

"Those creatures are mindless, senseless beings programmed by Rolf to steal and to kill. You can't reason with them."

I waved my hands. "He was different. He had hair and, I don't know. But he wasn't like the other Pinkys. Maybe..."

"No, maybe. None." He balled the papers from his burgers and stuffed them into the takeout bag.

"We have to try to get him back." I shucked my salad leavings into the bag, found a trash can and dumped it.

"Get him back," James said when I returned to the car. "I don't believe that's possible."

"There's magic in the world. Hadn't you heard? Anything's possible."

He started the car, then turned to face me. "No, it's not."

And we weren't only talking about Neddy.

I pressed my hands to his face, leaned in and kissed him. His warm lips were sensual, the way I remembered. I took my time, and even though I got no response, I gave it my best go. As I nibbled his chin, kissed his cheek, his temple, I searched for his song, our song and found only silence. I drew the tip of my tongue across his lips, then released him.

"You will fail," he said.

"You felt nothing."

"Nothing."

"I'm not giving up. Inside you is the man I..." Couldn't say the L word. Nope, not now. "Is the man I deeply care about. One who cared about me." I searched his eyes, saw emptiness. "You're worth the fight. He's in there. You're in there."

His flat stare said otherwise.

DRIVING up the Pacific Coast Highway was one of the most gorgeous experiences on the planet. On the left, blue sky and red cliffs that plunged to the Pacific. To the right, forested hills and more cliffs and, far north, mighty towers of redwoods reaching for the heavens.

As we neared the entrance to the Getty Villa, my *magic*, began to stir. I leaned my head against the backrest. The magic built a song, a sonata, a symphony, and soon words I didn't know, chanting, pulsing, intensified to an ache, a compulsion.

"Wait," I said, struggling to form words. "Turn. Go here. Here."

A hand on my shoulder.

My magic snapped.

No song. But the aftermath. And emptiness. I blinked.

"What are you talking about?" he said.

I looked out the window. We were traveling at a decent clip, the Getty Villa well past us. When I visited the museum, I'd sensed a pull, but never like what I'd just experienced. Rae was teaching me how to proactively access my magic, how to control it. Was I becoming more attuned to it?

"Did you hear me?" he said.

"Yes." I wouldn't tell James about the Chest of Stone, not with The Union's "improved" control over him. But after we found Him, I'd beeline it back to the Villa. "Just something in my head. I thought we should turn there and... Look out!"

I slammed my hand on the dash as James pumped the brakes. We jerked to a halt, nearly kissing the bumper of the red Maserati in front of us.

"Apologies," he said. "You looked pale. My attention was divided."

We began the L.A.-traffic-crawl, a mystical dance known well to the denizens of that fabled land.

"Where do you think Rolf is holed up?" I said.

"A good question."

"And...?" The Maserati inched forward, nearing the entrance to Topanga Canyon Boulevard.

"In his human life, Rolf grew up in California, farther north, where the redwoods grow tall. He always hated Southern California. Too many humans."

"So why is he down here, so close to Union headquarters?"

"I'm aware of no large shifter pack that far north. No pack, no victims to steal. Perhaps several packs exist, smaller than Arctos, but the wolves in L.A. hold the power, which is what's drawing Rolf."

I shifted in my seat. "You know a lot."

"About Rolf, yes. He's a construct like myself."

His expression never changed, yet the flavor of his mood did. Funny, although he expressed no feelings, I sensed the shift.

"Is he exactly like you?"

He didn't answer. I suspected each construct had different enhancements. "Now that you've been 'tuned up', as you call it, do you feel your fae spark? The wyvern's essence?"

He tilted his head, paused. "I do not."

Could they have programmed that knowledge out of him? Had they killed off the wyvern? Masked the spark? "So we're going north, to his home?"

"No. Have you been to Malibu Canyon?"

"I haven't."

"It sits in the Santa Monica Mountains National Recreation area. A few roads cross it, from the PCH to the civilization of Calabasas and Westlake. It's vast and wild. That's where he's hiding."

"You sound so sure."

"I am."

"If the area's so large and desolate, how will we ever find him?"

Our truck inched forward, but I was unable to see what was causing the logjam.

He swiveled his head to look at me, eyes bright with speculation and what I'd almost call curiosity. "You confound me. Something about you urges me to tell you my secrets and reveal information forbidden by The Union."

I allowed a slow smile to bloom across my lips, dropped my voice to low and husky. "So I say, go with it, baby."

Oh, gods, I would have killed to see him laugh, or even twitch those sculpted lips.

All I got was more deadpan.

"You're not going to, are you?" I said.

"No. I yield to the wisdom of judgement." He notched his head. "There's the tie up. Police."

Topanga Canyon Boulevard was just ahead, and a clump of uniformed cops clustered at the turnoff. A few cars ahead of the Maserati, then us. Beyond the sawhorses and yellow tape, the way looked pretty clear.

"Given the wilderness of the canyon, we should bring in the shifters," I said. "With their aid, we'll easily track Rolf down."

He grew still. "We discussed this. I don't want his death, just his capture. The shifters will kill him."

"They won't, not when you explain how damaged he is. Anyway, you're going to hand him back to The Union. That's worse."

"They can fix him."

Like they "fixed" you? But I kept my trap zipped. We inched along until we were about six feet from the cop directing traffic. And I wanted to either giggle or scream. Rae was playing cop.

"Let me do the talking," I said.

"Why?"

"Because you appear aggressive and you're scary as shit."

"All right."

We approached Rae, and everything froze, literally, except for that crazy mage and me.

He leaned on Larrimer's open window and spoke across the man frozen beside me. "Y'all okay?"

"I am, and thanks for asking. Have you told the wolves?"

He pursed his lips. "Now why would I be doing that?"

"Gee, golly, I don't know. Because they're pissed as hell, have a missing kid and three dead ones and—"

He raised a finger.

"Don't you dare shut me up."

He did that annoying laugh of his. "Feisty."

"Freaking out is more like it. We're going after the guy who killed the children. He's got Neddy."

Rae nodded, all sage and stuff.

"Are you coming with us? We could use you. That freezing bit is pretty cool."

He grinned. "Hell, no. This all's your path, not mine."

Oh, gods, the Zig Zigler of mages. Swellsies. "So why are you here?"

"To remind you of your true mission."

And now he was talking like James Earl Jones, same voice, same sonorous tones.

"I haven't forgotten, believe me. Is that all?"

"You take this. Learn it." He slipped me a white card with a phone number. "Might come in handy."

"Thanks. Can we go?"

"No. This one." He pointed to James. "He might kill you."

"No he won't, I—"

"I've seen it, Clea. If he doesn't, y'all are gonna kill him."

It took me a sec to find my voice. "I never would."

His ancient eyes sparked, then filled with sorrow. "You wouldn't kill your James? Not even to save a child?"

WE CAMPED that night in a lonely canyon where a necklace of stars spangled the sky and brine from the sea wafted on the breeze, and where I tried not to think about Rae's terrible words.

Though the temps in L.A. broiled, here the air was clearer, cooler. Only a coyote's yip, a hawk's screech, a lizard's skitter broke the deep silence.

We walked toward the shell of a decrepit house, fenced in by modern iron rails and surrounded by scrub brush and trees. The house's rough stone walls were broken up by a chimney and holes where windows and doors had once hung. Impressions like flickers of an old-time movie popped into my mind. I opened my senses to long-ago lives. They brushed me cotton-soft, the residue of emotions faded by time.

"We'll camp here." James tossed our packs over the fence, and I yelped when he lifted me over. He then gracefully hurdled the five-feet himself.

The sign read *Keller House,* and I walked the short path to the interior. The foundation was beaten up, but enough remained for us to roll out our sleeping bags.

I enjoyed camping, except for one thing.

I did a circuit for snakes. True, they shouldn't be about this chilly evening, but I always checked for snakes. Reassured we were the only residents, I dropped my pack and sat.

James began to build a fire. "You've been quiet since the traffic stop."

Not thinking about Rae's pronouncement. Not. "It's been a busy day. I'm tired, is all."

He reached behind, into his pack, and produced a lighter for the fire. As he did so, a piece of paper fluttered to the ground. I snatched it up before he could notice. With his back to me while he arranged the kindling, I clicked on my flashlight.

I held a dog-eared candid photo of me taken at Sparrow Farm in New Hampshire, where he'd stayed with us and we'd hunted a killer.

"Why are you carrying this?" I held up the photo.

The small fire blazed, and he produced two prepack meals and bottles of water from his pack.

"So I could identify you." He held out his hand for it.

"You know what I look like. So why carry it?"

I waited for his answer. And waited. Either he wasn't going to tell me or he didn't know the answer himself. I handed him the photo, and he slipped it into his pocket.

After we'd eaten, he sat against the wall facing the doorway, legs outstretched, ankles and arms crossed. I sat kitty-corner to him, legs folded, the fire between us.

As we'd driven that afternoon, I'd cooked up an idea to awaken his emotions. Sort of an exploratory mission. I was so damned tired, but this mattered.

I cast out my senses to read inside him and slammed up against his shields.

"Will you let me in," I said.

"No."

"Why not?"

"Protocol."

I moved to sit beside him, his warmth an intimate comfort. I didn't touch him, not yet. "You insisted I come on this hunt for Rolf. I deserve some payback."

"No, you don't."

I cupped his cheek with my hand. He banded my wrist with his and lowered it. "I've said before, I'd prefer you don't touch me."

"Remember our deal?" With my free hand, I brushed his chin. "Does it hurt?"

"No. I'm going to sleep. I suggest you do the same."

Instead, I slid onto his lap, leaned against his chest and wrapped my arms around his neck. I pressed my cheek to his. He was warm, his body hard, his chin stubble scratching my...

He shoved me away.

I flew through the air, landing on rough ground. Ouch. But worth it. Definitely. Melike'd thrown me harder, which said James hadn't nearly used his full strength.

I rolled to my side and bounced up. He sat statue still, hands fisted, which in my book said he was feeling something. I stalked back across the campsite, holding his eyes, insisting they link with mine.

He frowned. "Why did you do that?"

"Because I like it."

Fast as I could, I slithered back onto his lap, same pose, same result.

"Shit," I said as I landed. Yeah, this time hurt more.

I flipped to my hands and knees, got my feet under me and rose. "We had a deal. That wasn't cool."

He stood, lightning fast. I ran, leapt, clung to his neck, legs wrapped around his hips, face tucked into his shoulder. I inhaled, and his scent of pine and honey and James surrounded me, transported me. Any second I expected to be airborne.

He placed his hands on his hips, careful not to touch me. "Why are you doing this?"

"I want inside, James."

"Larrimer."

"Let me inside, and I'll stop."

He poured dirt over the fire, dousing it, and I hung on like some bloated tick.

I kissed his neck—oh, gods, he tasted wonderful, just like my James. I licked, sucked, nipped.

"What do you expect me to do?" he said.

"Kiss me back?"

"There's no point."

I almost lost it then, hearing that from a man who'd been crazy-hungry for me, just like I'd been for him. A man who'd once told me I made his life "bearable." Instead, I tilted my face up and kissed him.

Rockets blasted inside me. His lips were pliable, with that familiar taste I loved. Gods, I wanted inside. But I didn't try, didn't probe, just kissed him, nipped his lower lip, and pressed against him with all the longing, fervor, love I felt for him.

He tugged my hair, yanked my face away from his. His eyes were cool, not icy, not pissed. Just empty. "Satisfied?"

"Not even a little," I ground out. "Let me inside your shields. I won't hurt you."

"Obviously. Get down. Since this appears to matter to you, I will lower my shields."

I stood in front of him, focused my senses and unfurled my mind.

His shields were down, but the landscape was alien. A void of white noise. All white noise. I went deeper, searching for his fae spark and the wyvern. It was like traversing a landscape through a white-out blizzard. I probed and probed, sensing, yes, there, Charlie the fae's spark, dim and cold, almost doused. But without it, James would die.

I tried to get around it, under it, refused to believe the wyvern was gone. Any minute James would shut me out. My mind called to the creature—*Wyvern, where are you? Wyvern!*

I... AM... SHACKLED.

The pulse of a physical shockwave hurtled me away from the wyvern, from James, landing me on my bum, head reeling, stomach roiling. I rolled to the side and puked. Talk about a tilt-a-whirl of crazy.

"It seems you're done," he said.

"Not by half, buster."

CAMPING

ow to unshackle a wyvern? That ping-ponged around my mind as I tossed and turned in my down sleeping bag on the rocky canyon floor.

I got up, brushed my teeth yet again, peed, and climbed back into my sleeping bag.

How to unshackle a wyvern?

The creature had talked to me once, saved me from dying, brought me back. The wyvern had pulled me from the depths as I hovered near death from my twin brother's final blast.

The wyvern was James, but James was *himself*, too, a concept I wished I grasped.

Perhaps if I learned *how* they'd chained him, I could reverse it and free him. Perhaps that would free James' emotions, too.

James lay as dead atop his own sleeping bag. I rolled over, punched the pack I was using as a pillow.

Something tickled my foot. *A snake!* No, just a tickle. I scratched my foot, but as I did so, I replayed the mini-movie of an old friend jumping around the campsite when a milk snake had crawled into his sleeping bag. I jerked my hand out of the bag.

Boy, talk about knee-jerk reactions to old fears.

I rested my chin on my bent knees and studied James while he slept. He lay on his back. Sweat beaded his forehead and ran in rivulets into his long hair. He appeared relaxed in sleep, yet his hands were white-knuckled and balled into fists. I inched closer. He didn't need to breathe as often as a human, yet his chest rose and fell with near unnatural swiftness. His lips moved as if he were talking in a dream. He twitched.

The urge to touch him was strong, and I reached out... I snapped my hand back. He'd probably rip it off.

No, but there was something there. Something off with his "tune up." He was *feeling* in his dreams.

I'd begin my two-pronged attack tomorrow, to unleash the wyvern and reignite his emotions.

All while we tracked *Him*.

A RUSTLE AWAKENED ME. I froze, kept my breathing light. I remained on my stomach, but peered around the campsite. James hadn't moved either, but his open eyes gleamed in the moonlight.

Had Rolf found us?

The sagebrush to my left shook. *Don't be a snake. Please.* Quiet as a sigh, James drew his gun.

The bush quivered and out emerged...

A kitty! One with giant black eyes and a long, bushy ringed tail.

I flashed to James. He'd lowered his gun, understanding that the creature was no threat. Me? I was having trouble not laughing. The ringtail was adorable. The size of a large house cat, and so cute I wanted to take it home.

The ringtail walked closer, froze, then padded to James, seemingly curious about what he was. The creature touched its nose to his, and my laugh burst the silence. The ringtail scampered away, but I continued to laugh.

"That was the cutest thing I ever saw," I said.

"Curiosity," he said. "An interesting emotion."

"Are you no longer curious?" I said.

The silence grew until I sensed his contemplation, pinpricks on my mind.

He rolled onto his side, away from me, and said nothing.

James might have fallen asleep, but I couldn't. How angry would Arctos be that I'd gone rogue? Where was the chest? Where was Rolf? Would I recognize him? Would he go after me again? Could I protect myself? How would I...

My heart raced. My palms sweat. I grew woozy.

Stop. I inhaled, released my mind, sank into the vastness. Exhale. Inhale. Exhale.

I calmed.

A fragrant breeze tickled my senses. Peaceful, delicious. Here in the canyon, the world felt huge, endless. The land spoke to me. Bright stars dappled the sky, the air fresh and fragrant with sage, the rustle of nocturnal creatures, notes on a scale. And magic. A hint of it caressed me like dandelion fuzz.

"What's wrong?" came the granite-hard voice.

How had he known? James was always a puzzle. Now, even more so. "Nothing. I couldn't sleep, so I was enjoying the night." I scooched from my sleeping bag and walked across the distance separating us. I needed.

The earth was hard and lumpy as I stretched out on my belly beside him, turned my face toward his. In a whisper, I said, "I'm going to touch you. I'm going to pretend it's like it was before. Your arms around me, holding me, and mine around you, and I can drift away imagining what once was."

"No."

"Are you sure it doesn't hurt when I touch you?"

"It doesn't. Go to sleep."

"You may not understand this, but I ache for you, for the closeness we had. What we shared. What we meant to one another."

"My memory bank says you sent me away. Am I not correct?"

I'd been an unforgiving idiot. A fool. "Yes. A mistake. Which I corrected. Interesting which incident you recalled. After that, you forgave me, and I forgave you, too, for your deceit. You promised you'd find me. You cared deeply about me. Does your... memory bank recall *that*?"

His lips thinned, which I took as a yes.

"So why can't you pretend? Just tonight."

Long, endless minutes of silence. I began to push myself off the ground when steel arms banded me.

The euphoria made me dizzy as I scooched close to him, wrapped my arms around his waist, and nestled where the curve of his neck met his shoulder. Home. I was home.

He flinched.

I raised my head, saw his T-shirt dampened with my tears. "Sorry."

"I understand. Is this what you wanted?"

"Yes. Thank you."

"If it helps you sleep, that's a good thing. You need to be alert in the morning when we confront Rolf. Understood?"

"Yes."

But of course I couldn't sleep then, either, so I was awake when James tensed.

"Stay still," he said. "Humans are approaching the campsite."

"Rolf?"

"I don't believe so. They're making too much noise."

An instant later, guns chambering rounds snapped the stillness.

"Who the fuck are you?" came the growly voice. "And what do you want?"

"Mind if we sit up?" James said, his voice steel calm.

"Make sure we can see your hands at all times."

James unwound from me and straightened to a sitting position. I did the same, knees up, arms draped across them.

In the ghostly moonlight, five men and a woman wearing camo held AR-15s on us. A militia? Survivalists? Nut jobs, for sure.

I unfurled my mind, my empath senses stretching outward. Hate and fear overridden by fun, acquisition, money, with low notes of sex. No time to filter which thread came from which person. Didn't matter.

These were not nice people. Not even a little.

"We're camping," I said. "Isn't that obvious?"

The speaker notched his head. "Bethany, you take the girl." The four remaining men kept their weapons trained on James. "Get up."

The woman yanked me to my feet, her animus and fear a nasty cocktail. I could take her, and James would disable the four men, but for some reason, he was going with this. So I went with it, too.

They bustled us out the back doorway, away from the fence, through scrub, over rocks, and down a slope. We walked in silence for about fifteen minutes when the leader veered off toward a scrubby cliff to our left. He disappeared.

"Clear," came the disembodied voice.

James and I were shoved toward that voice. We moved upward, visibility near impossible, and I would have tripped but for Bethany's flashlight pointed toward the ground.

We stopped before the face of the canyon. And the creepy idea that they would push us against it and shoot us slithered into my brain.

Whenever I was with James, I seldom felt fear. Stupid, since Bethany plastered a foul-smelling cloth to my mouth. I elbowed her in the gut before the land of nod claimed me.

CLIMBING OUT OF SLEEPYLAND, the cold floor pressed against my ass, my arms constrained behind my back. My stomach heaved. I was about to barf. I hated puking, so I swallowed again and again, trying to clear the nausea.

"What the hell?" I said to no one in particular when my stomach settled. Something was thrust against my lips, and I turned my head.

"It's just water," said a male voice.

"Yeah, right."

"Promise."

I weighed the possibilities, opened my mouth, and cool water splashed inside. I sipped, spat, and sipped again. Even if it was another drug, at least it helped clear my garbage-dump mouth.

Dim lights illuminated a cement-floored cave filled with a table, two camo men in chairs, and James and me, side by side on the floor, his arms bound as mine and our ankles zip-tied.

Shelves lined the walls, piled with cans and boxes of food, jugs of water, and guns. An arsenal of guns.

On the table sat a neat row of guns and knives, which I recognized as ours.

To my left, James appeared a helluva lot more relaxed than I felt unless you checked his eyes. Yeah, these guys were dead meat if he deemed it so.

"What were you doing out here?" said Camo Man One, who reeked of acquisition, money, and sex.

"Hiking," I said when James stayed silent. "Camping. You have a problem with that?"

He snorted, not a pretty snort either, and picked up my Glock. "And these?"

"We always travel armed, just like you survivalists." Why was James letting me do all the talking?

Camo Man Two stood. He was broad-shouldered and lean, with a hook nose and eyes like marbles. He shoved his face close to mine, and his garlic breath almost made me hurl again.

Oh, this one... his feelings threaded with an oily miasma of evil, woven with a sense of entitlement and triumph behind that facade of authority.

He paused. I guessed he was expecting me to look away from his probing gaze, which made me giggle. I mean, come on. I'd stared down wolves, the Cardillo, and Anouk. Well, maybe not Anouk, but still.

So I giggled, and his face got darker and darker. But I couldn't stop.

"We're looking for Rolf," James said in that calm, even voice.

Camo Two's head snapped to James and his face paled. He swallowed.

James' heavy-lidded gaze held his, and I quieted, donned my mojo, and fireflied my bindings away.

"What the hell!" said Camo One.

Oops. Guess he'd noticed me rubbing the feeling back into my untied wrists.

"I repeat," James said, simultaneously flexing his hands, ending the charade that his wrists were also bound, which they weren't.

"Code Black!" shouted Camo One, standing so abruptly his chair toppled.

In a blur, James batted Camo Two across the room. Another blur, and my Glock was in my hands, my two knives sheathed my ankles, and I'd ended up behind James, who bristled with weaponry pointed at the assholes.

The Union had obviously upped his speed ability, too.

Camo men and women crowded the room, their weapons aimed at James.

"Where is Rolf?" James said.

This time, his voice was pure granite, low, growling, scary.

One survivalist fired. James caught the bullet.

Holy shit.

A half-dozen survivalists raised their guns. In a blink, my right hand was aloft and my fireflies pulsed outward to encompass the two of us.

I'd been a hare too slow as a bullet seared my arm.

A chorus of booms as bullets ricocheted off cave walls, bookcases, and arrowed straight for us, where they dropped to the ground about a foot away.

Camo Two raised his hand. The barrage ceased.

"What are you people?" Camo One said.

I moved out from behind James and stepped beside him. "Scary as shit."

The growl came from James' chest, up his throat to emerge from a face gone feral. "Another shot fired and you all die. Put down your weapons."

Our captors couldn't comply fast enough, dropping their weapons to the floor. Silence.

James' eyes cut to my arm. "Stop," he said to me in a hushed voice.

"Stop what?" I hissed.

He tilted his head. A bullet had furrowed his temple, the right side of his face a mask of blood. "Let the shield down."

"No."

"Your blood's dripping to the floor."

Yeah, my arm killed, but we'd be chopped chuck if I did what he said. Except a small wave of dizziness swirled through me. I blinked fast to clear my head. "I'm fine. I can hold it a while longer."

"I can kill them faster than they can retrieve their weapons."

"What about the weapons and men we *can't* see?"

"I'll make sure you're protected."

And what about you? But I didn't say it, just shook my head and held the shield. But he was right—we had to do something.

"He's here!" shouted someone from far back in the cave.

Camo Two smiled. The survivalists parted to make an aisle, and from the black maw of the tunnel, a seven-foot-tall Pinky emerged, *Neddy* emerged, drool dripping from that wolfie mouth now half opened so the lights gleamed on its pointed teeth and glowing green eyes.

The survivalists screamed, ran chicken-like, banging into shelves, toppling food stores, tripping over dropped weapons, careening into my shield, only to bounce off it like rubber balls.

Camo Two reached for an Uzi.

James barked, "Don't."

A voice near the darkened entrance shouted, "Quiet!"

Relief on some faces as they pressed against walls and crawled into corners. Camo Two wrapped one hand around his other wrist, maybe to stop his shakes, and stood his ground.

The Pinky walked forward, down the aisle. Behind him came a man, huge, beefy, and bald. I gasped.

My shield wavered, and I hung on. But not for long.

"James, it's—"

"Rolf."

The Pinky moved on the balls of his feet, his head swiveling right and left. Rolf strode into the room, eyes narrowed, glued to James, only James. Hands fisted, massive forearms bunched, he glided much the way James did, as if they walked in a space separate from the rest of the world.

My good arm trembled with my effort to hold the shield.

"Drop it," James said.

"No." It was a whimper, more than a word.

His hand came up, and he pushed my right arm downward, slowly, inexorable. It didn't take much. I was failing already.

I inhaled a sob, fisted my fireflies closed, and dropped my arm. I bowed my head—damn those acid tears, my fury and fear getting the better of me. I wouldn't let Him see me cry, couldn't let Him see me like this.

Except... I squared my shoulders, raised my head. Hell, no way would I bow to him.

My fireflies would recharge. James was with me. I was not a victim.

The Pinky stepped left, so we were up close and way too personal. Rolf moved forward, facing James. They embraced.

I jerked, as if from a gun's recoil. And saw Rolf's tattoo etched on the back of his neck, a lightning bolt with a star attached to its point. Just like James'.

"James," Rolf said, and another tremor shook me.

That voice.

James placed a hand on Rolf's shoulder. "It's good to see you."

Rolf did the same on James'. "And you."

They dropped their arms, but each held the other's eyes.

The two men's geniality disgusted me. Was Alex right? Had James betrayed me, led me right to Rolf? Or was this some complicated plan to capture Him?

The Pinky leaned in and sniffed me. I froze.

"You're bleeding," Rolf said to James.

James notched his chin. "Courtesy of your friends."

Rolf cracked each one of his knuckles. Slowly. Deliberately. "*They did this?*"

"Yes," James said.

I leaned back. The Pinky leaned forward, and a long sinuous purple tongue slid from its mouth and licked my neck. *Holy gods.*

A tornado exploded. Rolf.

James barked, "No!"

But the tornado didn't listen.

Rolf swirled around the room. Blood and bone and brains flew. And, oh, the screams. I covered my ears, closed my eyes. But I still could smell.

Ceaseless screams of pain and horror until the room finally quieted. I forced my eyes open.

To my left, He again stood before James, whose face remained frozen, stolid. Blood and bits of glutinous flesh coated Rolf's bald head, smeared his face, his chest, and dripped onto his work-booted feet. The room was painted in blood and brains, feces and flesh. I couldn't make sense out of it, not really.

My eyes flashed to James. Fluids and splinters of bone had splashed onto us, too.

Had any of the survivalists escaped? I hoped so. They might've been creeps, but their deaths were hideous.

"We should go now," Rolf said calm as could be and turned toward the cave opening. His booted feet made squishing sounds as he walked.

The Pinky followed.

"Oh, gods, James. What the hell?" My stomach spasmed.

"Come." He wrapped his hand around my uninjured upper arm.

I couldn't move. I couldn't.

He tugged, and I finally stepped forward.

NOON LIGHT BLAZED down when we emerged from the cave, giving a clear picture of the splatter that covered us. I staggered.

James and Rolf moved off to the side and talked quietly while the Pinky stood sentry. I wasn't fool enough to make a dash for it. Any of the three could easily catch me.

We'd sure found our quarry, all right.

Was James playing a long game or wasn't I meant to return from this jaunt?

If the latter, I'd never see Lulu and Ronan again. My guilt was trumped by my thanks they weren't anywhere near me right now. The one glass-full thing—I would help Neddy escape. When I took in the reality of what he'd become, I wondered if that even mattered.

Either way, I'd try to bring the boy back, free him from the monster. It *had* to matter.

Minutes later, Rolf and Neddy-Pinky disappeared up a steep path and James said we should hike back to our truck.

Once there, he pulled blankets from the trunk and draped them over the seats. Smart move, considering our disgustingness. If I thought about *who* that gunk had once been, I'd puke.

"I need a shower," I said. "More than a shower. A bourbon would be good. And a memory eraser, too, for what was left in that cave."

He got out a bottle of Purell, a white handkerchief, and a first-aid kit with antiseptic. "Bare your arm." He gestured to the injured one.

I complied, and he dripped the Purell onto the cloth and ran the handkerchief across my wound.

"Ow!"

"Buck it up, Clea."

A horrible wave of nostalgia flattened me. Why had he said that? Bernadette's words, a favorite expression, one he'd heard her say plenty, but... I dropped my eyes.

When he finished cleaning and bandaging me, I scrubbed my hands and face with the Purell. I reached for the bottle to do the same for his face wound.

"Not necessary."

Those Pacific-blue eyes, empty. "Let me. It'll make me feel better."

He paused, nodded. With a fresh white handkerchief, I cleaned his wound of blood and gunk. *My* Larrimer always carried colorful handkerchiefs—purple and red and green, with polka dots and stripes and zigzags.

Pressure in my chest, burning in my eyes. Memory was a bitch.

He started the truck, then pulled out a black kerchief from the glove compartment and tried to tie it around my eyes. I slapped his arm. "What the hell!"

"You want to live?"

I stilled. "What's that supposed to mean?"

"If you know Rolf's hideaway, he'll kill you."

"You rescued me from it, remember?"

"Not the same place."

"We found Rolf." I crossed my arms. "Why didn't you take him?"

"I have my reasons."

"Care to share?"

"You'll have to trust me."

"I thought we agreed you'd tell me everything about this op. Why should I trust you since you're refusing to do that now?"

"Because I've kept you safe. Because you are a priority to me. Because something more than my mission tells me you matter."

I stared long and hard at him, then waved at the black cloth in his hand. "Go ahead."

18

NOT AGAIN

E ven blindfolded, I could tell when we left the canyon's bumpy roads for pavement, and then hit stop-and-go traffic. Soon, the roads grew winding enough that I grabbed the "oh, shit!" handle above the car door. James drove like a madman. Some would say he was.

My fingers found a door button, and I lowered the window. I couldn't see, but I could smell and hear, the sea scents and caw of the gulls a constant accompaniment.

I sipped from the water bottle James had thrust in my hand, and every so often bit a chunk of a tasteless protein bar, knowing I needed the calories.

Onto even more curvy roads, then bumpy ones until we stopped. The air was cooler here, damper, too. We were near the sea and must have gone north, up the Pacific Coast Highway.

A creaking sound, like gates opening. As we drove downward, the whine of metal closing played a grim background tune.

I was closed in with *Him*.

We stopped, and I didn't move, didn't want to leave the truck.

"Don't anger him," James said.

I nodded, knowing I'd spew unhelpful words if I uttered a single one. I reached for my blindfold, to release it.

The creak of the seat, warm breath on my cheek. "Not yet." The hairs on my body rose in warning, the first time I'd reacted to him that way since we'd become lovers.

I dropped my hands to my lap, and he divested me of my knives and guns. I didn't mention my fireflies. He knew about them, but all of this was a costume we were donning so we wouldn't set off Rolf.

James understood that my fury might end the man who'd stolen children's lives and violated me.

"He won't hurt you while I'm here," he said.

"Don't bet on it," I spat.

INSIDE, he removed my blindfold. Except for the scents—rotten fruit and death—the house was incredible. Neddy-Pinky was our guide, something that said a spark of Neddy-the-boy might remain inside the creature. He led us through an atrium entryway into a sprawling living room, with vaulted ceilings and a bank of windows overlooking the ocean that roiled far below.

Where was Rolf?

Rain spattered the windows, and I shivered from the chill, wishing Rolf had lit the massive woodstove that crouched silent and cold in a corner of the room.

Beneath a wall display of large black-and-white photos, sat an L of the huge burnt-umber leather couch, the other L facing the ocean. A perfect spot for curling up with a bourbon and a book. Right. Someone had painted a modern abstract on the opposite wall. In front of the couch, a massive live-edged burlwood table flowed like a trout stream. I took a step back to peek into the kitchen, all stainless and mellow wood, the room's windows blacked out. Because they faced the front of the house, I guessed.

As I moved deeper into the living room, I took a longer look at the abstract art on the wall. Prickles across my shoulders. Not art, but spatter, blackened blood spatter, done by a Jackson Pollock gone mad.

I squeezed by eyes tight. Wherever Rolf had stashed the home's occupants, they were dead.

The mahogany floor cushioned my feet when I moved to the bank of windows. Beyond, an open-railed deck overlooked the rocks and sea far below. Not exactly a viable escape route.

James leaned a hip against the windowed wall, deceptively relaxed. The Pinky began sniffing me.

"I have to use the bathroom," I said.

The Pinky tilted his head, then gestured as if to lead me away. Neddy-Pinky understood my request, reinforcing that some of Neddy remained inside the grotesque exterior. I resisted the urge to ask James to accompany me and followed the creature through the kitchen and down a small hall. The Pinky stopped, and I almost stumbled into him.

I squeezed by him into a huge luxurious room done up in turquoise and pale pearlescent sea glass. After I took care of business in the private toilet area, I stepped to the sink to wash off the remaining blood that dappled my arms and face. I froze.

The Pinky was in the room. With me.

It, he, leaned forward. His black, shiny nose sniffed, ropes of drool dripped to the floor, and his eyes—Neddy's eyes—were glued to me. His black-clawed hands opened and closed. "Cle-ahhh," it said. "Cle-ahhh."

Was he recognizing me or was it because he'd heard my name? I walked closer, but stopped so suddenly I tilted back on my heels. What was I thinking? Was this Neddy talking? The Pinky? Or Rolf through the beast?

"Neddy?"

"Cle-ahhh."

Hand trembling, I reached out. The Pinky's mass of teeth snapped at my fingers. I fisted them. "Neddy." Hell, I had another hand, right? I uncurled my fist and leaned forward. "Neddy."

I brushed my hand across a patch of shoulder fur, one of many that dotted his pink flesh, like clumps of grass on rain-soaked earth. I pet him over and over, repeating his name. "How can I help?"

His jaws snapped at my wrist, but didn't touch it, then he turned and loped out of the bathroom.

I reeled against the sink, hands clutching the counter.

Gods, if Neddy was still in there, I had to return him to himself and to his human form. And I had to do it soon. My gut said the creature Pinky would soon subsume the boy Neddy. But how to bring him back? *How?*

WHEN I REAPPEARED in the living room, James and Rolf held brandy snifters, looking convivial as hell, while Neddy-Pinky crouched in a corner. James' clothes and boots bore the dried detritus of blood and guts, whereas Rolf had obviously showered. He wore a neat blue button-down shirt and clean, pressed jeans. His feet were bare, and his bald pate shone in the darkening day's watery light.

Rolf had taken the wall L of the sofa, James, the other. I sat to the right of James, as far from them as possible, my back against the couch arm, knees pulled up, as if they would shield me from Him. I forced myself not to clutch a throw pillow to my chest.

Rolf's graveyard eyes bored into me. They whispered pain and need and death. He'd poked and prodded my body, been inside my mind. I stared back at him, refused to drop my eyes, no matter how loud my hindbrain shrieked.

I expected James to say something, do something. His silence unnerved me.

Fuck it all. I unfurled my mind. First James, a cool pool of tranquility floated above his tightly clamped shields. Now, Rolf. A blast of static crazy enough that it hurt, but I caught a few high notes of hunger, too. But the bass notes shocked me. They hummed with pain. Desperate pain.

In for a penny and all that. "Why did you take the children, Rolf?"

He blinked, took a sip of brandy, sat it on the table. A slow smile wreathed his lips. "I know you. All of you."

My facade of cool held, and I shrugged. "There's not that much to know. Why the children?"

He glanced at Neddy-Pinky. "I needed their blood. For the creation of an army. We're making progress."

"An army," I repeated.

"Rolf hates The Union," James said.

I almost blurted out *Who doesn't?*

Rolf leaned forward. "With my soldiers, we can take them."

I processed that nonsensical idea. "Why take *me*, Rolf?"

"I need your magic."

As James had said. Another idea without reason or sense. "And how could you *possibly* acquire that?"

James growled low in his throat. A warning.

A smile curled Rolf's mouth upward, opened onto teeth broken and jagged. "Games. You're playing games. You know."

I sure as hell didn't. "What makes you think that?"

Rather than answer, he waved toward the blood-spattered wall. "How do you like it?" He smiled, open, friendly. "I made it myself. Organic. Like some of the art I saw in New York."

I had no words.

He dismissed me and turned to James. "You brought her for me. Thanks, bro."

"I did not," James said.

James' pose remained relaxed. The real James, the old James, had seethed with passion, something he was expert at hiding from the world, but I'd always felt those emotions. Now he was a fathomless sea of tranquility void of life.

I clenched my teeth, crawlies coating my skin from the thickened atmosphere. The room's tuning fork tension vibrated faster.

Rolf's face turned childlike. "But, Larrimer, I thought she was a present for me."

"She's isn't, old friend," James said. "She's mine."

Rolf's massive chest expanded, then deflated. He shook his head. "He was right after all."

I'M WEARING TORN JEANS, **work boots, and a green bra,** while all the other *women are in sequins and velvet. James looms before me and asks me to dance. He's gorgeous tonight, in a black tux, hair slicked back, blue eyes sparking. We dance, James and I. Then... That creep from the gala stands in front of me. The bastard wants me to sell him my goats. For meat!*

I smile up at him. "I'd be delighted." No!

"You're not dressed properly." He morphs into Rolf and holds out his hand.

Never.

I shrink back, but I place my hand in his. It's greasy, stained with blood. I expect us to move, but we don't. Rolf stares at my cleavage, and I'm a horse at auction. He pulls me tight, too tight, and his hand creeps from my waist to cup my breast.

James materializes from the ether. He smiles, all predatory male. "She's decent in bed. Take her."

I AWAKENED WITH A START, sweat-covered, breath shallow, tiny tremors shivering my body.

That dream sucked.

I tried to move, except... I was bound to a table. Shit, not again.

I lurched, pulled, tried to get free, and I... *No way, Jose.* But I wouldn't freak out. Not this time. And I wasn't drugged. Yippee.

Fluorescents lit the room's concrete walls and ceiling. In my direct line of sight, Neddy-Pinky stood against a wall about four feet away. Was he trembling?

On Neddy-Pinky's left crouched three six-foot-tall mesh cages. One cage was empty. Inside the second, a naked woman lay curled on her side, knees pressed to her chin, eyes closed. In the third, to the left of hers, a child appeared to be asleep in a bundle of blankets. Feces and what I suspected were puddles of urine covered both cage floors.

Rolf's handiwork. Where had he taken the woman and child from? Were they shapeshifters, too? If so, I knew only too well his plans for them. He wasn't in evidence, but noises came from another cellar room. Blowers wafted the air, unsuccessfully masking the sweet-copper smell of blood, the stink of excrement, the horror of cruelty.

Duct tape again bound my head to the gurney, hands pressed together above me and bound. This sucked.

I swiveled my eyes to my right. *James*, restrained on a steel table beside mine by massive chains that crisscrossed his legs, torso and head. Thank the gods they'd left his eyes, mouth, and nose free.

"James," I hissed. "James."

"Yes."

"Are you all right?"

"Yes. I miscalculated. Apologies."

Even now, his toneless voice drove me batshit. He must be figuring how to escape, but he lacked any emotional signature. *Fuck.*

James would do his damnedest to free us. But I didn't see how that was possible. Rolf, constructed of the same nanotech as James, knew all about his strengths and weaknesses.

This was bad. Very, very bad.

I focused on my fireflies, confident I could call them up. Unlike the last time, when he'd left my fingers free, Rolf had duct-taped my entire hands and wrists in that prayer position.

Plan B. I'd shoot fireflies out the soles of my feet, which were taped only at the ankles. I gathered my energies and whammo.

Yeah, not so much.

It might be possible. Trouble was, I didn't know *how*.

Time for plan C.

"Neddy."

His eyes snapped to me.

"Can you help us?"

He grinned, a glistening array of serrated teeth shining bright. Not a confidence builder.

"This is wrong, Neddy. Rolf is going to hurt us."

The grin widened, which was so not good.

"Neddy, we can take you home. To your mom and your pack. Help you return to yourself. Your mom, you remember her, right?"

Nothing.

"Neddy, remember your friend, Paul?"

Still grinning that awful drooly grin.

"Remember Cami? She always wore jeans, didn't she? And she had the prettiest blond hair. You loved her, didn't you, like a big brother? And she loved you."

His muzzle snapped shut. For the first time, I saw hints of confusion.

I couldn't firefly, but maybe... I unfurled my senses, sent feelings of warmth and love outward to Neddy-Pinky.

"Cami would want you to help us, Neddy. Please."

I felt him then—confusion, fear, and an ember of curiosity.

"Rolf killed Cami, Neddy. He killed her. She is no more."

If I could have scraped a hand through my hair, I would have. This was eating up long minutes.

"He ended her," I said. "You'll never see her again. She's gone."

A growl, much like a wolf's, erupted from his throat. He took a step closer. And then another.

"Help us, Neddy. Rolf killed Cami, but we're not dead yet. Help us."

Another step. He raised his right arm, his black-clawed index finger pointed at me.

He leaned forward dripping drool onto my belly, closer, so close he could rip off my face. The claw scraped my forehead, then pulled. The tape parted.

"Thank you."

"Cam-i?"

"She's gone. I'm so sorry, Neddy."

Neddy flew across the room, crashing into the wall ten feet away. He crumpled to the floor and didn't move.

I CLOSED MY EYES. Rolf.

"Hey, Sis."

Oh, no. Please, no. If I opened my eyes, I would see him. Seeing him would make it real.

Of their own volition, my eyes opened wide.

He wore a white linen shirt and black jeans and a beaming smile. His light-brown hair was longer, to his chin, and eyes were laughing. His dimples showed because his grin was wide. Except my once-beloved twin's handsome face bore red, marbled scars, I suspected gained in our last confrontation. His right eye drooped and its former smoky gray-green appeared milky in the harsh light.

"White shirt?" I said. "Not suitable for a torture session, brother mine."

He frowned. "Untrue. I'll be the observer. Rolf, here, will be doing the physical work."

Rolf stood at parade rest beside Tommy, towering over my brother's five-foot-ten frame. I hadn't even noticed him. Like always, Tommy filled my world.

Tommy stroked my cheek, then slapped me hard enough to bring tears to my eyes.

"Whoopee," I said. "The big man slaps his sis when she's tied down. Well done, Tom."

"I see you're still cavorting with the monster."

Pot calling the kettle black much? I snorted. "I know quality when I see it, and you ain't it."

He went to slap me again, but fisted his hand and whammed. Shooting stars, piercing pain, and then I settled. Blood filled my mouth, and I spat at him.

"Fuck!" Tommy said, plucking at his now red-dappled shirt. Tommy was always into clothes.

He pulled his arm back for another wham-bang punch, but stopped himself. "Rolf, go get me a Perrier, please. Then we'll get on with it."

He drew a pack of Gitanes from his pocket, along with a lighter, tamped one from the pack and lit up.

"French cigs, Tom? Really? A bit froufrou, don't you think?"

His eyes narrowed, and he leaned forward, waving the cigarette toward the scars on his face. "You did this," he said in a conversational tone. "I think a little payback is in order. Don't you?"

Every cell in my body froze, my eyes glued to the cigarette's glowing tip.

The glow drew closer.

Relax. It would hurt less if I relaxed, had control of my body. I unclenched my muscles.

Closer.

If he pressed it to my eye, I'd scream.

"This is payback for the fake Chest of Bone."

Heat on my cheek, then pressure, and pain spiked through me. I clamped my teeth tight. The burn. The sizzle. The smell.

"Hey, Tom," said Rolf. "What did you say you wanted again?"

Tommy jerked up the cigarette. "Perrier!"

Waves of pain undulated through my head. My tears literally added salt to the wound, my breaths out of control, frantic.

The spot, the burn, he'd done it where I had a small scar on my cheekbone from one of our childhood misadventures.

"And you, dear bro," I said, panting. "You killed Dave and Jason, kidnapped Lulu, and tried to kill me. Oh, and you killed our grandmother, a woman who only ever gave you love."

He inhaled, tapped the ash onto my face. "Not my fault she got in the way."

"Nothing's ever your fault, is it? Everything bad that happens is just collateral damage. Right?"

He dipped his head, again bringing the glowing tip close, this time toward my right eye. "This will hurt, and you'll be blinded. Sounds like fun to me."

"Did you say your coconut water?" boomed a voice from upstairs.

Tommy rolled his eyes. "He's losing it. Fucking brain cells dying faster than I can keep up. Too bad he's useful." He sighed. "The Perrier!"

Back to the cigarette. I'd closed my eyes so the ash didn't drift into them.

"Open 'em," Tommy said.

I did and hissed through clenched teeth.

"I think I'll do this instead, just because I feel like it."

The cigarette closed in on me.

Pain speared my other cheek, and every muscle in my body trembled. I might've whimpered. I probably whimpered. My eyes watered, and I blinked rapidly to keep him in my sights.

"Now they match, sort of." Tommy grinned. "You're a toughie, Sis."

Not really. But I was damned good at faking it. The burn continued, burrowing into my brain.

"Here, boss."

Tommy straightened, and Rolf handed him the bottle.

"Thank you." Tommy strolled off, out of my line of sight. He was cooking up something. Was he rolling out one of those leather wraps with all sorts of pointy devices of torture? I so wasn't up for this.

"He hurt you," Rolf said.

I ground out the word. "Yes."

"I don't like torture," Rolf said, "without a purpose."

He talked slowly, as if his mouth was having trouble catching up with his brain.

"I don't like torture, period," I said.

Rolf moved from the table, I guessed to follow his "boss."

I cut my eyes toward James. He was red-faced in his effort to break his chains, which seemed to have stretched. More likely my optimism coming to the fore. Either way, he'd never break them before Rolf and Tommy did their torture tango.

They were after something. I just wasn't sure what, at least where James was concerned. Me? Oh, yeah, Tommy planned to torture me until I spilled Chest of Bone's location. And wasn't that special? Rolf? He was lost in his own sad, crazy world.

But even if I caved and told them its location, it would do them no good. They could raze the Arctos den to the ground, and they still wouldn't be able to access the chest in the room between worlds.

I'd bet big bucks they hadn't a clue, and Tommy's master, Tatianne, hadn't informed them of that teensy-weensy fact. Her sick idea—screwing with the retwining of the worlds—wasn't gonna happen.

Even if I died, the chest would be protected, and Anouk and the guardians would anoint a replacement Key.

Of course, perhaps Tommy and Rolf had set their sights on the Chest of Stone. Until it was mine, anyone could acquire it. But activating it? Nope. Only I could do that.

They must think I knew its location and planned to torture it out of me.

Craptastic.

"Good to go," Tommy said as the pair walked to the foot of my table. They held no devices of torture, except Tommy carried a small hypodermic needle filled with a greenish fluid. I tensed, expecting them to approach me. Instead, Rolf took position next to James, while Tommy hovered beside him.

Plan C, or was it D, going into effect.

I expanded my mind, hoping James would allow me inside his shields. And they were locked up tight.

I broke the connection and turned my head. "James?"

His head was chained down, but he blinked.

"I love you," I said. "Please open yourself to that. I love you." Yup, I'd used the L word.

"Thank you."

Was there ever a worse response to a declaration of love? Now to see if he'd understood my message.

"Blah, blah, blah," Tommy said. "Pathetic."

"Maybe. But it's true."

Rolf stared at me, eyes curious. "Love. I knew that once." He turned to Tommy. "Are you sure? Did Tanya say—"

"Her proper name is Tatianne," Tommy said. "Use it."

I pushed them into the background and unfurled my mind. James' mind was... *Open!* I aimed for the wyvern.

19

DEEPER AND DEEPER

I delved deep into James, but the white noise fought me, blinded me. My mental breaths were ragged, my calm, fracturing. I plowed on through the blizzard, losing valuable seconds until I sensed the warmth of the banked fae spark. The closer I came to the warmth, the easier the going, until a nauseating tumble landed me right in front of the wyvern. Shaken, I looked upward. The immense red-gold beast crouched before what looked like a rocky edifice, shackled in chains reminiscent of oily black smoke.

Wyvern, help us. They're going to kill James. Kill me.

His clouded, dull eyes swiveled to mine. *I... AM... SHACKLED.*

I had to take the right tack. Play to my weakness or to his strength? I hadn't talked to the wyvern much, but I'd helped him when he'd been in pain. *Well, fucking unshackle yourself. You're a wyvern, not a wimp. You are powerful. You are transcendent. You can do this.*

Only another can unshackle me.

The only one trooping around inside here is me. Can I do it?

He shrugged and turned his head away.

I went deeper, projected standing beside the wyvern. And I was. I touched his red-gold hide. Warm, not hot, his hide layered with rounded scales dotted with silky smooth bumps. I ran a hand across one wing, its gleam of burnished-gold on the curve of each scale, dulled.

A hum, a tremble. A purr. The wyvern purred!

He was attuned to my fireflies, but... This might weaken me, make me helpless. Oh, screw it.

I poured my magic into him.

Molten gold dribbled from beneath his scales, his eyes, his nose. Gold-red liquid frothed from his mouth, and I jumped back.

Do not stop.

I pushed harder with my mind, pressed my hands to his flank, his head, his side, wished I could reach his spine, but he was too immense, at least my mind perceived him that way. His leathery hide grew hotter and hotter. My fingers began to burn, so different from that cigarette tip. Periodically I'd lick them to cool them off and tried not to think about the virtuality of all I was doing. Or was it?

His magnificent head slithered toward me, and I stroked those majestic horns now curled pathetically like a child's limp paper noisemaker. I pet and pet. My hands blistered and popped, skin ripped, became raw meat. I bit my lip and forced myself to continue even as I keened in pain.

I began to tremble, agony battering my will like a siege engine.

I kept on. I could do this. I must.

This was magic. And with magic, there was always a price.

And his horns sinuously uncurled, to arc mighty and huge.

Stand back.

I tried to release my hands, but the blood and fluids had stuck me to the base of his horns.

I pulled, ripped, stumbled backward.

The wyvern roared.

Warm blood dripped from my ears, my nose, but I laughed.

I am free!

Yes!

He swiveled to face me, and a thin, forked tongue emerged from his maw. He licked my hands, and the pain eased.

Now go to work, my dear wyvern, and save our asses.

As I spoke the last word, he roared.

An explosion of pain, the wyvern's fury, blew me from James' mind.

James was screaming. Screaming! His back arched on the metal table, hands clawed, face a rictus of agony.

"James!"

A hypodermic needle attached to an empty vial protruded from his neck, and Rolf and Tommy, both with arms crossed, stood passively watching.

Me, panicked, near hysterical over James' pain. I pushed, pulled, tried to rip my bindings. And I couldn't. *Couldn't!*

I was spent. Empty.

And the air charged. Brushed my cheek. Warmed me.

"What's this?" Rolf said, having to shout over James' screams. "I've never seen this before with the drug."

Tommy shrugged. "Interesting."

A hot breeze, a current of wind inside the cement enclosure. Energy surging. Varooming across the room.

James' back arched so high I thought it would break, his skin now a red-gold.

The chain across his chest snapped.

One across his leg broke.

Right arm, free, too.

I started to laugh, giddy, crazy with joy and fear.

Tommy frowned, raised his left hand to throw his deadly magical needles.

My taped-together hands burned deeper, my fireflies trying to release. Hungry to help James, to stop Tommy.

Tommy's palm hovered high. He was going to end James.

"No!" Rolf and I shouted simultaneously.

Tommy smirked at Rolf and pressed his power. But Tommy's calm transformed to fury. His face reddened, eyeballs bulging, mouth open in a soundless cry.

Not a quill arced from his palm. Not one.

He raised his eyes to mine, teeth bared. "You! You did this to me! You neutered my magic!"

"I'm glad."

Tommy stalked around the table toward me, a knife glistening in his hand.

Rolf's eyes never left James, whose screams turned to bellows as more chains snapped. Rolf remained statue still.

Tommy loomed over me, knife raised.

I blinked away the tears and sweat. The knife point gleamed, the blade serrated. His eyes said he'd do it, this brother of mine, his eyes a cocktail of pleasure and envy and fear. I bit my cheek. *Keep him talking.* He wanted me to beg, and I grinned. "I won't, you know."

"Won't what?" He said.

"Beg. You'd do it anyway."

"You know me too well. But, Clea, this hurts me."

"It'll hurt me more."

"True." His eyes, pools of melted chocolate. "I love you."

"Not as much as you love yourself."

The knife plunged.

Thick arms wrapped around Tommy's waist and flung him. Tom bulleted into the air, slamming against a wall with a crunch.

Rolf had saved me. Why?

The huge man sprang toward a darkened corner and dragged a whimpering Neddy-Pinky toward the door.

James shot to a seated position, his bronze color returned, blood oozing from his pores. A final chain bound his right leg.

"James, don't let Rolf get away!"

A look passed between them. Then Rolf ducked toward a door in the corner, lugging Neddy along with him.

A whoosh, and a length of chain wrapped around Rolf's neck. The huge man dropped Neddy to tug at the chain with both hands, even as James kept the tension taut. Muscles bulging, tendons distended, Rolf scrabbled to rip the thing apart.

They had bound James well, with strong, near-unbreakable links. Of the six, James alone had the wyvern's strength.

Rolf crashed to his knees, face flushed, tugging, pulling at the chain that wouldn't release.

My fireflies finally responded and sliced the bindings on my hands, and I used them to sever the tape holding me to the gurney.

I leapt off the platform and hung on, swiped a hand across my nose that came away red.

I was in lousy shape.

With one hand on the steel table, I fireflied. A knit triangle pattern flew from my palm and cut the final chain holding James' right leg.

He leapt down, his naked body dripping blood. Chest bellowing, he stalked Rolf.

Tommy. I whirled. A small pond of blood surrounded his still, broken form. I would end him, firefly him while he lay unconscious. How could I? I raised my palms. But my heart seized at the brief echo of what we'd once been.

"Clea, now," James said. "I need you."

I hesitated, then ran to James.

James crouched by Rolf, who continue to struggle, lips blue, tears dribbling from his eyes. James gently unwound the chain.

Rolf crumpled against the wall. Breathing, but... No, he was suffocating. The chain must have crushed his windpipe.

James rose to his feet, pressed a bloody hand to the wall, then pushed off the wall to weave across the room to a lab table filled with tools. Moments later, he hunkered down before Rolf and sliced his neck and trachea with a nasty-looking knife, then inserted a black rubber tube in the airway. I ripped a scrap off Rolf's shirt and wiped as much blood away as possible.

In seconds, Rolf's lips pinked. He blinked several times, as if a fog were clearing, and caught James' eyes. They stared at each other for long moments. I waited. Powerful feelings swirled between them. A slice out of time between two old friends, comrades who spoke the same language.

This man had kidnapped me, bled me, abused me. Yet he'd been raped and twisted and abused too—by The Union, by Tommy. I couldn't find it in myself to hate him.

A blur. Rolf's tube was ripped from his throat and he'd closed his hands around James' wrists.

It should have been easy for James to pull from Rolf's grasp. He didn't. I scrambled for the tube, tried to reinsert it. Rolf elbowed me hard enough that I gasped.

"No," he said, his voice mere puffs of air.

He was dying, suffocating.

"No," he repeated.

His eyes shined a clear gray-green, and they never lost contact with James'.

"No."

James growled when Rolf released his wrists, but didn't make a move to stop his friend's death.

Rolf frowned. "I wanted to be one of the good guys."

"You were," James said.

"Once."

Rolf toppled onto his side. His chest rose and fell twice, then he clutched his throat, shuddered, and died.

I closed the lids of his eyes.

Damn Tommy. This was his doing, one of his many schemes.

I whirled to where my brother lay sprawled on the floor.

Gone!

How the... I raced upstairs. Okay, "raced" was an exaggeration, but I made it to the first floor without keeling over. As I staggered around like a drunken zombie, I hoped when I found him, I had enough juice left to kill him. The house was big, but didn't have many rooms. I scoured the place, ended up back in the kitchen. Since the windows were blacked out, I opened the kitchen door.

The driveway was clear. Our truck was gone, and so was Tommy.

Hell.

I was tempted, so tempted, to shower off the blood. Instead, I searched for a phone, found one. Downstairs again, I surveyed the chaos. The caged woman and child remained unconscious. Neddy-Pinky stood shivering in the corner, and James...

I zoomed across the room. He lay on his back, eyes closed.

"James."

On hands and knees, I reached my left hand out with caution. But he didn't move when I pressed my palm to his cheek. Cool, whereas normally he burned.

His non-response had me diving inside. Pushed past the white noise, the cool sea, past the fae spark which was dimmer than ever, to the wyvern, curled in a ball with his massive spiked tail tucked around him. I touched his tail. He neither stirred, nor awakened. *Wyvern.*

I didn't sense any pain, but he felt... absent.

I withdrew and shook James. "C'mon, buster, wake up."

He was having none of it, so I tried to firefly him awake. I Flowed, which was a misnomer, since all my fireflies did was dribble to the floor. Pretty much used up. Good thing my brother was gone.

A moan from the woman's cage. Swell. It was me, Neddy-Pinky, a passed-out James, and a traumatized woman and child. Oh, and Rolf's corpse. Hell of a party.

Neddy-Pinky tilted his head, then all seven feet of him squatted and sniffed Rolf and James. He made a strange sort of yowl-yip sound.

I sat back hard on my butt.

Neddy-Pinky walked around Rolf's corpse and sat beside me, somehow folding up that huge body, hands on bent knees. Even sitting, he towered over me. He smelled awful. He sniffed me.

I guessed I smelled awful, too. Or maybe my scent was delicious to him. Hard to tell.

I pet a tuft of fur. "You're safe, Neddy. No one will hurt you anymore. We'll fix you." *How*, was the question.

He grinned, open mouthed, with those awful serrated teeth, like an alligator yawning. Perhaps he was thinking about food, with me as his next meal.

Gods. I reached for the phone to call Alex.

The pack would be thrilled at Rolf's death and Neddy-Pinky's return, well, perhaps not thrilled, but at least they'd know he was alive.

Except my fingers stilled on the keypad. James lay like stone, injured and utterly vulnerable. The pack despised him, Alex in particular. They were good, good people, but I didn't trust they wouldn't kill him.

I pressed my cheek to my knees, conflicted, indecisive and thoroughly exhausted.

Neddy-Pinky stroked my shoulder, his drool plopping onto my forehead.

Plop. Plop. Plop.

Which was when I remembered Rae.

I punched out the number he'd given me what felt like eons ago, but was mere days. Per his request, I'd memorized it. A good thing, since I had no pockets in my naked skin.

Answer. Answer. Why the fuck wasn't he answering!

"No," came a faint voice from one of the cages.

I moved to kneel in front of her cage. "Don't be afraid. I won't hurt you."

She screamed.

Neddy-Pinky had followed me, hovering behind me, which must have prompted that ear-piercing shriek.

"He won't hurt you," I said. "I'll find the key or something to break the lock."

"No," she said, her voice a rasp.

"Why not?"

She pointed at Neddy.

"No, he won't harm you." I looked over my shoulder. "Will you, Neddy?"

His grin had her scooting to the farthest corner of her cage.

"Okay, I won't undo the lock until the troops arrive. Are you good with that?"

She nodded.

Maybe I'd find food and water for her and the child, except that would mean opening the cage doors.

The boy slept on, so I went to check James.

Bloody or not, I lay beside him and began to kiss him. It had worked once before, months ago when because of the freezing cold, he'd "shut down," as he termed it. Except it might be chilly in here, but not freezing. I kissed him, talked to him, murmured love words to his still-as-stone form.

It was like déjà vu when we'd been trapped in that horrible refrigeration room, but this time, no response.

Rae's line wasn't answering. *Pick up!*

At the moment, no one was dying or on the precipice, so I trudged upstairs and showered, avoiding the vanity's mirror, then trolled for clothes. I found filthy ones, couldn't bear touching them. After more searching, I found others—huge, that would at least cover James', mine, and the others' nakedness.

Dressed in ginormous clean sweats and a T-shirt, along with my filthy socks and boots, I carried my bundle of clean clothes to the cellar... and found Neddy eating Rolf.

"No!" I raced over.

He didn't stop, didn't look up, just chomped on a...

"Neddy, stop!"

His head swiveled toward me, his jaws dripping blood and guts and grossness.

"Please stop, Neddy. We'll find you something upstairs to eat. Please stop."

He lowered his head, opened his maw and took another bite out of Rolf's belly. "Good," he said between chews.

My stomach heaved. "He was a human being. Try to remember what that is." I firmed my voice, tried to put some Alpha into it. "Stop eating. It's wrong."

Neddy bit a chunk out of Rolf's thigh.

I raced upstairs, trolled the Sub-Zero, and came away with a giant haunch of... something. It didn't matter what it was as long as it wasn't Rolf. I skidded to a stop in front of Neddy, barely able to hold the heavy haunch of meat.

"You can have this if you leave him alone. Permanently. No more chomping on him."

He looked back and forth between the haunch and Rolf. He sniffed and turned back to Rolf.

"Look, Neddy." I pitched my voice low and stern. "You're in there, dammit, and you're going to come back from this. I will help you."

He stopped chewing, purple tongue lolling, and those eyes, Neddy's eyes, bored into me. "Cle-ahhh."

"Yes. If you leave Rolf and don't chew on him again, I will keep you safe. I will stay with you and help you. But not unless you leave Rolf alone."

His hand crept to his tooth-and-claw necklace. "Pro-mise?"

I would promise him the world, a promise I wasn't sure I could fulfill. "Cross my heart. I promise."

Neddy pet my arm, smearing blood down it as he did so. "O-kay." He reached for the haunch, took it, and bit down.

Minutes later, I pushed a t-shirt though the cage mesh for the child, wondering if he was a shapeshifter and what kind. The child breathed with reassuring regularity, and while he was thin, he wasn't emaciated. When I squinched a t-shirt into the woman's cage, her eyes flew open.

"Are you sure you—"

"No!"

My hands flew up, palms out. "Okay. Okay."

I sighed, kneeled beside James, and pulled on the sweatpants I'd retrieved for him. I leaned forward and kissed his cheek. *Wake up. Wake up.* The phone rested beside me. I had to call someone. I looked at James, eyes closed, lashes so long they brushed his high cheek-bones, and back at the phone. I lay down beside him. Uncaring that he was coated in dried blood, I wrapped my arm across his broad chest, rested my cheek on his pectoral. I shivered. He was usually so warm, hot, even. Now he was cool, as if the life were leeching out of him.

I combed my fingers through his hair. So like the cellar prison, but worse, much worse. Then, I'd been frantic. Now, all was calm and quiet. Too much time to think, to fear.

A door closed. Upstairs.

I sprang to my feet, and weakness pulsed through every inch of my body. The knives I gathered were plenty sharp, then I snagged the chain that James had used on Rolf. Whoa—too heavy by half. I shucked my boots and socks, and on silent feet, I sprinted to the stairs.

With Neddy hovering an inch behind me. Great. Not.

"Stay here," I said, and put a finger to my lips for quiet.

He frowned, like a sulking child.

"I mean it."

He slapped his hands on his hips in such a human gesture I wanted to weep, then I flew up the stairs.

The whoosh of the fridge opening, closing, had me hugging the wall as I stalked toward the kitchen. Around the corner and...

"Y'all pretty quiet, but not to me."

My muscles relaxed, and I raced to Rae, skidding to a stop to see him forking a mound of chocolate cake into his mouth.

"Don't you gimme that look," he said. "I'm hungry."

I grabbed for the wall, the relief making me dizzy. "I've been calling you. Oh, Rae. Gods, Rae."

"I knew you were in trouble," he said through a mouthful of cake. "Damn, sugah, you get yourself in some fixes."

I threw back my shoulders. "Not what I need right now, mister."

He waggled a long finger at me. "Don't you go sassin' me, hear?"

I tilted my head back and closed my eyes. "I need help, Rae. We've got a mess. A big fat mess."

His "tut, tut" was not attractive. "Y'all sit down." He dragged me to one of the barstools and plopped me onto it, which was when I noticed Neddy hovering in the door. Swellsies.

I filled Rae in on the whole clusterfuck.

EIGHT HOURS LATER, around ten a.m., I lay on a down mattress within the open second floor of Rae's luxurious treehouse. Rae had healed the burns on my cheeks, the bruises, and most of my other injuries. A beautiful ceiling arched above me, made of natural boards curved to resemble a bower in some fantastical fairytale. The room's sandalwood and cinnamon scents invited relaxation. The air was soft, the breeze from the windows soothing my skin. And Rae had placed a few lit candles over by the burlwood dresser for ambient light. I sighed with discontent.

A virtual boulder pressed against my chest, suffocating me. All the ambience in the world couldn't erase the fact that James lay beside me, alive, but as still as a corpse.

Like untangling a skein of yarn, Rae had managed the whole operation with precision and skill, and faster that I could have imagined.

He'd contacted the woman's and boy's pack, both some type of large cat, left them at a mutually agreed-upon spot. He'd also erased their memories of Rolf, Tommy, and captivity, a talent which scared the hell out of me. Each might have a bit of a headache, he told me, but they were healthy enough and would be minus the horror of what Rolf and Tommy had planned for them.

In my bower, Neddy had his very own pallet in a nearby corner. Rae had intended to put him on the third story, but Neddy would have none of it, and I'd insisted Rae not force him.

Not wanting The Union to reanimate Rolf, if they could even do that, Rae had vaporized him with those black motes he used on me, fortunately not with the intention to vaporize. Since the tiny motes weren't attacking me, I watched carefully, noting how they sparkled with a rainbow of colors, like chips of obsidian. When he'd dropped his hands, nothing remained of Rolf, including all signs of blood and guts where Neddy had been noshing on him.

"Wow," I said.

He nodded, but I saw a hint of weariness in those ancient, smoky eyes.

We discovered the oceanside home's true owners, decomposing in a guest room bathroom. He'd vaporized them, too.

"But their family won't know what's happened to them," I'd said.

He shook his head, sorrow marking his features. "I know it's tragic for that family. But we can't leave any trace for The Union or Tatianne's minions to find."

Neddy helped us carry James upstairs, although I suspected he'd rather eat him, and I bathed him, shampooed his hair, and re-dressed him. Rae's magic motes scoured, then purified the house after I forced Neddy to shower and leave his filthy jeans to don a fresh pair. And then we were off to Rae's.

Now I curled onto my side to stare at James, to pet him and to talk to him while waiting for Rae, who did whatever mages do when they weren't helping me or working a shift at an urban streetwear store.

He materialized beside the bed, again a young black man in jeans and a tee. He held a small stack of neatly folded clothes.

"He still out cold?

I nodded.

He handed me the clothes, and when I shook out the leggings, my eyeballs nearly popped.

"Neon pink?" I said. "With tacos on them?"

"They're cool." His wide grin would melt steel.

"Cool, my ass. I swear you found the most hideous pair in the store." At least the top was black. Except it was cropped, made of some spandex crap that would fit unnaturally tight and cut low enough that my boobs would threaten to burst out. A black jean jacket with a leopard-fur collar—faux, thank heavens—completed the ensemble. "Where's my neon nail polish?"

"Hehehe."

"Not funny." I stared at the taco leggings. "You must really hate me. Are you ready?"

"I am."

"You don't have a problem with helping James?"

He frowned, but then said, "He's important."

"Thank you."

His eyes narrowed. "I don't just mean to you, Miss Lovelorn. He's important to the retwining."

"How? He's—"

"I know what he is, sugah."

"But you said one of us was going to kill the other."

He had the courtesy to look guilty. "I mighta lied 'bout that."

"Why, you—"

"Now shut your pie hole and let's get on with it. This boy's got other stuff to attend."

Rae stood by James' side of the bed and raised his palms waist high to hover over James' supine form. He closed his eyes, pressing his hands closer, and his black motes swirled outward, to encompass James like a swarm of black flies.

I swallowed, waiting, hoping.

"Join me," he said.

I kneeled on the bed and mirrored Rae's hand motions. My fireflies came to my call and streamed outward, the moss stitch pattern, making a net, then blanketing James.

I breathed in, breathed out, held the net for I don't know how long—ten minutes or ten hours, time fluid as a rippling river.

"Release!" Rae said.

I fisted my hands, my Flow vanishing with a snap, and stared at my lover.

James' beautiful form lay before me, passive, unmoving, unnatural for someone usually so kinetic with life. "Rae?" I said, voice roughened by unasked questions.

"Now, we wait."

20

AN UNEXPECTED MEETING

Twenty-four hours, and James hadn't moved but for the occasional rise and fall of his chest. He'd once told me his breathing cycle was set to a different rhythm than a human's. If he hadn't, I would believe him dying. Perhaps he was.

Courtesy of Rae, today I wore lime-green leggings adorned with black skulls and a baggy white t-shirt with L.A. scrawled across the front, a considerable improvement over yesterday's outfit. Rae had been gone for most of the day, and I'd worked with Neddy on social skills. In other words, not eating everything in sight, including a neighbor's black Pekingese-mystery mutt, Bash. All the while I obsessed about James' wellbeing and continued to fret about not being there for Lulu, Ronan, and our menagerie. I hated that, and they were most likely worried sick about me, but until James rose to consciousness, I feared contacting them or the pack.

While I waited for James to wake, I'd cooked up a plan to fix Neddy. Here, my magic mojo was decent. Rae and I had tried to change Neddy back. No joy. But if I took the boy to the magic world, where I was seriously amped, I bet I could fix him. With Rae's help, we'd do it.

Except I worried about what Alex had said—his pack being too long in the mundane world to venture into the magic one. Given that Neddy was changed, and Rae said he'd been magically "enhanced," he possessed more magic. He should survive in the magic world just fine. It was worth the risk.

Footsteps down on the first floor. The emotional signature told me Rae was home.

Neddy growled, and I narrowed my eyes. "Stop that. It's Rae, and you can scent him." His eyes brightened, and a string of drool plopped onto the floor. "No, you can't eat him. He's our friend. And you can't eat Bash either." I glanced at the dog, who was asleep beside James on the bed.

A fireman's pole coursed through all three floors of the treehouse, and I zoomed downstairs just as Rae opened the fridge and pulled out a beer.

"At ten a.m.?" I said.

"Sayin' that stuff don't get on my good side. Y'all got a question for me."

Smartass. "I do." With careful reasoning and a judicious use of flattery, I detailed my go-to-the-magic-world idea for Neddy.

"No." Rae finished his beer and reached for another.

"You can't just say 'no.'"

His head bobbed. "Just did."

"We need to help him."

He morphed into a six-foot-five, muscled black man wearing tight jeans, a snug t-shirt, and a badass expression. He poked a finger at me. "First of all, not 'we'," he said in that James Earl Jones voice he sometimes affected. "Second, you will die. That bitch will eat you alive and own your soul."

I slid onto a bar stool by the counter. "How can I not help him? I met him before his transformation. He was a good kid. Tough. Caring. Determined. Neddy had a life. He deserves a chance to grow and explore, to be a kid again, and to become a young man."

He took a swig of beer. "All of that may be true, Clea. But the danger to you, to us, to our mission, isn't commensurate with returning the boy to his natural form."

"I get that Tatianne's powerful. Yeah, I understand it, but how can I live with myself if I don't try?"

He expanded his massive chest and exhaled slowly. "You cannot access the magic world without me."

"I get that, dammit! Which is why I'm asking you to come with me or at least get Neddy and me there."

He compressed again into the skinny black boy. "No."

I'D WALKED the path for more than an hour. James still slept. Neddy was napping, too. Ray had disappeared. The sun beat down, but a breeze from the Pacific cooled the air. I hoped the walk would center me, and it had, somewhat. What it hadn't done was dissipate my anger. How could Rae just say no?

I sipped some water and tucked the near-empty bottle into my pouch. Trees and scrub dotted the mountain ridge, and beyond, vistas of a stormy Pacific, the color of James' eyes when filled with passion. Would I ever feel that passion again?

I turned away, left the path, and sat, my back braced against a tree trunk.

Alex and his pack couldn't access the magic world, so they were out in terms of helping me get there. Charlie the fae might help, except I had no idea where he was. Anouk... She could open the portal, except she never did anything I asked of her. I didn't have a clue where she was, either. So I'd learn how to enter the magic world on my own. Except that might take years. Years we didn't have.

The Chest of Bone would do it, I'd bet. But the thing was more dangerous than an atom bomb. I'd bet big bucks Rae wouldn't tell me how to use it to get there. So, okay, I'd figure it out.

Helping Neddy felt right. Necessary. An urgency in my gut burned hot and insistent. I had no clue *how* to help him transform back, I just knew I could. The longer he stayed a Pinky, the slimmer his chances to change back.

Decided. I'd use the Chest of Bone.

I stood and wiped the dust from my butt.

A solo hiker rounded the bend carrying a six-foot staff, long legs eating the distance between us. Not in the mood for chitchat, I turned away and stepped back onto the path.

And bumped into the hiker who towered in front of me, leaning on the staff, a knowing smile lifting her lush lips. Anouk.

"What are you doing here?" I said.

"You called me."

"Didn't."

"Well, oh powerful Key, I sensed you needed me."

I snorted. Where was she when Rolf and Tommy were playing their torture-the-mage-games? I spread my arms, annoyed as hell. "Queen of all I survey. Why are you really here?"

She tilted her head, reminding me of her eagle form. "*You* wanted *me*."

"Say I do..."

"Come." She waved a hand.

We hiked down a small hill to where a tree sheltered a large, flat boulder. She removed her pack and withdrew two sandwiches, cookies, and two bottles of water.

"I didn't think you were the picnic type," I said. "But thanks." I took a sandwich and chomped. Chunky PB&J, with raspberry jam on 12 grain. Divine. The fresh water was heavenly, too, chilled and bubbly with just a hint of lemon. "You're buttering me up for what, exactly?"

She held aloft one long index finger. "I do not talk while I eat."

I did a lot of thinking while we polished off the meal with chocolate-chip-and-walnut cookies, my fave. When she lit one of her smokes, I waited until she'd taken a few drags, which always mellowed her out. "You're going to help me access the magic realm with Neddy."

Smoke streamed from her nose. "I am." She produced a tin cup from her bag and tapped the ashes.

"Why?"

Her brow crinkled. "Is that not what you want?"

"Yes. But you have more agendas than a Google meeting."

More brow crinkling. "What does that mean?"

She didn't get tech. "Unimportant. There's always a price with you, especially as you're hot for me to find the Chest of Stone."

"Hush. Not aloud. Never aloud."

I put as much drama as I could into my sigh. "Fine. Just lay it out, plain and simple."

"I have learned a sliver of the chest remains in the magic realm."

"Which chest?"

Smoke swirled out her nose. "That which you imprudently mentioned."

"Convenient."

She shot me a furious look. "Not so. Tatianne is not aware. If she were, she would have already possessed it, and consequently, would find the chest. You must retrieve it."

"You said all the chests were here, in the mundane world. You told me I alone could bring them together and reboot them."

"Reboot?"

"Reignite, start, get them to work in concert again."

"Ah. Yes. Only you. That is correct."

My Spidey sense said she wasn't lying. But she wasn't telling the entire truth, either. "And the other part, about *all* of them being in the mundane world?"

She gave me the side eye.

"So," I said. "You're not sure about that now." Which just added a whole new kink to this weirdass business. "How did this splinter get there?"

"A mystery!" she hissed, and feathers sprouted from her forehead. A first. Wow.

I raised my hands in surrender. "Okay, okay. Sorry. So how do I find this sliver in the vastness of the magic world?"

"It will call to you."

"And what if it's thousands of miles away?"

"You will find it." Swear to gods she took out an iPhone. She stabbed the Home button so hard, I expected the glass to crack. "It is

Anouk," she said into the phone, apparently unaware of Caller ID. "Are you ready and willing?"

Pause.

"Good." Then she spoke in a language, an old one of mystery and magic, one so strange, chills skated up my spine.

After she'd jabbed the red End button several times, her sloe eyes cut to mine. They'd changed from chocolate to amber. "Be ready to leave in four hours, or so."

"What's 'or so' supposed mean?"

A snarky smile lifted her lips. "So when I find it, how am I supposed to carry the shard? In a box, like the chests?"

Her forehead feathers fluttered when she shook her head. "No. You must wear the shard."

Wear? "How...?"

Her waggled finger shut me up. She wouldn't tell. She was done. "I need to understand something."

"No time."

"*Make* time. I get the wobble, the dangers of the worlds retwining without the chests orchestrating the 'braid.' There's something else you fear. I need to hear what that is."

Her eyes narrowed to pinpoints of amber. "You *need?*"

"Yes. Something's off. Something *more* that makes you and Rae and whoever else is working with you fight so hard for this."

Her nostrils flared. "Perceptive. All right. Since the worlds separated, diversity has been leeching from the magic realm. Unlike the Mundanes, who come in many shapes and sizes, magical creatures within each species have evolved in an insular way. Fewer births. Creatures fading away. That resulting sameness is killing us, or so our... what would you call them... scientists believe. You and your like—"

"You mean my mixed fae-mage heritage?"

She nodded. "You are rare. Inter-matings were once common, or so I have been told, and included human-magic ones. I am aware of only one other—"

"Who?"

Her slow blink said nothing and everything. I suspected Lulu. Her father was mage, but memory told me Lulu's mother had the pointed ears of a fae. Then again, memory often lied. She'd left when Lulu was a child, and I was an almost-teen. My nickname for her, Cruella, said it all. But why wouldn't Anouk say her name aloud?

"Without the proper retwining of the worlds," she continued, "not only will epic disasters occur, but the magic realm and her creatures will die off. We will fade to but a memory."

A leveler. "But Tatianne...?"

Her hand sliced the air. "She and her kind do not believe that. Fools. They refuse to see what stares them in the face. Which is why she appropriated your brother."

Something was bugging me. "Why isn't he The Key? Tommy was born first. Why me and not him?"

"That is the way Tatianne thought. She imagined, I suspect, that your brother also had the power to gather the chests. You were twins, after all." A mean smile split her lips. "Idiot. There can only be one Key. *You* were chosen. She failed to understand. He could have been more. Not The Key, but more. Then she dug her claws into him. The boy was dark to your light. Balance, you see. Or the gods playing with us. If gods exist."

The deck was always stacked against my brother, which made me sad. "And so we have this war for the chests." She'd been forthcoming, unlike her usual opaque self. She must be really worried about me going after the sliver. "Where shall we meet you?"

She flowed to her feet, all elegance despite the cutoff jeans and tank top. "You'll know."

"I'll *know.*" She was back to the Anouk who drove me nuts. "Dammit, Anouk, I..."

Smoke curled about her until a massive six-foot-tall golden eagle stood before me. She spread her wings, leapt, and arrowed into the air. The sun glinted off that immense feathered body as she banked and turned east, transforming her into golden light.

Annoying? Yes. But I couldn't deny Anouk was glorious.

I ARRIVED BACK at Rae's, checked on the still unconscious James, and stepped into the shower. He'd awaken soon, he *would*, and he'd be himself, stoic and passionate, kind and protective, and focused as hell. Neddy would be okay, too. Now he napped on his pallet. Was he dreaming Pinky dreams or Neddy ones?

As I dried off, I spotted a small stack of folded clothes on the dresser in our room, ones I recognized. I put on underwear, jeans—soft and well-worn—a lime-green tank, and fresh socks. Across the desk chair back hung my leather jacket, an ineptly sewn rip in the arm from the bullet I'd taken months ago.

Which is when it penetrated my thick skull that those same clothes should be hanging in my closet at the den.

I slid down the pole to the living room and followed the low voices coming from the wraparound deck. Out the window, Alex and Melike sat talking between sips of what looked like piña coladas, including umbrellas, which was odd in the extreme. Rae—nowhere in sight—must have phoned them. Shit. I could imagine how ticked they were that I'd taken off with James. Their anger was justified. Time to suck it up.

Alex raised his eyes and zapped me with a wrath bright as new gold. He'd smelled me, of course. Melike must have, too, but I assumed she didn't care or was so furious she wouldn't look at me.

Peachy.

I stepped outside, and the blast of their fury almost made me stumble. Boy, were they pissed. Once I corralled my own zigzag emotions, I strode across the deck and reached for the clean glass that sat beside the pitcher. A hand snapped to my wrist.

"*I'll* do that," Alex said, voice a growl. "Why don't you take a seat?"

I plopped into the one remaining chair.

He handed me my drink, his cool fingers brushing mine.

"Thank you," I said. "How are Lulu and Ronan and the critters?"

"Oh, you remember them," Alex said.

"Sarcasm doesn't help, Alex," I said.

"They're worried sick, but that didn't seem to concern you when you took off with that prick."

I squeezed my eyes tight, opened them. "I had reasons for leaving that way."

His eyes burned. "Ones I can understand? Doubtful."

"I knew you'd take good care of my kids and critters. I miss them."

"You're coming back with us *now*."

My stomach clenched. "Not just yet. I can't."

He leaned closer, his face inches from mine. He spoke slowly, and with great deliberation. "You have a responsibility to Lulu and Ronan."

My frustration and guilt made for a nasty brew. "Yes, I do."

"It's that thing we saw asleep in your room, isn't it?" Melike spat disdain.

Did she mean Neddy or James? "Oh?"

"Why didn't you kill it?" she said.

Neddy? James? "Because… why would I?"

Her lips curled. "It's an abomination."

"He's not."

Melike raked a hand through her hair. "That grotesque thing killed our children."

Neddy. "That thing *is* your children."

The glass slipped from her hand and shattered.

"I'm sorry. I didn't mean it to come out that way. It's not Paul. That Pinky is Neddy."

Alex raised his brows. "Not anymore. And you didn't kill it because…?"

"Did Rae tell you what happened? How this whole kerfuffle came about?"

"Yes," Alex said. "He repeated what you'd told him about the survivalists, Rolf, your brother, the house in Big Sur."

Melike ran her hands up and down her thighs. I grasped her hands. "I'm sorry I startled you so." The look she cut me would curdle milk.

"Pinky-Neddy isn't like the other Pinkys," I said. "How so?" Alex said.

"Rolf… He was unhinged." I explained why he took the children…

and me. They knew how the first Pinkys were created from blood and DNA. "But Neddy is still Neddy. He wasn't killed, but transformed. And, no, I have no idea how they did any of this." Except I was sure my brother was involved. And Tatianne. I took a sip of my drink. It could've used more rum. A lot more.

I leaned back in the chair, waiting for the billion-dollar question.

"*They*?" Alex said.

I wanted to look away, forced myself to meet his eyes. "Rolf and my brother, Tommy. A powerful mage. Evil."

I explained about Tommy and Tatianne. "Just like The Union, Tommy wants control of the magic in the mundane realm." He'd said he imagined himself like Jeff Bezos, the creator of Amazon. "Tatianne is using him. She likes the status quo, with the worlds separate. Their unnatural obsessions are harming both worlds."

"I knew this," Alex said. "Not about your brother, but Tatianne."

"How powerful are they?" Melike said.

"I don't think Tommy is, not anymore. But Tatianne?" I shrugged. "I suspect very powerful."

Alex's face tightened. "Can we bring Neddy back?"

"I hope so," I said. "I plan to try."

"How?"

"You can't tell Rae," I said.

"Why not?" Melike said, voice whip furious.

"He doesn't want me to go, says it's too dangerous. But I have to try. Promise you won't tell him."

Alex gave me a sharp nod. "We'll go with you."

"*Oui*," Melike.

Their eyes brightened. Oh, how I'd love to have them with me. "I'm sorry, but you can't. I'm going to the magic realm. You told me that any pack member who entered would die."

He stiffened, frustration pouring off him. "What makes you think it won't kill... Neddy?"

"Because he has so much magic in him now, much more than when he was simply a shapeshifter. I believe he'll be okay."

"You 'believe'?"

A shadow in the door frame. James stood on the deck, an immense presence, chest bare, in a gray pair of sweats that rode low on his hips. I gasped, and those Pacific blue eyes found mine and remained. I rose and walked toward him, the redwood boards hot beneath my feet, the breeze cool on my skin, the rustle of leaves, a background song.

Words tumbled around my head, but I couldn't seem to get them past my lips as I breathed in James' honey and pine scent.

Inches away from James, I raised a hand and rested it on his chest. The pulse of his heart warmed me. "James?"

He wrapped his large hand around mine.

A joy so fierce my breath hitched. Tears blurred my vision, and I blinked fast to clear them.

His face never changed, his eyes cool and distant. Alien eyes. He lowered my hand to my side. "You recall I don't like being touched. We've completed our errand, so the agreement is off."

My heart cramped. "Don't you *want* to feel again?"

His eyes darkened, but he paused, as if troubled by my question.

I waited.

His lips finally parted. "I don't know."

I took that inside me, held it close, and I might be a fool, but hope budded. "I'm glad you're finally awake."

"A hard reset. It happened once before. This one took longer."

"How are you feeling?"

He nodded, but his eyes moved to the shapeshifters. "I'm leaving."

"What? Why?"

"I need to return to The Union and Taka to report about Rolf."

"You're going back there? How can you?"

"Where else would I go?"

Given shapeshifters exceptional hearing, I stood on tiptoe to whisper in his ear. "Come with me to the magic realm. Help me bring Neddy back to himself."

Animus slapped my back, virulent and savage. I pivoted.

Eyes aglow, Alex and Melike rose as one. "We can't let you go to The Union, Larrimer."

"Oh?" James said.

"You know about the den and about Clea," Alex said. "You know too much."

James nodded as if he was thinking on Alex's words. "What you say makes sense."

Both shapeshifters prowled closer. "We're sorry."

"I suspect not," James said.

I stared at Alex. "You can't—"

"We can," Melike said through gritted teeth.

"I will tell none of that," James said, in that monotone voice I so hated. "I go merely to report on Rolf. Taka has proven her duplicity one time too many. I may be their creature, but I am no fool. I intend to rejoin the five..." He paused, and I wondered if he felt something over the death of Rolf. "... the four, and lay before them options of whether to continue with The Union or strike off on our own. They are my brothers and sister. I will not abandon them."

He's always had incredible loyalty to his fellow "freaks," as he'd called them, a loyalty that seemingly no longer extended to me.

"Let him go," I said to Alex and Melike. "He'll keep our secrets."

"No." Alex lunged.

I was knocked onto my butt as all three blurred into a whirlwind.

Seconds later, James towered over me. He lifted me by my shoulders to stand. Alex and Melike lay on their backs, unbloodied, breathing, but unconscious.

"I removed the threat. They'll be fine."

I gripped his arm. "Please stay," I said.

He shook his head and blurred again.

Gone.

21

KNOCK, KNOCK

After thirty minutes, I finally convinced Alex and Melike I hadn't engineered James' escape.

When growls came from our bedroom, I realized Neddy was awake and unhappy. His fear reached me out here, too. It was time. I doubted he'd come outside on his own, so I went indoors, Melike and Alex following me. That was all it took for the seven-foot-tall, pink-and-furred Neddy to cower behind me, his breath hot on my shoulders. I opened my arms to Melike and Alex, a plea to show understanding, kindness. Melike's eyes widened, like she'd seen the bogeyman. Gray smoke curled around her sprinkled with motes of gold. She changed to wolf, looked to Alex. He growled, but nodded. She sprinted out the doors, across the deck, and over the railing, and ran.

Alex took a step toward us. "Neddy."

The boy shivered and made snuffling sounds that telegraphed his fear.

The alpha held out his hand, but Neddy didn't move from cowering behind me. Sadly, it didn't take an empath to feel Alex's waves of disgust.

The alpha was trying. But he wasn't cutting it.

"Would you wait for me on the deck, Alex?" When Alex was gone, I turned to face Neddy and placed my hands on each side of his muzzle. "We'll fix this. Promise." He crushed me to him, hiccoughs of growly-sobs coming from his throat. "We will."

Alex hands clenched the rail, white-knuckled. I walked over, and he whipped around and snapped at me, stopping a millimeter from my face.

"Whoa," I said. "You're scary."

"Sorry," he ground out, voice gruff with the wolf ascendant. He fisted a hand over his heart. "I couldn't feel his pack bond, Clea. Nothing. Man, how the hell can that be Neddy?" "It is." "I wanted to be accepting. I love that kid. But I felt nothing. You really think you can change him back?"

"I do." "Fuck, I hope you're right."

"I've got to go, Alex."

He ran his hand up and down my arm. "Wait a bit."

"Neddy and I have to be ready when the call comes, and I'm not."

He leaned forward, slid his hands around my shoulders and kissed me, just a brush of the lips. His desire threatened to drown me. His scent, that delicious sunshine and sea, brushed away cobwebs of fear and worry. If I succumbed to this relationship, I'd be cared for, loved, protected. Treated as a woman of worth. So easy to love and admire and want this man. To be touched, and to touch him in return. To offer him comfort and a surcease from his duties.

The James I loved was gone. What Rae and I had done had failed. I'd lost him. It was done. Over.

Alex kissed me again, deepened it, a delicious melding of our lips, our tongues. When we came up for air, he said, "I want you, Clea. All of you."

His hand on my breast. Tingles of need. He plucked and massaged, and my hunger bloomed.

Except when I closed my eyes, I saw a man bulkier than Alex, with raven-black hair and sea-blue eyes. I pushed away, stuttered in a breath. "I won't deny my body wants yours, Alex. My heart?" I shook my head. "I'm sorry. It's not mine to give away."

RAE HADN'T RETURNED, which was odd. Then again, *he* was odd.

An hour later, my backpack filled and awaiting the call, I explained to Neddy where we were going and what I was going to try to do to help him. His eyes gleamed with pleasure. "Cle-a, good." He was eager to go. I couldn't say the same for me. Anouk hadn't told me he'd die. Then again, she hadn't said he wouldn't. That thought terrified me.

Dave. Bernadette. And now James. All gone. I'd be damned if I'd lose Neddy, too.

"Time, Cle-a?" came the sibilant voice from a corner of the room.

I walked over to Neddy and took his hand. "Soon. We have to wait for the call. It will come. How about we go outside?"

He shook his massive head and drool flew. "Weee wait." I almost laughed at the glimmer of stubborn boy he'd been. The true Neddy was beginning to emerge. A seedling of hope. "Okay, we wait."

The breath I chuffed was angry. At myself. I had the guts to help Neddy, but I'd given up on James? Dave and my grandmother were dead. No return ticket from that trip. James still lived, breathed.

Bernadette's *Buck it up, cookie* chimed in my head. Hell, yeah. James might be gone, but he wasn't dead. And we weren't done.

AT NINE THAT NIGHT, I wondered if we'd ever get "the call." Alex and Melike were long gone and Rae was still MIA. I walked into the bathroom to take care of business, but when I reentered the bedroom, a shadow stalked me. Now what? Neddy chittered, and I slid my Bowie from my boot, rolled to the balls of my feet, and prepared to fight.

The shadow darkened, deepened, and the scents of licorice and menthol tickled my nose. I laughed.

"It's okay, Neddy."

In moments, a man materialized. Well, not a man, but a fae I'd met once before in the New Hampshire woods. As tall as James' 6'4", but far more slender, with a long face of ethereal perfection he could mask. But not today, although his board shorts, fitted tee, and high-top Jordans added new meaning to "idiosyncratic." Since I'd last seen him, he'd cut his yard-long, wheat-colored hair and wore it tied back into a neat ponytail

"Charlie." I stepped forward, arms raised for a hug.

He held up a hand. "Don't. I'm not all here yet."

Neddy walked over to me, still chittering.

"It's fine, Neddy," I said. "He's a friend."

"Done!" Charlie said, and the smile on his elegant face spoke of triumph. "Gods, the wards around this place are absurd." He tilted his head, and I noticed his small, pearlescent horns had grown about an inch since our last meeting. "You want to hug me, do you not?"

I shrugged. "Maybe."

He opened his arms, his silver eyes laughing.

I rested my cheek on his chest. "This feels good."

He stroked my hair. He had a thing for my dreads. "Yes, it does, Clea. You're not well."

I looked at him. "I'm fine."

"Your heart is not."

He got that one right. "Are you our transportation?"

"I am."

I stepped back. "Wait a minute. Your betrayal, working for The Union, won't the magic police be after you?"

He eyes sparkled. Literally sparkled. "Even before I met you, I made peace with our queen." His grin lit up his face. "Well, mostly. I should be fine."

"'Should' is not my favorite word." He'd animated James and the other five at the behest of The Union and Taka. The fae queen sounded incredibly forgiving, and I had trouble picturing the fae all sweetness and light. But what did I know? Still, something was off. Then again, Charlie wore big-boy pants.

"How are we going to do this?" I said.

"Simple. I'll hold your hand and, um, that thing's—"

"His name is Neddy."

"Neddy's hand. Click my heels together. And whoosh."

Neddy's chortle sounded more like a cough, but he was laughing, the first I'd heard. It delighted me.

"So you caught that *Wizard of Oz* reference, eh kid?" Charlie said. Neddy nodded.

"Maybe there is hope for this bizarre excursion," Charlie said.

"I thought you could no longer teleport others," I said.

"Anouk made some deals and juiced me up."

"Hence the longer horns?"

He nodded.

Had she told him about the splinter from the Chest of Stone?

Charlie extended his hands, when a whirling dervish twirled into the room.

Rae, in full woman mode, in five-inch heels, a pink Chanel floor-length gown, and a fall of auburn hair. She wagged her finger at me. "You are not going anywhere with that fairy and pink Gollum."

"Talk about pink. Look at you! And Neddy and I *are* going with Charlie."

She gripped my upper arms. "You're not ready."

"Bernadette said that to me about two billion times. She had the right. You don't."

She released me so fast, I stumbled back, and she minced over to Charlie. "And, you! How dare you enter my domain without permission?"

Charlie scratched his cheek as if contemplating great thoughts. "Oh, I don't know. I *felt* like it."

Neddy had taken up his new favorite position, cringing behind my back. I patted his arm. "It'll be okay."

"No, it won't." Rae began to wave her hands, glittery black motes swirling in her palms.

I touched her wrist. "Don't, Rae. Please."

The world shimmered, and the skinny streetwear salesman appeared, complete with snarky attitude. He poked me. "So now y'all being nice and stuff?"

"You've been good to me, taught me a lot. You think I want to do this? I don't. But Neddy deserves a chance."

"I can't come to help y'all over there."

I nodded. "You said that, and while I don't understand, I accept it."

He backed away from me shaking his head. "Y'all gonna die. Gonna die."

"I'll be with her," Charlie said.

Rae snorted. "Big pile a help that'll be, traitor."

Charlie flushed, but remained silent.

"I'm gonna be lookin' for another Key, sugah. You've been dickin' around instead a doin' your job." He gave me his back as he droned on and on about my shortcomings and acquiring another Key. "Y'all got one job, and you can't even..."

I placed Neddy's hand in Charlie's, took Charlie's other one.

"Even if you live, y'all gonna be screwed!" Rae's last words followed us into the ether.

FOR SOME REASON, I expected us to arrive in the magic world. Topanga was, after all, a thin space. Magic lived there. Made sense.

Not. We landed in the Bradbury Building's atrium, one of L.A.'s most iconic architectural landmarks and creepy as hell at night. The scenes from *Blade Runner* kept looping in my head as I peered up several stories through filigreed railings to the top floor.

The Bradbury had appeared in about a billion movies, TV shows, and music videos. The halls, which were open-air balconies, surrounded the atrium. Staircases zigzagged upward, while wrought-iron elevators stood at the ready. Victoriana at its finest.

I started to open my mouth, and Charlie shushed me. He leaned close and whispered, "It might be late, but L.A.P.D.'s internal affairs offices are on the second floor. Most likely someone's here. Marvel Comics have offices here, too, and you never know when those dreamers are working."

We took the pink marbled stairs to the third floor, and were so exposed by all that filigree I was sure someone would exit an office and see us. Charlie and I could fake it. Neddy? Not so much.

Charlie stopped on the top floor and tilted his head. I was supposed to be all magic and stuff, but I sensed nothing. Above, the glass roof canopied us. Charlie tugged us along until we reached one of the brick arches with an oak door inset about three feet into the brick.

"We have ten minutes—on the dot—or I lose my window. Don't wander. I'll be right back." Poof. Yeah, he could poof, too. So irritating.

A whine burst from Neddy.

"Hush. We can't make any noise."

"Gone."

I nodded. "He'll be back." No way was Charlie leaving us here. I hoped.

THEY SAY time flows like a river. If that was true, ours was stagnant as we waited for Charlie's return. Neddy jittered, while I checked the time, again. Five minutes gone. Where the hell was he?

Neddy undid his jeans' button.

"What are you doing?"

"Pee."

Seriously?

He unzipped his fly.

I gripped his hand. "No," I said with a hiss. "Come with me."

Earlier, I'd seen a bathroom around the corner. I tugged Neddy from the alcove. "Hurry."

"What the fuck are you doing here?" a voice boomed behind me.

I whirled, and Neddy chittered. This beefy middle-aged guy was all human and didn't scare the Pinky one bit. Neddy'd distended muzzle rose to show an impressive number of teeth.

We didn't have time for this. "We're... we're here for the audition."

The guy's head bobbed forward, like a bird's. "Audition?"

"Yes," I said, thoughts frantic. "For Marvel."

Neddy crouched, his elongated arms almost brushing the floor. He was getting ready to pounce. I just knew it. Was he seeing food?

Over my shoulder, I hissed, "Stop it, Neddy. "I turned back to the man. "My friend's in costume. He's a Method actor."

"Actors. Christ." The guy grunted, threw up his hands.

"We need a bathroom, like, right away. It's challenging when he's in full regalia."

He jerked his thumb toward the corner. "Right over there, kid. Boy, whatever character he's auditioning for is disgusting."

I gripped Neddy's wrist, and we raced.

WHILE I PEED, I checked my phone. Two minutes. *Damn.* We did a cursory wash-up and slammed out of the bathroom. "Run, Neddy. We're late."

We almost careened into Charlie, who paced in front of the archway. He slapped his hands on his hips when he spotted us.

"Humans need bathrooms," I said, a little breathless. "So do Pinkys."

A man stepped out of the alcove. My breath hitched.

"James," I said as we reached the two men. He was beautiful, dressed all in black. The handle of the katana strapped to his back poked up beyond his shoulder, and he wore about a gazillion knives.

His face was flat, his eyes, empty. "I pledged you protection. Perhaps you've forgotten."

"But you... I..." He'd come, and something inside me settled.

"Let's go," Charlie said. "We're almost out of time, so this will take even more energy. Keep still."

We all smooshed into the alcove, and I would have found it funny if I were in the mood.

I held Charlie's left hand, Neddy his right, while James gripped his shoulder, as if to stop the fae from escaping.

A smoky mist curled around us, and reality shimmered spectrum colors like funhouse mirrors. Charlie stepped forward, and we fell.

WE LANDED STANDING in bright daylight. Beside us, Caribbean-colored waves lapped an ocean shore rimmed with black sand. Emptiness for miles, dotted with rocky promontories and angular cypress trees, ones with red leaves. Did the magic world's geography mirrored the mundane's? Was this the shore of the Pacific in our world? Which would mean we'd traveled not only worlds, but distance, too.

Thinking about it made my head ache.

Neddy's pink-tinged skin had taken on a gray cast. I hoped he didn't barf. But other than that, he seemed fine. "How do you feel, Neddy?" His jaws opened, and he stabbed his clawed finger toward his mouth.

"Like you want to puke?"

He nodded.

"Other than that?"

"O-kay."

James and Charlie were okay, too, each standing sentinel beside me.

I sat on the soft sand, raked my fingers through the glittering black crystals.

The other three joined me, which was when I realized how easy it was for me to read them in this world. Neddy felt feral and frightened, Charlie, worried. James? Ever watchful and wary.

"What's wrong, Charlie?" I said.

He ran a finger back and forth across his chin. "Where are we? This isn't where I planned for us to emerge."

Perhaps we'd arrived here because the Chest of Stone's shard was calling me. "We'll find our way. I need to tell you something. We're here to see if I can change Neddy back to his natural form with my magic," I said. "But I also need to find something."

"What?" Charlie said, his voice diamond-hard.

"I can't say."

He huffed. "Nice of you to inform me of this. Where is it? How do we even know we're near it? Why can't you say what it is?"

"Because I promised secrecy." Anouk said I would know where to go. I held up my index finger and unraveled my senses. Power brushed me, gleeful and bright. "I believe it will draw me to it."

"How utterly special," he said, sounding perturbed. "You're aware I'll help you any way I can. I simply dislike not knowing our location."

"Can you get us back to the mundane world?"

"I can."

"So no worries. Which should come first? Neddy or my hunt?"

"Your hunt," James said, his granite voice definitive. "At present, he has teeth and claws far deadlier than a wolf's to protect him here. He's stronger and faster, too. We'll have to leave quickly if you succeed with Neddy. He'll most likely be afraid here in his human skin."

As was typical, James made sense. I tried not to think how Neddy's "normal" skin might kill him in the magic realm. "Okay, follow me."

"Why?" Charlie said.

"Because I think the thing is calling to me."

WE TOOK a narrow path that began where the cliffs met the sandy beach. An hour later, having traversed a slot flanked by two towering black rock walls, we spilled out onto a grassy patch. Before us, a small thatched cottage stood shaded by a windblown cypress on a rocky promontory high above the turquoise sea. Roses perfumed the air, yet none were in sight, and the fierce wind threatened to rip the scarf off my dreads.

The place had an oddly thick aura that sent tingles across my skin, like little spiders traversing a fleshy landscape.

Neddy started chittering and inched his way behind me.

I stepped forward and raised my fist to knock on the carnelian-red door. James stopped me with a hand on my arm. "Wait. I'll go."

I shook my head. "It's got to be me. You guys are right here, so it's all good."

Charlie's snort sounded very un-fae like. "Nothing about this is 'good.'" He shrugged.

I knocked.

The door cracked open, and the splinter's vibration hit me rock-slide hard. I staggered backward into James.

"We're leaving," Charlie said.

"She won't," James answered.

He was right.

Still in shadow, a slice of light revealed an aquiline nose with a sweet little hook on the end. The door widened enough for us to see the woman's face. She was beautiful, faintly Asian looking, with tousled brown locks and eyes the color of oranges. Rosy cheeked, tan skinned, her lips tilted into a smile.

"May I help you?" she said, her voice soft, yet assured.

I smiled back. "I think so. I've been sent here to retrieve something. I believe it's inside your home."

Her smile widened. "Do you?"

I nodded.

"Well then, come in." She widened the door, which now shielded her, and of course this felt all hinky. Nonetheless, I moved forward into the house.

The door slammed behind me. I lost all connection with the shard. Oh, hell.

I whirled.

Yup. We were alone. Just me and a creature with the body of a lion, the wings of a great bird, and high, bare breasts topped by that beautiful face. The Sphinx.

22

SCARY RUGS AND AWKWARD KNITTING

I blinked a couple times to make sure I was seeing what I really was seeing. "You're a Sphinx."

"Call me Sophy."

"For wisdom," I said.

She winked. "I'm going to eat you, you know."

I sighed. At least she didn't drool. "No, you're not."

She prowled past me to the cottage's interior, a large rock cavern with a ceiling of crystal stalactites sparkling like icicles. The curved wall on my left held arched bookcases filled with hundreds of books and an efficiency kitchen beyond, complete with a small oven, extra-large sink, and fridge. A really, really big fridge. *How did they power those things in the magic realm?* On the right side of the cavern was an expansive window which didn't exist when I'd stood outside the "cottage." Through the window, the woods opened into a rolling verdant valley, nothing like the seaside promontory where our group had stood. Made no sense. None.

In the center of the room sat a wooden trestle table and chairs, beyond which two massive Zebra-covered futons faced each other, a coffee table in between. Braziers burned rose-scented incense, and rugs were scattered across the stone floor. Not rugs, but skins of deer and zebra, antelope, and *human*.

Bile burned my throat. No upchucking in magic land. Check. Given my cold sweat, I unzipped my leather jacket.

The Sphinx padded across the room. I followed, careful not to step on the human skins. She led us to the two futons and crawled atop the one on the left. I took the one across from hers.

"You treat all your visitors this well?" I said.

She grinned, that lovely face alight with joy. "Of course."

I couldn't stop staring at the skinned redhead, whose long curls brushed the floor.

"Oh, *her*," Sophy said. "She was arrogant. Thought she knew everything. She was sadly mistaken."

"Trust *me,* I don't know everything. Anouk sent me here."

"Who?" She dipped her face into a large ewer filled with what looked like red wine. Sucking sounds ensued.

"Anouk? The shapeshifter Guardian."

She surfaced, her tongue licking the corners of her lips. "Never heard of her."

"Do you know why I'm here?"

She wiggled her lion's body, hunkering further down on the futon. "Of course. They all come here for the splinter. They don't leave."

"Who are they?"

She shrugged. "Fae, a few. Shifters, vampyres, mages, the ones who aren't smart enough to avoid me because of my rep. Oh, and mundanes. I've had several of those, too. Poor suckers."

"I see. So let's get on with it." I had no clue what "it" was, but her windup was way too slow for my liking.

"Thirsty?"

I wasn't stupid, was I? "Thank you, but no."

"Wine from Napa? Perrier? Mastiha?"

"No, but thanks."

She ruffled her feathers. "You're no fun. Here we go. A man

visiting the island of Ikaria comes upon three fishermen and they ask him this:

'What we caught, we threw away; what we didn't catch, we kept. What did we keep?'"

"Seriously? We're doing the whole riddle thing?"

"Of course. Nothing's free, girlie."

I was Bilbo Baggins. Or Oedipus. Oh, dear. Ikaria. Greek. Named after Icarus? Yeah, that worked. Greek riddles. Right in her bailiwick. I'd read some Sophocles. Plato. Homer. *Homer. What did we keep? What did we keep? What did we...*

"Lice!" I shouted.

"Ow. Hurt my ears. That was an easy one. Next up..."

"Do I have a choice in the goings-on here?"

Her smile said I was being absurd. She took a deep breath and continued. *"'Out of the eater came something to eat, and out of the strong came something sweet.'"*

Oh, shit. My eyes itched, and I rubbed them. I'd heard this one. I had.

"You should have taken a drink," she said in a sing-song voice. "Not much time. Yum. You look delicious. I could add some pommes frites."

I rested my head in my hands. The riddle wasn't Greek. I didn't know much Norse mythology. It sounded old. Biblical? David killed a lion. But he didn't do any riddles, did he? No, so why had I thought lion? Samson. Samson told a riddle about a lion. That still didn't *answer* the riddle.

"Time's almost up. I'll go get the mustard. It goes awfully well with mage. When I get back, chow time."

Nothing was coming to me. Not a damned thing. She bustled about another part of the cavern. She'd be back soon. I quieted my mind and let it unfurl. I tried to read her.

"Fat chance," she said, her words bouncing off the walls.

Calm. Soothing. Buzzing. Why was I hearing buzzing?

Bees! Bees make honey... in honeycombs. The dead lion Samson had killed.

Her breasts swayed as she carried a small bowl in her mouth. Must be tough with no hands.

I hoped I was right. I'd better be right.

She sat the bowl atop the table between us and clambered back onto the futon. Her orange eyes glittered. "Well?"

I took a huge breath and blurted out, "Bees making a honeycomb in the belly of a dead lion."

With a swipe of her paw, the mustard and wine bowls flew into the air.

I wiped my wine-soaked face with the hem of my t-shirt. "Your manners stink."

Her eyes narrowed. "I wouldn't if I were you, especially since you got the second riddle right and that's quite annoying. I'm planning on a good meal, remember. Maybe I'll delete the third riddle."

"You wouldn't dare," I said.

"I might."

"Look. I'm a mess, on a mission, and it matters for all of us, not just the mundane world."

She fluttered a wing. "I know. So?"

"You're with Tatianne!"

She gave me teeth. "Never with that bitch."

"Then why don't you just give me the splinter?"

Her face crimsoned. "Don't you think I would if I could? There are rules in our world. Many rules. I must ask riddles, complex ones. I have to be fair. It's not a matter of choice. There are no passes with the sphinx. Not allowed. Which is why I'm in charge of the shard."

"So you *must* ask me the third riddle."

She huffed. "All right, yes. This last one is the hardest. Get ready. No magical creature has yet to answer correctly.

"*One windy and rainy night, I'm out driving my car. I pass a bus stand and spot three people waiting for the bus. The first is an old shapeshifter, a bear, bleeding from a head wound and in dire need of medical attention. The second is my best pal, a centaur who's crying. The—*"

"There are *centaurs*?" I said.

"Yes. I'm not finished. *The third is the sphinx I'd loved since I was a child, who is now wobbly because one of his back legs is gone. It's very sad. By the way, my car is a two seater. It only fits one other creature."*

A smartass smile tilted her lips upward. *"So who do I help?"*

I threw up my hands. The whole thing was preposterous. A centaur, a bear, and a sphinx wouldn't even fit in the car. What a ridiculous mashup of magic and mundane.

"Tick tock."

"Oh, stop it and let me think."

As I understood it, no cars existed in the magic world. Perhaps this riddle had originated in the mundane one. The answer eluded me until... I pictured it with humans and grinned.

"What?" she said.

"Easy! The sphinx driving helps the old, injured bear into the passenger seat. She then gives her car keys to her buddy, the centaur, so he can drive the shapeshifter to the hospital. She stays behind to be with the three-legged sphinx who she's always loved. Well?"

A deer-in-the-headlights expression froze her face. "How did you... Ah, of course. Anouk told you the answer."

"You do know Anouk! And she didn't tell me the answer."

"She's a bud. So how did you figure it out?" She tapped a paw to her lips and smiled. "Anouk said mundanes have big, squishy hearts. You're a mage, true, but you were raised mundane. You went with your heart."

"Yes, I did."

Antsy as hell to get going, I asked her for the shard.

"Not yet."

"Look, Sophy, I have another task to complete before I leave this realm. If I stay too long, Tatianne will feel my—"

"No!" Sophy insisted I have a glass of wine to celebrate my victory.

New bowl of wine for her. A glass for me. I poured, sipped. "Delicious."

"My own grapes. Now, I have one more question for you."

Would I ever get the damned shard? Or was this like a P.S. riddle, where if I failed, she'd eat me?

Her brow furrowed and her lips thinned and whitened. She looked like she was in pain. Two tiny, frail hands appeared beneath her wings. And grew. In minutes, she possessed two human-like arms with fingernails painted a flashy turquoise.

She flexed her hands a couple times, then leaned over the side of the futon and retrieved a bag with handles. Out of the bag came the beginnings of a robin's-egg-blue triangular shawl dangling from knitting needles.

"*Knitting?*"

Her grin was wide, eyes brimming with smiles, she began to knit. "Love it."

"You have arms."

"Well, duh. How else could I knit?" She patted a wing. "With these?"

"No, um, I see your point." I took a hefty swig of wine.

"It hurts like a bitch to create them, which is why I only grow them in emergencies or to knit."

Watching a lion-eagle-braless sphinx with arms who was knitting made me long for my phone. Talk about a photo op. Would that even work in this realm?

"I really have to leave," I said.

"One second." She reached the middle of the row and paused. "Short rows. I have a terrible time with them. They're scary."

She wanted my help with her knitting. *Inconceivable!* I leaned forward and fingered the shawl. Cashmere, perhaps. Her stitches were beautiful, even, with good tension, but holes abounded where she'd tried, and failed, to make proper short rows. "Scooch over."

I took a seat beside her, her warmth seeping into me, and demonstrated how to make the wrap and turn, so no holes would appear in her short rows.

"Fantastical!" she said. "I've heard you have this thing called YouTube, where you can watch on a machine to see how things are done."

"Yup. You could have watched and leaned how to do short rows."

Which got me thinking. "When the worlds retwine, will all the magical creatures become part of the mundane world?"

"Oh, no," she said as she knit with blurring speed. "Many will stay where the magic's strongest. Although I can't really say. The worlds were last plaited together before my time. As you said, that creature Tatianne doesn't want this to happen. Nor do others. They all fear a loss of power. But I want it. It's natural and right. And I can learn all sorts of things from those YouTube videos."

Which was a chilling thought.

She reached inside her knitting bag and pulled a small Tiffany-colored box sized to hold a ring. "For you."

"Why couldn't I feel it?" I said.

"Because the lid was closed. I'd had it open to draw you here."

How special. Boy, was I an easy mark.

When I opened the lid, I sputtered out a laugh. The metal band, a dull charcoal, held a teensy-tiny red chip of what I presumed was the Chest of Stone. My laughter cut off when power burst inside my skull like Fourth of July fireworks. Ripples of that power skittered up and down my arms and torso and legs, much like the feathery feelings I got when I touched a magical object. Times a hundred. Whew. I closed the lid.

"No," Sophy said. "You must wear it."

"But the power—"

"You'll get used to it."

That's what *she* said. I hesitated, then plucked the ring from its box. It was too big for my ring finger, so I slid it down the index finger of my left hand. As I did so, the power reached up and *zonk*.

I came to with a skull-splitting headache. A wine glass hovered in front me. It smelled great. I snatched it from Sophy's hand and gulped. The headache softened to tolerable, but I was still woozy as hell.

I lay sprawled on the futon beside Sophy, who'd resumed her knitting. I raised my hand to admire the ring. "Holy shit!" My finger had turned the color of burnt charcoal.

"It'll turn back. I think. But it's interesting, don't you agree?"

"No, I don't." I tried to take the ring off. It didn't budge.

"You can't remove it," she said.

"Why not?" I tugged harder.

She shrugged. "Because."

"That's a helluva explanation."

Another shrug. "Until you reunite it with the chest you have no choice but to wear it."

"That just sucks."

She raised a front paw to her mouth and chewed a claw, like a nailbiting nervous kid. One of the oddest things I've ever seen, since those hands she'd created still clutched her knitting.

"Something bothering you?" I said.

The paw thumped to the futon. "Maybe."

"Well, out with it."

She whooshed out of breath. "Anouk said I wasn't to say anything. That it would only make you nervous and interfere with your hunt."

"Look, time's a-wasting. Either out with it or I'm gonzo."

I searched my jacket pockets for my leather mitts. At least when I tugged them on, the damned ring was covered. My blackened fingertip sticking out could only be described as disgusting.

"It'll kill you," Sophy said.

"*What* will kill me?"

She notched her head toward my hand. "The ring. The black will creep up your fingers, then to your wrist, and to your arm. You know, pretty much all of you. When it reaches your heart, you die."

I should've guessed. I should've frickin guessed. "How long?"

Her forehead wrinkled. "A month? Um, three weeks? Or two. It's really hard to say because of the formula. It depends on your power level, combined with your physical fortitude, combined with your will. But the good news is, none of it will hurt until you die." She smiled, wide and open, as if this were the best news *ever*.

Of course it was. I mean, it all sounded great. I was simply wearing an instrument of death on my finger and couldn't get it off.

"Will I die if I reunite the shard with the chest?"

"I don't *think* so."

I giggled.

"You're taking this very well. Far better than Anouk anticipated."

Tears ran down my face as my laughter boomed off the walls of her home. Lunacy.

She held up her knitting. "Which do you like better, the blue or this?" The color changed to a fiery red.

"The blue."

"Yes, I agree." Once the blue reappeared, she replaced her knitting in its bag, her arms retracted, and she slid off the futon to stand on the floor. I stood, too, and walked to the bookcase. When I brushed my fingers across the leather spines, magic sparked. I smiled and whirled on Sophy. "Do you have an, um, encyclopedia on the magic realm? One I could study?"

I'd been looking for a book on magic forever. Perhaps I'd learn how to cheat my death sentence if I didn't find the chest in time. Or maybe it'd be good bathroom literature.

She padded over, her muscled lion's body undulating with power. "Perhaps."

"Would you lend it to me? Please? Grrr. If I have to answer another riddle, I'll—"

"No." Her wink was evil. "But be careful what you ask for."

"I need a book that explains the different elements of the magic realms, the inhabitants, the creatures, its history, the chests, the rules, and—"

"Whoa there, girl!" Her wings fluttered. "That's about a thousand books. More."

I chuffed a breath. "You guys need a database."

Her eyes ran across the stacks. "There. *You* get it. Pain in the ass to grow my arms."

I followed her gaze to a row of books and reached for the immense one bound in blue.

"No, no, no. Two books to the right."

Two over sat a tome bound in purple leather, maybe four-by-four inches. I stood on tiptoe, plucked it from the shelf, and opened the cover.

Except it failed to budge. When I'd first tried to read the Story-book, the same thing had happened. "The key?"

A secretive, slow smile meandered across her lips. "That's you."

Geesh. "I mean the key to open the book."

"Ah." She nodded, all faux serious. "One and the same."

I didn't have time for this. "*Fine*." And, okay, my voice might have been a little sulky.

"Guard it well, Clea."

I vowed to do so and slid it into the zippered pocket of my jacket. "Thank you."

"You're most welcome."

She walked me to the door. Her lion's fur shimmered in the diffuse light, like a ripple of the finest velvet. Beautiful. "Can I pet you?"

"I would enjoy that."

Her coat was so soft it tickled. "Oh, it feels lovely. You weren't really going to eat me, were you?"

She tittered. "Yum. I was so looking forward to it."

When we reached the door, she said, "You do it. I'm not in the mood to open it with my mouth again."

I turned the knob and cracked the door.

"One more thing."

Dear *gods*! I paused, uttered a soft, "Yes?"

She frowned. "I'd watch my back, if I were you."

"Is this a warning? Or a threat?"

"Riddle me this, which do you think?"

She winked and shoved me out the door.

I STUMBLED out into the gloom of a pine-ish forest. Vivid periwinkle pine needles, black barked trunks, beneath which neon yellow and pink mosses grew. Clusters of mushrooms dotted the earth, a few with long, waving tentacles colored in a subdued fuchsia. Small flowers, too, laid out as if in a checkerboard pattern.

I'd obviously stepped into a vat of LSD.

As I walked on, mist curled across the ground, around my legs and up the tree trunks. From within the mist, the fronds of bright green ferns glowed like holiday lights, their tips reaching up through the fog to twine around the trees. Haunting and surreal.

"James! Charlie! Neddy!"

I listened, but no one answered.

23

OZ, WITH NO TOTO

I called to my companions again and again. No joy.

Alone, except for forest creatures that would probably scare the shit out of me if I saw them. I sensed no eyes on me, which I counted as a good thing.

I paused. Breathed deep. Found comfort in the magic licking my senses, the sensations pleasant and oddly comforting.

I walked in a widening spiral. The earth was smooth and spongy beneath my feet as I wove beneath the towering trees, the air dry and thin, as if I were at a higher elevation than when we'd arrived, the topography undulating and gentle. I caught no hint of the sea.

As I continued my spiral, the mist dissipated. Rocks of crystal, colored amethyst, peridot, and topaz dotted the ground. I reached for a purple one, heavy and thick with magic, stroked its smooth edges, temptation urging me to keep it. When it pulsed like the beat of a heart, I almost dropped it.

I laid it back down, wary of bringing something so magical to the mundane world.

"Holy shit!" I jumped backward.

A small humanoid head, maybe a foot off the ground, bald with ginormous pointy ears peeked around a tree trunk. Its eyes were huge and black, and when it blinked, its two lids met in the middle.

Hell if I knew how to react, so I waved. "Hi."

Its eyes widened, and it scampered off. Well, galloped, actually. While it had humanoid arms, its body was that of a perfectly proportioned tiny horse.

Wowsa.

With the worlds retwining, how much magic flora and fauna would appear in the mundane world? Yeah, that was something to contemplate later. Much later.

I jogged forever, at least it felt like that, lost as to how I should proceed. I would be stuck here without Charlie. I still had to help Neddy. And I definitely didn't want to encounter Tatianne.

When I climbed a small rise, a valley spread out below, with a pond that glistened purple in the pale light. To its right, a meadow with tall pink-tipped grasses undulated like the back of a sea serpent, while to its left, deep-green grasses covered the earth.

I'd never felt more like Dorothy in Oz. So where was my Tin Man? Gods, *James*. Ouch, way too close to home.

I half-stumbled down the craggy hill, and...

Eyes. I sensed eyes.

With a shudder, I scrambled the rest of the way down, aiming for the meadow which would give me cover.

At the meadow's edge, I scooted into the fronds and flattened. *Whoa*. Tatianne was not Sauron. And I was mixing my fantasies like metaphors.

Two legs, hairless and muscled and wearing a pair of Jordans appeared in front of me. *Charlie*. At last.

"Why are you lying on your belly amidst the shushgrass?" he said, offering me a hand up.

I jumped to my feet, peered around. "Because I felt a 'something.'"

He tapped a finger to his lips. "Ah, the ever-elusive 'something.'"

"I'm glad you found me. Where are Neddy and James?"

He notched his head.

They emerged from the same forest I'd just left and seeing them —a spring rain after a long drought. Neddy spotted me and raced forward on those fast, spindly legs, James striding behind him.

"Did you retrieve your *thing*?" Charlie said.

I didn't answer, just tucked my hands into my pockets. Neddy reached us, and he began to pet me.

I smiled. "I'm glad to see you, too, Neddy."

"I see you're in one piece," James said as he came up beside us.

"Luckily, if you consider almost getting eaten by a sphinx one piece."

James raised a singular eyebrow.

"Now that you guys have arrived, I'm a-okay. Let's go back into the forest. I feel exposed, and it's time to bring Neddy back to himself. I'm babbling. I think I'm a little drunk from being here." I turned to James. "Do you feel that way?"

He shook his head. "I don't—"

"Feel. I know."

"No," he said. "I do not feel disoriented."

Charlie's face turned solemn. "You realize using your magic thus will bring you to Tatianne's attention."

"We're here for Neddy. It's a risk I choose to take."

"It's a bad idea," Charlie said. "From how I understand the dynamics, it most likely will fail."

"What do you mean, 'the dynamics?'"

"All the magic realm rules that you've yet to understand."

Why was he balking now? "Look, we agreed to do this. You *agreed*."

He nodded. "I did. But my world is unsettled. As much as the mundane world is changing, our magic one is changing, too. Are you aware the top of a skyscraper landed here? It crushed an entire village."

The Sears Tower. "The village's people?"

"Dead."

"I'm sorry. What about those in the skyscraper?"

"Also dead."

Terrible. Yet my instinct says transforming Neddy-Pinky would work. "I won't leave without trying."

Two spots of color dotted his high cheekbones. "You do recall I'm your transportation, correct?"

I chuffed. "Obviously. But Neddy deserves a chance."

He leaned close, almost kissing my cheek, his breath warm, scent a sweet licorice. "Know that I've warned you. Whatever happens, remember that."

Well, that creeped me out. "I will."

"Where's the portal, Charlie?" James said. "We'll need fast exit."

He reached for one of my dreads, massaging it with his fingers. "Thinking."

"Don't." Larrimer pulled Charlie's hand away from my hair. "Best not to touch her."

Might this world be affecting James' emotional asphyxia?

The fae's chest expanded. They were of a height, but James' bulk was twice that of Charlie's. "And why shouldn't I touch her?" Charlie voice was both musical and deadly.

James paused. "I don't know."

Charlie laughed and slapped him on the back. "No, you don't, do you? All right. Let's go. Hang on to me. We're headed for the nearest portal. And keep your eyes closed."

"Why?" I said as I gripped his shoulder. Larrimer and Neddy did the same.

"Because you'll go blind."

I didn't believe that, but... As I closed my eyes, his laugh faded and reality iridesced—blues, purples, yellows—with that dizzying funhouse mirror smear.

We tumbled.

Naturally, I wanted to peek.

We arrived ass first, which hurt. I squinted open my eyes, and the black-sand desert that surrounded us bore no resemblance to our original arrival locale. Charlie hadn't taken us to that seaside, which bugged me.

I rose. We stood atop a hill, an endless black desert of sandy waves rolling before us. Directly below us lay a willow-treed oasis, the water a dark, murky navy with bioluminescent fronds waving like ostrich feathers beneath the surface. The trees' blue-green leaves fluttered in the wind, yet I detected no breeze in the chilly air.

An alluring lavender-ish scent tickled my nose, accompanied by hints of lemons and pears.

I wished I had time to explore this world, with its exotic plants and creatures and rules. It sung to my magic. Yet I felt apart from it, an alien intrusion it tolerated, but didn't welcome.

I brushed the sand off me, as did the others, except for Neddy, who didn't seem to mind it sticking to his drool-coated muzzle.

To my unfurled senses, we were alone, but Charlie's vibe had changed. Since he was magical, rather than mundane, I wasn't as skilled at reading him. I focused, felt his jagged edges, where before there had been none, and a pinpoint sharpness to his intent. Disturbing.

"Why here?" I kept my voice casual.

Charlie shrugged. "Why not?"

I cut my eyes to James, whose rigid jaw and tight lips sent a message of warning.

"Why not, indeed," I said lightly, remembering all too well Sophy's final "riddle."

I brushed my butt one final time. "Let's get started."

Growling from behind me. I whipped around. Neddy's huge black-clawed hands were extended toward me, his muzzled lips a snarl, his massive canines shining in the harsh sun.

In a blink, James was beside me.

"It's okay," I said to him.

"Doesn't look that way," James said.

"This is our purpose. Don't interfere." I walked toward Neddy. He shook, tremors shivering his body. My Basset Gracie did the same thing during thunderstorms.

"I don't know if it will hurt or not." I closed to within a foot from the shaking teen. Drool poured from his muzzle, and he kept swallowing. I placed my hand on his pink-fleshed shoulder. "I hope it won't hurt. Do you still want me to try?"

The snarling continued, as did his shivers.

"Neddy?" His green eyes, so full of terror. Would he shred me when I attempted to change him back? James and Charlie wouldn't be fast enough to help.

A tear leaked from one eye, his nod, hesitant. But it was still a nod.

He was so tall. To make things easier, I inched my arms around his pink and tufted waist and pulled him close. The sun beat down, the silence absolute, as if the creatures of this world paused to watch. The weight of James' and Charlie's stares pressed against me.

I brushed all sensation away and focused on Neddy. Only Neddy. I aimed to replicate what I'd done months ago when I'd pulled James from a killing fury. I'd taken his pain inside me and partially healed him. My gut said that would be the path to take with Neddy.

I rested my cheek against Neddy's chest, above his beating heart.

With all that I was, I projected outward, the pain and pleasure and power of my magic coursing through me as I pushed caring feelings and spirit toward Neddy. Simultaneously, I inhaled his terrible wrongness, pulling it to me, dragging it inside.

My spiral tattoo blazed and in a blinding rush, fireflies streamed from my fingertips, my palms, my wrist. They tornadoed around us, gaining power, leaching Neddy's otherness, drinking it in, deeper and deeper. I remained standing, though my knees threatened to buckle. Neddy's wrongness, splinters beneath fingernails, razors on palms...

I threaded my fingers at his waist so as not to inadvertently release him.

My fireflies knit together, again forming a Tree of Life pattern, thick trunked, sinuous branches that bowed and swayed, where meandering roots dug deep, then surged upward to meet the branches. Branches and roots met to weave Celtic knots. The fireflied tree mantled around us, blurred faster and faster.

Pain blinded me, bowed my back. Neddy's pain. Dizzy, I pulled the cyclone tighter as the golden fireflies swirled into a vortex. A scream bubbled up, my body shaking with its force, scalpels scything flesh, scoring bones. Release it. Release it. I must.

No.

The tempest intensified, malevolent, hungry, sucking me in, swallowing me, blinding me. My silent scream poured into the blackness.

And then I saw it, down in that spirit-deep place within the boy, his Pinkyness clinging to his Neddyness, a carnival candy of yellow and pink twisted into one. It writhed, screeched.

The blackness absorbed that, too. No light, no scent, no fireflies. Only pain. I pulled and tugged and squirmed between the Pinky essence and boy essence.

In a boil of flesh, a break of bone, a mouth of blood, the boy and the Pinky separated.

Stars exploded.

Consciousness flickered, brought on by the scents of honey and pine, a comforting balm. I breathed deep, noted the ache in my chest.

A body scan said I had all my fingers and toes, the rest of me ached like the Hulk had given me a good pummeling. When I cranked open my lids—which also hurt—I stared up at James Larrimer's chin. He needed a shave, his scruff turning to beard. My head lay in his lap, which was perfectly wonderful. It had been a long time since he'd cradled me.

"You're awake," he said, his eyes on the horizon.

"I am." I sounded like a frog.

He handed me an opened water bottle, and I drank.

"Neddy!" I panned my eyes, found Neddy on the sand, held by Charlie. From the tips of his toes to the cap of his tousled hair, he looked like the boy I'd met at the den.

Tears accompanied the moist laugh that bubbled up. "It worked."

"Yes," James said. "He hasn't awakened, but he's breathing normally." He looked down at me, eyes laser bright. "You did that for me once."

"I did." The emotionless words flayed me but he'd remembered. I raised an arm. "Help me up. We need to leave."

He pulled me to a stand, and I wobbled, but stood on my own aching feet. I walked to Neddy and Charlie, kneeled, and pressed a hand to the boy's cheek. Dampened with sweat, it was warm and soft and human.

"Neddy." I kneeled by the boy and pet him. "Wake up, Neddy."

Not a twitch.

I raised my eyes to the fae. "What do you think, Charlie?"

He stared down at the boy. "What you did. Incomparable."

I sighed. "Just a talent. Everyone's got something."

James kept silent, his eyes scanning the horizon.

A rippling in the air.

In the distance, the sound of bells, high and light. Charlie's face tightened, and my senses brushed against regret, sorrow, determination.

"I'm sorry." Charlie stood, the boy in his arms.

I leapt to my feet.

A distant screech, and I moved to face the oasis.

James turned, too, his stance battle ready.

A purple-green cloud roiled in the distance, too bright, its swift forward movement unnatural. Those odd willow leaves fluttered, and the wind increased until white caps foamed the oasis' dark water and the trees bowed in the gale.

"What have you done, Charlie?" I said.

He handed the boy to James, and with a flick of his wrist opened a murky portal maybe fifty yards away and glowing with sparks of light. "Take the boy back to the mundane."

James rumbled low in his throat.

"Run, James," I said. "Take Neddy home!"

"You won't be safe," he said.

"I'll be right behind you. Now run!"

James raced toward the portal carrying the boy, but he wasn't using his bullet speed. My aches and pains vanished as I ran after him, juiced by adrenaline.

She was coming. Tatianne. Tommy's Tanya.

Charlie had betrayed us.

A peal of laughter, and a woman at least eight feet tall towered over me. Her hair as blond as mine, long curls flying behind her like a cape, her head was crowned by foot-long, pearlescent horns that arched forward.

I skittered to a halt.

She emitted a golden glow, which sure didn't fit with the tight jeans and flowy blouse that clung to her as the wind whipped around her. A face too stunning to be real, round and sweet, with a pointed chin, full red lips, and eyes that tilted upward. And for some reason, bizarrely familiar.

Her lips pulled into a feral smile, revealing four-inch-long canines.

Beautiful. Terrible.

I took a step backward. I really didn't want to die at this monster's hands, but... no way could I reach James. She stood between us. James turned back, Neddy limp in his arms.

"Go!" I screamed. "Go!"

Tatianne's smile widened. She thought I'd spoken to her.

"You really think your words could make me *leave*?" she said. "You delicious girl, you."

James shook his head and lowered Neddy to the ground.

Tatianne flicked a hand, and they flew thirty yards, crashing into the black sand.

I widened my stance. "Wow, you're going for the big entrance thing. Been reading too much fan fiction, have you?"

Her eyes, marbles of black, narrowed. "You—"

"At a loss for words?" If I kept her busy, James and Neddy could escape through the portal where Tatianne was unable to follow.

From the corner of my eye, James got to a knee. He slung Neddy over his shoulder and drew his katana.

The sliver of the chest on my finger blazed in my head, and I shoved my hands into my jeans. Why didn't she sense it?

She held out an arm and curled her hand, as if summoning me.

"Come to me, little Key. Come to me. Join with me. Imagine how amazing we will be together."

Join with her, my ass. More like end me. Idiot tried to compel me with Voice. As with Anouk's attempt, her Voice didn't affect me. I waved, grinned. "Hi there. Sorry, but I'm not the joining kind."

She made a little moue of disappointment. "A shame. You were such a pretty baby."

What? Pretty baby?

Her eyes turned the color of congealed blood, and she repeated, "Come."

Movement to my right. Charlie. Why had he done this to us?

I took another step backward. *Let's see what happens if I walk away.*

The earth beneath me vanished.

I fell, hands scrabbling on the sides of the crevasse for purchase, for anything that would stop my fall into the void.

Fireflies shot from my fingers, tendrils of light wrapping around the huge roots of a willow. My descent stopped, and I bounced as if tethered to a rubber band, my fireflies the only thing holding death at bay.

Given my efforts with Neddy, my reserves were ebbing fast. And then I'd plunge.

Laughter from above, near hysterical.

A fiery ball from above shot downward. I wrenched on my firefly tether, slammed against the wall just as the fireball blazed past me.

Except it wasn't a ball. It was Charlie, *aflame.*

I hooked my arm around the exposed tree root.

Oh, Charlie.

And now, like in the movies, she'd snicker and walk away, and I'd be able to save myself.

James and Neddy. If Charlie died, they'd die, too, at least James would for sure. *No.* James would save them both.

Tatianne floated downward, a feather drifting on the current.

"I wonder if I could bite you," she said.

"Oh, do try."

She hovered. "I think not. Your Flow is impressive."

I stared into those black, black eyes, willing her to feel my loathing, my revulsion.

"Your Flow wilt dissipate," she said.

"'Wilt?' No one uses 'wilt' anymore."

She growled. "Too cheeky for your own good. But your arms will grow tired. You'll exhaust yourself. Then I will inhale your essence, and you will scream. And I will transform into The Key. Sadly, you will drop into the abyss."

How to stop her? I'd die before I'd let her absorb me.

She smiled, and her arm shot out.

I smiled, too. "Try it."

She fisted her hand, drew it back. Curious how not all her powers worked on me. I suspected I'd be dead before I solved that mystery.

"Why fry Charlie?" I said. "He was your ally."

Her brows raised. "He opened the portal so your compatriots could escape me."

I prayed James and Neddy had made it to the mundane. "I'm glad they did."

"But you shalt not."

24

THE DRIP OF TIME

Hours trickled by, Tatianne crouched atop the crevasse like a bloated spider. My arms wrapped around the willow root wearied, my fireflies dimmed.

I couldn't climb up. I'd tried. So I hung, as the otherworldly sun dipped lower on the horizon. Day became twilight, then night. Down here, the wind stilled, the only sounds the occasional fall of earth from the sides of the crevasse. I never heard them hit bottom.

Tatianne's glow softened, then extinguished, but I wasn't naïve enough to believe she'd left.

Exhaustion crept from my toes to my fingers. So very tired.

Did it matter when I let go? It was inevitable. The end result, the same. Even if Tatianne left, I was powerless, nearly out of Flow. With each passing second, I weakened further. My arms trembled.

Fear dried my throat. I wasn't sure if death was what scared me or the pain that led to it. Or the aftermath. Emptiness? Or would my empath senses feel the sorrow of those I'd left behind? The ones I'd failed. I tried to swallow. My mind circled back to James over and over. My breath hitched. I wish he'd held me one more time, looked at me with eyes that blazed with love. I pictured...

"How are you faring, little Clea?" came the sensual voice from above.

"Better than you will when I get my hands on you." It came out a husky croak.

"So feisty. So pathetic. I have a surprise for you. She's coming. An old friend."

I moistened my sandpaper throat. I coughed. "She couldn't be worse than you."

"Let's wait and see, shall we?"

The crevasse would claim me long before any monsters could.

Time dripped.

Fingers near numb slipped, inched me down the root. I leaned my head against the wall, loosening dirt. If I waited Tatianne out, she might get bored and leave. At least then, I could die in privacy.

Why was she allowing me to die? If I was dead, she couldn't suck out my essence. Ah, but she was still afraid to touch me. The shrew was waiting for my surrender. Expecting it.

Keep waiting, you creep.

A sound from beneath. Slithering. I lowered my hand, glowed it with my Flow.

There. Far below. Ooze, that pulsed with greenish-yellow light. It moulded into a woman's face, crown alight. I shuddered.

The Cardillo.

I'd thwarted her with the help of the wolves in the mundane world.

Snake-like tendrils differentiated and rose upward. Red cobra heads, black forked tongues flicking from poisonous mouths. Weaving up the crevasse wall.

My hand slipped, and I clenched the other one in a death-grip on root.

Greasy laughter tumbled downward. "Prepared to join with me, Clea?"

"The Cardillo's gotta be an improvement on you, asswipe."

A huge presence filled my mind, one both furious and hungry. Something I knew. Something that...

I peered down. The Cardillo, perhaps fifteen feet below my toes, snaky tendrils inching upward. Hissing.

The creature who'd brushed my mind drew closer and closer.

The sky. It came from the sky.

I looked up.

Limned by the light of the half moon, Tatianne lay on her belly, head resting on hands as she peered over the edge at me.

That presence filling my mind, so silent, so lethal. Yes, I'd tasted it before. When...

Something huge dived toward Tatianne, immense claws glittering in the moonglow.

Holy shit! My heart soared.

Sophy thudded onto Tatianne's back.

The monster screamed.

The Cardillo... I looked down. Gone!

Screams, shouts, and another voice, low, commanding. "Clea."

A voice from across the crevasse. I slitted my eyes, but saw nothing.

"Clea, tuck your head into your body."

James.

I obeyed and a thunk reverberated to my right. I jerked, my slick hold on the root, sliding.

"Hold on!" he said.

"Trying!"

A nearby thud shivered my bones.

The screams and caws and growls from above escalated.

Energies pummeled me, from above, from below.

"Grab the grapnel," James said.

Where the hell had he gotten that thing? I gathered my energy. With my right hand, I released the root and inched my hand toward the metal, felt the grapnel's curve beneath my fingers. When my fingers crawled up it, I tickled the twist of rope. My left arm shook, straining to keep my grip on the root.

"I can't come get you," he said. "Too heavy. You need to cross hand over hand."

Oh, swell. Where was Tarzan when I needed him?

Did I have the strength to do that across the chasm? I remembered that old movie where a girl was doing just that. She fell, screaming. Of course I recalled *that* movie. Now.

"Hurry," he said.

Yeah, yeah.

I was paralyzed, afraid to release the root, to trust the thing dug into the dirt wall, to trust my arms and hands.

I curled my one hand around the rope. Numb. I flexed again and again. Drove through the pins and needles. My hand curved around the fiber beneath it. Okay.

Now or...

I let go of the root, swung my other hand up and onto the rope. *Yes.*

Oh, shit. I dangled above the black maw that held the Cardillo and who knew what else. "There's no way I'll make it across this thing."

"Then tug the grapnel out," he said. "Swing over the crevasse. I've got the rope. You won't fall."

Easy for him to say.

I pulled. The earth held the grapnel tight in its grip. Think, think. I couldn't swing across one handed. No, I couldn't. But... I began to swing back and forth over the crevasse. Except I was parallel to the grapnel which wasn't good enough.

Hands and arms shaking with fatigue, I got my momentum going. Back and forth.

Growls, screeches, curses as the creatures above fought.

On a good backward swing, I swiveled my hips, lifted my legs high, thigh muscles burning, and kicked with all my might away from the cliff wall.

The grapnel released. *Yippee!* Except now I swung free and zoomed toward the opposing wall of earth. I'd go smoosh. Over the painful protest of my abs, I hugged my legs to my chest, the soles of my boots facing the fast-approaching earthen wall.

Hold on. Hold on. Hold...

Smack.

The jerk of hitting the crevasse side jarred my hands. My jaw tightened, I whimpered, but I clung to the damned rope, slid lower, gripped tighter. I crunched to a stop.

Drooping, I rested against the earthen wall.

A female shriek from above.

The rope started to rise, thankfully with me attached. My heart stuttered. A few more pulls, and I'd be out of the chasm. Free. Safe. Just a little longer.

Tatianne would notice us soon.

Time crawled in teensy increments as I rose. Burning behind my eyes. How much longer could I hold on?

"Hurry," I said through gritted teeth.

Above us, the growls and screeches reached a fevered pitch. The pair were at the crevasse edge, rolling, clawing, biting. They toppled.

My hands slipped.

The pair tumbled into me, and I swung wildly.

Claws bit into my thigh, around my waist. Tatianne's.

"Let me go, James. She'll bring us both down."

A flash of silver from above, and the hilt of a knife protruded from her eye. Blood sprayed, coating my face, my hands. She jerked, and one arm holding me fell. Sophie's weight dragged her down, and with Tatianne's claws sill deep in my right leg, she furrowed my thigh as Sophy dragged her downward. Daggers of pain scored my flesh. I squeezed my jaw, grunted with pain, tears streaming from my eyes. The sphinx bit and clawed her, trying to get her to release me, while Tatianne pulsed power bursts into Sophy.

Again, I slipped. And again. The grapnel's cold metal bit into my fingers. I squeezed tight.

Sophy screeched, Tatianne bellowed, and her claws tore from my leg. Blinding pain shot me toward blackness.

I bit my lip hard, tasted blood, didn't pass out, and I squeezed that metal tight.

I rose, higher and higher, shaking my head, grinding my teeth, desperate to stay conscious.

And then in one mighty tug, I flew upward. James' arms caught me, held me tight. He was standing. I was a boneless doll drowning in pain.

"Thanks for the lift," I said with a whisper.

He rose to his feet and ran.

THE PAIN IN MY LEG, unbearable. Yet I had to bear it, to fight for that consciousness that I so wished to escape. Wind brushed my cheek, and a dollop of sweat, James' sweat, landed on my lips. I licked, eager to take something, anything of him inside me.

If only the pain would stop.

"Don't die on me," he said through puffs of breath.

"Why do you care?"

Silence.

But something had changed, made him fetch Sophy, return for me. Duty? Honor? Compulsion?

I wanted to cast my senses, to feel him. Too weak.

My leg's agony forced me to close my eyes and grit my teeth. But a glow lit the inside of my lids. I cranked my eyes open.

The portal.

Closer, closer. My heart thudded. Almost there.

I spotted Neddy, who stood beside the portal, hands fisted, leaning forward.

"Why didn't he go through?" I said.

"He refused to leave."

"Charlie's not dead," I said.

He cut me a sharp look.

"He told me when he dies, so will you."

The wind whipped, sand a dervish. I craned my neck to look behind us and saw...

A haboob, an immense storm of dust the size of a tsunami, was headed for us.

"James!"

In front of the storm, glowing, jeans ripped, dripping blood, Tatianne. "Not so fast, James Larrimer."

He skidded to a stop and turned.

She walked closer, the haboob at her back keeping pace. "I know all about you, James Larrimer. My Tommy told me. Everything. Leave her, and I'll let you and the boy pass."

He whipped me around like a discus thrower and tossed me. "Catch her, Neddy. Take her through."

I thudded into Neddy and we tumbled to the sand as a shriek of fury burst my eardrums. Neddy scooped me up and leapt.

From behind us, a blinding flash of light, then a boom powered us into the beyond.

I AWAKENED TO BIRDS TRILLING. And pain so fierce I ground my teeth so I wouldn't cry out.

My other senses gradually came back online.

The smells of thyme and juniper surrounded me. The soothing hum of bees and the thrum of harmonic tones filled the room. A desultory breeze cooled my face. I reached for those sounds and scents, but the dissonant spikes of pain failed to retreat. I licked my parched lips and opened my eyes.

A wood roof arched above me and huge open-air windows lined the walls to the left and right of the large four-poster bed. The bed sat in the center of the octagon-shaped room. Out the windows, leaves fluttered.

I was at Rae's. Back in the mundane world. Alive.

I lifted the water glass on the bedside table and froze. Pain scored me like serrated steel. I remembered Tatianne's claws digging deep into my leg. I brushed back the sheet. Heavy gauze encased my leg up to my crotch.

"Y'all awake?" Rae stepped into the room. He wore a dotted swiss blouse and white shorts printed with four-leaf clovers. Given it was Rae, nothing odd about that. But his legs. For the first time, I saw him without jeans or a full-length skirt. Each lower leg bore a plastic-and-metal prosthetic from knee to foot. I forced myself not to flinch.

I mustn't have had my game face on, because he said, "Happened a long time ago."

"But why haven't I seen them until—"

He slapped a hand to his hip. "Now why you think?"

"I'm sorry. But your magic. You can fix..."

"No. I can't. And that's why I can't be spendin' lots of time in the magic world, either. They don't work so good there. How you feelin'?"

The subject was obviously closed. I pushed myself up, so I rested on my elbows. "Weird."

He chuckled. "Y'all weird, all right." He pointed to my leg. "Hurt much?"

I nodded.

"Drink this." He reached for some pills and the pitcher beside the bed.

"Wait." I sucked in a breath. "Neddy?"

He jerked his thumb. Neddy slept on a pallet in the corner of the bedroom. He looked all boy, and I smiled. "Still on the floor?"

"Kid wouldn't leave you. It's all I got."

I whispered, "He's good?"

He tapped an index finger to his temple. "In here, fine." Then his palm tapped his heart. "Not so good."

No surprise, that. "I'm so grateful my magic worked. Thank the gods he didn't die."

Rae's fingers tugged at his lower lip. "Yup. He's changed, more magic than shapeshifter."

"Shapeshifters *are* magic," I said.

"You know what I mean. He's different."

I didn't like the sound of that. "Help me scooch up, Rae."

He pulled, and I bent my good leg and pushed until I was sitting up, resting against a pile of fluffy pillows. Sweat beaded my face, and it took several seconds before the galloping pain receded.

"My leg?"

He dragged a chair over and sat beside me. "It'll heal."

I nodded, holding off on the one question I was afraid to ask. "How many days?"

"You've been here two. Found you and the kid before anyone else could. In the store hall. Bloody. Out of it. And a damned good sight to these old eyes."

I smiled. "Thank you."

He leaned closer, his eyes scrunched, and frowned. "That's some finger you got there, sugah."

Still wearing the ring, still black. Except the black seemed to be leaching onto my "screw you" finger at its base. Shit. "I think it'll go away once I—"

He shrugged. "You did good."

High praise from my snarky teacher.

"Wanna hear all about it," he said.

I wrapped my arms around my waist, screwed up my courage to ask. "Did James—"

"No. No sign of the creature."

I looked away, eyes squeezed tight.

Rae might not have seen James, but that didn't mean he was gone. No, it *didn't*.

DAYS PASSED. A blur. Each day, Rae's healing treatments eased the stiffness and pain of my leg a bit more. It was good of him to do this, to use his energies that way, especially since each healing wiped him out. When I'd thank him, he'd shush me and order me to keep exercising the leg. I obeyed, even did a few upper body ballet movements and stretches, although it hurt like a bitch.

My new best friend was books on tape while I knit. Using the needles and yarn I'd forced Rae to buy, I did up a beanie for Rae in bright crazy colors. He was inordinately pleased with the gift. Next for Lulu, a lacy pair of mitts in cotton-linen. I knit a new pair of black mitts for James, too, out of a hardy Merino to replace the mitt he'd lost. I was sure he'd been the one watching my practice sessions with Rae. I had to be ready for his return. Had to.

As often as I relived the magic realm's horrific events, I'd occasionally drift to that feeling of calm, of surcease that had brushed my senses in that strange forest. When the worlds fully retwined, would that sensation be diluted? Or more powerful? Alex visited, and Neddy hid. Neddy and I talked about his disappearing act, but I wouldn't force the boy to meet with his alpha. Fortunately, Alex agreed. We'd wait. Neddy's mom had been told he was safe, and she couldn't understand why he wouldn't see her, either. Alex smoothed things over with Svana, but it had to be hard on her.

One morning, I woke up to humming. Eyes closed, I listened while the person bounced around the room. Lulu. No one bounced like Lu. She hummed the lively French drinking song, *Chevaliers de la table ronde*, I'd taught her.

I was about to crank open my eyes, when she pulled a chair beside the bed, sat, and began to sing.

I adored the tune, and when that girl sang, the world stopped. With each note that glided out, soft and sweet, an unearthly resonance grew, enhancing the notes, the lightest of embellishments. It was her singing voice that had alerted me to her part-fae heritage. Only the fae possessed that extra, lyric layer to their song, an aural manifestation of their otherworldly essence.

O ye'll tak' the high road, and I'll tak' the low road,
And I'll be in Scotland afore ye,
But me and my true love will never meet again,
On the bonnie, bonnie banks o' Loch Lomond.

As Lulu sang, warmth filled me, and locked-away emotions geysered out. The last note hung like a hummingbird, airborne. I waited for it to fade, got myself under control. Finally, I sniffled and turned my head toward Lulu, noting as I did the tear-snotty mess on my pillow case. Gross. I smiled up at her. "Hey."

She smiled, too, but her lips wobbled and *her* eyes moistened. "Hey, yourself."

I pushed up to a sitting position, muscles protesting from yesterday's leg exercises. "Remember, Lu, there's no crying in baseball."

A watery giggle. "You should talk."

I swiped a tissue, blew my nose, and gave her a hard stare. "I *always* cry when you sing. What's your excuse, eh?"

She tucked her hands beneath her armpits. "Are you okay?"

"Lu." I opened my arms wide.

She hesitated, face mulish.

"Lulu, I'm fine. Healing."

She pounced, her taller body sprawling over mine, hugging me tight. "Promise?" she said, voice muffled by my shoulder.

"Promise. My leg still sucks, but it's getting better."

She sat up, taking care not to bonk my bad leg. Her eyes narrowed. "Rae's mean. He won't let me stay here with you."

I wondered why, but shrugged. "Rae's house. Rae's rules. I'll be home soon."

Ronan and Neddy entered through the deck sliders. Neddy carried a basketball, and sweat dampened both boys' t-shirts.

"Playing horse?" I said to them.

Neddy tossed the ball into the trash basket by his floor pallet and grinned. "Ronan's good. But I'm better."

Ronan punched Neddy's shoulder. "What do you expect, shifter?"

Neddy snorted.

I turned to Lulu, about to ask her and Ronan to stay for lunch. The words died in my throat. She was staring at Neddy, her face awash with rancor, eyes glittering. "Why don't you dial it back when playing with humans, Neddy?" She spat his name like an epithet.

Ronan jerked. "What's your problem? He offered. I declined."

She stood so abruptly the bed bounced. "Let's go, Ronan. I can't stand to be in the same room as him."

Ronan, a bear of a boy, stalked over to her with red-splashed cheeks and thinned lips. "I haven't visited with Clea yet."

Lulu tossed her head. "Too bad. You chose to play some stupid basketball game. I drove. I'm leaving." She stomped over to the table and scooped up her keys and backpack.

"Lulu," I said. "Stop it. What's the deal?"

She twisted to face me and jerked her head toward Neddy. "He gets to stay. But I don't? He gets your attention, but I don't? He gets—"

"Lu, it's complicated," I said. "He's been through hell, and you know that."

"All I know is..." She sighed. "I just... I have to go, Clea." She kissed my cheek. "I'll come back for another visit soon."

At the door, she peered back. "Coming or not, Ronan? I'm gone."

He slapped his hands on his hips. "One sec."

She nodded and slipped out the door.

Ronan came to my bedside, dropped to one knee and hugged me. He lowered his voice to a whisper. "She's a pain in the ass, but she's been having a hard time of it. She's jealous, but she'll get over it. She always does. Love you." He kissed the top of my head and followed Lulu.

After Ronan left, I hobbled to a white-faced Neddy and brushed a hand through his hair. "It okay. Not your fault, Neddy. Teenaged hormones. Lulu hormones. She misses me being at home."

He stared at the floor. "I miss being home, too."

25

MIA

Lulu tore up my heart. She was my kiddo and my responsibility. I loved her madly. I even understood her being jealous of Neddy. But without Rae's daily healing, it would be months before I fully recovered. So I stayed.

When Melike arrived on a rainy morning, and she bitched that I'd done this just to get out of our practices. I agreed with her, of course.

"*Zut!*" She said. "Those fingers are disgusting."

The black on my hand had risen to the knuckle of that second finger. It didn't hurt, but I found it deeply disturbing. Rae was baffled, too, and I purposefully didn't mention how the creeping black would kill me. "Yup. One of my gifts from the magic realm. Fancy, don't you think?"

Melike's smile didn't reach her eyes. "That's one way to put it."

All the while, when any visitors other than Ronan arrived, Neddy hid. We were working to alter that, but so far, no joy.

Although we talked often on the phone and texted, Lulu stayed away.

The mage became Nurse Rae. Swear to gods, one day she appeared in my room wearing an old-fashioned nurse's uniform with a high-peaked nurse's cap. I laughed. She frowned, berating me for being unappreciative, which made me laugh harder.

My leg healed slowly, the agony often waking me in the night. But I managed to muffle my groans so as not to awaken Rae or Neddy. I stopped taking any meds. They made me woozy.

I was a fast healer, but even with Rae's help, it took a week before I could handle crutches. Neddy was attentive and sweet, and he allowed me inside his mind and soul to use my abilities to soften his heart pain. He hadn't shifted, not once. I understood his fear, that he wasn't able to, so I tried to help with that, too.

With each passing day, *my* heart pain grew. Most days, it was a tight band around my chest, squeezing, suffocating. But James would return. He would. I called to him both in my mind and with speech, which was silly. I begged him to come home.

If he were dead, I didn't know where I'd find my next breath.

Rae wouldn't talk about the Chest of Stone, not until I was healed, he said. And so I waited.

Rae's aerie was beautiful inside and out. Situated by a burbling stream, shaded by tall trees—a place out of time. But I was sick and tired of being indoors, and even the expansive view didn't offer what I needed.

On a sunny morning filled with promise, two weeks after our return, I'd grown desperate for alone time. That band, that steel corset squeezed tighter each day James failed to return. I slipped a bottle of water, energy bars, and the small leather-bound book Sophy had loaned me into a lightweight backpack. I took my phone, too, wanting to do some research. I strapped one of my knives onto my good leg and then my gun and shoulder holster.

Since my return, I hadn't even attempted my fireflies, and though the land surrounding Rae's place was warded and safe, I wasn't going anywhere unarmed.

Alone in the large bedroom, I hobbled to the French doors, intending to do my research out of prying eyes, in particular those of the mage.

"Going outside," I hollered to no one in particular.

I reached for the door's handle, ignoring the leg pain and that beneath my arms from the stupid crutches.

"I'll come!"

Neddy varoomed into the room, long hair flying, wearing red Cons and ass-slung jeans that emulated Rae's. His eyes sparkled, one hand clutching an unopened can of Red Bull.

"Not today, Neddy," I said. "I'd like some alone time. And you know you're not allowed more than one can of Red Bull a day."

"My first can. Promise." His open features squinched into stubborn. "You don't need alone time. You're broody. That's what Rae calls it."

I sighed. "I know I am. I'll try to be better, but I want to be alone, outside."

His eyes widened. "You're not leaving, are you?"

"No!" I ran a hand across his hair, his curls bouncing with my fingers. "Not even a little."

He crossed his arms, his jaw rigid. "I don't believe you."

I tiptoed up, which killed my leg, and kissed his cheek. "I will never leave without telling you. Never."

"Okay, *fine*," he said, voice sulky.

"I promise."

Mouth thin, he stayed put as I went outdoors.

I sighed. I'd have a hidden watcher, for certain.

I CLIMBED the hill beside the house. Swing, step. Swing, step. Once I got to rougher terrain, I slowed. The last thing I needed was to re-injure myself.

I again saw Tatianne's claws ripping downward from thigh to ankle. The furrows had been wide and deep and gushed blood, and when Rae changed my bandages, I'd sometimes look away so as not to see my shredded flesh. But sometimes I peeked. The sight was so gross it reinforced why I never considered becoming a doctor or a nurse.

Now, they were inch-wide, jagged red gashes. Victory scars. Of a sort.

It was early, not yet ten, but I was sweating by the time I'd climbed the step-stoned hill to a large willow that grew beside the bubbly stream. I might inhabit a crazy world, but it was lovely here, serene and quiet.

Sitting with my leg and the crutches was always problematical, but I managed, making sure I was positioned on the flat rock so I could get vertical without too much effort. I awakened my iPhone and went to work.

The Getty. The Getty. The Getty. I'd become more certain that the Chest of Stone was at the Villa, hiding in plain sight.

What I'd sensed during my Villa visit had overwhelmed me, the sheer age and number of artifacts, intense. I'd been stalked by a watcher I now believed was Rolf and protected by another I was sure was James. If not for their ruckus, I might have found the chest that day.

My intense feelings when we drove by the Villa on our hunt for Rolf reinforced my certainty. My reaction had been virulent. Even with the urgency of our mission, I'd wanted James to turn into the museum's drive.

Memorizing the layout wasn't difficult. Designed to resemble a Roman villa, the museum was a rectangle surrounding a large open-air courtyard. The building enclosing the gardens was divided into precise themed rooms, such as Monsters and Minor Deities, Greco-Roman Egypt, Athletes and Competition. The chest could change shape, I understood that. But a naked statue without embellishment was just that unless it gave off vibes I'd recognize as the chest. So although the Getty housed some 44,000 artifacts, I should be able to swiftly eliminate many of them.

The damned crutches impeded me. I'd be off them tomorrow. Okay, maybe the next day, and then I'd be ready to hunt. Since working with Rae and my visit to Magicland—like Disneyland, but not as fun—my abilities had grown, my control of them improved. Plus I wore a splinter from the chest.

I held out my hand, with its blackened fingers—now two completely charcoal colored—and neon-green nails courtesy of Rae. I could barely see the Chest's fragment that nestled in the band that surrounded it.

Yup—I had everything I needed to find the chest except for one thing...

A tickle in my mind. My phone slipped from my fingers.

Gone. Nothing.

No, it was something.

As I spread my senses, I slipped my phone into my bag, tucked the food and water inside, too. Putting both crutches together, I used them as a brace to stand. Once they were fixed under my arms, I unholstered my gun and held it in my left hand, my right hand wrapped around my crutch.

Gun aimed straight ahead, I drew in a breath and focused. There, to my left, down the path. A hum, one shielded in a way I didn't trust.

Someone was trying to hide his or her essence from me.

Had Taka found me? *Oh, gods, disastrous.*

With the crutch tip, I shoved my backpack behind the tree, then hobbled behind the same tree. It wouldn't completely hide me, but it was good enough.

Whoever was approaching was a friend. Sure it was.

Except they were shielding. Doing a good job of it, too. Rae, Neddy, Alex, Melike—they'd *want* me to know they were approaching.

Maybe it wasn't human, but...

Tatianne?

My mouth dried.

No. She was unable enter the mundane realm.

Anouk? Knowing her, she'd poof in.

Birds hushed, as did the small sounds made by forest creatures. A predator approached. Animal?

Gods.

Wait. What was wrong with me? My fireflies would take care of business. For a moment, I'd forgotten them, not having used them since Tatianne. Rae was a pain in the ass, forbidding their use because they'd *allegedly* leech energy my body needed to heal. Crap.

What if I'd used it up helping Neddy and fighting to stay alive in the crevasse? Could I be tapped out?

I gripped the gun tighter, then consciously forced each muscle to relax. A too-tight grip would only make matters worse.

A predatory animal? Coyotes, eagles, foxes, even bobcats didn't scare me. Nor would they bother with me. A mountain lion, that was another story. I could use my gun, but I didn't *want* to harm one. I was in her territory, not mine.

Damn, but these crutches compromised me.

The hum's volume increased.

James!

Of course not. I'd sense him anywhere. Or would I if he were shielding?

I moistened my Sahara-dry lips.

A "someone" mundane? Mundanes didn't have strong shields and hadn't enough practice.

The Cardillo!

A groan of fear escaped me.

Stop.

I was being ridiculous, driving myself batso. This wasn't me. Fearful. Paranoid to the nth degree.

I inhaled a deep breath and slowly released it.

Just wait. And see.

A shapeshifter stepped around the bend in the path.

Reidar. Zach's dad, who'd lost his son to Rolf's insane experiments. I relaxed a fraction, but not completely. The hum continued, yet it wasn't coming from him, and Reidar's shields were tight as Tupperware.

"Reidar, hi! How are you?" I let my body and face droop to appear exhausted.

He took another step forward as if moving to hug me.

I held up a hand. "Much as I'd love a hug, everything still hurts." I gave him a wan smile.

He nodded. As always, his hair was pulled tight into a long braid that reached his waist. Aviators shielded his eyes against the bright noonday sun. He was a handsome man, his muscular torso clad in a grey t-shirt that moulded to his body, jeans hugging his strong thighs.

"Want to sit?" he said, giving me a smile. "You look tired."

I shook my head. "I've been out here for a while, sitting. My leg needs to stretch."

Except for Alex, Erick and Melike, when the other pack members had come to visit, they'd always come in groups. Alex insisted. He understood one-on-ones exhausted me. When I thought back on those visits, Reidar hadn't been among the wolves.

"What's up, Reidar?"

He shoved his hands into his pockets and took a step closer. I forced myself not to mirror him and back up.

"I wanted to thank you properly, for avenging our pups' deaths and bringing Neddy home."

I nodded. "I had lots of help, and some luck, too."

"Which is why this is so hard." His hands flashed, fully clawed, as he leapt.

My right palm shot up, and my fireflies streamed outward. Motes of yellow-white light surrounded me like a shield. His trajectory toward me was so powerful, he bounced off my Flow, landing five yards away, to lay supine on the path.

He sprang to his feet, stance aggressive.

"Don't!" I said. "You won't get far. I can contain you."

His sunglasses had fallen off, and his shields might still be up, but his eyes glowed with a combination of regret and anger.

Lightning fast, he came at me again.

I flowed my fireflies to cage him.

He screamed as they cycloned around him, encompassed him, swirling in the knotted-rib stitch pattern to trap him.

"No!" he barked. His shields fell as his clawed hand blurred to his chest. *It dug!*

"Reidar!"

Fast. So fast.

I clenched my hand, dissolving my fireflies.

Reidar lay at my feet, arm outstretched. Empty eyes stared skyward, one clawed hand curled deep inside his chest to pierce his heart. His face was a peaceful mask, though I'd swear I saw sorrow there, too. The ever-widening pool of blood surrounding him dampened his braid and reached for my purple-painted toes.

LONG MINUTES LATER, I sat slumped on my ass, injured leg straight, good leg bent, hands clasped around my knee, where I rested my cheek. I kept processing over and over what had just happened.

My horror and sorrow at Reidar's death was only matched by my confusion. What had compelled him to hurt me? Why would he kill himself? Why not try to escape? To reason with me? Something. Anything.

I felt the displacement of air when Rae poofed in front of me. "I've got this. Didn't want the boy to see."

I raised my face. "You were watching."

He nodded.

"I don't understand. Not at all. I'd wondered if the pack had a traitor, but Reidar was the dad of one of the dead children."

He cocked a hip. "Sugah, I expect The Union offered him something he couldn't refuse. Alex'll find out the truth of it."

After a slow exhale, I said, "So sad. So pointless. He had to know I wouldn't kill him. It reminds me of..."

"What?"

Blondie, The Master's minion, a stone-cold killer who'd also suicided rather than be taken. I told Rae about his death.

He pinched his lower lip as he listened, then nodded toward Reidar. "Your brother's handiwork?"

Tommy. A brother I'd loved with all my heart. A powerful mage with a twisted soul. My twin, who'd tried to destroy me. "It wouldn't surprise me."

"Your Flow be damned fine today."

I gestured a tip of the hat.

He lifted Reidar as if he weighed twenty pounds, not two-twenty. With a wave of his hand, his shiny black motes, *his* Flow, streamed out and erased the blood that covered the earth. "Y'all comin'?"

"In a minute."

The hits just kept on hitting, and I needed to process, needed to feel something other than empty and confused and lost.

In seconds Rae disappeared with his sad burden.

Telling myself to cut the tiny violins, I pushed to my feet and hobbled to retrieve my pack.

A shadow moved by the scrim of trees down below bordering the stream.

I whooshed out a tired breath.

I didn't even bother to hide. I leaned my weight on my right crutch. With my right, I pressed my palm outward to face this latest threat.

I could call Rae. Should call Rae. I didn't damned well *want* to call Rae.

The shadow stepped from the trees. I couldn't see him well, his face still in shade, but my breath hitched. I *felt* him.

But was it a lie?

Same height. Same breadth.

He leapt across the stream and strode up the rise toward me.

I began to shake.

James Larrimer stopped two feet away from me. Black cargoes, tan button down, Ray Bans—in a blink, I took it all in. Took *him* all in.

My shaking increased, and I tightened my grip on both crutch handles to stay vertical. Mouth dry, eyes burning, I absorbed the reality of him.

His cheekbones bladed his taut skin, the crosshatch of scars white against bronze. His ragged raven hair brushed his shoulders, a lock falling across his forehead. His strong arms lay relaxed against his sides, but the pulse at his neck beat a frantic tattoo.

He'd lost some weight, but not much.

Hope. I tamped it down. I'd hoped before.

We stared at each other for long minutes in a world gone quiet with too much emotion.

He raised his right hand and removed his Ray Bans.

Those Pacific blue eyes *burned*.

My mind failed to comprehend what my heart knew as truth. Home. He was *home*.

I licked my lips, swallowed, but my voice still came out as a croak. "I would hug you, but I'd fall on my ass, so I'll do this instead."

I leapt.

His arms shot out and seized me. Fiercely. Protectively. Possessively. "I will always catch you, my Clea."

Thought fled. The hard tension of his body. The sun-heat of his skin. His scents of honey and pine. I inhaled it all.

He opened his shields.

I drank him in. Our soul song, that incandescent harmonic melody we shared, one I hadn't heard in eons—it soared. Sweetness and love, power and strength, blending, rising, complementing. One. Tethered. Us.

I raised my hand to cup his face, needing to touch more of him. A blast of warmth and hunger and love washed over me as our song crescendoed.

His arms never faltered as he crushed me to him. He buried his face in my neck and breathed deeply.

Tears burned my eyes and became a whirlwind, a storm.

His hold tightened, and he lifted me off the ground. We soon sat braced against the willow, me in his lap, his arms a cradle, one hand stroking my hair over and over and over.

"Sssh," he whispered. "I'm here. I'm here."

I gripped his shirt with both hands. "Are you really?" I said with stuttered breaths.

He peered down at me, eyes laser bright. "I am."

"I... I can't seem to stop crying."

Mouth stern, he leaned in and whispered in my ear. "That's because you're such a girly girl."

I jerked. "I am not!"

The laughter in his eyes, those beautiful, beautiful eyes.

Tears still flowing, I grinned. "Button pushing already, James?" Like always. Like *him*.

I hugged him tighter, so tight I'd swear I'd break a lesser man.

He kissed my neck, my cheeks, my eyelids, my temples, the tip of my nose. Feathery kisses. Butterflies.

I stroked his chest, his shoulders, his face, his hair. Answered his kisses with my own.

Time, glorious time, spread before us.

"Hey!" came the shout. "You two lovebirds comin' down anytime soon?"

"Clea!" Neddy called "Larrimer!"

"We'll be there in a minute," Larrimer said, his rumble of voice hoarse.

"No, we won't," I said with a whisper.

His lips tipped into a smile that grew and grew. "You are as you always were, Clea."

I kissed those lips, and he answered me in full. Our tongues tangled, our teeth clashed. We ate each other up.

"Hurry!" Neddy said.

I sighed. After seven months, we'd earned more time. Our frenzy slowed to something softer, tugs, then sips, then a pause, with each of us breathing like marathon runners.

"I have a billion questions," I said.

His callused fingers traced my face. "We will have time."

"Time. Yeah. Except for those nags at the house." I smiled.

He set me on my feet, then scooped up my pack. He turned to me slow and sexy, body relaxed. Well, most of it relaxed.

"I have to know... How?" I said. "How did you return? I don't mean physically, but...?"

His face tightened. "It was all you. You scraped and sanded away much of the shell encasing my emotions. That's what it felt like each time you went at me with a kiss, a touch, a glance." He rubbed his thumb across my cheek. "When Tatianne shot her fire bolt, the casing shattered."

For long moments, I breathed him in. I was so damned glad. My leg buckled, and he caught me.

With bedroom eyes, hot, needing, he said, "I could carry you."

"You could." I looked at him, from his tousled hair to his broad chest to his huge erection. "But we'd never make it to the house."

He chuckled softly. "True."

"Plus, I need to walk, to move. I have too much energy inside me right now."

His head dipped, breath moist on my lips. "I have a fix for that."

I stole a kiss. When it finally ended, way too soon, I grinned. "Yeah, me, too."

His nipped my lower lip, then dove for my mouth, hands digging into my back, pressing my cleft against his hardness. We moved to the soft earth, him on his back, me sprawled atop him. His hips moved, as did mine. This here, this now was what mattered.

I broke the kiss to peer down at his beautiful face. "I missed you so much. All of you. Everything. So much."

His eyes flared, fierce, relentless.

"We gots company!" shouted Rae.

I went limp, though I couldn't say the same for him. "Damn."

In one fluid motion he rose and set us on our feet, his insane strength startling. I'd forgotten how our song fed not only us, but each other's abilities.

After he'd handed me my crutches, and I'd positioned them, he cupped my cheek. "Soon."

He'd said that in the dream, eons ago. Crap. No more tears.

With James' hand resting on the small of my back, I hobbled down the hill to the house.

A panicked thought. "You're not going back, are you? To The Union, I mean."

"No," he said, his honeyed-granite voice a growl.

I sighed as a weight vanished, comforted by his words, but even more by the song, that at rest wasn't a song, but rather a soothing purr—a fullness—living inside me.

"Neither will the remaining four return to The Union. We'll be shadows, their waking nightmares. We won't forget what they did to us, to Rolf. We won't forgive, either."

He stopped walking. Rae and Neddy waited on the treehouse's deck, our watchers' furious impatience prickling my skin.

James paused, his face stoic and jaw tight, eyes hot with anger. "What's wrong?"

"When I left you in New Hampshire," he said, "I made you a promise, one I failed to—"

"You didn't fail."

He pressed a finger to my lips. "My promise went unanswered."

So grim. He took his oath as a profound commitment. No one was harder on James Larrimer than himself.

I pressed a hand to his chest. "Oh, James, I don't blame—"

"They're here," shouted Rae, "and I'm coming up there to get you two! Don't make me do it."

Down below, a grim-faced Alex and Melike stood alone on the deck staring up at us.

26

CH... CH... CHANGES

We sat on the terrace, an uneasy truce hovering between the five of us, and talked of Reidar's betrayal and death. Angered and grieving, Alex affirmed that he would find answers, no matter how distasteful the process. During the discussion, James remained a silent, but a vibrant presence at my back. I knew what was coming next, and I dreaded it.

Alex notched his chin. "I'll speak with you alone, Clea." Not a request, but a command.

"All right," I said, fighting the snippy answer that begged for release. He understood how this would raise James' hackles.

Melike excused herself and vanished indoors. Rae followed. James leaned down and kissed me, gave my shoulder a squeeze, then gifted Alex with teeth. Lots of them. He left the deck, too.

We were alone. Across from me, the shade of an overhanging tree dappled Alex's face. He leaned back in his chair, crossed one leg to rest his ankle on the opposite knee. A deceptively relaxed pose that belied the fury he wasn't trying to hide. He opened his mouth and...

Rae bopped onto the deck, banana earrings bobbing, her red caftan swishing with the thrust of her lush hips. She carried a tray of glasses, a pitcher of lemonade and a dish holding three pills.

I frowned. "No pain kil—"

"Ibuprofen."

I downed them with the lemonade, which wasn't a great combo. The tension in the air spiked.

From the living room, the inferno that was James boiled onto the deck. A balm to my soul, an incendiary to Alex's.

Rae waved his goodbye. "Sorry to interrupt, ladies."

"No, you're not," I said.

He tossed me a wink.

Alex growled. I zipped my lips, so as not to laugh at Rae's antics, my nerves banked to manageable levels.

Gods, I didn't want to hurt this man. But I had. I did. I would.

"James is changed," I said to Alex.

"More like a costume he wears to deceive you. To give you everything you've been hoping for in order to get the chest."

I could tell him about our song, how it couldn't be faked. But that was private, ours. "He's whole again, feels emotion again. James isn't going back to The Union. In fact, he's vowed to fight them."

Claws sprang from his hands. "How can you be that naïve, Clea?"

If I hadn't felt his pain, I'd have gone at him for that one. But he was hurting. "This isn't about James or the chest. It's about us. And I'm so sorry, Alex. You're the most wonderful—"

"Cut the crap." He leaned forward.

When you care for someone, their pain matters. Easy for me to reach inside this man I'd hurt and smooth the edges, but that would be a violation. If James weren't in the picture, I could have fallen in love with him.

"I hurt you." I dared to wrap my fingers around the clawed one dug into the table. "But you knew my heart was engaged elsewhere. I'm sorry."

"Man, this is fucked up. He's an artificially constructed *thing*, Clea." His clawed hand closed on mine.

James' rage nearly knocked me sideways. "I love him."

A savage growl low in his throat. "You don't really mean that."

"I do. You're frustrated and hurt and angry." I squeezed Alex's hand, with its lethal claws that would never harm me. "He's my heart. I'm not sorry for that, only that I've caused you pain."

Long moments passed before his golden eyes no longer pulsed fury. The Alpha snapped into place. "Okay. I accept your apology. I will try to accept *him*." A wolfie smile. "But I haven't relinquished the field. Does he know how to play? I do."

Oh, hell. "But..."

He raised a hand, sans claws, and grinned. "My choice. I'm aware of the pitfalls."

He'd never seen James, the *real* James, in action.

Rae reappeared waving a small piece of white kerchief taped to the end of a straw.

"*Really*?" My laugh bubbled out.

Alex snorted. "Man, that's damned measly if you ask me."

Rae slapped her hands on her hips. "What? I spent hours on this DIY project."

Alex snorted. "You need to get a life, Rae."

"Hey, y'all, I've got a life. Problem is, y'all is in it."

The alpha checked his phone and his smile faded. "Where's Neddy?"

Rae pointed upward to the treehouse's third tier.

"Svana will be here in fifteen minutes," Alex said. "Neddy's mother is done waiting."

I PUT my foot on the stairs, but hesitated. James stood in the living room, so beautiful, so *present*. I couldn't stop staring, didn't want to lift the other foot. Bizarre how hard I found it to climb those stairs away from him. Having him out of sight jangled me. It wasn't like he was going anywhere, yet I was terrified that when I came back downstairs, he'd have vanished.

He closed the distance in two strides, ran a hand down my face, brushed his lips across mine. "I'll be right here."

"Promise."

"I vow."

I wound upward as I climbed the open-air stairs, crutches paired in my left hand, bannister supporting my right. Though shielded from the sun by the trees' leaves, sweat beaded my forehead by the time I reached the third level.

The trunk supported a giant oval of open space beneath an arched ceiling of mahogany boards. Huge rectangular windows interrupted the octagonal walls, pouring diffuse light into the room. Rae's space. A large desk, mounded with papers, a Mac laptop, and a sculpture of a sphinx hugged the wall to my left. A long sofa faced the massive bed directly across the room, and to my right a door I presumed led to a bathroom or closet.

I couldn't see Neddy, but I sensed him. Deep notes of fear and wariness, with high ones of longing. The lowest notes held anger, like an underground flow of lava that threatened to erupt.

I hobbled to the foot of the bed and turned to face Neddy, who sprawled on his back along the sofa's length. He stared at the ceiling, arms crossed tight above his head, muscles straining. I leaned my crutches against the bed and hoisted my butt onto the mattress.

"She's coming," he said.

"Yes. That wolfie hearing is pretty acute."

"I heard the stuff with you and Alex, too. My alpha's one cool dude, but I saw you with Larrimer. I get it." He licked a finger, held it up, and made a sizzling sound.

I chuckled. "How about you sit up and look at me? Not much fun talking to you this way."

He chuffed out a breath, but complied, resting his forearms on his thighs, fingers woven tight together. "I don't want to see her."

Not the wolves to hear, I leaned forward, waved him closer, and whispered, "You've been afraid to try to shift into your wolf form."

He jerked back, eyes wide.

"I know, Neddy. I understand." He didn't protest when I maneuvered off the bed to sit beside him. I spoke in whispers. "Answer me this—what's the worst thing that could happen?"

His teenaged shrug, so familiar, so real. An ache spread from my heart. Lulu. I missed her *so much*.

"Now that you've got your human form back, you're afraid you *can't* shift to wolf."

A tiny nod.

"You're also scared your mom won't want you anymore because of what happened to you." I slipped an arm around his shoulders. "And maybe of what Alex thinks of you?"

Another small nod.

"Never forget your bravery in helping me when Rolf held us captive. Never forget you always retained some of yourself while transformed. Never forget your courage in the magic realm."

His snapped me a look of surprise. "I wasn't brave."

"Of course you were. You went to the magic realm, knowing it might kill you. When Tatianne attacked, you could have run through the portal, but you refused. You caught me when James threw me to you, saving my life."

He rested his head on my shoulder. "But, Clea, I—"

"But nothing. You are Neddy, and no matter what shape you assume, you are a brave shapeshifter wolf." I pressed a hand to his heart. "You are a member of the Arctos pack and my good friend."

He peered up at me. "Am I? Your friend, I mean."

I hugged him. "Oh, yes, Neddy, a beloved friend. As I hope I'm yours."

He squeezed me tight. "Heck, yeah. You helped me so much when I was... different." His arms tightened

"Can't breathe, Neddy."

He loosened his grip, and I kissed his forehead.

He grumbled and pushed me away. "Hey, that's for babies."

Hard not to smile at his adorable blush. "Sorry."

"Aw, I guess it's okay. You're like a big sister, and they kiss their brothers. I guess."

My smile widened. "I like that, being your big sister."

We fist bumped, and Neddy grinned.

He stilled, and his eyes flashed with panic. "She's here."

I struggled when I started downstairs, a much more challenging project than climbing upward. Behind me, Neddy snorted, and he swooped me up, crutches and all, and pounded down the two flights.

Halfway there, Alex's potent command of "Sit!" from the first floor, had Neddy plopping us down on the steps.

"I don't think he meant you, Neddy."

He was breathing hard. "I can't help it. He's my alpha."

"Alex," I said in a normal voice knowing he'd hear me. "Release Neddy from sitting, or we'll never make it to the living room."

"Shit," came his voice from below. "Come, Neddy. At your own pace."

MELIKE, Alex, and Svana sat on one of the two semicircular couches that faced each other. She was average-sized, with wild, brown curly hair much like her son's.

Rae was somewhere nearby, but absent from our convo.

When Neddy carried me into the room, Svana bounced to her feet.

"Please sit, Svana," Alex repeated, a request, rather than a command.

She growled, full lips pulled back into a snarl, but did as asked.

Neddy focused on his mom. He set me down, and I hobbled to a seat beside James on the couch that faced the wolves. James slung an arm around me, and my clenched muscles relaxed.

The boy straightened his shoulders, eyes blazing. "Hi, Mom."

"Now?" Svana said.

Alex nodded.

She ran to Neddy, who backed up so fast he bounced into the wall.

Svana stopped, held her arms forward in supplication. "Neddy?"

Neddy's panicked eyes cut to mine.

I made a shooing motion, and he flowed into his mom's embrace.

I blinked, fighting those stupid tears. James lifted my palm to his lips, a profound comfort. I allowed the soft tears to flow and smiled up at him. The warmth and gentleness in those ever-watchful eyes undid me further.

Alex stood. "It's time." He notched his head at Melike, and she disappeared outside. He did the same to James, who didn't move.

I whispered in his ear. "It's fine. Really."

He nodded and offered me a hand up.

"Clea stays," Alex said.

James shot him a look hot enough to melt steel. Once he was outside, Alex moved the massive coffee table as if it were driftwood, then threw the faux fur rug aside.

"It's fake," came Rae's disembodied voice.

"Idiot," Alex said with a mutter. "You think I don't know that?" He waved Neddy over.

The boy's spike of fear was a gut punch.

Both Neddy and Svana swirled with so much emotion, prickles danced along my skin. I projected waves of calm, but they had little effect on the electric atmosphere.

Neddy strode toward his alpha, head erect, back straight. Svana moved forward in concert, but Alex halted her with a shake of his head.

The boy faced Alex. This was it. Alex shot me a knowing look, and I nodded.

When others' emotions ran this high, affecting them was a delicate thing, but for Neddy to change this one time, the participants needed a tranquil environment.

I closed my eyes and traveled deeper inside myself to where my magic lived. I pictured a gentle breeze wafting over a still lake, projected that soothing calm outward. I raised my lids and watched.

Alex and Neddy stood in the center of the room. Neddy's mouth tightened, but he managed to hold on to his alpha's eyes.

Alex placed squeezed the boy's shoulder and commanded, "*Change.*"

Neddy's flash of alarm, then smoke swirled around his feet, his ankles, his knees, his thighs. Sweat beaded his forehead and dampened his t-shirt. His eyes widened, grew panicked.

"I can't!" he said.

"You can." Alex took Neddy's right hand in his. "You will."

The smoke rose higher, swirling around the teen faster and faster, his eyes glowing a vibrant green. A spark of green light flickered inside the smoke, then brighter, as if Neddy were a miniature world with his own lightning storm.

Alex stepped back.

Just before the swirling vapor encompassed him, he reached for the tooth and claw that hung around his neck.

The teen disappeared in a gray-green smoky swirl.

The smoke bent, twisted, writhed. Neatsfoot oil and cherry scents burst in the room as the smoke assumed the shape of a four-legged wolf, then grew.

Neddy screamed.

I jerked to my feet. Svana raced forward.

The three of us encircled the boy whose smoke now dissipated to...

A seven-foot-tall Pinky stood before us.

"No," Svana whispered.

Between patches of shiny pink skin, gray-brown fur bristled his back, legs, arms, and immense black-clawed paws. His chest heaved, head hung low.

A terrible whine came from Neddy's throat.

The lupine jaw dripped strings of drool. He reached again for the claw and tooth around his neck and fisted his hand around it.

His pained leaf-green eyes found mine.

I moved closer, dropped my crutches, and wrapped my arms around him.

"It's okay, Neddy." I looked up at him. "Okay. You're Neddy. You're unique and powerful and amazing."

His tears pooled and fell, scoring those pink tufted cheeks. Teeth glistened, dripping saliva. I tightened my hold.

"You are now and for always, Neddy," I said. "A strong shifter with a brave heart."

He took a deep breath, howled, and tore out of my grasp. In seconds, he was outside. He disappeared into the forest.

Alex shifted to wolf and leapt after Neddy, with James blurring as he did the same.

Neddy's *mom*. I whipped around.

She stood trembling, arms wrapped around her middle.

I limped over and took her hand. "Svana, he's still Neddy. He really is."

She withdrew her hand. "I have to go."

"He desperately needs your acceptance."

"Acceptance?" she said.

I brushed her forearm. "C'mon. Let's sit down. I've spent a lot of time with Neddy in this form. He saved my life, Svana. He's good. He's Neddy."

"Acceptance," she repeated.

"Yes. When they bring him back, he'll need both your love and your acceptance."

She shook her head back and forth. "He's a monster."

I couldn't help but think of James. "Monster" was a catchall for things people didn't understand. "Neddy's not a monster. Just changed. You saw him as a boy, embraced him. Try to understand. None of this was his fault. He's a soldier who's come through the wars. He needs understanding, support."

"She's right, Svana." Melike's voice commanded Savana's attention.

"How can you say that?" Svana spat at Melike. "He's no longer wolf, but a creature. A warped, twisted thing."

Melike stiffened. "I would give anything, my entire world, to have my Paul back. I wouldn't care what he looked like. Just to hold him once again—anything."

Svana slipped her purse over her shoulder and walked toward the front door.

"Don't go," I said. "Be here for your son."

She faced the door, her head angled toward us. "I don't have Melike's strength. I never did." She shut the door quietly behind her.

"What can we do?" I said to Melike. Her face pale, she shrugged. "Nothing. She's right. She's weak. I loved my Paul. So. I will love Neddy in Svana's place. It won't be enough, but it will help."

She'd probably bite my head off, but I hugged her. Just had to do it. "I love him, too."

"*Merde!* Don't give me that touchy-feely crap."

But she hugged me back before shoving me away.

Four hours later, I watched what may have been the all-time strangest basketball. James, Neddy, and Rae played a game of horse. Neddy's had no trouble shifting back to boy, a small comfort, so Alex had left. It would be okay. It had to be okay.

After dinner, Neddy and Rae disappeared to Rae's "cave" upstairs. I showered, scrubbed, depilated, and pretty much everything else one could do to one's body to prepare for James coming to my bed. Finally.

Because of my bum leg, changing the sheets took forever, and I alerted Rae and Neddy that under no circumstances were we to be disturbed. I retrieved the bottle of James' favorite bourbon, Blanton's Original, that I'd been saving for months, a talisman for his return Melike had brought over from the den. I grinned. She knew me too well. I hummed a tune while I wiped the bottle free of dust. Cut crystal glasses, courtesy of Rae. A platter of cheese and fruit, also from Rae.

I looked longingly at the stone hearth. A fire would be perfect, but in the heat of L.A.'s fall, we'd roast.

Last, I donned the sinfully sexy nightie Melike had smuggled in and waited. And waited. And...

Ninety minutes later, I tossed aside the book keeping me company, doffed my nightie and donned pajama pants and a tee. I bagged the crutches and went a-stalking.

I searched the house and failed to find him. When I opened the glass door to the terrace, the brush of cooling air braced me.

Had he left?

I dialed down the panic. He must have gone outside after dinner.

He had to know I wanted him. Didn't he? My desperation bordered on maniacal. He had to sense how I longed to hold him, touch him, love him until we erased the past months and replaced them with new memories. Except...

Maybe *he* no longer wanted *me*.

27

STONE WALLS AND MOONLIGHT

B efore I walked outside, I pulled an umbrella from the closet for my cranky leg. I wobbled, but it was a helluva lot better than those damned crutches.

He wasn't on the terrace, and I stepped to the edge quiet as a cheetah. Which wouldn't make much of a difference, given his enhanced hearing. He'd suss me out long before I found him.

"James?" I said in a whisper only he would hear.

"Yes."

I followed the deep timbre of that one-syllable word, down the steps, over the sandy soil, and climbed for several minutes, then skittered down toward the stream. Until I banged my shin on a tree stump. "Fuck!"

No answering chuckle or offer of assistance.

The moon-bright night led me to a half-crumbled stone wall a couple of yards above the stream. James sat on a fragment of wall, iron-rod back broad and tight, facing away from me.

I rested a hand on his shoulder. "I missed you."

He said nothing.

I hitched my butt onto the wall, then swung my legs over so I sat beside him. The moonlight carved his profile into planes and angles, reminding me of that first night in New Hampshire. He'd thrown pebbles at my window, his face stony as the rock beneath us.

Tracks of his tears glinted in the light, silver blades of anguish. They meandered across those shards of cheekbones, over scars, to his proud chin, where they fell like bitter gems onto his weathered jeans.

My hand rose to cup his cheek. I dropped it.

He didn't want or need my sympathy. He needed something else from me. Now to figure out what.

The soft scent of mingled honey and pine evoked memories both harsh and sweet.

His fists rested on his thighs, and I slipped my arm through the crook of his elbow. I laid my cheek on his shoulder.

"Tell me?" I said.

Long minutes passed, neither of us looking at the other, but straight ahead to the hilly rise and beyond. We sat there long enough for his now-stoppered tears to dry.

"I killed, Clea. Again," he said.

He expected me to turn away. He'd never understood I loved him even more for the naked truths he shared. This moment, it could change everything. I rifled my brain for the right reply, the one that would soothe him, wouldn't push him deeper into his own personal abyss.

And nothing would be right. Nothing I could do or say would make any difference. It was all up to him.

So I stopped thinking and went with my heart. "I'm sorry. For them. For you."

In that emotionless voice I would never get used to, he began. "One woman I killed... Three months ago. She had two kids. Twins. Eight months old. A single mother. A lawyer building a case against The Union. After her, I kidnapped an old man Taka used as leverage against his son, a scientist. I executed him, too. There were others."

As much as I grieved for those he'd ended, I wanted to hold him, comfort him. I didn't. "You know what I'm going to say."

He nodded.

I wished he'd look at me, so he could read on my face all that I felt. Before I spoke, I made sure my voice was steady. "All right, I'll say it. You weren't responsible. They stole your emotions and your will, and you acted on their orders, not of your own volition. You were the weapon. *They* were the killers."

Silence. I wrapped my hand around his bicep. "Talk to me, James."

"I have culpability. When I left you, in my arrogance, I *knew* I was untouchable, that they couldn't reach me." His laugh was bitter. "I was fucking wrong."

"You made a mistake. Whoa. Shocker. That arrogance, that confidence, has saved your life, saved *mine*, many times."

He ran a fist up and down his thigh. "I see them. A movie. Fucking again and again."

He was withdrawing from the world, from me, seeing himself as that monster again. The Freak. How much more could they twist him until his soul died? He was such a *good* man. A strong man. Kind. Gods, he was so kind.

The image of Rolf pulling the breathing tube from his throat blazed through my mind. Hell no, not my James. Never my James.

I eased closer. "Don't fight it. Accept it. You'll remember them. They won't be erased. And you will avenge them."

"It won't be enough."

"You stubborn man! You're good and kind and courageous—that's the true you."

"Bullshit."

"Dammit, Dragon Dude, I love you! Would I love a load of bullshit?"

A lip twitch.

I slid from the stone wall, making sure to land on my good leg, and faced him. He might refuse to look at me, but he sure as hell would feel me. I poured love and desire and need at him in waves. A softening. Maybe. Just a little. So I poked his chest with my finger. "You listen to me, mister. I've been horribly alone without you."

He tucked his chin and peered down at me, his eyes black pools of darkness.

"See," I continued. "I've had good people around me, which was pretty nice. But they weren't *you*. Because you live inside me. Get it? You once said I made your life bearable. Well, you make *my* life bearable. So buck it up."

I held my breath. I was scared. Had I pushed too hard? Said the wrong things? Would he turn away? Vanish? Embrace that long goodnight?

He hopped off the stone wall and faced me. I tilted my head, questioning. Gods knew what was coming next. He held out his hand. My breath hitched.

The hand I placed in his trembled. His warm fingers curled around mine, eyes locked on me. His brief smile was half joyful, half poignant as he tugged me closer. His right arm slid around my waist.

My head, tilted up. His, bent down. Us, tethered to each other.

He moved, swayed into dance steps slow and lithe, just like that evening at the policeman's ball. I pressed my cheek to his chest. His kiss to the top of my head was lighter than air, stronger than steel.

My throat was thick, my heart painfully tight and full.

We danced beneath the moonlight, silent but for the rustle of nocturnal creatures and the hush of wind in the trees.

"Remember the last time we danced?" he said.

"I do." I could barely get out the words.

"Clea."

His whispered voice shivered through me. I squeezed him tight, my tears cleansing me.

"I dreamed," he said. "I dreamed of this, of you. In my dreams, I felt so fucking much I wanted to take a knife to my gut. Every night. And when I opened my eyes each morning, it was gone. I was empty."

The dreams I'd had just before he returned. I'd suspected. Now I understood I'd been living *his* reality.

I pressed my hand above his heart, which beat strong and sure. My eyes moistened. No more tears, dammit. "I'm sorry."

"I remembered. My mind *knew*. Sensed the *absence* of feeling."

My fingertips brushed his lips, my eyes ensnaring his. "Not anymore. Never again."

He dipped his head, took my lips, kissed me deep and long and slow. It burned so damned good.

When we surfaced for air, I was desperate for naked, fast and furious, and hot and sweaty. The whole magilla. "Tell me what you want, big guy."

His grin flashed. "A ham salad sandwich with Worcestershire sauce."

Definitely not what *I'd* imagined. "You hate those."

"Not when you make them, baby." He winked. "I want you cradled on my lap, content and happy. I want to lick the bourbon you've sipped off your lips."

Need seared me.

"I want to see your face, that goddammed beautiful face, aflame with temper when you're pissed off at me," he said.

"Well, that shouldn't be hard."

His grin widened. "True."

He lifted me, bodies pressed together, as our hauntingly beautiful song rose between us.

"What I really want to do," he said, "is bury my cock in you deep and watch you come."

Me, too, I almost screeched.

"And lick you 'til you scream."

Oh, geesh. My mouth dried, my core throbbed, my folds liquid, swollen, aching.

He carried me to a mossy bank beneath the old gnarled willow draping the stream and set me gently on my feet. Shirt doffed, he spread it on the moss, then lay me down. I pulled him with me, and he settled his weight atop me, my arms tight around his naked torso, hand spread across his back.

Where I traced the raised ridges of scars, new ones. I flinched.

"You okay?" he said.

The past. That was the past. *Never again.* No one would hurt my James ever again. "Better than okay."

He raised his head, eyes sparking, but face so serious. "If I take you, I won't ever let go. Not ever again. Can you handle that?"

"Sounds perfect."

His lips twitched. "It does, doesn't it? You've got too many clothes on."

"Bossy." I grinned. "Gonna do something about it, Dragon Dude?"

"Perhaps." My Mr. Stoic outside, but inside his laughter and delight filled me up. His big, calloused hand grazed my face. "I'm admiring you, Clea."

"Well, hurry up."

He smiled, slow and easy. "Always hot off the mark."

"You bet I am." I slid my hands beneath his belted jeans and cupped his ass, squeezed.

His lips exploded against mine, fierce and possessive and wild.

My hips jerked, and I widened my legs to nestle his hardness where I ached for his touch.

He broke the kiss. "Jesus, woman. Too many fucking clothes."

A blur, and he was standing before me naked. Moonlight glazed that gorgeous torso, the vee of his hips, his erection, thick and proud.

Gods. "Wait."

That one eyebrow arched.

Damn, I loved when he did that. "And now *I* need to look, to admire, to touch."

I moved to my knees and stood.

He crossed his arms, biceps flexing, as I drank my fill of his beauty. His naked body was tall and broad-shouldered. I drank in his scarred chest with its light dusting of black hair, his hips, and those gorgeous thighs. So bitable. "You are beautiful."

"Jesus, baby." Chin lowered, eyes narrowed. "This isn't only *your* feast."

"For now it is." I brushed my palms across his face, his cheek-bones, his lips. Our song, its double-helix twining, twisting, twirling around us. I closed my eyes, scraped the bristle of his scruff, the soft-ness of his neck where it joined his torso. I splayed my fingers across his smooth shoulders bunching with muscle. My body vibrated like a tuning fork. Torture. How long could I keep this up? Didn't matter. My fingers searched, found his lightly furred pectorals, his nipples. When a ridge of scar stopped me, I leaned forward and kissed it.

"*Christ!*" he bit out.

I meandered lower, to the muscled vee.

Hands caught my wrists.

My eyes flew open. His face, tightened with need, melted me. But I managed to quip, "I want, James."

He tugged us down to our knees, pulled my shirt over my head, tossed it. His hands trembling, he smoothed them down my arms, then cupped my breasts.

Those calloused-rough, hot hands roved across my breasts, insistent. I arched. A stuttered sob. "It's been so long." I wove my fingers through his thick raven hair, pulled him to me for a kiss.

His thumb flicked my nipple, and I whimpered. Then he slid his palms across my ribs, down my waist, and his fingers meandered inside my pants, over flesh that ached so bad. For him, always for him.

"We're going to go slow," he said, as he tugged off my pants.

Then one finger found my clit and strummed.

My nails dug into his back. "Inside me. I want you inside me *now*."

His thumb stroked my nub while his fingers feathered my opening, exactly where I needed his cock so desperately.

If he didn't hurry, I'd explode, I just knew it, and he *had* to be in me when that happened. I slipped a hand between us and found his pulsing cock. I squeezed.

"Shit!"

His bark of pleasure, another kind of music. I laughed, and our song heightened our desire, our need, our pleasure.

He lay me down and covered me with his body, wrapped his hand around one swollen breast, his other guiding his cock to my entrance. The pressure of that hot tip pushing against me—I thrust upward.

He pumped forward spearing me in one smooth, blazing stroke.

His lips muffled my cry, one arm cradling my shoulders, the other hand holding my hips in place.

He stilled. My eyes snapped open, and I'd swear his were sapphire flames. "You," he said, his voice gravel. "You. Not that witchy bitch, not the explosion, *you* brought me home, baby." A devil of a smile spread across his face. "Now you're stuck with me."

I went to speak, and he stole my lips, his tongue piercing my mouth and mine answering. I held him tight, and he moved. Oh, *gods* how he moved.

Sinuous and slow, so slow. I squirmed and pushed, trying to get him to go faster—and the laughter I heard came from inside him as he spiraled us higher. His thrusts deepened, quickening, pounding, taking me, possessing me, *giving* to me, his hips changing angle just enough so my clit, oh, *gods*...

Our song crescendoed, and I shattered, fireworks on a velvet star sky.

My rhythmic waves of orgasm drove me higher still as James thrust again and again until he froze, body granite hard. A groan escaped him. Echoes of my orgasm squeezed his cock as he pulsed inside me.

We were home.

Our bodies, liquid, the beautiful hot and heavy weight of him resting atop me, his face buried in the crook of my neck, his chest a bellows, his breaths, music.

He lifted his head and shook it like a dog, spraying droplets of sweat from his hair and face.

"Good workout," I said.

"Mmmmm."

Inside me, his cock twitched, hardened. There was something to be said for nanotechnology. I snorted and ran my hands up and down his delicious sweat-slicked back. "Let's get even more sweaty."

His rasped chuckle made me clench. Gods, he cranked me higher with a mere chuckle. His smiles, his laughter, his joy melted me.

Feather kisses dappled my mouth, my temple, my cheeks. "Let's."

"Y'all scarin' the wildlife!" came the shout from the house. Rae. "Are you two done?"

James smiled down at me. "Not by half."

I'm not sure how we made it to the bed after our shower, James' kisses drugging my universe. I poured his Blanton's into two glasses, while he retrieved a tray of chocolate-covered strawberries from the mini-fridge.

He raised a single eyebrow as he set it on the bedside table. "Been practicing your cooking skills?"

I handed him his bourbon. "Yeah, like that's gonna happen. Never."

He unfolded the paper on the tray, read, and handed to me.

Rae and I made these for you and Larrimer.

Don't be so loud! Neddy

Giddy with laughter, cheeks blazing in embarrassment, and maybe a few sniffles from the sweetness of it all, I plucked a strawberry from the tray and waved it in front of him. Bourbon in hand, he slid beside me onto the bed and took a giant bite.

"Greedy," I said.

Eyes fused to mine. "Very."

I put down my glass, did the same for his, and tossed the strawberry remains. I slid my arms around his neck. "Me, too."

With a tug of my waist he pulled me closer, studied me as if imprinting each inch of my face on his mind. "Open to me."

My forehead crinkled. "I am."

He shook his head, and I had to—just had to—rake that silken hair, each part of him, a precious gift.

"All of it," he said. "Open your shields."

I lowered my eyes. I didn't want that, would hate for him to learn what Rolf had done to me. "Not tonight, okay? Plenty of time tomorrow to muck around in that... mess."

He pulled me tight, his erection fierce between us, and cradled my face between his palms. "Listen to me, baby. I don't just want the sweet, but all of you."

For once, I didn't want to talk. So I smashed my passion into my kiss.

It proved irresistible to James Larrimer.

I AWOKE with James staring down at me. The singular intensity of his gaze undid me, and I burrowed my face into his chest, arms clamped around his waist.

"Don't hide, pretty Clea."

"How can I not when you look at me like that?" came my muffled reply.

Kisses, so many kisses, across my cheek, my shoulder.

"Plus, I have morning breath," I said. "I can smell you've already brushed your teeth. Not fair."

His laugh, a sweet vibration against my cheek. "I never play fair. How's your leg?"

With caution learned from pain, I moved it. An ache, dulled by time, Rae's healing, and James. "Not bad, actually." No, it was other parts of my body that reminded me our sexual gymnastics had played havoc on my muscles.

"Sore?" he said.

I was tempted to lie, but... "A little."

He kissed my forehead and withdrew.

"See?" I said. "That's exactly what I was trying to avoid. Honesty isn't all it's cracked up to be. About certain things, at least." I sighed. "Well, we've got a plan to devise, so I guess we should get to it." *Would we ever have time?*

He took me in a long, drugging kiss. When he finally released me, he said, "We will."

"Will what?"

His hand stroked my dreads, fisted them. "We will have time."

I should be joyous. Instead the tired, cranky me asserted itself. "I have four chests to find. Tatianne to defeat. Tommy. A world—"

"We're together, baby. We've got this."

I nodded, but wasn't convinced.

He cupped my chin, raised my face. "This isn't you, oh great and indomitable mage, but exhaustion and overload talking."

I snorted, but for some stupid reason, stuttered a sob. I ran light fingers over those beloved scarred cheeks.

"You're afraid I'll vanish again," he said.

He got me, he *so* got me. "I can't help it."

"I know. But I'm here for good, Clea. Believe it. Now open your shields."

"And yours to me?"

"Already done."

He cradled me, but I shuddered. I hated him seeing those truths that would heighten his pain. So I dropped my shields while I delved deep inside him, past his brightened fae spark, and deeper still to see how the wyvern fared.

Around me, the world was mist and shadow, except for the wyvern, his golden glow limning the air with light. He slept, in all his immense red-gold fabulousness, but cranked open a gold-flecked emerald eye.

I prepare, he said in my mind. *My time comes nigh.*

Do you have to talk all cryptic?

It's who I am.

Yeah, when you want it to be.

The world around me quaked with his laughter.

You're preparing, I said. *Are you going somewhere?*

I have no plans to vacate the premises.

James was the premises. Would the wyvern leave? *Could* he leave?

And where would I go?

I reached out a hand, pet his snout, then ran my fingers up between those glorious eyes.

Scratch there, please.

I did as requested.

Ah, yes. Perfect. I had a dreadful itch.

I reveled in his healthy glow and satisfied sigh. Both lids drooped. I continued to scratch.

Remember this—If you command, it will be so.

What? *What?*

But the great beast had fallen asleep, and I knew I'd be unable to wake him.

28

HOLY MOLY

Neddy shot hoops outside, having inhaled two Pop-Tarts in record time, an inappropriate breakfast that would change once I had my say-so.

Rae, James, and I sat around the kitchen table. Rae had gotten take-out, and he and I ate bagels, lox, and cream cheese, much to James' disgust. Ever prepared, Rae conjured up a steak and baked potato with sour cream and bacon. So why the hell hadn't he poofed our food?

"James need his veggies, too," I said.

"Po-ta-to," Rae said.

"You know what I mean. And why didn't you conjure our breakfast?"

"I've got my eye on that sexy bagel delivery girl." He winked.

"Of course you do."

James ignored our banter, focusing on the humongous steak he was devouring.

"The Villa will be watched," I said. "By Tommy, and any minions he's managed to collect. From what I saw when he was directing Rolf in that basement, Tommy's magic isn't working right."

James cut me a sharp look. "We can't count on that holding."

I sighed. "It'd be nice, but no, we can't." I crossed my fingers and turned to Rae. "Will Anouk help?"

His eyes narrowed. "That one, she's sassy. But I question whether she can join the party. It's y'all's mission. Your chore."

My mind shot to the Chest of Bone, which was safely tucked away at the Arctos compound. I wondered who the chest's guardian was. He or she hadn't come forward, and while I was to gather the chests, I didn't see why I couldn't just hand off the ones I collected to their proper caretakers. "Rae, why can't..."

Neddy walked inside and grabbed a seat.

"Shower," I said.

He scowled. "I don't need—"

"Oh, yes you do," I said. "You've been playing hoops for forty-five minutes. You're sweaty and smelly."

He looked to James for rescue.

James notched his head toward the stairs.

"Fine," Neddy said in a tragic teenaged tone that implied he was heading for the guillotine.

After Neddy left the room, James crossed his arms. "He's a good kid."

"He is," I said, my thoughts darkening on his mother's rejection. When I'd told James about it, he'd gotten quiet. Deadly quiet. I lowered my voice, shifter hearing and all that. "How could she? I don't get it. Not at all."

"I know you don't," James said. "It's that squishy heart of yours."

"Maybe she'll—"

He shook his head. "She won't come round."

I bristled. "What makes you so certain?"

He donned his Mr. Stoic mask. Not the dead one he wore when he was emotionless, but the face he'd worn often when we'd first met, the one that effectively shut out the world to his emotions, whether volcanic or polar. "He's like me now. Other. Pariah."

"But you're—"

"I get her type. The kid'll be okay. He's got you and—"

"And me!" Rae stabbed a finger at his chest. "What else could he be wanting?"

James' lips twitched. "I can't imagine, Rae. That other shifter woman, too."

"Melike," I said. "And Alex."

"No," James said. "Arctos *is* the pack and *of* the pack. He will always choose pack over the individual."

"You're wrong."

He arched an eyebrow. "Perhaps."

"Even with all of us, it's not the same as his mom," I said.

He tilted back on his chair, lifting its two front legs off the ground. An annoying habit, which he hadn't broken even with my grandmother's haranguing. That was my James. The James *before*.

Eyes dancing, he said, "What are you smiling at?"

I leaned forward and poked a finger into his chest. "You know *exactly* what I'm smiling about."

He captured my hand, kissed the palm. The devil danced in his eyes. "I do."

"Get. A. Room!" Rae said.

I chuckled. "We *have* a room."

With another kiss, James released my hand. I was glad it wasn't the one with the two blackened fingers, a blackening that now crept toward a third, my ring finger. A bag of chuckles to see death inching closer.

"All right," I said. "Back to business. So how do we approach the Getty?"

THE FOLLOWING MORNING, James led me up the path to the Getty Villa.

Today, I wore a pretty little sundress with strawberries on it, and cowboy boots, high ones that hid the gun strapped to my left ankle and my small Bowie strapped to my right. Knives on my thighs beneath the flowy skirt of my dress. Under the bodice rested a lightweight bulletproof vest, courtesy of the blissfully unaware Union, since Larrimer had raided one of their supply depots. My light cardigan disguised the gun nestled at the small of my back. Not an ideal position, but a shoulder holster wouldn't work with my casual getup. And we were going for casual as we walked the path from the parking lot to the Villa proper.

I'd braided and bound my distinctive blonde dreads and shoved them under a straw cowboy hat. To complete the look, I wore thin red leather gloves, an affectation the denizens of eccentric L.A. wouldn't even notice. The better to hide the ring, its shard, and my creepy black fingers. Yes, fingers—the black covered one hand and circled my wrist. Quite the accoutrement.

Compared to James, I was underarmed. He wore more weapons than a SWAT team, disguised by faded jeans, shitkicker boots, black bullet-resistant t-shirt and leather vest. He'd even roughed up his black Popular Demand snapback hat to age it.

For all that I was anxious as hell about our mission, my hormones remained in overdrive. James looked positively lickable.

"Stop that," he said under his breath.

"What?" I answered in my most innocent tone.

"You know what I'm talking about, baby." His restless eyes scanned the path with a predator's intensity.

"I can't help it."

"*Help* it. It's distracting."

Good to know. "Later."

"Yes." His chuckle was husky and deep.

And that laugh of his wouldn't calm *my* libido one bit.

"You'll pay for that," I said.

"Hope so."

Our high-tech sunglasses, another giftie from The Union's supply depot, could be switched electronically from day to night vision, something we'd need after the Getty closed.

Rae said he would meet us inside, along with a trusted friend. A friend, huh? I wasn't happy about the latter, but had no way to prevent his plus-one from joining our little caper.

Sweat dampened the inside of my gloves. My gut said our time was running out, that I had to take possession of the chest, or others would beat me to it. Not to mention how I'd die, a fun fact I'd kept to myself.

We left the path to stand by the small outdoor amphitheater, perpendicular to the museum entrance. Minutes later, we blended into the group tour about to enter the museum. With my hand in James', I stepped forward. His arm went rigid, and I bounced back.

"What?" I said.

He dragged me to the cafe flanking the museum shop. It seemed like decades ago when I'd questioned the woman about the dolphin earrings.

Once seated, and we ordered and were served my iced tea and his coffee, James squeezed the bridge of his nose.

"Something's very wrong," I said.

A hiss of breath. "The wyvern spoke to me."

My eyes widened. "Is this the first time?"

He nodded. "It was weird as shit."

He got that I talked with the wyvern, but it was always when my senses traveled deep inside him. "What did he say?"

He stretched out his legs. "The entrance is warded."

"Against you?"

He shrugged. "All he said was 'Stop. Wards.'"

His words made me instantly ravenous. The Chocolate Budino should do it. My nerves had amped up, and I needed fuel. Sweet fuel.

When the server delivered my dessert, I dug in with abandon. "Plenty of people have knowledge of the chest. But that it's here at the museum? Tommy may suspect. But I doubt he can place wards."

He growled. "This is a deadly op. I don't like it. If I could retrieve this thing *for* you, I would."

I rubbed the back of the white-knuckled hand he'd curled into a fist. "I know. But you can't. So here are the possibles. Rolf was working with Tommy, who is Tatianne's minion. So does *she* know the chest might be here and did she set the wards? Except she can't enter the mundane world. At least she couldn't."

He leaned back in his chair and crossed his arms. I waited. His finger traced the long scar that ran down his face. I still had trouble grasping the real James was back.

"Rolf was following you." His face tightened, white lines bracketing his mouth. "Nothing to do with the chest, but just him trying to get his paws on you."

His fist tightened, and I was sure his mind had traveled to Rolf's assault on me.

I took his fist, pulled it close, and kissed it. "You *came* for me. I'm over it. Sure, it's going to take some time to process. But it's old and done. I refuse to carry that burden of what he did. Don't *you* carry it either, please."

He tugged off his sunglasses—deliberate, calculated—to reveal those Pacific blues blazing with heat. "Let's find a corner. A dark one."

Gods. My body liquefied, an inferno that speared right to my groin. "Geesh, James. Seriously? We can't!"

His arms stretched across the table to cup my face. He leaned closer and took my lips, slow and hot, his tongue probing and teasing.

The world vanished to only his lips, his tongue, touching, flicking, delving deep. When we surfaced, he kissed the tip of my nose, the chocolate on top.

His eyes smoldered with a fiery hunger much like the wyvern's.

"You destroy me, Clea Reese," he said. "Every fucking time. Then you recreate me. Each breath I take is for you."

Wow. How did a girl even deal with that?

I wished I smoked. *Really.* Or brought my knitting. Yeah, that would help. I shoved another bite of dessert into my mouth, a pale substitute for the taste of James. "Maybe..." Geesh. I sounded breathy as all get out. "Maybe it was Anouk."

"The crazy mage from the diner in Midborough?"

I nodded. "She's powerful. On our side. Mostly. She might have warded the entrance and keyed it to us or against The Union or Tommy."

"Or any magic users," he said.

"Yes. Could The Union produce wards?"

"Sure. They've got magic connections, twisted ones. Their

specialty is blackmail and bribery. Consider that they might be in league with Tatianne."

I stopped chewing. "No. Why would you think... But it makes a sick sort of sense. She doesn't want change, and she's trying to thwart us. The Union might be pretending to agree to her agenda. Oh, that would just be so special. Not." Tatianne and The Union teaming up would make things... I squashed that nasty thought.

He brushed his thumb back and forth across my hand. "Doesn't matter. True or not, we can beat them." His intense certainty gave me shivers.

"We've got to go," I said.

"Now we find another way inside. Not a problem."

"You're so damned sure of yourself."

A lip twitch. "This is news?"

I wanted to find a dark corner. Instead, I deliberately licked a dollop of cream off the corner of my mouth. He replaced his sunglasses, but the burn of his eyes remained.

Six hours later, we'd come up with a plan to elude the magical wards, along with the mundane alarms and security guards. We planned to jump over the wall into the Villa.

When James had saved Bernadette and Lulu, he'd leapt twenty feet into the air, straight up. He'd get us both over the wall. We were betting that the wards only extended to the exterior doors. Why ward walls, right? Fingers and toes crossed and all that.

I texted Rae, explained the plan, and he got onboard.

James and I waited until night enveloped the Villa. We'd hidden in the shadows as the museum grounds emptied. While guards patrolled, there were few enough to easily avoid them. Now we moved along the side of the main building.

The fact that the Villa was a re-creation of a first-century Roman country house worked in our favor. Beyond the Villa's main building —a square with a wing to the right and a small interior courtyard— sat a long rectangular section, the outer peristyle. Inside, a long reflecting pool and gardens were flanked by a row of colonnades. The door at the base of the rectangle was probably also warded, but not the peristyle itself. The structure's roof was about fifteen feet high, as opposed to the much taller main building.

James stopped about halfway down the peristyle's outer wall.

"Ready?" he said, grinning.

The man who'd worked in covert ops for years was eating this up. I smiled. "Sure am."

He tapped his back. "Climb on."

I jumped, and he caught me beneath my thighs, while I wrapped my legs around his torso and my arms around his neck. I just had to kiss his ear.

"Tickles," he said.

He bent his knees and jumped.

We landed at the crest of the gently sloping roof. Silent. Amazing. Then he leapt again, and we were inside the Villa. I slid down, and we moved on cat feet into the walkway covered by the columned roof.

"Simple," he said.

"Easy peasy." We would wait through the night—chancing the Getty's alarms and guards was too risky—until the museum reopened in the morning. And thus avoid the wards.

I stood on tiptoe and kissed him.

He hooked an arm around my waist and tugged me against his chest. Bathed in inky black, my love pressed close and swooped down for a long, luxurious kiss.

My hands roved his muscular back, his ass, and I pressed myself tight to him, desperate to be closer.

Long moments later, he said, "We've got all night."

I didn't need my senses to tell me he was smiling one of those salacious grins, one brow raised. His marble-hard erection said it all.

"And we've found a dark corner," I said.

His hand brushed my breast, and he rubbed with a light touch that made me ache for more. I ran my hand down the front of his jeans to find him stiff and long and throbbing. I squeezed.

"Jesus," he said. "I planned to take it slow, baby."

"Forget slow."

He lifted me by my waist, plundering my mouth, while his other hand delved inside my panties to the center of my aching need. He cupped me, and then his one finger hit my sweet spot and stroked.

I sucked in a breath, inched my hand beneath his waistband and wrapped it around the velvet of his cock.

"Here's a fifty. Get a room."

James' hold tightened before he eased me to my feet. He held me until I steadied, then I rounded on Rae.

"A fifty? Dammit, Rae, you know that's not enough for a room in L.A.!" Rae's eyes widened, to my great satisfaction. I chuckled. "Per usual, your timing sucks. You said you were going to wait until later."

"I changed my mind," Rae said in a plummy British accent that I instantly hated.

A near-silent whoosh to our left. James shoved me behind him and morphed into attack mode.

"My compatriot," Rae said, his snide Brit voice making me want to throttle him.

For a brief second, moonlight glinted off long, ghost-white strands of hair that fluttered in the soft breeze.

Alex. The plus-one he brought was Alex. Swellsies.

It would be a long night.

THE NEXT MORNING, we pressed our backs to the wall in shadow, as workers, guards, and docents filtered into the Villa the next morning. I suspected Rae helped with the invisibility thing, as no one came near us. When the doors opened at ten, we were ready.

Alex and Rae walked into the bright California sunlight around the pool in the center of the peristyle. Alex wore a surfer get up—board shorts and Hawaiian shirt—while Rae was dressed in a bespoke grey suit. He was also lily white, with curly cropped blond hair. We waited until they entered the main building's double doors, then moments later strolled up the colonnade and slipped inside by one of the side doors.

Which is when I realized the ring felt dead, inert. So did my fingers. Unlike the magic world, where the shard had called to me, now I sensed absolutely nothing. I curled my left hand, the one not clasped in James'. Yup, fingers no feely. Shit. Not only did I not sense the pull of the ring, but with my left-hand fingers numb, my dominant hand would be useless wielding any weapons.

Crap.

A slight tug on James, and he followed me to the lobby's bench. We sat side by side, his arm slung over my shoulder. I leaned close and explained my awful lack at sensing the chest.

"Nothing?" he said.

I shook my head.

"We can come back another day."

I rubbed the ring beneath my gloves, a ring that now felt cold and dead.

My nerves were on fire, alarm bells clanging. Boy, I wanted to leave. I squeezed my eyes tight. "No. We do it now. Tatianne's getting close. Or Tommy. Maybe the Cardillo, too. And I'll be..." *Dead*, I almost blurted out. "I just know it has to be now."

I started to rise, but he held me, his breath brushing my ear. "What aren't you telling me?"

"Nothing important."

"Then why won't you tell me?"

"Later. Promise I'll tell you later."

"Christ," he said. "I could do without you driving me nuts."

I smiled up at him, batting my lashes, all innocent eyes. "You love it."

He lips twitched. "Maybe I do. Let's go." He wore that intense face that said we were unstoppable.

I groaned inside. "Forty-four thousand artifacts and counting."

THE CHESTS WERE mutable constructs that defied description. I'd first seen the Chest of Bone as a girl's plastic jewelry box, complete with musical innards and a ballerina that twirled when opened.

When I'd touched the chest with my flesh, it had morphed into its true aspect—an unforgettable experience that altered my perception of reality. The slivers of souls in each chest, along with the Evermore Queen's magic, had been freely given. The chests were universes, and an aspect of them was to organize a particular species magic, which made them essential to the mundane and magical worlds' orderly retwining.

My inscrutable friend, Anouk, was the Chest of Stone's Guardian. She'd instantly suss out the chest. But her questionable ability to join our hunt made that moot. I often found the magical world's rules quixotic and strange.

As The Key, I was the single being who could reunite the chests, which was why Tatianne had tried to steal my essence and why The Union wanted me.

All of which was scary as shit.

Except now I had allies, strong beautiful ones. We would succeed. We must succeed.

"Let's start on the second floor," James said. "We'll work our way downward." We climbed the stairs. "Do we have any idea which object to look for?"

"Not really. But keep an eye out for the dolphin earrings. I'm betting whatever's preventing me from sensing the chest will dissipate the nearer I get to it." I sure as hell hoped so.

HOURS LATER, we'd made no progress. None. Rae and Alex were our satellites, unseen and ever watchful. James had texted Rae with an update every half hour, and vice versa. We had zip.

My bad leg ached like the devil, and I'd sensed nothing magical. Not a thing.

Dammit, I would find the frickin' chest.

"Sit," James said. "You look like death."

"You've got to stop with the compliments." We found a corridor bench, and I made a point of keeping my back straight, chin up.

"You're exhausted," he said.

My pose, a fail. "Let me think."

He leaned against the wall, his eyes moving, searching for danger, for threats.

I knew, *knew* the chests in our mundane world appeared nonmagical. I'd been so sure the shard would lead me to the Chest of Stone. Stupid.

The chest could appear as a statue. A necklace. A glass vial. A painting. Anything. Think. Think. Think.

Which is when I remembered the middle-aged man in the blue shirt. A docent. I'd asked him about the earrings. What was his name? Mr. Singer? Mr. Player? "Mr. Harper!"

"What?" James said, although his eyes continued to scan the corridor.

I jumped to my feet, or I would have if James hadn't put a hand around my waist. My ass stayed planted on the bench.

"What's got you so fired up?" he said.

I explained about Harper. "Let's go."

"No. Send Rae to find this Harper."

"Good idea." He also asked Alex to bring us some water. I'd been so certain we'd find the chest fast, we hadn't brought any fuel. Once James ended the call, I said, "We might as well wander around the room, and I'll touch stuff. See if I have any reaction."

Rae found us fifteen fruitless minutes later. He shook his head, then smoothed a very Caucasian hand down the lapel of his suit. "No joy, my dear."

"In what way?"

"No one works here by that name."

Damn. "Who did you talk to?"

"A Ms. Yevtukh."

The Villa's chief of security. I remembered her. Then again, she'd be hard to forget. "And why," Rae said, "pray tell, were you looking for this Mr. Harper?"

While I explained, a disgruntled looking Alex appeared with our water.

"Thank you," I said, as he handed me the bottle.

He brushed a finger across my hand. "Always a pleasure to serve m'lady."

James snorted in his dragonish way. Alex snapped around and cut James a nasty look. I rolled my eyes. "The last thing we need is you two getting your knickers in a twist."

Rae plucked his lower lip. "Perhaps you could do up a sketch, and we will query the docents here about said earring. One may know where it lies."

Good thing his vibe felt like Rae, because with that fussy accent and white skin, he sure didn't look or sound like him. "A hell of an idea, since I'm fresh out of them."

From his pocket, he produced a pad and pen.

"How did you do that?" I said.

"My dear Clea, you could do that, too, if only you *practiced*."

"I've been busy." I yanked the pen and pad from his hand and began to draw with my right hand, which felt like a monumental task.

I drew the earring—a pearl attached to the ear bob of a gold dolphin, about an inch and a half long, with another pearl dangling at the bottom of the S.

I held up the sketch.

Brit affecting though he might be, Rae gave that "He, he, he" laugh filled with smugness and irony. And drove me batso.

"Tell us," I said.

"I have seen those earrings." He pursed his lips. "They're not on the premises."

My heart stilled. "Where then?"

"Damned if I know." He tucked a finger beneath my chin. "What I do know is their representation is here."

Patience apparently flown, Alex growled.

Rae flapped a hand. "All righty, then. I've seen them on a painted Egyptian Fayum mummy portrait."

James raised an eyebrow. I had no clue, either.

Rae opened the guidebook, flipped pages and pointed. "Right down the hall. A mummy, and a bunch of mummy portraits."

The book showed portraits painted on what appeared to be wood or maybe stiffened linen. The strangest thing about them, one of many strange things, was that they looked more Greek or Roman, than Egyptian.

"How could you possibly remember those earrings?" I said.

His finger stabbed an image in the book. "That lady, she looked like my auntie, who's one scary mage bitch."

Holy moly.

29

GOTCHA

We stood outside room 209, the Men of Antiquity room. I checked my map. Down the hall were the Fayum mummy portraits. To reach the room, we'd turn left, enter a large room and hook a right to reach the small Arts of Greco-Roman Egypt room, which had no windows and no access to the hall.

Around us, individuals and groups, kids and elders perused the art, chatted and did what folks did at museums.

I steeled myself. This was right. Felt right. I worried my lower lip.

I wanted to press out my senses, see if any of the myriad museum-goers were a threat. Except if I did that, someone with skills might sense me. Which was an unacceptable scenario.

"Lots of people," I said. "Maybe we should wait until near closing."

"No," James said.

Alex bristled. "Who the fuck are you to say no?"

"The longer we wait," James said. "The better the chance we'll be hunted down."

Alex gave him teeth. "Okay. Yeah, okay."

We ambled down the hall, Alex and Rae at our backs. We didn't hold hands, didn't talk, just one step at a time.

The hairs on my neck rose. A familiar someone moved into the broad doorway to the room facing us.

Taka.

We stopped. James remained loose and relaxed. I wanted to scream.

Black cargo pants and t-shirt, black lipstick and hair and black glasses that remained as crooked as the day I'd met her. Her thin mouth widened into a smile. Her whole Goth thing was cartoonish, except she wore no weapons. Disturbing.

Taka nodded a respectful bow at James. "Thank you for bringing the mage to me, Larrimer. Sandra Yevtukh, a friend of The Union, alerted me to her earlier visit. We've kept watch."

His motionless body belied his hum of fury. He smirked, and Taka reacted as if slapped, the return of James' emotions an obvious shock.

I sensed Rae and Alex melting into the background.

Her eyes slithered to mine, sleepy, yet they gleamed with arrogance and avarice, and I didn't need my empath abilities to read her distaste.

"Ah." Her black-nailed index finger tapped her lips. "I see you are changed yet again, Larrimer."

A blast of animus so fierce I nearly choked. James despised the woman. But he held his words for long moments, until, "Leave, Taka. While you have the chance."

She pressed fingertips to her lips and tittered. "I will. With the two of you."

Purple-red flames spewed from her mouth.

Holy hell, magical fire!

James pressed me against the wall, covered my body with his.

Screams and shouts, gunfire and alarms!

Pandemonium.

James whirled, a-bristle with guns. I did the same, to see the corridors peppered with black-clad men and women pointing Uzis directly at us. Three bodies littered the floor, leaking blood. Security guards.

Shit.

And one idiot California cowboy holding a 9mm directed at Taka.

He pulled the trigger, and fire blazed from her mouth. Much as I wished to shield my eyes, he deserved my witness. The man in the cowboy hat screamed, writhing as he burned to death.

I shuddered.

By the time the body stilled, the corridors were clear of life, except for Taka's troops and us. The alarms abruptly cut off.

The poor cowboy was a pile of gray-black ash, his weapon melted metal beside him.

Taka returned her attention to James. "You see? I am changed as well."

I could contain James and myself in my firefly bubble. For a while. Where were Rae and Alex? Had they been shot? Were they alive?

Even using my fireflies, I doubted James and I could take out Taka and her crew before my shield failed and they disabled or killed us.

Think.

I looked at James. Red suffused his face, a disturbing first, and his eyes weren't blue, but emerald green, like...

The wyvern. *If you command, it will be so*, the wyvern had said.

I wrapped my arms around James, as if terrified. Not taking his eyes off Taka, he tilted his head to the side, closer to me.

"Keep her talking," I whispered to James. "And open your shields."

"Risky," he said. "She could take me over. Like before."

"Trust me?" I said.

His eyes softened, then, "What did you do, Taka? Fuck a fairy?"

"You are not the only one," Taka said, "with unique abilities now, James Larrimer."

If you command, it will be so.

I went fast and deep into James... and found the wyvern roused. He stood on his two legs, neck stretched, head snaking from right to left. I had no frickin' idea what I was doing, but I held his eyes. *Now, wyvern. I command it. Now!*

A blast tossed me from the wyvern, out of James' mind, to jolt back into myself. I reeled. James steadied me, then moved several feet to the right. Half the gun barrels tracked his movement. Red-gold smoke swirled, coating his legs from the knees down.

Taka smiled. "What's this, a new party trick?"

"Last chance, Taka." His menacing voice had taken on an even deeper timbre, strange and melodic.

The smoke, opaque and kissed with green flame, rose around him in a curling sinuous motion. I slammed against the wall as gunfire erupted.

"No!" I screamed.

I fireflied, tried to encompass the smoke, but my Flow hit some barrier and dribbled to the marbled floor. I leapt at James, but I was frozen. No, more like I'd been wrapped in Saran and stuck to the wall.

"James!"

"Stop!" Taka shouted. "Her! Point them at her! Fire at my command!"

I sensed the guns swivel to me, but my eyes remained fixed on that writhing smoke. James was gone, obscured behind the swirl of red-gold that rose eight, ten, fifteen feet in the air.

A roar. Deafening. The building shook, marble statuary trembling. A bust crashed to the floor.

Green flame shot from the dissipating smoke, turning several of Taka's gun-toting minions to ash. Heat seared my face, but the flame never touched me.

I braced for a hail of bullets.

"Kill it!" Taka screeched, then shot flame from her mouth toward James.

A barrage of bullets. The noise. Taka's flame.

The bullets found their target as the smoke vanished from...

Ohmygods.

The wyvern. When we had talked, our sizes hadn't seemed so disparate. Now, James' wyvern stood fifteen feet high, twenty feet long, his head almost pressed to the Getty's ceiling, his eyes glowing beacons of hate. Two golden horns arced backward from his triangular head. Foot-long spikes protruded from his spine, and red-gold half-moon scales covered his body and immense folded wings. Two trunk-like legs supported him, while black claws curled from his feet. The wyvern's jaws opened to reveal double rows of pointed, serrated teeth. He bristled with magic.

Again I went to move, but the damned invisible force holding me prisoner didn't budge.

Bullets rained onto the wyvern, and they bounced off his hide like cotton swabs.

Another ear-splitting roar, and then chaos, with smoke and flame blasting from the wyvern's maw, taking out uniformed men and women, armaments and ancient artifacts.

Heat seared me, the wyvern's sweeps deadly. The Union forces broke, running. The wyvern snaked its sinuous neck, and poof, those fleeing became ash.

It was all crazy insane.

The wyvern moved, fleet and shockingly agile, straight after Taka who'd disappeared into the exhibition rooms.

I tried to move, too, and fell forward, released from my prison. I landed hard, but leapt to my feet. Gods, I wanted that bitch Taka. But the artifacts! If they were destroyed...

Would the wyvern care? Was he James? The wyvern? Both?

I raced into a large exhibit room, skidded to a halt.

The wyvern's immense bulk took up a quarter of the room, its tail extending into the hall. Quiet, sniffing, gray smoke curling from its flared nostrils.

Then it moved, and I mean *moved*.

Through a second, much smaller room into another large one.

There! Taka rounding a corner into another room.

The wyvern followed.

Oh, gods. Pompeii. It was the Pompeii exhibit. If he flamed her, he'd destroy thousands-of-years-old artifacts.

I stepped inside, near the wyvern's right leg. Rae and Alex stood in the arch of the room's far entrance.

Taka had nowhere to run.

She faced the wyvern, her eyes cut to me, and she flamed.

The wyvern leaned and blocked the flame before it hit me.

Tickles, the wyvern sonorous voice bubbled with amusement inside my head.

I moved to his shoulder by his folded wing. Rae and Alex didn't budge.

"You're done, Taka," I said. "Surrender."

The wyvern raised a ridge above its glittering right eye, like it was an eyebrow. *Surrender? I think not.*

I understood. "Don't, wyvern!"

Oh, he said, a breath mingled with smoke chuffing out of his maw. *I'm afraid I must, my Clea.*

Taka flamed again, yet only embers dribbled out of her mouth. "Fuck you all. *She* is coming. *She* will end you. The Union will—."

A focused blast of green flame encompassed Taka.

A final shriek.

Gone.

I EXPECTED Taka would look like a crispy critter. Nope, she was gone. Erased. I walked to where she'd stood moments earlier. Only a small mound of black ash marked the woman who'd relentlessly hunted me.

Shame on me, but I was glad.

Rae approached, still white, still wearing his bespoke suit. "Y'all be badass." He stared at the ash pile, then his eyes rose to the wyvern towering over us.

The immense beast dipped his red-gold head to mine. Close up, he smelled of chicory. Staring into his eyes was seeing a kaleidoscope of age and knowledge, with a healthy dose of feral arrogance thrown in. He wasn't James, yet...

I stood on tiptoe, reached up, and snugged my arms around as much of his neck as possible. "Thank you."

His nostrils flared, and his burbling growl held notes of affection, not to mention a fine bit of preening. *You're most welcome, my Clea.*

His caring undid me. It scared me, too. *James?*

He is with me, and I, with him.

Don't start that cryptic stuff, okay?

His snort gusted over me, a little too warm for comfort.

"What're you two discussin'?" Rae said.

"Not now, Rae," I said.

"What you mean, talkin' to me like..."

The wyvern's head snapped up, lips pulled taut to expose those glistening teeth.

Rae's jaws clamped together.

"I need James," I said to the wyvern.

The wyvern's faceted eyes glittered. *I enjoy this form.*

Oh, damn. "Others nearby, they shouldn't see you, and we've got to find the chest."

He dipped his head. Moments drizzled by.

For now, I accede.

I didn't much like that "for now" business.

Step back.

I did as ordered, and the wyvern straightened. Red-gold smoke rose from his clawed feet, to funnel around him until it encompassed his gargantuan form.

See you soon, my Clea.

Soon? Nope, didn't like that one bit.

Seconds later, James stood before us, clothes pristine. He dropped to his knees. "Fucking hell."

I rushed to him, wrapped him tight in my arms, and peppered kisses across his face. Could the wyvern really *keep* James inside him? *Would* he?

His arms banded around me. "Baby," he whispered, "that was one insane trip."

"Are you okay?" I said.

He growled. "If you call looking out of sky-high eyes and shooting flame okay, yeah."

A laugh erupted from my mouth. "What was it—"

"I am *tired* of all this lovey-dovey shit." The voice was all Rae, the body all upper-crust Brit. "Y'all should be finding us a chest."

The four of us raced back down the shambles of corridor, through the large Women and Children in Antiquity room and into the small one that held a glass-cased mummy and a myriad of funerary portraits hung on the black-painted wall. I jerked to a halt. My blackened hand tingled. But not good tingled. Weird, never-before-felt tingled. Hurt like crazy, in fact.

Rae was staring at one of the portraits, hands clasped behind his back.

And there she was, preserved behind glass, one third of a tryptic. Big round eyes, blacker than black, gorgeous thick crimped hair. Red lips, heavy brows. A strange flaring flower-like headdress. The earrings—gold dolphins with pearls, just like the replicas.

"That's my auntie, Isis," Rae said.

"How do you know it's your Aunt Isis?" I said.

"See that frou-frou headdress? That knot's called an 'Isis knot,' which says that's my auntie."

"Like the goddess," I said.

"No, sugah. Auntie *is* the goddess."

Oh-kay. I lifted my fingers to the glass, but the tingle didn't increase. Huh.

"Clea," James said. "Time is of the essence."

"I know." Should we break the glass so I could touch the portrait? I didn't want to do that. Not yet.

I raised my hand, circling the room, brushing it against the glass of each wall portrait. The tingles lessened, but didn't dissipate.

I dove deeper inside, homing in on my magic as Rae had taught me. My throat dried, and I grew faintly dizzy. Sounds deadened, until a singular thread tugged. On trembling legs, I turned and faced not the portrait, but the supine mummy resting in its case. I fisted my hands and kept them at my side.

"His face," I said. "It's so alive, like it was painted yesterday. He looks more Greek or Roman than Egyptian."

"He does." James bent over the case.

The famed Mummy of Herakleides. He'd been a young man when he'd been painted. Handsome, with a strong nose and full lips I'd swear almost smiled. He wore a mustache, and a gold, leafy circlet bound his curly hair. I'd read that his name, Herakleides, was written on his upturned feet, while painted Egyptian symbols and mythological scenes covered the wrappings that bound his body. Although it had faded, red paint covered his shroud.

"An ibis." I pointed to the one depicted on the funerary wrappings.

"Yup," Rae said. "That says he's got a mummified ibis inside his shroud."

I unclenched my left hand and raised it to the case.

Arrows of pain speared from my hand to my heart, which thudded in a mad rhythm.

"Here," I mouthed, unsure if I'd made sound or not.

James' hands braced my shoulders, grounded me. "Is the entire mummy the chest?"

"I don't know." I stripped off my gloves.

"Let's remove the case." James bent to me. "You have to move, Clea."

I took a step back, another, eyes glued to the mummy. Alex and James each took an end and began to lift the rectangular glass encasing Herakleides. They broke the case's hermetic seal used to preserve the remains. Unfortunate, but my only way to access the chest... if this *was* the chest's home.

Noises rose from downstairs. Law enforcement would pour in any minute. We had to rush. How could we rush? I cursed the pain knifing my body, sharpening my impatience.

"How much time do we have?" I said.

"Working on that," Rae said.

The men eased the heavy glass case to the floor.

The mummy was fully exposed.

I stepped forward, and of its own volition my blackened hand rose. I didn't fight it, my hand numb, my body on fire.

My legs buckled, and I fell.

James moved toward me.

"Don't!" My knees crashed onto the stone floor.

The pain was irrelevant compared to the horror of my hand as I watched the ring carve through my index finger.

"Holy fucking shit!"

"Clea!"

"Hells bells!"

Everything was white noise compared with the agony of the ring cutting off my finger.

Spots danced before my eyes. I couldn't black out. Wouldn't.

Finger gone. But little blood. Where was the blood?

My finger with the ring flew to the mummy's throat.

I pushed off the floor with my intact right hand and stumbled to the mummy. I'd prepared for this. I drew a pair of nitrile gloves from my pocket and held out my hands to James.

"Put them on me," I said, eyes focused on the mummy.

He tugged on the gloves and the world darkened to a pinprick. Done. I caught my breath, then held out my good hand. "Give me a knife."

A hilt slapped into my palm. I curled my fingers around it.

Shouts from below. Gunfire? Woozy, I shook my head and leaned my thighs against the platform's black base. I had to hurry.

Gods forgive me, I stabbed the mummy in the throat, then ripped the knife downward. The five-inch incision just sat there. Nothing.

I ripped off a glove. Touched the mummy.

The ring, bound to my amputated finger, slid into the opening I'd made.

My hand moved atop the slit, and the wrappings began to glow and throb in tune with my heart.

My body's pain eased.

The slit widened of its own accord. Striations appeared, broke open, and triangles peeled back like an orange skin.

My hand cooled, as if shoved in a freezer.

Cooler still. Icy. I kept my hand in place.

I couldn't touch the chest with my naked hand. It would recognize me, and we were too exposed. I tugged a glove back on.

All too slow. *Oh, screw it.*

I dug my fingers inside the mummy wrappings and curled them around an icy hardness. It felt like a knife was scoring the bones of my hand. The urge to jerk my hand free nearly undid me. But I couldn't. Wouldn't.

Whatever I held was hard and frigid. Pain shot up to elbow. I groaned.

My fisted hand was too frozen to move, so I bent my arm and pulled upward.

And the queen cried stones of silver.

A necklace dangled from my numb grip.

Comprised of matte red beads interspersed with gold ones, its large focal pendant, a red stone set in matte gold, the color a symbol of the goddess's bloodlust.

The necklace wavered before me. I swayed, clutched it to my breast.

"We go!" someone said.

That same someone lifted me. Scents of pine and honey.

I fell.

30

HOME

I awakened to James' warm arms and strong chest. *The necklace!* Still clutched in my left hand, which pressed to my heart.

"Where—"

"Still at the museum."

"Why?" My voice sounded distant and disembodied.

"We have a problem." He leaned close. "The bitch is here."

Tatianne. She who couldn't cross into the mundane world apparently *had*.

"Where?" I said.

"On this floor. Down the hall: the room where I ended Taka."

'I ended Taka?' How much was James melding with the wyvern? "Take out the box from your pack, please." Where the hell were the police? The SWAT teams? The National Guard? We'd made a shambles of the museum. Cameras had to have seen.

James produced the ebony oval box Anouk had given me. I removed the glove on my right hand and touched the seamless box. The lid sprang open, and with my left gloved hand I slid the necklace inside. I wondered at the chest's true form, but now wasn't the time to find out. I tapped the lid again, and the box closed. Simply a block of wood with no access to anyone but me. James slid the box back into his pack. Safe.

Pain beat a mean rhythm in time with my heart. I refused to look at my four-fingered left hand—the one I wrote with, the one that held a gun, the one... *Shit.* No time for pity parties. "Where is everybody?"

"Rae and Anouk are—"

"Anouk?"

"Now that you have the chest, she can approach. Apparently." His voice, dust dry, held a world of annoyance, most likely at Rae. Or Anouk. Or Alex. Or all three.

"Kiss me?" I said and opened my shields.

An intense stare before his mouth swooped to cover mine. Yet his kiss was gentle, a fusing, a searching, his tongue feather light as it licked and probed my open mouth. Wet and delicious and real. Our song twined, the spinning helix not building, not today, but a melody that hummed along my senses, my heart, my soul. It warmed me in a way nothing else could. Too soon, our lips parted. He nuzzled me. And I inhaled the moment's sweetness.

"Love you, baby," he said.

"Me, too."

She comes. Wait. Don't flow until we make our move.

Rae's voice in my head. I couldn't answer him. Another trick I had to learn. Where were Rae, Alex, and Anouk? Out of sight and primed for action, I didn't doubt. And I was supposed to wait?

"She's here," I said. "Help me up."

With assistance, I stood and reviewed my body parts. All systems seemed onboard. Yippee.

Okay, I so wasn't up for this next confrontation. Like I had a choice? And while I also loved the wyvern part of James, a deep knowledge told me not to call him forth, that the more often he subsumed James, the less chance James had of resuming his human form.

We moved down the hall to a corner near the openings to two exhibit halls, where we'd have escape routes and a wall at our backs.

He pulled out his katana, and in his other hand he gripped a hand-held automatic.

I braced myself. No knives or gun. But from the energy frothing inside me, my fireflies were good to go.

He tilted his head. "You ready, baby?" I smiled up at him. "I am." Truth.

His low chuckle felt *so* good.

Movement far down the long corridor. A being appeared, ambling toward us, all arrogance and superiority.

Tommy. But not.

I narrowed my eyes.

He wore a slick black suit, white shirt open at the collar, blond hair to his shoulders. And once he caught sight of me that devilish grin split his face. A grin that still made my heart hitch.

Why did I fear him so? From what I'd seen in Rolf's basement, his magic was damaged, unable to throw his lethal silver needles. *His* Flow. Or had he recovered?

But surrounding him an aura projected outward and *through* him, a translucent form in a long flowy dress and crown. A shadow, but *more*.

I stepped away from the wall.

"You shouldn't have come," I said, not knowing to whom I spoke —Tommy? Tatianne? Both?

My brother slipped his hands into his pockets and moved closer.

"I missed my little sis," he said in echoing voices. Tommy's and *hers*.

"I'm not your little sis. We're twins, Tommy."

His grin widened. "But I was first, Clea. I'll always be first."

"Oh, get a grip."

I was glad James let me do the talking, not that I knew what the hell I was doing.

In the pantheon of strange things I'd witnessed since learning about the magical world, this was at the head of the line. I raised my hands in front of me, palms out, and let my power build.

He drew closer, maybe six feet away, and stopped. "You look a little beat up, sis. And that hand. Nasty."

"I'm aiming for the Frodo look."

He threw back his head and laughed, then abruptly stopped, his face hardening to that nasty grin. "You have something we want."

"Yeah?" I grinned. "Come and get it."

He moved.

Alex, Anouk, and Rae appeared in the doors to the exhibition rooms. Anouk and Rae pounded Tommy with their magic, and Alex's wolf leaped.

Tommy deflected all three, and they flew backward, followed by the sounds of crashes.

My brother hadn't even tried to fling his needles.

I unleashed my fireflies, while James rocketed toward Tommy-Tatianne, gun blazing, katana arcing toward his head.

My fireflies flowed around James, bounced off Tommy and rebounded.

I gritted my teeth as James and I smashed back toward an exhibit room. With a wave of my hands, my fireflies reversed to soften our landing. Even so, we smashed into display cases, shattering glass, destroying artifacts. Pain sliced up my back and my head rang from hitting the floor. I grunted, thankful for the adrenaline dulling the damage and for my fireflies which had somewhat cushioned our crash.

Tommy stalked closer, sauntering as if he hadn't a care in the world.

I used the back of my arm to swipe the blood from my eyes.

James lay beside me. He leapt to his feet, lifted me to mine, his face rigid with fury.

"Will the chest work to deflect them?" he said.

I shook my head. "I don't think so. It's a thing of power, but I don't know how to wield it. If I failed, the blowback might kill us."

He slipped off the pack and handed it to me. "Run."

"You've *got* to be kidding me," I said. "There's not a prayer—"

"What matters, Clea? Think about it?"

He was right, but... "I can't. I just can't run away from this. From them."

He kissed me hard, and in a blaze of speed, gathered his katana and gun and sprinted from the room toward Tommy.

I raced after him, but something, some*one* blocked my way. I skidded to a halt, prepared to firefly until I saw...

"Charlie?" I stepped back.

He wore jeans, a sword at his hip, a pink Grateful Dead t-shirt, and a bandolier of knives. His silver eyes were sleepy, as if we had eons of time. Wind rose around us—whipping his long hair and mine —to scream above the sound and fury of the battle. But inside the whirlwind, all was quiet and serene. The eye of the hurricane.

"What?" he said. "You imagined I was dead? Takes more than that shrew to end me."

I raised my palms, just in case I had to firefly him. "Charlie, help us. Fight with us."

"Can't, m'dear." A slow smile. "Not until I get free of that bitch. Thought I'd see how things were progressing, though."

The gale battered my dreads and they whipped my cheeks. "Why do you care? You betrayed us."

"Did I?" Legs akimbo, he punched his fists to his hips. He glanced at his bandolier.

His eyes deepened, and within his ageless gaze I saw a choice, my choice. And I knew the dark sorrow he was offering me.

I plucked two of the knives from the band across his chest.

"Good luck." He winked and poofed out.

The wind died. I stared at the knives, one gripped in each hand. They were black, with the mellow patina of polished bone. Charlie had given James their twin for our previous battle with my brother.

Since Tatianne was piggybacking in this realm on my brother, they wouldn't affect her. But they would *end* Tommy.

Kill my brother, end this now. Kill my brother, end him *forever*.

My choice would always come down to this. Except I could fight only using my fireflies, with James and Alex, Anouk and Rae.

A bitter laugh escaped me. *Oh, Charlie, you bastard.*

If I simply used my fireflies, we'd lose. Fail. Die. And Tatianne would take possession of the chest.

My grip on the knives tightened, my prayer to the gods instinctive. I pressed my back against the wall and peeked into the corridor.

The battle was silent. Tommy-Tatianne lobbing power at my four companions, sending them flying. But they were making progress, as they'd begun to stagger their assaults, divide Tommy-Tatianne's attention.

Except Tommy's suit remained unmussed, his hair precise, his smile bright. As if this were the best fun. As if he were toying with them.

I'd have one chance, one moment before he saw me, to throw Charlie's knives. I was good with knives. Better than good. But would my mangled hand work? Would my bruised and bloodied body respond to my mind's commands? Would I be accurate enough to kill?

That flashed through my head as James' body arced high to slam against the ceiling.

No! I stepped into the hall, legs wide, arms at my sides.

Tommy saw me and grinned.

I released the knives.

They parted Tommy-Tatianne's power like a spoon through butter. One buried itself in his shoulder, the other found a home in his heart.

A female screech shook the building, made the floors tremble and cracks appear. Her shadow outline vanished.

I ran forward. *Tommy* buckled.

Mouth agape in a shocked O. Blood flowing from the wounds. Knees crashing to the floor as he plucked at the dagger in his shoulder. Falling backward, a doll crumpling. Raising hands to unleash his deadly needles.

But nothing came. Nothing at all.

His arms flopped to the floor, as if their weight was too much to bear.

I slid to my knees in front of my fallen brother. "Tommy."

His eyes blinked. "Sweetness."

My breath stuttered.

"Are you going to end it?" he said, voice a whisper. "You missed my heart by a sliver. Bad aim."

I took his hand in mine. "My Frodo hand isn't quite up to snuff."

He closed his eyes, a small smile teasing his mouth. "End me, will you, beloved sister? I hurt."

"I..."

"Your heart's soft and loving. Always was. Do it. You don't want her to win, do you?"

My left hand shook, but I wrapped it around the hilt of the knife in his chest. I twisted.

His eyes flew open, laughing eyes that faded to emptiness. His body shuddered and went still.

A scream inside my head. Not Tatianne's, but...

You killed my son!

Mother?

My head exploded in agony. The world turned black.

I AWAKENED IN BED, covers tucked to my chin. I did a body check. Achy, sore, my bad thigh ablaze. And my hand. Not gonna look.

I wasn't in Rae's four-poster. My eyes panned the room. My katana hung on the wall, my Nantucket basket atop the dresser, the magic book from Sophy... on James' lap?

I sighed. The compound. I was back at the Arctos compound, with James in a chair, magazine covering his face, legs sprawled. Was that a snore?

I'd woken up like this back in New Hampshire, after The Union had poisoned me.

Shit. The chest. Where was the chest?

Since James was here sleeping, it must be safe.

Memory pressed a boulder to my heart.

I'd killed my brother, my twin. Tommy was gone. Forever.

I'd come to loathe him this past year, but for so many more years he'd been my lodestar, my best friend, my go-to guy. I relied on him, and he on me.

I'd loved him forever. Now, he was no more.

Maybe I whimpered, because James was beside me in a wink. He lowered himself onto the bed and tucked me to him.

He nuzzled my neck. "Hey," he said in gravelly voice.

"Hey." A burn behind my eyes. My lips wobbled. "I killed my own brother."

He brushed a hand across my hair. "You did."

"My twin."

"Yes."

He knew. I knew. It was the right choice. "It wasn't a choice, baby, but an imperative. He was wounded to the death." The burn continued, but no tears fell, something damming them, denying me the release I so desperately needed.

For once, I *wanted* to cry. I couldn't.

I wasn't ready to tell James of my mother's, my mam's voice inside my head. The enraged one I'd heard when Tommy had died. "I need to sit up. I'm so sick of finding myself in bed."

He chuckled as he helped me rise to a seated position, fussing with the pillows and blankets until I had to say, "Stop. I'm fine!"

His face tightened, the bones of his cheeks, blades. "You're not fine."

"I'm fine enough."

He filled me in on our escape from the wreckage. I'd passed out, gone some place he couldn't reach, which disturbed him.

I brushed my right hand down that beloved face. "Sorry."

He nodded. No smile.

"I'm okay now."

A rumbled growl. "Got it."

James told me Anouk and Rae had combined their powers to render our escape invisible before the authorities reached us. No one saw us. No one heard us. No one remembered us. The pair had fried the video and audio feeds, disappeared all bodily traces of us, The Union's dead, Tommy, and the dust that was Taka.

Everyone had been wounded, Alex the worst, but all were healing. And now the mysterious battle of the Getty Villa would weave into the lore of L.A. since not a single thing could be found to account for the massive destruction, one missing human in cowboy hat, and several dead security guards.

All was well. I reached for James, except I'd used my left hand. My maimed and disgusting one.

Holy shit.

An articulated gold digit replaced my amputated finger. Jointed, shaped like flesh, but made of metal, it moved with the rest of my hand, which was back to its normal coloring. The gold finger nestled against the small stub of flesh with no visible attachment, and even when I moved it, clung, as if the metal were melded to my skin.

Holding the hand up, I flexed my fingers.

Wowsa.

I touched the finger to my lips. Cold. No feeling in the artificial digit. I wiggled my fingers. They responded, even the metal one.

"How, James?" I said. "And how the hell is it attached and working?"

"Magic," chimed in Rae, who'd just poofed into the room wearing his streetwear uniform. Thank the gods he'd lost the British dude.

"Couldn't you walk through a door?"

Face smug, he looked like a smartass 22-year-old. "Where would the fun be in that? Y'all react so bad when I apparate in."

Don't tell him to screw off. Don't say it.

I wanted to kill this mage.

Except I loved this mage.

"So..." I said. "Magic is holding my metal finger on?"

"Sure is, sugah." He nodded. "Pretty cool, huh?"

"Thank you, Rae."

"He, he, he. Yeah, it's damned cool. My present to you, Ms. Mage. And unlike my legs, it won't curb y'all visits to the magic world."

I bit my lip. "Um, why can't you give yourself magic legs?"

His nostrils flared. "That's an iddy biddy finger. Legs? Uh-uh."

"Thank you. For everything."

"You did good with your Flow." He pulled a chair beside the bed, leaned forward, and narrowed his eyes. "Where did'ja get those knives?"

I told them about Charlie.

He reared back. "Well, bite my ass."

"Unappealing," James said, not even a twitch to his lips.

Rae frowned, and James and I burst out laughing.

"Where's Lulu, James? Neddy? Alex? Anouk? Ro—"

"They've all been in to see you," James said.

"He beat 'em back with a stick," Rae said. "Even me, if you can believe it."

I snuggled closer to James, ignoring Rae's grunt of disgust.

James kissed the top of my head. "When Grace tried to crawl onto you, we had to close the door."

I couldn't wait to see Grace. And everyone else. But most especially Lulu, Ronan, and Neddy. "The kids are okay?"

James nodded. "Fine." He cut Rae a dark look.

Rae held up his hands. "I'm leavin'. Right now. I've got piles of stuff to do."

"Tatianne," I said. "She's back in the magic realm."

He nodded.

She'd thrown Tommy away like a piece of refuse. I wanted her to suffer, to see her writhing in pain without end. I longed to find her, to make her pay for the many lives she'd...

"Hey, baby?"

James' waves of worry lapped at the shore of my mind. I inhaled a deep cleansing breath. "I'm not rational when it comes to her."

Rae frowned, his eyes simultaneously concerned and afraid. "You forget about her for now, yeah?"

I paused, nodded. "For now."

Rae leaned forward and kissed my forehead.

A first. Wow. "We got more practice to do, darlin'. He, he, he. Lots more."

He poofed out on my groan.

"Melike will want to beat me up, too," I said to James.

A grin. "Count me in."

"What!"

"Only the katana, baby. I'll work with you on it."

"Okay."

He leaned over me, his eyes darkened to midnight. "How about a shower?"

"I like that idea. A lot."

He scooped me up and stood.

"Hey! I can walk!"

"Sure you can." His eyes laughed. "But this is more fun."

He kicked the door to the bathroom closed behind us, and I stretched out my arm and twisted the lock. "In this place, it's always best to have insurance."

In a blur, my clothes vanished, as did his. A nasty red pucker marred his right hip. I feathered my fingers across it.

"It'll heal, baby."

"It must've been—"

"Not a big deal." His hands captured my breasts, and he dipped his head to suck the left, then the right.

My arms clung to his waist, and I slid them lower to hug his perfect ass. I trailed one hand lower still, found his balls, cupped them.

"*Clea.*"

He lifted me against him, skin to skin, walked us to the shower, and turned on the tap. James. If I had him, I had everything.

His chest hair sent waves of friction straight to my clit. His flesh, delectable, as muscles moved beneath the smooth skin. I wanted to taste every inch of him.

Each time we touched was new, yet familiar, my hunger for him insatiable.

He stepped us inside the shower and slid me down his body inch by sinuous inch until I stood on the warm tiles.

His hand tilted up my chin, and our eyes met, our song rose.

"This fae thing between us," he said.

"Our twin sparks, tethering us."

"It grows."

My eyes burned hot. "Yes."

His hands clasped my face, his erection hot between us. I ached for him.

"You burn me up, baby," he said.

"And you, me."

He waited, increasing that burn, that sizzle, that longing as our song built., and then slowly lowered his lips to mine.

My breath hitched, anticipation a living thing.

His eyes chained mine as he brushed his lips across my parted ones. Gentle, light as air. Again. And again.

Water sluiced over us.

The muscles of his back beneath my palms tightened.

His eyes, phosphorescent.

My body tremored. *Oh, gods, tongue me, lick me, take me.*

He did. His tongue spearing into my mouth, fingers finding my clit, mine answering as I wrapped them around his cock and squeezed. Pumped and pumped again, and again.

He devoured me. Little bursts of pleasure erupted where his fingers pressed into my waist, my breasts, my back. His other hand relentless, massaging my clit, dipping into my folds, inside me, penetrating deep.

My head fell back, water cascading across my face. My nails dug into his shoulders. Fiery ripples from those talented fingers. Pleasure spiked. I came and came and came.

He pressed me to the wall and eased his cock into me.

I squeezed. I was full. So gorgeously full. His cock throbbed inside me, but he didn't move.

Why didn't he move? Oh, gods, he had to move.

I hugged his shoulders, wrapped my legs around his hips, and he snugged me to him, pushed deeper inside me.

My eyes snapped open, and I stared at that adored face, jaw tight, eyes fiery and so alive.

I ground my hips. His desire flared, but he still didn't move.

More. The beast of a man was torturing me with pleasure. I

reached up and my teeth snagged his lower lip. I nipped him, and he jerked. And my tongue dove deep inside his mouth, mirroring his cock, but I couldn't get enough, wanted moremoremore. "James."

He thrust.

I stuttered, almost coming, then he withdrew and thrust again. I caught his rhythm as he pounded into me, his hands bracing my back.

James, me, our song, a madrigal of sensation, rising higher, higher.

His finger touched my clit, pressing, rubbing. I inhaled, dug my nails deeper into him, head flung forward, hips jerking as waves and waves of pleasure roared through me.

His thrusts grew frenzied until he tightened, froze, and his cock pulsed inside me. His groan of completion made me shudder. He rested his forehead on mine. "Home."

31

WHAT A TRIP

W hat felt like hours later, the high gradually subsided, and, damn, if the water wasn't still warm. Yeah for us.

James braced a hand against the wall, the other circling my waist. "It only gets better, baby."

"Think we might catch fire one day?"

His laugh, melted honey across my flesh. "Be worth it."

I hugged him tight, and beneath the spray, we soaped, rinsed, and dried each other off. Afterwards we lay on the bed wrapped in each other's arms, I said, "I don't want to let go of you."

His eyes darkened to a sensual navy. "Not even for...?"

Oh, boy, I knew just what he meant. "If you insist."

He prowled down me, dropping kisses along the way, lifted my legs over his shoulders, and feasted. My mouth grew desperate for his cock, so I twisted around as he stretched lengthwise, and I fisted his cock and drew him between my lips.

My tongue played with the tip, and I sucked him into my mouth, my hand circling the base of his cock and pumping.

His groan against my nether lips evidence of his pleasure, I clenched, almost went over. Licks and sucks and long, long strokes, my clit alive to the sensations of his mouth and tongue. Tingles began, then a crest of ecstasy. *Gods, the pleasure.* I sucked harder, pumped my hand as my body undulated with my orgasm, and he spurted into my mouth, salt and tang and James. *I ate him up.*

We lay entwined for long moments, catching our breath, until he gave me a final lick and climbed atop me, bracing his weight on his forearms. He took my lips, kissed me, the delicious taste of *us* mingling.

"Clea Reese, you wreck me." His hand smoothed my hair.

I played mine across his scruff, then trailed my fingers through his long hair, stroked him, loved him. "I want to see Lulu and Neddy and Ronan. Everyone."

"We will."

"I wish we were normal, had a home. You'd arrive from work, maybe late sometimes, and so would I. Lulu would careen in from school, the dogs yapping at her arrival, Calico Kitty jumping on the windowsill. Ronan would be there, too, and Neddy, and we'd all sit around talking about our day. I wish—"

"Hush. We will. There's time. We have time. Sleep. I love you, baby."

"Love you, too. So much." I nestled impossibly closer to his big body, his arms surrounding me, and closed my eyes.

I SHRIEKED. James had moved lightning fast, katana and gun in hand. I found the hilt of my knife between the mattress and wrapped my fingers around it.

A column of smoke, sparks of red and blue and yellow at the foot of our bed.

I relaxed. "Geesh, Anouk, couldn't you knock?" Nudity didn't bother James, but I pulled the covers to my chest before I flicked on the bedside light.

The smoke dissolved and Anouk stood tall, arms crossed, head shaking, fully dressed in shorts, and a beaded, midriff-baring bustier. "You two are like rabbits."

I pointed to the chair. "Have a seat."

She shook her head. "I cannot stay. The chest is safe?"

"It is," James said.

Those sloe eyes of hers found mine. "Have you activated it?"

"I don't understand," I said.

"Of course you do, inside your soul memory. When you activate it, it is much like a lock that unlatches. It is a deliberate action, one filled with purpose. Without that..." Her lips thinned.

I recalled holding the Chest of Bone, how I'd felt that click inside me, how something had changed, and even though I didn't get it then, I'd started something.

At least now I knew what.

"I haven't activated the chest yet. But I will." I drew up my knees, rested my cheek on them. "You're its guardian, but you won't take it, will you?"

"I will not. You must gather them. And then it will be time for the Guardians to take possession and reunite the worlds."

"I just don't see—"

Her lush lips pursed. "You *saw.* Dave took his chest, which then was much as a homing beacon for those who wished to acquire it. You witnessed how that ended poorly."

Talk about an understatement. Dave's death had been horrific. "Two down, three to go."

"Activate it now."

"Yes, oh, mighty Guardian."

Her Cheshire Cat smile appeared, then smoke swirled, the giant bird emerged. It tossed us a wink and was gone.

WHILE JAMES CHANGED for the cocktail party and celebratory dinner, Lulu texted she'd meet us at the dinner. She had a surprise for me, so I wasn't to see her beforehand.

My phone read five-fifteen. I still had time to activate the Chest of Stone and put it in the safe. *Two down, three to go.*

Given my strange experience with the Chest of Bone, I decided to wait for James. But I'd get everything ready. I retrieved the plain box on the dresser that held the Chest of Stone, kneeled before the safe in the corner of the bedroom, and pressed my palm to the door. It whooshed open, and I reached inside for...

"James!"

James crouched beside me. "What?"

"The Chest of Bone is gone." My hand scrabbled around in the safe and came away with a piece of paper.

No worries. It's all cool. Come to my suite. Alex

"What the hell?" I said.

James' jaw tightened. "The fuck is that shifter up to now?"

WE STOOD before Alex's door, James holding the box with the Chest of Stone. I wasn't about to let it out of my sight.

Alex opened the door looking a little worse for wear, but in tight worn jeans and black silk shirt, his long hair cascading around him. A beautiful man, but I was fuming.

"Well?" I said. "Where is it?"

Alex scrutinized me head to toe, so much so the hum of James' annoyance escalated.

The wolf raised my left hand to his lips and kissed my golden finger. "Hurts?"

"Cut it, wolf," James said. "Answer Clea."

Alex snarled. "What are you two in twist about?"

I hissed, voice low. "You took the chest!"

He cocked his head. "Of course I did. Anouk's instructions."

"The why didn't she... That Cheshire grin. Damn her games."

He crossed his arms. "She didn't explain, did she?"

"No," James said.

"Follow me." Alex widened the door.

We walked through his luxurious suite, fitted with old Spanish-style furniture, Navajo rugs on the walls, and a sprinkling of artifacts I suspected he'd collected in the field. A rapier, an African mask, a massive sword, and other objects hung on the stucco walls or rested on a table or in a corner. A mobile of odd keys, two decorated with old runes, dropped from the ceiling. My fingers pulsed with the urge to touch it.

"Viking or Celtic," Alex said. "Old."

I fisted my hand. Now wasn't the time.

At his bedroom door, he notched his head at James. "He stays here."

James' inner hum grew dissonant, but not a muscle stiffened. "I go with her. Always."

I bit back an aggravated sigh.

The wyvern stirred. Crap. "He knows everything, Alex. In the fae sense, we're mated, tethered. He'll never betray us."

The wyvern preened with utter smugness. Fortunately, James did not.

Alex snorted. "I doubt you have the fae song."

"*Enough*," James said. "We have the song, not that it's your fucking business."

Alex's glowing eyes shot to me.

I nodded.

He stepped inside the bedroom, but I'd caught the look of pain he'd instantly masked. Once he closed the door, I looked around, but saw no chest.

The room was dominated by a massive black-oak bed that would hold his pony-sized wolf form. He led us to the far wall, hung with a large signed photograph by Ansel Adams. I expected Alex to lift the photograph or swing it outward. Instead, he pressed his hand on the wall to the left of the frame. A seamless door pivoted open.

Soft light leaked from inside. And sound. A harmonic hum. Two different notes, the song unfinished, yet its beauty resonated deeply within me. Close encounters of the magic kind?

Alex gestured. "Lead the way." Another press to the wall, and the door whooshed closed behind us.

Inside the ten-by-ten room stood five plinths crafted from a burled wood I didn't recognize. A black box rested atop one of them. Every molecule in my body eased. I inhaled and moved forward to stand before the rectangular box that held the Chest of Bone, its hum of presence soothing.

"As I said, Anouk's doing," he said. "The room is warded. You're aware the boxes encasing the chests are, too. The first guardians programmed..." He shook his head, hands on hips. "Man, this is weird. The way Anouk put it, those first guardians *told* the chests to obscure themselves. She built this room a couple of weeks ago for the safety of the activated chests. The room is... between worlds."

"What the fuck does that mean?" James said.

"Haven't a clue." Alex notched his chin toward the chests. "We've got a party to get to, so do your thing, Clea."

Okey dokey. I took the plain oval case from James.

When I touched the top, the lid bloomed open. Inside, coiled serpent-like, lay the Chest of Stone, its gold beads mellow in the light from the wall sconces.

Feathers tickled my skin and pulses tugged at my flesh. That feeling moved across my palms to the backs of my hands and up my forearms. Fireflies swirled and power pulsed through me. My wrist spiral flared to life.

Been there, done that. At least this time, I was somewhat prepared. With my right hand, I reached inside the box and drew out the necklace so it draped across my palm.

The chest came alive.

Like awakening a numb limb, tingles slid up and down my arm. The chest began to change shape.

The necklace morphed into a rectangular box with a curved lid, about five inches in diameter. A box of stone that iridesced with rainbow colors like Labradorite. It throbbed to the beat of my heart.

Silver runes slid across its face and down its sides, their swooping letters echoing the Chest of Bone's Tolkeinesque ones. The Ouroboros, The Dragon, The Eye. When the runes and symbols covered the entire box, it stilled.

I touched it again. It hummed, the sound oscillating inside me, a half-remembered melody I'd heard... when?

Yes, I'd heard it with the Chest of Bone, too, but before that, it had sung through me, somewhere, somewhen.

I had to lift its lid.

I sensed James moving forward, shook my head.

The smell of air after a lightning strike filled me, a cloak of black surrounded me. I *must*. I dove into the abyss, infinite and unfathomable.

I saw nothing.

I saw everything.

Cascades of lava... Stars birthed... Scents of patchouli, amber, and oakmoss... James, Anouk, Bernadette... Callisto, Polyphemus, Eurydice... Turquoise, ruby, diamond... Truffles, wheat, corn... Thunder, a burbling brook, a bass drum... Wolf-men, panther, crow... The Storybook, the Queen, the *souls*... Golden fireflies swirling around, around, a galaxy, a spiral nebula, dancing fast, faster, and worlds upon worlds upon worlds upon...

"Clea." Hands banded my upper arms, pulled me back to warmth and reality.

I snapped down the lid, clutched the chest between my two palms.

A snick. A click. Activated. Alive.

Wait... Blackness dotted with stars and moons arced across my horizon.

That luminous song. I held onto it, held on, held...

"Clea. Come back."

But why? So much to explore, to see.

Breath on my neck. "Come home."

Home. Yes. I ripped my mind back to our world, our life—the plinths, James holding me, the Arctos compound, Lulu, Alex, Neddy, *here*. Home.

I sloughed out a long, tired sigh and placed the chest back in its container on the plinth.

The luminous runes and symbols faded, and with a snap, it again became an ancient gold and carnelian necklace. Stunning and inert.

Active, but sleeping, awaiting its Guardian's touch. I pressed the container's lid, and it sealed shut.

James turned me in his arms, and I rested my cheek against his heart, took a moment to steady myself.

I straightened. "I could sure use a drink."

SHIFTERS LOUNGED ON COUCHES, a few in wolf form, and Alex leaned against the fireplace mantle talking to two attractive women, while Rae in a purple floor-length mermaid skirt topped by a pink twin set sashayed from one conversation group to another. The air was festive, laughter easy and often, drinks plentiful, and nibbles galore.

James and I sat on a leather sofa. I was still recovering from my dive into the chest, so I nursed my blended turquoise margarita, courtesy of Erick's skills as unofficial bartender.

I was starving, and since I couldn't wait for dinner, downed way too many vegetarian empanadas and grilled polenta bites.

Melike and Carlos arrived, and she zoomed over to me.

"*Bon!*" She slapped her thighs. "You look good."

"Thanks. I feel good."

She leaned closer, notched her chin at James. "*He* looks good, also. Very good. Yum."

"Carlos!" I said, calling for reinforcements.

Her low laugh tickled me. "Jealous, much, *ma petite chatte*?"

"I am *not* your *pussy*."

Melike roared with laughter. Carlos appeared and handed her a drink. "*Merci*," she said to him and smacked a kiss on his cheek.

Ronan and two older teens breezed through the door. I walked over and gave the huge boy a hug. Although not so much a boy anymore, but a man.

"You okay?" he said.

"Swell."

He grinned.

"Clea, you get over here, girlfriend!"

I gave Ronan another squeeze and obeyed. As I crossed the room to Rae, James, Melike, and Carlos looked to be deep in conversation, James warm eyes telling me all was well. Many wolves still saw James as a nanotech "thing," but Alex had quietly passed the word that he was something *more*. In other words, don't rouse the beast. You'll lose.

"What's up," I said as I approached Rae. My stomach rumbled. Guess I was still starved, so I snagged another empanada.

Screams. Yips. Growls.

I whirled.

Neddy, in full-on Pinky-wolf mode.

I yelled, "Don't hurt him!" and raced across the room. What the hell was he thinking? Why come to the cocktail party as the Pinky?

By the time I reached the boy, Alex, James, and Melike were holding back the crowd gathered before Neddy, now cowering on the floor.

I slid to my knees in front of him, put my hands on his shoulders. "It's okay, Neddy. No one will hurt you."

The palpable fear in his eyes made me want to hug him, but something bad had happened.

"What wrong, Neddy?"

"Gonnnne."

His garbled Pinky voice. Oh, dear.

"Who's gone?" I said.

His mouth moved, but he didn't seem able to form the words.

I ran a hand across his head. "Can you change back?"

"Scareddddd."

"It's okay. These are friends. You just startled them. Change back, Neddy. Please try."

He bobbed his head, took another scared look around the room, then smoke enveloped him.

It took forever to dissipate. Finally Neddy-the-boy appeared, wearing khakis and a black button down. He'd obviously dressed for the celebratory dinner. He'd combed his curls back from his face, and those bright leaf-green eyes shimmered with fear.

"Neddy?" I said.

"She's gone."

"Who?"

"Lulu."

I froze. "Explain 'gone,' please."

He bit his lip and slipped a hand into his pocket, to pull out a sheet of paper.

I reached for it.

Had she again been kidnapped? My hand shook so violently, the words on the paper smeared together.

Someone plucked the paper from my trembling fingers.

I twirled around. "No!"

James' eyes, calm and terrible, hushed me. As he read, his face tightened. He ran a finger down his scar.

"What?" I said. "*What!*"

He leaned toward Alex, whispered.

Alex cleared the room except for Melike and Carlos, Rae and Erick, and Neddy.

Ronan argued with him, and Alex nodded his agreement that he could stay.

By that time, I'd morphed to warrior mode. We'd get her back. Oh, hell, yeah. And whoever had taken her... "Who took her? Who took Lulu?"

"No one," James said.

I tilted my head. "Neddy said she was gone."

James nodded, his eyes tethered to mine. "She is. She's run away."

THREE DAYS LATER, we gathered in the courtyard of the den where I'd arrived months ago with Lulu and Ronan, our pups Mutt and Jeff and Gracie, and Miss Calico kitty.

Today was different. Today we were saying farewells, not hellos.

James and I stood to the side, geared up with small satchels and armaments. Alex, who was accompanying us, was talking to Erick. He'd be in charge while his alpha was away from the den. Lulu was considered pack, thus under Alex's aegis, and he said it was his responsibility to find her and see her safe. Melike's arms circled

Carlos' neck. Then she hunkered down by Bron. Alex had charged her to come with us as my protector, and Carlos and Bron agreed, even though James and Alex were overkill in that department given where we were headed—to Charleston's fae court. According to Rae, the court bridged the mundane world to the magic one.

Carlos and Bron weren't the only ones staying behind. The dogs and Miss Calico were left in Ronan's and Erick's caring hands. Both had wanted to join our party, but Ronan was too human and Erick needed to stay for the pack.

Why? Why had she run away? Stuck on rewind, those words looped through my head. Even *after* we'd found the letter tucked between mattresses. The one allegedly from her mother.

From the letter's contents, it was obvious this one wasn't the first letter, nor, I suspected, was it the last. Lulu may have forgotten she'd put it there, perhaps in haste when someone surprised her in her room. Or maybe its placement was intentional. We wouldn't know until we found her.

The letter was signed "Mother," AKA Cruella, a nickname I'd given her as a child. I never liked her, met her a bare few times when I'd been a kid. She'd disappeared years earlier from Lulu's and Dave's lives when her child was very young. She was presumed dead. Dave had loved her, yet he'd hidden things from her for his own, opaque reasons.

No urgings to flee in the letter we'd found, yet I knew Lulu had gone to this woman. Or some woman she *believed* to be her mother.

Lulu presented as mundane. But I'd suspected what she was, her otherness artfully hidden by her father's magic. Ever since she'd sung to me those many months ago, I'd been pretty sure she was a mutt like me—fae on her mother's side, mage on her father's. And somehow the woman in the letter had convinced her to join the fae court.

My gut said I was dead on.

We'd tried to find Charlie the fae. He hadn't answered my summons, nor had he responded to Anouk's, who was miffed we'd disturbed her while she was doing *important* Guardian business.

Rae'd chuckled when she'd said that, which prompted her poofing out.

James peered down at me. "How about we put that in your pack now?"

I clutched Blue Monkey tighter. Her father's last gift to Lulu, we'd discovered it beneath her pillow. A bomb blast had ripped the fuzzy creature apart and my grandmother had sewn it back together again, the stitches neat and precise. There'd been a powerful bond between Bernadette and Lulu. Blue Monkey was precious to Lu, and the stuffed toy had sat on my dresser since we'd found it.

My finger rubbed across its back over and over. Had she deliberately left it or had she forgotten it in her haste to flee?

A bump beneath the pad of my finger.

When I parted the fur for a closer look, I saw the seam, one *not* repaired by Bernadette.

The stitching was crude, lacking the artfulness of Bernadette's careful hand. I slid into the shadows, dropped my pack, and removed my tool knife. Three snips, and I widened the breach with my fingers, then poked inside.

I wiggled them around Blue Monkey's cotton batting, wormed them up toward the head. There. Paper. I pincered it between fingers and gently pulled. A note. Folded many times.

My hands dampened as unfolded it again and again until a letter-sized lined piece of paper rested in my hand. Typed. But with Lulu's inevitable doodles of cats and creatures, purple-inked in the margins.

I read Lulu's words.

32

WE HUNT

Dear Clea,

I bet "big bucks," as you always like to say, you'll find this. I placed the bet with myself because you weren't around to bet with me.

You're mad at me. Too bad. I'm mad at me, too.

But I had to do it, I had to go, even if my mom is bulls—tting me.

How come? I need to prove to you that I'm worthy. You're such a Big person, Clea. You do Big stuff. Dad did, too, but, with him, it never felt like it. I'll never be good enough. Not unless I do something Big. I have to try.

Please don't be super mad. (Even though you probably will be. And freaking out.)

My mom wrote me, which I bet big bucks (another one!) you know by now. She said she knows where a chest is. A different one. She's probably full of... you know... but I have to go.

Because if it's true, I'll make you proud.

And if it isn't true, no loss.

I know you love me, but...

Oh, never mind.

I'll be back soon. I'm not leaving forever.

I'm glad James is back. Tell him I said that. And tell Neddy I said "Bye," *and that I'm sorry I was so mean. Say "Bye" to Ronan for me, too. Pet pups and kitty, too. Okay?*

Please don't be really mad.

Love,

Lulu

MY BACK PRESSED against the wall, holding me up. A "Big person," my ass. I was just trying to get through the day and do what was right. The same as Lulu. The ache in my heart grew and grew until I bit my lips to hold it in.

Voices raised in argument. Rae, wearing low-slung jeans and a bright red t-shirt, was going head to head with a similarly dressed Neddy. And it looked like Neddy was winning. *Whoa.*

Minutes later, the pair ambled over. Well, Rae ambled. Neddy hopped like he'd jump out of his skin.

I straightened, swiped at my eyes with the heel of my hand.

I kept half an eye on James, who'd gone to talk to Alex. No help from that quarter. At least they hadn't killed each other... yet.

"What?" I said to Rae.

He jerked his thumb at Neddy, who was trying very hard not to grin. "He's comin' with us."

"No!" I said.

Rae's sleepy eyes blinked. "Yeah, he is."

I opened my mouth, and found Rae had once again rendered me voiceless. I gave him a one-fingered salute.

He turned to the boy. "You go over there and make sure those two alphas don't explode." He pointed to Alex and James.

After Neddy trotted off, he gave me the stink eye. "Now y'all listen. These people here, not bad people, but they don't get that boy."

"Some do," I said, thrilled I could speak again.

"Most don't. They're scared of that Pinky-wolf. Scared bad."

"Yes." I sighed. "And I know what happens when scared people overreact. But he's young. Only just turned sixteen."

Rae bobbed his head. "He sure is. But, sugah, he's been through a lot. Too much. He's becomin' a man fast."

Truth. Neddy, James, and Alex stood in a huddle, the boy with the curly hair nodding, hands clasped behind him. He was almost as tall as James and Alex, skinny as a toothpick, but when James squeezed his shoulder, Neddy's thin chest puffed out and he smiled.

"You're right," I said. "He comes."

I DOZED on the private jet, unable to sleep, unable to stay fully awake. I needed to be ready to rock 'n' roll when we landed. We'd red-eyed it across the country to South Carolina. If Lulu wasn't there, we'd discover where she'd gone with her "mother."

If the woman writing really was her mother.

James had gone icy cold when I'd shown him my letter from Lulu. Then he'd kissed my forehead and stroked my hair, and I'd leaned against his welcoming warmth.

The guilt I felt—he understood. James got me so good.

I hadn't done enough for Lulu, hadn't been *present* enough, so she'd reacted to some stranger's words in a bid to make me proud. I was *always* proud of her, dammit.

But I suspected she also longed for her "real" mother's love. And that bitch had played right into Lu's longing. Some power game, I'd bet. The woman I remembered had been a scrooge about the love she gave her daughter.

The thrum of the engine relaxed me, but sleep remained elusive. I reached for my knitting, except the pattern was a complex one, and I was so tired I'd make a mistake. I could open a juicy novel, but the words would blur. Maybe I'd dive inside James to see what the wyvern thought of all this. I'd bet his pithy comments about our metal means of transport would be amusing.

I raised my eyes to James. Beside me, his body a furnace that kept me warm, he read the book on magic I'd borrowed from Sophy's library. Thankfully, I'd figured out how to open it. My head rested on his shoulder, the fingers of my left hand threaded through his right one.

He didn't seem bothered by my lack of an index finger. I was.

When he turned to me, his eyes glittered with questions. An idea popped into my head. I smiled.

"Uh, oh," he said with an answering smile. "I know that look."

"Ever hear of the mile-high club?" I said.

He chuckled, all sexy and hot, and slid the book into his pack. When he stood, his proffered hand told me he had.

We walked hand in hand down the narrow aisle, passed Alex-as-wolf and Neddy-as-Pinky cuddled in sleep. When we reached Melike, those sharp, gray eyes slid to mine. Her slow, sexy wink made me blush. Thankfully, Rae wasn't with us, since he'd poofed to Charleston to do recon. I could only imagine what he'd have to say about our jaunt. I'd never verbalize it, but I missed the crazy mage—the Guardian of the Chest of Bone.

Leave it to Rae to casually drop that little bomb on the way to the airport as he stunk up the car puffing a joint he insisted was medicinal.

And why hadn't he told me earlier he was its guardian?

Because it was *fun* to watch me try to figure it out.

He was lucky I didn't stab him where he sat.

Lulu's absence reinforced how much I loved her. When we found her, I'd do better at this parenting stuff. If she'd come with us. If she was unharmed. If...

James tugged me inside the tiny bathroom and lifted me. I wrapped my arms around his neck, legs around his waist.

Instead of sexy, his face was serious, his eyes deep as the Pacific. "We'll find her, baby. We'll find her."

This man knew my heart. Speech failing me, I nodded.

"Together," he said, his smile fierce.

I answered it with my own. "Together."

And that was all I needed. For now.

~ The End ~

THANK YOU! AND NEWSLETTER

Thank you for taking the time to read this book!

If you enjoy a book, leaving an honest review where you purchased the book is one of the best things you can do to support an author. I'd so appreciate you taking the time to share your thoughts with others.

I'd love for you to sign up for my newsletter at my Website, and receive my bonus novel, *Body Parts*. My monthly newsletter contains info on the Afterworld Chronicles novels, my other works of fiction and non-fiction, reviews, and lots of yummy stuff.

Come visit with me... VickiStiefel.com
Facebook • Instagram • Twitter • Ravelry

ACKNOWLEDGMENTS

Thank you, my readers! You give me energy and inspiration each and every day. You're the best. I offer deep bows and sincere appreciation to so many for helping me see *Chest of Stone* through to publication.

To the amazing Rosemary Hill who read the manuscript pre-Beta, post-Beta, and beyond. To my fabulous Beta readers, Ro, Richard, Debi, Ericka, Kathy, Abby, and Alisa. There would be no book without them. To my incomparable writing partner, Camille Cotton, who waded through early drafts of the manuscript. Such a mucky road! To Colleen Vanderlinden for her editing skills. To my agent, Paula Munier—thank you for helping me steer this storm-tossed ship!

To Isis of Helheimen Design, who painted a stunning portrait of Clea and Larrimer, and for her marvelous cover work. I continue to swoon, Isis! To Grace Draven, Tiffany Roberts, Mel Sterling, Monica Enderle Pierce, RJ Blain, Amy Cissell, Elizabeth Hunter, Jeffe Kennedy, the late Lora Gasway, Kimberly Trochesset Ladd, Pilar Williams Seacord, Genevieve St Yves, Colleen Vanderlinden, Cate Rowan, Alicia Treat, Emma Hamm, Parris Afton Bonds, Susan Emans, and Colleen Champagne, who continue to inspire me with their warmth, humor, and magic.

To Monica Lin and Kiona Stowers, who cheered me on, to Sarah Van Berkum for her invaluable graphic expertise, and to Nadia Banuelos, who got me out of many a scrape. To Norah Gaughan, Ro, and Karen Clements, for their friendship, support, and knitting expertise. To Sheila Ryan, for her constant support, love, and joy, and her brother, Marc Ryan, who inspires me. To my students at Clark University, who always moved me to grow and reach. To Cynthia Michaels, who took me in, and, more importantly, took in Gracie, Penny, and Cranberry.

To my wonderful family: Peter, Kathleen, and Summer—I can't thank you enough for your enduring support and for your deep and abiding love. Love you so much. Finally, to my beloved sons, Blake and Ben—for all that you are, for all that you have gifted to me, and for all your abiding love. I am the luckiest mom in the world.

Without these folks, this book wouldn't have happened. A writer's journey is never easy. It's sort of like climbing Mt. Everest... in shorts. Would that I could turn my "thanks" into stars and gift them to you.

Please know that any errors, screw ups, or messes are mine alone, and not those of the wonderful and supportive folks named above.

ABOUT THE AUTHOR

My fantasy romantic suspense series, The Afterworld Chronicles, launched with *Chest of Bone*. The second novel, *Chest of Stone*, hits shelves Nov. 2017. My mystery/thrillers—*Body Parts*, *The Dead Stone*, *The Grief Shop*, a Daphne du Maurier winner, and *The Bone Man,* a du Maurier finalist—feature homicide counselor Tally Whyte. All are now in ebook format. Tapping into my love of knitting, I wrote *Chest of Bone The Knit Collection*, a pattern book based on my novel and in collaboration with Karen Clements, Norah Gaughan, and Rosemary Hill. I also co-wrote (with Lisa Souza) *10 Secrets of the LaidBack Knitters*. My late husband, William G. Tapply, and I ran The Writers Studio workshops.

I grew up in professional theater—the Ivoryton Playhouse—and planned to become an actress. Instead, I've slung hamburgers, managed a scuba shop, and became a college professor. I'm a mom to two wonderful humans and a furry pack. My passions for scuba diving, fly fishing, and knitting pop up in my novels. As do vinho verde, bourbon, Maine lobster, and chocolate, not necessarily in that order. I sing musical comedy scores in the shower, unfortunately not an Equity venue, and I write daily. I adore teaching, having taught fiction and modern media writing at Clark University, and so I mentor writers and students in a variety of writing genres. Currently, I'm playing with my pup, Penny, going wild in L.A., and pounding the keys on the series' third novel, *Chest of Air*.

Come visit with me...

www.vickistiefel.com

vicki@vickistiefel.com

ALSO BY VICKI STIEFEL

The Afterworld Chronicles

Chest of Bone

Chest of Stone

Chest of Air (2018)

Tally Whyte/Homicide Counselor Series:

Body Parts

The Dead Stone

The Grief Shop

(Daphne duMaurier Award winner)

The Bone Man

(Daphne duMaurier Award finalist)

Nonfiction:

10 Secrets of the LaidBack Knitters, with Lisa Souza

Chest of Bone The Knit Collection by Vicki Stiefel, Karen Clements, Norah Gaughan, and Rosemary (Romi) Hill

Visit with Vicki:

Website • Facebook • Instagram • Twitter • Ravelry